Demŏnware

The Spiritual War Within

(a love story)

by

Sōl Una Amé

For more information, visit:
http://www.solametales.com

Book and cover design by Sōl Una Amé

ISBN - Paperback: 979-8-218-78103-3

This Edition Second Printing 2025

DEDICATION

With immense appreciation to Michael Angelo.

For illuminating the darkness,
while tethering me to this world.

CONTENTS

TRIGGER WARNING

This book is for adults only.

Please be advised that the characters in this book discuss and seek to heal from traumas that include sexual assault, sex trafficking, occult rituals and childhood abuse.

This is a work of fiction; however, these traumas do happen to real people, and reading this content could trigger a heavy emotional and psychological response.

While detailed accounts of the traumas are avoided, and often only alluded to, for the characters to heal and understand the darkness they are up against, they must recognize the damage and revisit the crimes, which are portrayed with some specifics.

This book seeks to inform through the eyes of a storyteller who is innocent and naïve, without assaulting the audience. However, everyone's individual comfort levels are different. This book is a science fiction romance novel and could also fall under the paranormal and horror category for some of its content.

Proceed with caution if you are a survivor of abuse.

EPIGRAPH

At the end of the Second Edenfall all that is malevolent will be taken up and cast down. The powers that rot our age will be rooted out. Pacts broken, whispers silenced, ripping up what was hidden in plain sight.

The enemy of the dark will carry the fire to burn the brambles of their present; and a sword for what comes after. The land will be made ready; stones swept from the path; the thorns pulled from the earth. Humanity's greatest healers will walk faithfully and leave the fields clean for the sowing, at the arrival of first light.

The shadow, that always returned before, is now keen to sleep eternal. Let those who follow, rise without chains and face the coming dawn, with no more ghosts upon them.

- Fragments of *The Veiled Testament*,
from the *Book of the Second Evenfall*
(Sealed Archive, *Silent Era*)
Inscribed by an Unknown Hand

PROLOGUE

When I awoke to this world I was fully grown, with no memory of me or how I'd come to be. The only information I had about my lost perception of reality came from a recurring dream.

A masculine presence floated above me, with a crimson aether rolling off his skin, like living smoke. All parts of him were mysterious and alluring, a most beautiful and terrifying vision. So perfect, he looked iconic, but his expression was covered in a shadowy gloom that trailed off him as if the gloom itself were alive.

His eyes shone a bright light, disguising his true face, and when his hands reached out for me, my body immediately responded.

I relaxed.

How bizarre.

When his reaching hands grew closer, a sphere of light lit up around me, becoming a forcefield. I was encased in a protective bubble, separating me from him. Palm to palm, we tried to push through the wall of energy between us, but the forcefield was like liquid glass that moved with us, unbroken.

I was impossible to reach, and it made him angry.

That's when a glowing orb of darkness awakened inside his head and came alive before me. It was both beautiful and ugly as it spun within him, within his head, its shape constantly shifted.

The orb caused him pain, and he changed because of it.

Suddenly, he wanted to hurt me. The darkness inside him was in control and his hands broke through the forcefield around me and wrapped around my throat. I felt frozen, until my anger made me move. Using my own aetheric hands, I reached inside his body and seized the dark orb within his head and pulled it free. The darkness fell away from him, from us.

I gasped!

I can breathe!

His hands released my throat and moved gently to my face, the crimson haze blown away, and our lips met. The illumination between us was so bright and the feeling so familiar and wonderful that my body felt it all. We were alone, naked limbs intertwined; his darkness gone.

After my rebirth into this world, and all the pain of surviving, I relished this escape into dreaming, and how in my dreams he could make me forget everything but him. I wanted to stay inside that place, but no amount of sleeping pills or pain meds could bring the visions back once he was gone, once the trauma of my mother's death stole him from me too.

In all that time, never did I ask myself if he was real or if a curse like that could go so gently from the realm of humankind.

It was a dream, I told myself.

Yet, for all its fantasy and make-believe, in that place with him I would have given anything for his freedom from the darkness, and the feel of his soul near mine.

1

THE MASQUERADE

Between unconsciousness and rising, I saw a silhouette with a familiar face. She stood above me like an angel and wrapped me in a blanket of light.

"Wake up," her voice said.

I could see a glow all around me until I blinked, and it faded into a full moon brightly shining through skylight windows above.

What the hell happened? I asked myself.

Trying to adjust my eyes to the dark room, my thoughts were jumbled as I sat up. A mix of images flashed before me from not so long ago. The visions played over and over.

Guests hidden behind Venetian masks; a limousine ride into the countryside; ornate ball gowns and party masks; a ballroom covered in gold and gloom; a dance with a shrouded man who towered over me.

Nothing else was coming back to me.

I'd been laid out on an ornate chaise lounge, still in the white ballgown I'd worn to the black and white masquerade. The moonlit room was a study or a library, and the window view wasn't on the first floor. There was a wall of windows nearby and my only other source of light beyond the moon was coming from the lights below.

My head hurt, my mouth dry. The jeweled heels tied up my legs were too tight, as I fumbled for the closest wall of bookcases and followed it around to a doorknob. The door was locked and there was a faint sliver of light below the solid wood door. I kept going.

The second door opened, but the light switch didn't work. The bright white of a bathroom sink reflected inside. The faucet poured quickly, and the water choked my throat while I gulped. There was a flickering outside, beyond the horizon of the windows, on the ground. When I reached the windowed wall, below me was the backyard of the castle-like mansion, and a bonfire raging with lit torches.

It seemed as if the entire party had gathered outside and were attentive to the scene before them. A stone-built stage sat farther back on an ornate lawn. Red and black cloaked figures were gathered there; someone was moving between them, in shimmering white.

I looked from the cloaked actors on the stage to the crowd, also cloaked and masked and all watching. Some guests were more invested than others. The hooded movements became more apparent the longer I stared.

"What is this?" I gasped in a horrified whisper and backed away, tripping on a rug and falling on my butt.

I needed both arms to hold my shaking body up as I scrambled back, compelled to watch the perverse scene from the edge of the windows. The cloaked ones moved violently over the white shimmer, and it looked like a woman in a dress, the shimmer torn from her body. She was stretched across a stone slab, tied and gagged and naked, each ankle and wrist forced into a corner.

It was obvious, even to someone as simple as me, that this was no ordinary spectacle. When the first cloaked and masked man began, I covered my mouth to stifle the horror.

It's just a show, Gellion, I told myself.

I couldn't understand why I couldn't stop watching. I had to be sure it wasn't real, so I scanned the crowd again.

Three steps below the stone slab, a woman in a red robe pressed her hand into the shoulder of a man, also in a bright red robe. They were standing closest to the stage. Their masks were ornate, one-of-a-kind, and familiar.

I remembered them. I remembered him. Before the couple announced their engagement that night, the fiancé pulled me onto the dance floor and glided me through a waltz. I didn't discover until later that the man's grandfather owned the estate and had thrown them the party. Mr. Jairus was my old boss and the CEO of the company that recruited me out of college.

It was impossible to tell through their masks, or from my viewpoint, if they were entertained by the scene before them, yet they stared at it. When I found the courage to watch the altar again, a second or third man had moved to take the first man's place. The tied-up woman was struggling.

Nausea swept over me.

What am I doing here? Locked inside this room?

The engaged couple were unknown to me. In my years at Jairus Industries, and in the short time I was an assistant to Mr. Jairus, I'd never known him to be perverse. He could be cruel, but not perverse.

As my mind searched through the events from earlier that night, it had been a never-ending stream of raunchy shows, and I began to wonder if maybe the "victim" was a prostitute, who would be well-paid for the debauchery.

Why not? The naked bodies had been everywhere upon entering the masquerade decorated estate. Nude models painted to look like statues stood on pedestals lining the great hall. Masked dancers touched guests and each other, as part of their choreography. I saw full grown adults crawling on the ground with jeweled collars around their necks.

"It's just a show," I whispered to myself.

I sighed and lay down on my back, the Persian carpet beneath me was soft and clean, and I pulled each foot up to remove the laced shoes. I tried to calm my breathing. From that angle, looking up at the windows, I noticed a large telescope nearby and stumbled toward it. A comfortable stool was perfectly placed, and I sat down.

The view of the scene had been too far away for my naked eyes to correctly comprehend, and I couldn't be sure of what was really happening.

This might help me allay my fears, I gulped.

The telescope was pointed at exactly where I needed to look, and it was focused correctly.

Ew! Disturbing.

The woman on the slab was bleeding now! A knife had been used to slice her stomach and arms. She was tied so tightly; all she could do was hold onto the ropes.

Could it be fake blood? I wondered.

I held a quivering hand to my horrified face, but I also couldn't stop watching. Silent tears of fear poured quietly from me as I strained to see her. I truly couldn't tell if it was just a show. At some point, I felt deeply that it must be real. And though I never prayed, I found myself desperate enough to call out.

"God, please help her," I whispered. "Help her please."

I shook, yet kept focus on her thrashing head, her inability to scream through a gag, or pull her arms closer in defense.

And then something happened. She gave up, and her face picked a spot out in the night sky, and she stared out into the stars. With her face so calm, I could see every line and expression of her.

"No!" I screamed without caution, and stumbled backwards, knocking myself and the stool over. "It's not possible," I whispered as I fell to the floor.

My mind could not comprehend what I had just seen. Her face...

...I got up and stumbled back to the telescope, looking for her face, desperate to verify my eyes were lying.

Her face...there's just no way. No way!

"No!" I cried.

Her face, the woman on the altar, bleeding...it was my face!

"She can't be me. I'm me," I whispered in sheer terror.

6

I had to be hallucinating, yet my eyes were not deceiving me. As she braced herself for what hit her next, I could see every scar on her body; they perfectly mirrored my own. I traced my own scars with my finger as I traced her scars with my eyes.

Lines across the top of my forehead, from center heading left, through that temple, and back to the edge of my left cheek and jaw. The neck was spared a deep wound, but still held a line, until at the neck base it started again near the left collar bone, then down my shoulder, into my chest and along the left side of my stomach and torso. Scars I covered with clothing, hair, hats, scarves, and makeup.

The scars I stared at were bright red on her face and on her naked body too. I couldn't control the shaking of my legs, not well enough to stand up and watch anymore, so I slumped down and stared blurry-eyed through the wall of windows that began at the floor, watching without any finer details.

When all the men were done with her, they removed her gag, but not her restraints. I heard her scream through the window. The obvious master of ceremonies drew everyone's attention. He wore a horned-demon mask that covered his face, in black and red cloak with upside-down cross markings embroidered on his robes. He stood near her body on the altar as the fiancée walked forward with a chalice in her hands.

In his demonic mask, wielding a knife, he stabbed into the naked ribcage of my doppelganger! I felt my own ribs burn with pain!

The fiancée quickly collected the flowing blood from the open wound and walked the chalice back to her fiancé. First, she held it above her head for everyone to see, took a gulp, then offered it to her fiancé. He too drank the blood, and the crowd cheered and moved closer to the couple whose bloody lips met one another.

But the woman with my face wasn't yet dead.

The master of ceremonies had called out for their attention as he moved to the other side of the altar and raised a long blade and stabbed her in the center of her chest.

I sobbed and shook but couldn't pull my eyes from the horror.

It's a nightmare, I kept telling myself. Just a nightmare.

When the knife was removed, the blood poured out from her wound, and she screamed out, lifted her head and spoke directly to her killer, who leaned toward her.

Poof!

A cloud of smoke came wafting from her mouth and into his mask, lingering there between them. He stumbled backwards and dropped to his knees as the whole crowd of people started to gasp, move, scream, then panic, some running toward him, others running away. I found myself pulling my body to the telescope again, searching for the face of the monster who'd murdered...my doppelganger.

He'd pulled off his own mask as he was surrounded, his hood pulled back. I instantly recognized his face, as white froth came from his mouth. As he was convulsing, his eyes were staring in my direction.

I felt sick.

The host of the party, my old boss, lay dying. Mr. Jairus, the billionaire, convulsed until dead, as those around watched helplessly. Motionless, both he and the woman on the slab of stone; the woman with my face.

I got up, and went to the bathroom, where I found the toilet and puked. Then I drank water and puked some more, until I was dry heaving. When I was done, I pushed myself against the wall under the long bathroom counter and waited, my mind wondering when they would come for me.

It felt like a long time had passed before I heard noises and the door to the hallway quietly unlocked and opened.

"Gellion?" I heard a female voice whisper.

"Gellion, it's Katherine. Are you in here?"

Katherine? Where have you been!? I screamed inside my head!

I pulled myself up and fumbled my way through the doorway.

Katherine was holding her cellphone out, shining it my way. When it hit my face, she rushed toward me, wrapping her arms around me.

"Thank God, I found you!" She panted into my ear.

I pulled away from her.

"Something terrible..." I trembled, barely able to get the words out as I pointed toward the window.

"Gellion, listen to me," Katherine said quietly. "Don't move."

Handing me her cell phone and positioning my hand to point the phone's flashlight toward us both. She stayed close to me, her hands working her way around my dress.

"What are you doing?" I asked.

"We need to go," she said, still tugging at my clothes gently. "I'm changing your dress."

When my hand moved instinctively toward my stomach where she was touching, Katherine slapped my hand away. Then she unlaced the side torso of my shimmering white ball gown and pulled slowly down on a thread.

"Were you in the courtyard?" I screeched quietly at her.

Her eyes fluttered and her mouth drew down as her jaw dropped to her neck. It was her "I'm disgusted" face. We were practically face to face with only her phone lighting us, but I knew Katherine so well. She kept tugging and then pieces of the ball gown started to fall away.

I had a lot of things I wanted to say, including asking her how she knew where I was, but she beat me to it.

"What did you see, Gellion?" she asked softly.

Oh my God! She was there!

My best friend was a stranger to me!

"Fuck that!" I scoffed at her. Like hell I would describe that scene. "You saw."

Her shoulders went up, along with her eyes to the ceiling as she both rejected my question and winced.

"How could you watch that?" I felt the tears welling up in me.

She mumbled something in Korean while putting up her hands to ask me to stop.

"I'm compartmentalizing everything right now, Gellion," she complained. "I didn't think I'd have to watch. Cut me some slack."

"You already knew it was going to happen?" I gasped at her.

Complete stranger!

9

"We knew you would be safe up here," Katherine countered.

Who was she talking about?

"I hoped you would wake up in time to see the truth, so you could take my words seriously," Katherine said sternly.

"That was my face," I stated.

"Yes, that was your face."

"She died. That was real, wasn't it?"

"Instead of you, Gellion. Instead of you."

"And you watched," I said, realizing she was trying to tell me that I was supposed to be the one who died that way.

Katherine sighed and rolled her eyes as if to call me dumb and make me stop asking her questions. "Do you think those sick fucks were gonna let me look away?" Katherine's face grew sad.

I was horrified for her, as remorse stuck in her expression.

"Who are 'they'?" I asked, understanding Katherine knew "them" well enough to know a lot more than me.

"We don't have time for this."

"Make time," I hissed.

"I'm trying to save your life," she said, but I just glared at her, so she started rambling. "Look, it's not my fault. My parents are in the club. Their parents were in the club. And in the club, you do what you're told, or you're sacrificed."

I gasped. *What fucking club?*

"What club?"

But she just kept tugging at my ball gown.

"It's just an expression," she whispered.

"If I'm still here, who's on that slab?" I asked her.

She scrunched her brow at me, like she was disappointed I was asking.

"Your clone."

"I have a clone?"

"You did."

And at that moment Katherine's and my relationship suddenly felt like a performance. My brain could not ignore the flood of images arriving from the last decade of our friendship. All the movies, TV shows, books, YouTube videos, and conspiracy theories Katherine had been shoving my way all these years were popping back into view. Flashbacks of famous actors playing clones started to flood into my mind, making me think about all the different versions and options of clone available, supposedly.

"Look, if it makes you feel any better, they have everyone's blood in their system," Katherine mumbled as more pieces of fabric fell from me.

Memories of Katherine came flooding in as well, of her looking out for me in college.

"Never assume the person before you is not a clone," she quipped.

"How would that make me feel better?" I asked.

I pushed her hands away, and she scoffed and ticked her tongue at me, like her Korean mother would do. It was a message to do as I was told and not dawdle, when I was a guest at their diplomatic home. Katherine's hands had covered me everywhere, working to release me from the gown, but not to disrobe me. I could sense her purposefulness in touching my pressure points too, points on my body she had touched before to calm me.

"I'm getting you out of here," she said into my ear, as the last piece of white garment fell to the floor.

"I'm in danger," I stated, finally allowing the truth of that statement to settle in.

"Oh Gellion, you have no clue. He never should have left you this ignorant."

"Who?" I asked. Who the hell was she talking about?

Underneath all the handsewn costume perfection I wore was a silky black slip-dress that hugged every curve of my body. I had felt "held" by the strong silk that I thought was just a liner, yet the sheerness of the silk made me feel naked and vulnerable, like the dead clone on the slab.

I could easily die tonight, all over again, in literal horror.

Katherine produced a red sash and red satin cloak with a warm liner, then she fixed my hair and fastened a new half-mask to my face, leaving my mouth and chin exposed. She handed me black shoes and collected the others which she shoved into a lidded trash can under the bathroom sink with the dress remnants. In the full-length mirror by cell phone light, I looked exactly like someone at the party. My mask, my cloak and my dress were a carbon copy of the fiancée who'd brought the blood-filled chalice to her betrothed, to drink my DNA.

Katherine pulled me toward the exit and dragged me into the hall. Then she retrieved her phone and started texting. The hallway was just as massive upstairs as it had been downstairs, but there was no one in sight. Katherine put on her full-face Venetian mask with a small opening in the mouth and eyes.

"We're on the third floor," she said, walking with purpose, without shrinking or hiding, to the elevator. She kept checking her phone as she pressed the elevator button and pulled out a cigarette. She played with the filter nervously.

"Why am I wearing this?" I asked, flustered.

"Don't say anything," she said, ignoring me. "Just be silent and I'll do the talking."

We got into the elevator, and she sent a quick text and lit the cigarette through her mask and held it to her plaster lips.

I coughed. "Who are you texting?"

"Don't talk, and don't slouch. That woman..." she said, referring to my dress, "...is an heiress who will soon be worth hundreds of millions. Try to act the part."

The smoke accumulated quickly and then the door opened to the first floor. We stepped out, surrounded by smoke, and saw a man in the middle of the gigantic foyer. Just ten feet away was the fiancé heir to the Jairus empire, his mask unmistakable.

I grabbed the trim of the elevator doorway to steady myself as the terrifying vision of him, discovering me in "her" dress, hit my chest. He drank the blood of my doppelganger and God-only-knows what else he did while I wasn't watching. He would spot me as an impostor for sure!

He was looking right at us.

I took a deep breath.

Katherine walked quickly toward him while I stood back.

"Why haven't you left?" he said to her in a low growl.

"I got trapped and dragged to the courtyard," Katherine said to him. "I couldn't get away until it was over."

"She was upstairs the whole time?" he was growing angrier at her.

"She saw everything," Katherine whispered back to him. "She's jostled."

What the hell?

"Mmm," he grumbled, then looked over at me as I held myself tightly to keep from shivering.

"I think it's better this way," she said to him, submissively. "She understands it's not a game."

They were speaking as if I weren't even there.

"No Kat, it's always a game, remember?" he warned her with a smirk.

Then he turned to me.

"Katherine?" I asked her, worried.

He walked my way and almost reached me when an unfamiliar voice called out.

"Daphne!" A voice yelled from the hallway of the great foyer.

He was talking to me, but I wasn't Daphne.

"Shit!" The fiancé mumbled. "It's Tom," he said to Katherine, then turned away from us and started to walk toward the man.

"Back off Damon! I'm talking to Daph," Tom said from afar, as he looked at me.

Katherine walked back toward me, keeping me close to the elevator, shushing me, as she blew smoke around us.

"Tom is Daphne's ex-boyfriend, slash best friend, slash not-so-secret stalker," Katherine said under her breath with a tone of boredom and irritation.

Tom shoved Damon, but Damon just held onto him, unmoved.

"She doesn't want to talk to you, Tom," Damon said. "What are you still doing here? You need to leave."

But Tom ignored Damon and tried to move toward me, when Damon's large hands grabbed Tom's lapel and dragged him down the great hall toward the doors. Tom resisted, pulling Damon's mask down in the scuffle as he slammed Tom to the ground. Damon looked up at me with his mask down, staring at me as Tom squirmed beneath him.

Why does he have to look like that? I grumbled internally. *Of course, the psychopath would be striking.*

Damon was tall, with broad shoulders and a slim waist, but his perfectly chiseled face was surprising. I expected him to look like a monster somehow. Then I felt sick, mostly at myself for finding him attractive.

"You ruined her perfect night, Damon!" Tom squawked at him. "She doesn't want to stay with you. She isn't safe with you!" Tom screamed toward me. "Daphne!"

Tom pulled himself off the ground and broke free and made a run for it, but Damon caught him by his lapel and forced him into a face-to-face confrontation.

"If anyone had reason to ruin our night, it was you," Damon retorted. "You're insane with jealousy. I will find out who did this to my grandfather! And if you had anything to do with it, I'll put you on the slab myself."

Tom's face looked confused, and then he grew belligerent, except he was slow to respond, probably from drunkenness. He shoved Damon and backed away, fixing his jacket.

"That's ridiculous, and you know it," Tom scoffed. "I'm not leaving here without her."

Damon punched Tom in the face and the crunch of his nose breaking was immediate and loud. He fell to the ground, blood pouring from him. Damon picked Tom up by his jacket and dragged him away.

"She doesn't love you," Tom blubbered at Damon.

"You're bleeding on my carpet," Damon smirked as they reached the doors. "Daphne's family is marrying her off for power and money, or don't you remember the bylaws of her inheritance. Maybe you shouldn't have squandered your birthright, Tom, then Daphne would have more choices."

"Daphne, this is your last chance!" Tom screeched at me from the ground.

Damon barked back. "She's not going anywhere with you."

The mass of Damon's body and strength were obvious, as Tom vehemently protested the removal until he'd been hit one too many times in the head to keep fighting.

An Asian man stood at the entrance, without a party mask. He took Tom's collar from Damon as Tom screamed out one more time.

"Daphne, come with me right now!" he shrieked.

I closed my eyes and felt weak, wondering how much wealth ruled over these people. Damon and the Asian man shoved Tom out the front doors and into a waiting limo.

"Make sure the driver knows not to return here for any reason," Damon growled then turned back toward us.

We stood and waited for Tom's car to depart as Damon came closer.

"Tombo called your limo," he said to Katherine. "You need to go."

When he turned to look at me, I instinctively took a step back. He stared at me and put up his hands, trying to reassure me, then removed the mask that hung around his neck and tossed it away. He was beautiful, tall, and strong, with perfectly symmetrical features and glowing skin. He was like a Greek God with big blue eyes, a strong jaw, and dark hair. He was at least a foot taller than me, without my heels.

As he came close, my fear made me weak. My knees buckled in the six-inch platform heels Katherine made me wear to be as tall as Daphne, and I wobbled. Damon swooped me up and held me closely to him, walking us toward my escape, Katherine already in front of us.

"I'm sorry," he said softly, begrudgingly.

"Why is this happening?" I croaked out.

"It's my fault it went this far."

My breathing sped up in his presence, but he was walking so

deliberately that my masked head leaned into his chest and listened to his steady heartbeat as he slowly carried my traumatized frame down the hall.

The doors were quickly approaching, and I felt the breeze wake me, and I wanted to know more.

"Why did they kill me?" I asked, with a terrified quiver. "I'm nobody."

He took a deep breath.

"Because Gellion," he said, looking down at me through my mask, "I dared to love you a long time ago."

What?

Love?

...Me?

I pulled my head back, astonished. The hood from my cape fell away from my head and I took a swift breath in, as if my body wanted to cry, and then held myself still.

"You don't believe me?" he asked.

I couldn't answer or move because I couldn't remember, so I looked down. Damon stopped walking.

"Breathe Gellion," he said gently into my ear.

I took a breath and looked back up at him.

"I don't know what to believe," I said, because it was true.

His lowered chin turned forward and he began walking again. I tried to memorize the features of his face, as his cologne covered me in honeysuckle and musk. Then he stepped over the threshold, and the autumn night air hit my chest.

"I'll see you soon," Damon whispered.

As he placed me in the limo his lips brushed past my jawline, before he disappeared. Then the door closed, and the engine sped us forward.

2

BODY WAREHOUSE

Katherine and I stared at each other, our silent eyes aware of the overwhelming emotions within.

"Who the hell was that?" I trembled out.

She burst into tears.

Once we reached the main road off the long driveway, the coming red and blue lights told us the ambulance and police had finally arrived. We'd left just in time.

As I replayed the scene of Mr. Jairus killing my clone and then dying, I wondered if I could go home.

Could I?

What would happen next? The words of "love" were throwing me off. That someone had loved me was entirely unfamiliar. I should have been the first to cry, but Katherine sat back and heaved for a while. We'd been friends for a long time, and I'd never seen her cry like that. She was more than sad, she was afraid. Her moans of fear and relief allowed me to save my own strength. It felt as if she were crying for both of us as my physical pain increased, my body swelling and aching.

"I need my pills," I whispered, eager for relief.

Katherine knocked on the window between her and the driver, and the window opened.

"Pills," she said to the man, and he handed her a large bag. Inside was my purse, which she handed to me.

Quickly retrieved and swallowed, I took a deep breath and sat back and sensed the car beneath me as I tried to plan. Katherine was emotional all the way back to her parents' downtown residence. She didn't say anything until we arrived in the driveway then went back to her normal sternness.

"Here, take this," she said, handing me the first masquerade mask I'd worn to the ball. "Give me that one," she commanded of the other mask. She took off her black cloak and handed it to me as she motioned for me to remove the red one.

Katherine came nearer and reached out for the red lace sash and unhooked it from behind me. Now my dress was plain black, no more recognizable than anyone else. I was no longer pretending to be the fiancée. Katherine shoved Daphne's mask and sash and cloak into the bag and pulled out my cell phone and car keys and handed them to me.

"Put your mask back on, and your hood too," she whispered.

But I wanted answers.

"What now?" I asked, aware her instructions meant something.

"I have to have plausible deniability. I must be able to say you went home right after we got back," she said, nodding to cameras outside her parents' house.

"I'm not going home?" I was guessing.

She didn't answer. She looked out the window at two men sitting in the front seat of a vehicle, parked on the street by the large embassy house Katherine had spent years of her life inside.

"Aren't you going to tell me what's really going on? Or explain what I saw?"

Katherine squinted and took a deep breath and shook her head.

"Am I your best friend?" She asked me.

"I really thought so," I replied, but clearly that was up for debate.

"I'm really not," she sighed again. "The reason that I've been your friend is because Damon Jairus paid me."

She might as well have shot me in the gut.

"Excuse me?" I guffawed, open mouthed.

"Me being your friend and looking out for you meant so much to Damon that I'm now financially set for the rest of my life."

"Seriously?" I stammered; it was a major blow to my reality. "But we were roommates in college."

"Yeah, and how did that happen? Someone like me, from a wealthy and connected family sharing a room with you? On scholarship. Come on. I don't share."

Now she was just being mean. It was hard to fathom. I tried to understand, but that was the problem. Before my long recovery from the car accident, I'd lost all my history. Still, it made no sense.

"That was ten years ago," I said. "How did Damon make that happen? We weren't very old."

She squinted at me, and then looked around, calculating what she could say. "You lost two years of your life learning to walk, right? By the time you got to college, Damon was twenty-one and had inherited all his parents' money. He paid me to request you as my roommate, and then he kept paying."

"For what?"

"For every detail about you."

I audibly gasped. "What the hell! Katherine?" I was growing angry. "How much did you make for lying to me for ten years? For pretending to be my best friend?" I demanded!

I truly didn't know how much that was worth. She didn't like the question.

"Look Gellion, you saw those people. That's one part of my grandparents' world. My parents managed to get away from it by making me participate. I can't do it anymore. There's no way I can walk away without help."

"You were there for me through everything! How much was that worth?" I was genuinely curious, and desperately overwhelmed that anyone would do that for me.

"I don't think Damon would want me to tell you."

"Screw Damon! I've never met him before. How much was it worth, Katherine?"

"Gellion, he put you in that room so you would be safe, but in the end, it helped you see the truth. You can't be spared this."

She was right, but I didn't yet care about him.

"Did you ever love me?"

She swallowed hard. "People like me and Damon, we don't know the meaning of love, not really."

"So, he lied about that?"

She was flabbergasted. "You do get it, right? I wouldn't want you to leave here not understanding what's about to happen."

I looked again at the two men in the front seats of the SUV, waiting, and I wondered where I was going. My stomach started to hurt, and I pulled my arms into me.

"Gellion, he didn't save you just to let you die," Katherine said, reaching out a hand as if to try to comfort me but landed short of even touching me.

The chauffeur knocked on the window and Katherine rolled it down a few inches.

"Not yet," she said softly to him, then she looked at me.

"I have to go inside that house and get my bags and get out of here."

"Is that why you made such a big deal in front of my dad about your trip to Korea, and saying goodbye?"

"It's easier to field someone else's pain from far away."

"And safer for you too."

She didn't look hopeful, she looked afraid.

"It's the only way to avoid whatever is about to happen."

"What's about to happen?" I pleaded to know.

"I don't know!" she exasperated. "Gellion, how could I know? Mr. Jairus was a high-ranking member of the..."

Her face grimaced as she trailed off.

"...the what?"

She was mentally searching for the right word. "The elite. They're called many names."

"Like?"

"Whatever you like. Like all the damn movies I made you watch!"

"I knew it," I shocked myself.

"Freemasons, Illuminati, Satanists, Luciferians, the Ninth Circle, and a million other names. Whatever you want to call it. Whatever it's called, Mr. Jairus married his children into the bloodlines long ago and moved up. He oversaw multiple groups and projects, then Damon went and killed him in front of a crowd full of wealthy and powerful people tonight. That doesn't happen, ever, not without approval, and certainly not over some 'nobody.'"

Me, the "nobody."

It hurt, all of it, and my stomach churned again, and I wanted to vomit.

"I didn't mean that," Katherine corrected.

"So, I just go wherever my murderer's grandson tells me to go? I'm supposed to trust him with my life?"

"It's his fault you're in this mess. He's the only one who can get you out of it. You don't have a choice Gellion. This isn't just about you. They'll kill your dad and Brian too if they find out you're alive. Maybe me. They might not figure it out right away, but you can't hide without his money."

They'll kill my dad and brother?

I didn't even consider them. I shook my head. It was too much. I walked into a horror movie and had no idea what to do. I couldn't think my way through it. I wanted to curl into a ball and cry. I'd earned a breakdown but couldn't stop for it. To lose all composure, even if it was exactly what my brain needed, wasn't going to benefit me. I took some slow breaths to try to recenter myself.

"Will I ever see you again?" I whispered.

"Depends on what happens after I leave..." she shrugged but couldn't find the words to finish her sentence.

I looked at her, bewildered. I had no idea what she meant.

"...like if Damon doesn't survive this," she finally confessed.

My jaw dropped and I felt sicker, like the pressure of the horror was finally settling deep inside my stomach like a poison I wanted out.

"I'm sorry, I didn't mean that," she corrected herself as my shoulders caved into me and I bent over shaking.

"I'm dead, aren't I?" I sniffled with my head between my legs. "It's just a matter of time."

I wished I could go with Katherine to Korea, but then she wasn't really *my* Katherine anymore. I sighed, and covered my face, and was slowly aware of all the times I felt safe in her presence, and when she always knew what to do, it was because she was reporting to someone else. She was good at her job. We had gotten along well.

"You will feel safer with Damon, I promise," she encouraged.

I nodded, numbing to it. So, this was goodbye.

I sat up and put my hand out, palm up, and looked at my best friend and said, "Your music player please."

It had been the soundtrack of much of my remembered life so far. The device was small; she'd always had it with her. It was more than ten years old yet had been the latest technology from Japan when we met and was still good tech. Katherine pulled the player out of her purse and handed it to me, with some earbuds. It felt eerie to see it, like she had already planned to give it to me. I knew she had a copy of the music on her computer. My request, and her offering, was her way of saying goodbye as hugs were no longer an option.

"Get into your car and drive to the Cabin John Parkway and pull over to one of the trail parking lots," Katherine said. "Leave your phone and keys in the car and get out and start walking. They'll follow you and take you the rest of the way."

"Why can't they just drive me?" I asked.

"The security cameras need to see you leave alone. Though canal paths don't have many cameras, if you park near a camera it needs to see you abandon your car."

"Okay," I said, opening my pill bottle to take another dose of pain medication. I wasn't going to make it through this while struggling with so much discomfort.

Then I pulled my party mask down over my face, covered my head with the cloak and opened the limo door and got out. The SUV followed behind me after I pulled out of the driveway.

I did as instructed and headed south into Georgetown to get to the canal road out of the city. I drove slowly, trying to fiddle with my phone, until I realized the password had been changed.

No way to contact Dad.

Once that sunk in, I took my time driving and felt sorrowful as I looked around at the late-night city streets. A city I knew and loved no longer existed. The altered truth brought disenchantment, as the distress of a different understanding of the world started to sink in.

Clara Barton Parkway was dark and quiet with lots of places to pull over and park, to walk the C&O Canal trails parallel to the Potomac River, that divided Maryland from Virginia. I pulled over to one of the parking areas where both the Canal and the Potomac River were visible on the Maryland side. My car and cell phone, wallet and keys were abandoned there, while I kept my purse with my makeup and pills and music player.

I hadn't walked far before the SUV arrived to snatch me up. I sat in the back and found the music player and earbuds. I wanted to cry without sound, but needed help, so I put on my favorite playlist. The beat took over my worried heart and the lyrics helped the tears flow, but tears from the good memories too, not just the recent bad. It was the release of some emotion without the chaos of actually crying out in terror, like I really wanted.

It was meaningful to me to have been able to do some purging and still watch the road for our destination. The first part of the trip took an hour, into a small Northern Virginia suburban town. We pulled into the underground garage of a moderate-sized building. There was a second SUV waiting for us.

The Asian man was there, the handsome one I saw helping Damon at the estate, and he opened the door and took my hand to help me out of the car. His hands were large and strong, and he was gentle and clean, and smelled very powerfully of something one might find in a temple somewhere, an incense both bitter and sophisticated.

I instantly wanted to trust him, so I didn't know if I could trust myself to read things right. I'd rarely been around a well-dressed, well-groomed man as this, except hours before, around his boss. With straight, spiky hair that practically covered his eyes in the front, yet military short in the back, he was both mysterious and charming, like Damon.

"Tombo, right?" I asked, remembering how Damon referred to him.

He nodded at me and squinted his eyes and opened the back seat door to a different vehicle. I reached to pull myself in and stopped.

"That's blackened out," I complained.

"It's safer not to know the location," he said calmly.

I just shook my head. "Why?"

"It's for your protection," he said kindly. "And ours."

I still wouldn't budge, so he got in first. Then he pointed to the light fixture. He played with the settings. "You can make it bright, dim, or dark. You can control the air. This button here calls the driver. You can get some rest if you want."

"How long will we be driving?"

He shook his head. "No details. It's better if you sleep."

My mouth started to quiver from the fear.

Tombo's eyes softened. "I promise, no one will hurt you. Damon would never allow it."

I grimaced at the thought of Damon protecting me, as the memory of him brought fear and exhilaration, and the combination of chemicals pumping through my body had inflamed everything, making me dizzy as my muscles and joints burned.

I needed to rest, so I climbed in, and the seats were padded and covered in soft fur. There was a pillow and a blanket.

After Tombo exited and closed the door, I reached for the handle and was surprised to find it unlocked. Somehow that helped the panic, knowing I could get out. The light was set to dim, and it was there, in the blacked-out backseat on the softest cushion covers, that I succumbed to the sleep I needed despite the shaking in my legs.

I must have been delirious from exhaustion because I vaguely remember being carried out of the vehicle somewhere. Flashes of light hit my eyes as I tried to fight sleep, and though I knew at some point I was on a gurney, why that gurney felt like it was rocking was beyond me. I lost all consciousness to the slight swaying I felt.

I woke up to pressure on my head, like someone was squeezing me, and the room around me looked like some kind of makeshift hospital. Curtains closed me off from whatever else was going on, but I could hear voices talking quietly around me. I cleared my throat.

"Excuse me?" I called out, trying not to feel so alarmed.

The voices stopped mumbling nearby and footsteps approached.

A woman, who looked old enough to be my mother, pulled back the curtain. She was wearing a white doctor's coat. She had long, dark copper hair and blue eyes.

"Hello Gellion," she smiled. "I'm glad to see you."

"How long was I asleep?"

"A few hours. You really should get more rest if you can. We should've let you sleep in one of the private quarters, but we didn't want you to wake up all alone."

"It's kind of hard to sleep when everything is so..." I couldn't find the words.

"...terrifying?" she finished my sentence for me.

"Yeah."

"I'm sorry we woke you. There's been a lot going on."

"Who are you?"

"Damon is my nephew. You can call me Rosie."

"Was Mr. Jairus your father?" I asked.

I didn't know why I needed to know.

"He was," she said, her head bowed slightly.

I took a deep breath at how much it hurt to mention his name.

"I'm sorry for your loss," I said instinctually.

Her expression was confused, and she quickly put her hand in mine.

"You haven't changed much. Oh Gellion, here you are giving me condolences for a man who just tortured and killed you. He was a monster. No apologies necessary."

I smiled sheepishly at her.

"Do you know me?" I asked.

She nodded in agreement.

"I'm sorry I don't remember you," I replied.

"All you need to know is I'm not like my father."

I recoiled at the memory of my old boss shoving a knife into what he thought was my chest. She noticed my movements in defense of myself.

"Damon wanted to be here when you woke up to explain everything, but he's not back yet," she said, looking over her shoulder as if she expected him somehow. "I can have him wake you when he returns."

"I don't think I can go back to sleep right now."

"Of course," she nodded. "There are a couple of other people nearby you should meet. Calder? Eamon?" she called out to them.

Calder was an easy enough name to remember, but AY-mon was not. The names belonged to two extremely tall and handsome men, who looked like father and son.

Calder had a full head of orange-red hair, and Eamon was entirely bald, with a short beard filled with orange, brown and white strands.

"This is my son Calder," she said.

"It's nice to see you," Calder said without reaching his hand to mine.

He spoke with just a slightest Scottish accent. He was over six feet tall and looked like Rosie, but his physical build was like a larger size of Damon, with broad shoulders and a large chest. He was clean-shaven and wearing a lab coat like his mother.

"I'm Eamon," the older gentlemen said as he reached forward and shook my hand. "It's nice to see you again, Gellion."

His Scottish accent was much thicker, but he had the brightest blue eyes I'd ever seen. He too was tall and built but took up so much more space in the room, and his voice was strong. He wore blue scrubs, and his hand was large and warm and gentle as he shook mine with a genuine smile.

"I wish I could remember," I said, exasperated.

"We understand," Eamon replied, calmly.

"Where am I?" I asked.

Before they could answer my question, a piercing wail of an alarm sounded overhead as red emergency lights flashed inside the room. All three of them turned and ran toward the door without a word. I jumped out of bed and grabbed the pair of slippers on the floor, and ran to catch up with them, still wearing the black silk dress from the night before.

"Gellion, go back to the lab," Rosie yelled back to me, but I was close behind her, dragging my slippers and trying not to trip.

We ran through a long hallway that eventually curved and sloped down, as if we were descending a long ramp that took us from one floor to another. Then we reached a series of doors close together along a circular curve. Calder, Eamon, and Rosie ran inside the door with the flashing red light above it. Inside there was an unconscious man on a bed.

He was shirtless, with wired monitors attached to his chest and head. Calder wheeled over a medical cart with a defibrillator and then joined Eamon, who was putting something hard inside the man's mouth, as his body jerked about. Rosie was snapping open smelling salts and putting them under the man's nose.

A TV screen attached to the wall was playing a security feed from the Jairus mansion, where the masquerade was held. The TV showed a bedroom. Daphne, Damon's fiancée was there. She had a knife and wounded Damon badly!

"Damon!" Rosie yelled at the unconscious man on the bed. "You need to wake up now!"

In the mansion, Damon was struggling to move. Damon and Daphne were still wearing their evening attire, and there was blood coming from Damon's arm and thigh. As he stood before her, facing off, he kept backing away as she moved closer. She came at Damon again and again, and I screamed.

He couldn't keep up with how fast she was. Every third or fourth strike was a stab that whipped in and out of him, or a slash. I shook each time she moved toward him and found myself moving closer to Rosie and the distressed body on the bed, looking harder at him.

It was Damon on the bed, but he had darker hair that was longer, with a full beard, and his body was covered in tattoos along his torso and arms. The monitors were attached to his trimmed chest, and he was wearing thin, black sweatpants. His muscles were toned and tight and strong, and his body was shaking from the pain.

"Give him the shot," Eamon said to Calder.

"Not yet!" Calder yelled.

"What's wrong?" I demanded.

"His avatar wasn't designed for a martyr disconnect. He can't just leave without the right protocol," Calder said.

"What does that mean?" I demanded.

"If she kills him while he's in his body, it could stop his heart here," Eamon barked at me. "The bodies are too connected."

"But if we administer the adrenaline before his heart stops, we could kill him," Rosie said.

"No!" Eamon argued. "His heart has a better chance if we jump start it now, before the damage takes hold."

"It only worked to mitigate damage that one time!" Calder argued. "When his heart had slowed down too far."

Eamon stared at the heart monitor, seeing Damon's real heart still beating.

"Damon, wake up!" Rosie started shaking him while in the middle of the bed. "Leave your clone. Please wake up."

"What if I speak the protocol?"

"He won't hear it over her screaming!"

I had moved closer, onto the bed, next to Damon's stomach. I put my hand on Damon's heart and leaned down to his ear.

"It's Gellion," I whispered into his ear. "I'm here. Please wake up."

"Get out of the way, Gellion!" Eamon yelled.

But Calder held him back as we all watched the screen in horror. Daphne was on top of Damon, like a mad woman, stabbing him over and over. Damon's body shook under us. I felt like I was in a movie scene, too unreal to believe. Yet there I was trying to wake up the hero, stuck inside a horrific reality.

What happens to me if he dies?

I'd never been a fan of sports, but suddenly I understood the seriousness of rooting for someone to be physically tough. I needed this guy to wake up for my own survival, not because of love, but out of sheer terror. Sure, I also felt a burning desire to know who I'd been before, but to stay alive now felt entirely dependent on his survival too.

"Damon, wake up!" His aunt yelled. "Why aren't the protocols working?"

"He didn't do any of them," Calder answered his mother.

"Too much trauma," Eamon added, reaching his hand out for Rosie's. "He's always half-way out when things end badly, but she snuck up on him."

They all watched the TV in anticipation, as Damon bled out. Calder was waiting for his heart to stop beating. Eamon was watching the heart monitor too. They were all frozen.

I closed my eyes and thought of my grandmother, who had always answered the phone when my night terrors overruled the sleeping pills. She would say that part of my consciousness was stuck in the nightmares, and I needed to save myself. So, I'd allow her voice to help pull the rest of me back into myself, where I was safe. Always she spoke of calling on light beings and the divine.

I was so afraid I couldn't help but do that too, leaning down closer to Damon, saying it in his ear gently, as his family waited.

"Come back to yourself!" I said in his ear. "It's going to be okay; come back to this body, come back and be healed," I said the words she'd say to me.

His convulsing body stopped moving, and I moved in closer again as his family gasped out in horror at the screen behind me. I put my forehead to his, to do for him what my grandmother would do for me when the pain from my body was so out of control. I kept imagining. Suddenly I could see it all, that I was a giant looking down on him bleeding out at the manor as I towered over him. I saw his soul lifting out of his dying body, and I imagined there was an invisible power coming from my hands, like how a sorcerer would look in a visually stunning movie or game.

In my mind I created a sphere of light with the power of my hands, and I captured Damon's retreating spirit, and carried it in that sphere through the wilderness, to where we were deep inside the ground.

Wait! We're in the ground?

I didn't know how I knew that, but I set that knowledge aside to continue seeing Damon come back to himself, to his original body, covered in tattoos and hair and scars. The Earth opened for me in my imaginings, and I delivered Damon's spirit back to his real body.

"Wake up now," I whispered next to his ear, my eyes closed, still stuck as a character from my imaginings.

"Ah!"

Damon's heart never stopped beating, so when he bolted upright and yelled out in pain and anger, we were shocked. Rosie was knocked back onto the bed as he rose, and I was shoved back too, as my torso and head were brought upright with him.

By the time I realized I'd been repositioned, face-to-face with Damon, he had his hand wrapped around my neck and was panting like a man who'd just outrun a monster on Halloween. He turned his head and stared into my eyes with a rage that scared me, yet I grew immediately distracted when I noticed his eyes were no longer blue, but a different color entirely.

Instead of fear at his rage, his real eye-color made me feel quizzical. What once were blue eyes at the masquerade, had turned a translucent green grey that glowed back at me as if lit in warm amber. His expression turned to recognition at seeing me.

"Your eyes are different." I said, peering deeply into them.

30

"Gellion," he said, catching his breath and hovering his mouth near mine. "Everyone out!" He panted out to all of them, and they all complied.

"Damon," Rosie said, warning him. "Gently."

He took a deep breath again and sighed, turning his head away from mine. He never let go of the back of my neck and held onto my arm too from across his chest. My breathing became heavy even while avoiding his stare, as his breathing slowly calmed.

He was just stabbed over and over, blood everywhere, his body on the monitor showing him bleeding out, yet now he was here, right in front of me. His face was just inches from mine. He sniffed my neck.

"Shalimar," he said softly, inhaling the air around me. "I knew I smelled that at the manor."

"How'd you know that?"

"You always wore it to special occasions."

"Well, Mom left me a ten-year supply, so now I wear it all the time."

His face fell back at my words, and he let go of my neck and arm, and moved to the other side of the bed where he stood up and removed the monitors off his torso. He looked up at a darkened window above and behind the TV screen in the room.

"I need a status report, Caitir," he said to the air. The TV screen changed channels from his dead body to another part of the Jairus mansion. Suddenly the darkened-window, behind the TV, lit-up and there were two far-off faces inside, a man and woman.

A female voice spoke through an intercom. "Daphne's moved to the front entrance. Tombo is trying to contain her now."

We could see it onscreen, just like the intercom-voice had said. Daphne had made it to the main foyer at the entrance of the manor and was facing off with multiple security guards employed by Damon, with Tombo leading them.

I felt completely overwhelmed by watching this confrontation. The horror I'd seen with Damon's clone just moments ago made me feel sick inside, the racing adrenaline too much. This whole evening was creating shock within me. I was breathing heavily and backed away from the screen to steady myself against the wall, my eyes glued to images I didn't want to see.

Suddenly, Damon's face was in front of mine, staring down at me from his height above. He put his finger under my chin and gently made me look away from the screen to meet his eyes.

"Aren't you worried?" I asked him.

"This isn't our first rodeo with death," he said. "It won't be yours either."

He was cavalier and threatening all in one breath. Yet even with Damon right in front of me, I could see Tombo on the screen. He repositioned around Daphne's body and pinned her to the ground as the other security disarmed her. She fought and then gave up.

I sighed, and looked up at Damon, who was studying my face.

Then Daphne broke free, as she kicked her legs like an Olympic wrestler and spun around, releasing her arm from Tombo's grip, and pulled something long and sharp from her hair. My eyes grew wide in horror, so Damon pulled at my chin and brought his mouth to mine. I closed my eyes as he kissed me.

The whole room went silent inside of me, every sensation completely blurred by his lips, and a feeling of deep connection, a knowing or a long-lost memory.

Another alarm blared out! My heart jumped almost out of my chest. I opened my eyes to see the back of Damon's head and Daphne stabbing Tombo, and I screamed! My stomach was making my mouth water with nausea anticipation.

Damon grabbed my arm and pulled me with him, almost carrying me as he maneuvered us through a door on the far side of the room below the window-view. He practically carried me up a spiral staircase, his hands on my waist, as he moved and got me through another door.

Inside was a circular room with a frameless window all the way around. The opening was lit up in most of the room that overlooked sleeping quarters. The whole room looked a bit like a spaceship, or maybe a captain's bridge or a command center of some kind.

There was a dark-skinned man seated, typing, and looking at the monitors all around. He looked Indian or Middle Eastern, of maybe even Indonesian. I couldn't be sure. An auburn-haired woman with pale skin was seated nearby working at another station. They were clearly running multiple computers and managing streams of information.

I tried to step forward, but Damon held my wrist and kept me next to him. In front of us, and above the circular window were detailed computer screens where information was displayed about many different things. First, I glanced at Tombo's medical readings and heartbeat. Then I saw satellite connections and cell phone communications.

Front and center, where Damon was staring, we could see the indoor security camera feeds at the Jairus estate. I couldn't watch, but knew it was still being displayed, Daphne killing Tombo, live. The other security men had all backed away but kept a circle around her as she wielded her weapon on Tombo, stabbing over and over, slowly, with a twisted glee.

Through the observatory view we could see Eamon ready with the adrenaline shot over Tombo's chest as Calder, younger and stronger, held Tombo's shaking body down.

Damon squeezed my wrist and looked down at me, his brow furrowed.

"Why didn't my heart stop?" He questioned me. "I hadn't done the protocols. I should have had a heart attack."

I stood there stunned, unable to say what I visualized or where I'd learned it from. Both the brown-skinned man and the auburn-haired woman had stopped typing and turned to look at me. They were very attractive too, but I had a hard time making eye contact.

Damon sat down at a computer terminal and then a video displayed from not long ago inside his room. He'd rewound it when his body lay twitching on the bed, and I'd bent down to whisper into his ear.

"What did you say to me?" he asked, stopping the playback.

And I just blanked. I really couldn't remember, so I just shook my head. I could recall something about nightmares and being lost or leaving pieces behind. But once Damon woke up and held me and kissed me my mind was a whirlwind and none of it included what I'd said to him to bring him back to himself.

Damon picked up an earpiece.

"Malik," he said. "Patch me in."

Malik furiously typed and as I stared at him I wondered if maybe he was from a different country entirely. The phone call came up on speaker.

"Autolycus here," Damon said. "Stand down."

Daphne glared at one of the security cameras and stared into it with her tongue hanging out, and both middle fingers in the air. Then she licked the blood off her tiny hair-pin blade while she pumped Tombo's bleeding lungs, torturing him until the end.

I couldn't stand the sight of it, and I couldn't quite shake the unsettling feeling of Damon's questioning expression toward me. His expectation of me was surprising, and I felt I was letting him down. Watching Tombo die felt wrong.

"Did he do the protocols to bring himself back" I asked.

"It wasn't supposed to be that kind of mission," he replied, remorsefully.

I had no sense of right or permission, but I felt deeply Damon wanted more from me. The room felt overwhelming with expectation, so I got up and walked for the door to the stairs and went down, my feet carrying me so much faster than I thought possible, but I stopped at the doorknob, looking through the glass window at Tombo inside. Damon was behind me, right away, his hand on the door, holding it shut.

"I didn't mean to suggest you do this," he said. "He'll be fine."

I took a deep breath and stepped back. He was there, his massiveness behind me and I leaned into him to see if I could. He didn't move until I was done leaning, then he pulled me away, back up the stairs.

Malik had connected Damon to the security-communication line and each guard in the foyer could hear Damon.

"Let her leave," he commanded. "Let her get in a limo."

The security men closest to the door opened a large space for Daphne to walk through. She moved quickly out of the manor.

"The cleanup crew is on their way," Damon continued, disconnecting from the violence of the crimes. "When they're done, close-up the manor and return to base. We'll be back before midday. You know the drill."

The security footage went dark, and Damon turned to me, looking for a reaction. I clutched my stomach and found a chair and kept my mouth shut, staring out into the distance.

Suddenly, Tombo entered the room, followed by the others. All of them were a bit breathless. I took a large, deep breath, slowly, and watched the two shirtless and tattooed men who'd been stabbed to death embrace hand-to-forearm, and hand to shoulder. I could see they were telling each other they were okay.

Like Damon, Tombo was covered in scars and ink. This Tombo, like Damon, had longer hair than his avatar clone, and the slightest stubble on his face. He was moving his head a bit, seemingly shaking his body out, like trying to brush off all that suffering that swept over him. It reminded me of the Bruce Lee movies, where he was always moving, preparing for another battle.

"How did the 'it' get out?" Tombo asked Damon.

"It?" I repeated back, confused.

Damon ignored my question. "She's been locked in a lot of cages. She knows some tricks and clearly doesn't care who she has to kill. With grandfather dead, we're no longer bound by his arrangement with her family, but that will have to be dealt with carefully."

"You're just going to let her go?" Eamon asked.

"I'm not making it worse by adding a missing fiancée to the possible scandal that's about to hit. What can she do?" Damon said.

"She can tell everyone about Gellion," Rosie complained.

Me? I felt sick again.

"She doesn't know," Damon countered Rosie's argument, and rested his hand on my shoulder. "She saw Gellion die like everyone else. Tom was the only one who saw Gellion, and he was convinced she was Daphne. Besides, even if I took Gellion around town on my arm, do you think any of them remember the faces of the victims? Daphne's too busy staring at her fingernails to remember the details."

I found myself stepping away again, putting some distance between myself and their conversation, and found a chair a bit farther back.

"You can say that all you want," the auburn-haired computer tech named Caitir chimed in, "but you don't know what she's trained to recall. She's been M.K.'d."

"What's that?" I asked, but no one answered.

"She woke up tied up in a bedroom, after knowing Grandpa Skip was murdered."

"And when you flaunt Gellion to everyone and Daphne realizes what you did, then what?" Calder argued with Damon.

"I'm not flaunting Gellion!" Damon yelled at everyone, as if they were insane. "She's here. She's safe. That's all."

Rosie walked toward him and took his hand and held it. "Of course, Daphne wasn't invested in your arranged marriage, Damon, but please be careful. You don't know who's watching."

"Actually, we do," Malik said, in a slight British accent. "We know every move all the guests make. All their phones are cloned, and we've already been through every device."

Damon looked at me curiously, then turned his attention. "Malik, track Daphne and when she lands, send her a bouquet of flowers to remind her about the blackmail we have on her."

"The limo is taking her to Tom's city apartment," Caitir said, as an image of a phone's screen popped up. "But Tom's at the hospital, getting his broken nose looked at," she said, in a slightly chiding tone.

Damon ignored her scolding.

"Eamon? Calder? Can you prepare our clones for transport? Tombo, stay on coms for anything incoming, and then prepare for transfer-port. Rosie, could you pick out clothes for when we transfer? Caitir, Malik are we sure anyone there didn't backdoor a recording of the event?"

"Damon, I've got it," Caitir whined at his lack of trust. "We've been working with MARI since the beginning of the party to do the searches. Already erased videos off multiple devices and their clouds. Only two devices can't be accounted for or went offline immediately after, but Malik already dumped a virus to eat the contents when the phone turns on again. We'll update you when they come back online."

It sounded settled and before anyone could question him, Damon said, "Let's go! We can all catch up later." And they immediately scattered. Everyone left except Caitir and Malik.

"Oh my gosh!" Caitir squealed out loud as she got up from her seat. "It's Gell, in the flesh."

Auburn-haired to the mid-back, with pale skin and freckles, Caitir came at me with open arms. She was adorably short, even shorter than me, but thinner and almost pixie, unlike her brother who was massive.

She came in for a hug. "I'm gonna cry," she squealed.

Damon put his hands on both our shoulders and Caitir stopped rocking me.

"Gellion, you've met my family. Caitir is Calder's sister and they're my cousins. Their mom, Aunt Rosephine is my dad's younger sister. Tombo is the head of security. Uncle Eamon and Calder specialize in cloning and medical research. Malik, our most talented engineer, wants to marry into this."

Malik waved at me a little and reached out his hand to take Caitir's. Caitir kept one hand over her mouth, smiling at me.

"Gellion, we need to explain some things," Damon said, taking my hand and pulling gently at me to walk with him.

"Malik, can you take us up?" Damon said.

Malik and Caitir sat down at different workstations. Malik worked with some controllers on the center console in the middle of the room. Suddenly the floor began to shift, and we were rising. The circle window that overlooked the bedrooms fell away and the vacant space was replaced with darkness as we moved up.

One large floor above where we'd been, we stopped. A glass wall came into view, and beyond it was a gigantic facility. From that view the large room was visible, filled with rows of clear pods with liquid and human bodies inside. The faces were far off yet familiar; most of them. It was like a farm. I walked to the edge of the command center and leaned through the window-opening to get as close to the glass wall as I could. It was amazingly beautiful and horrifying too.

"Why do you have so many?" I asked quietly, as I stared in awe at them.

"Survival. War," Damon quipped.

The weight of his words brought heaviness to my mind. "Are you at war?"

His eyebrows raised up at my question, and slowly he nodded. When Damon finally looked at me, his face was contorted, his brow line squeezed by squinting eyes.

"Since the day they tried to kill you," he confessed.

3

THE QUANTUM SPECULUM

The words echoed in my ear. Damon's voice telling me when his war against his grandfather had begun.

Since the day they tried to kill you, he'd said.

It sounded so ominous the way he said they'd killed me, like he was speaking of a far-off time.

"They did kill me, last night," I replied to Damon. "Is that what you mean? Has a war started?"

"No," he grumbled out.

"When then?"

"A long time ago."

"How long?" I asked, my mouth was trembling.

He shook his head and put his hands up as if to feign ignorance.

"Tell me," I demanded!

My mind started to consider his words. Because I had died, in a car accident. I was told it was a miracle I survived. It was the last thing I expected to consider. To have my reality reframed, that the accident at the end of high school was deliberate. I went silent, absorbing the idea

I had been targeted all along, which made the damage my body suffered all that more understandable. I wasn't supposed to have lived.

When I finally made eye contact again, the only thing I could think to say was, "So, I'm a casualty of war. Hmm. All this time I just thought I was cursed."

"We were cursed," Damon mumbled.

"If I'm down here with you, does that mean the war is over now, or just beginning?"

"Well, my greatest foe is finally gone."

"Your grandfather."

"Yes, but we have no knowledge of how it will affect our safety, not yet. My cover may be blown. I don't know."

"Playing a double agent is nearly impossible without help," I surmised.

"Who better to help me than myself?" Damon said, pointing out all the far-off clones.

"And if I hadn't arrived at the masquerade?" I asked.

"We knew you were coming," Damon redirected and shrugged. "Grandfather vowed to relinquish his war on my past associations, in exchange for my submission and fealty. The moment he broke his word I had no choice but to plan for an end to his power over us."

"Yeah, it was so odd to be assigned to him," I reminisced. "To end up in his office, see the wealth of it and be so small in his presence. Is there any chance of winning the war?"

"Surviving is winning. A long time ago you told me the darkness of Earth would be leaving, and if I was smart enough we could survive through it."

"That sounds made up," I retorted, scowling at the words which sounded nothing like me.

"I know you don't remember, but it's true."

"And you believed me?" I asked.

He smirked. The longer I stood there staring, the clearer it was to me that some of these pods were like gazing into a mirror.

"How many of these clones are of me?" I asked. He didn't answer.

"And what do you do with them?"

Damon looked down at me and raised an eyebrow at my accusatory stare, and his nostrils flared.

"Eamon and Calder can give you a tour," he said and then he got closer to me. "You can count the clones for yourself and find out all about them. They're a recent addition."

He was so close to me I could feel the warmth of his breath in my face, but I didn't know how to get past his brutish demeanor.

"Why'd you save me, Damon?" I asked gently.

I felt so strongly at that moment that the real version of me was ugly and damaged and too afraid of society that I rarely valued my own life very much. Damon's eyes softened at my words, and he sighed. Then he reached out and touched my mouth with his thumb, and I let him, as he pulled gently at my bottom lip. He moved his hand to stroke my cheek but stopped himself, hovering his fingertips there. His hand was warm, almost hot on my cool skin.

"We need a moment," Damon said to Malik and Caitir, as they moved to leave the room.

We do? I thought.

Damon's hand was so large, he was able to hold my neck and touch my cheek too. I could hear everyone leave but didn't see them. I was enraptured. He pulled my face close to him, hovering over my lips.

"You changed me. You brought me into the light, the light I'd forgotten existed, while I brought your life into the darkness. I regret so much," he said, pulling my neck toward him, his lips touching my forehead. He sighed and kissed my forehead again. "You shouldn't have seen it, Gellion," he said, mournfully, confusing me. "I thought you'd left the manor already. To watch your own body, die that way..."

What?

That's not what I expected to hear, at all...and the images of the torture his words hurled upon me came flashing before my eyes.

Why do you keep doing that? I asked inside my head, frowning.

My vision was exhausted again, and I closed my eyes and took a deep breath.

"Enough!" I chided him and went to push him away because I didn't want to remember. However, Damon held onto me and pulled me back to him.

"We made promises to each other a long time ago, you and I," Damon said softly in my ear, his cheek brushing up against mine. Then he pulled away from me to stare into my eyes. "I'd already failed you once. It wasn't ever going to happen again."

"You're a stranger to me, and none of this seems real," I said, removing myself entirely from his hold.

"Don't Gellion," he said low and frustrated. "I didn't save you and bring you down here just so you could pretend like none of this is happening."

I glared at him and said the most obvious thing I could think to say, "I'm in shock!"

"You'll adapt," he replied coldly.

"Gee," I lamented. "Explain to me why I was on that chopping block."

"I told you why."

"So, you liked me. I get it; you're the main character, and I was your crush."

"Did you ever wonder how you ended up the assistant to one of the most powerful CEOs in the world?"

"I didn't. Back then I could barely think at all, just making it through the day, the week, waiting until I'd need to be cut open again."

My brow was scowling at how much his words triggered my memory. I couldn't meet his eyes because it was true, how I ever got that position never made any sense to me. I told myself it was Katherine's connections, but the company had sought me out, gave me scholarships and grants, internships, and jobs.

My job at Jairus Industries permanently set that feeling of worthlessness deep inside. Mr. Jairus loved to degrade me, while also complimenting me at the same time.

"I was told to walk away from you, and I tried..." Damon continued, "...hoping that desolation would be enough to keep you safe, but he was never going to stop playing with my affection for you. And he wouldn't be satisfied until I was willing to burn my humanity to the ground, and you with it."

My face twisted in disgust at the shifting thoughts of Mr. Jairus.

"Why?"

"It's just their way."

"What does that mean?"

"They don't believe in loyalty through love, or love at all. Only loyalty to bloodlines that work together to maintain power through a shared allegiance to the dark. The dark that requires blood sacrifices in exchange for reward. Many of the world's most powerful, rich and famous belong to this club. It's required for some of them."

I shook my head; it wasn't possible.

"It's the truth," he stated. "You saw it with your own eyes."

"Is that why you drank the blood?"

"I'm one of them. I belong to one of the thirteen families. My father's marriage to my mother secured my grandfather's future as blood-bonded to the people who rule," he said, trying to explain something I couldn't understand or conceptualize.

"So, the vampires rule the world," I whispered to myself, and Damon chortled at my words.

He couldn't disagree. My mind was stuck there, in that thought. The most disturbing movies I'd ever seen were some of the truest. How awful.

"Did you?" I wondered, redirecting my brain to ask for more information.

"Did I what?"

"Burn your humanity to the ground?"

He squinted at me and looked around before returning my gaze.

"I stood by and watched while my grandfather stabbed your image to death and then I drank your blood."

"My clone," I realized.

"Yes. And that was the closest he was ever going to get," Damon said with a quiet rage.

My body was having a hard time processing all the information. My ears felt clogged, and my head felt foggy. I was overloaded at who Mr. Jairus had really been and why I'd really been hired all along, as a trophy of some kind, in a twisted game. Damon looked angry, and maybe ashamed, and it made me wonder what I didn't know.

"How many times were you forced to stand by and watch while someone died?" I asked him bluntly.

His face was surprised by the question, so he took a step away, resting his arms on the railing, stretching against it to relieve something deeper.

"It's going to take time for us to get to that part, Gellion," Damon said, somberly, quietly, like he was reminiscing bad times. "You're not quite yourself. Neither am I. We're not ready for those stories."

"Who could ever be ready?" I whispered, feeling my chest tightening.

He was right, of course. I could barely handle anything anymore, but my body was also wired from the adrenaline of so much terrifying information coming my way. I took deep, slow breaths to refocus.

"Since it was my clone that killed Mr. Jairus, where does that leave you, with all those powerful people?"

"There's already a plan in place. You need not worry about it."

"Maybe, but I still overthink everything, or was that not your Gellion? So, sorry but this Gellion can't and just won't trust you yet. Like, you're just gonna fix it?"

"Hmmm," he hummed, then chuckled. "My grandfather had a lot of enemies." He chuckled again. "It gave me great fellowship to discover how many people wanted him dead, and how much fear he started to live-in because of his backstabbing."

"Wasn't the masquerade invitation only?" I asked.

"It was, and I invited his enemies," Damon laughed. "The people who would take issue with his death are going to have a hard time figuring out what happened for a while."

"I'm glad you're enjoying this," I said, disgusted, "but I'm not."

"You're safe. That's the best I could do, Gellion. He made plans to sacrifice you and see if I would flinch or lose it in front of a crowd. If I'd fought it, I would have lost my life on the spot. He would have made sure of that."

"You would have been killed?" I was surprised, "But you're one of them."

"Either you play by the rules of that world, or you die. You rarely 'get out,' no matter how much you sacrifice or how far away you run from society. He was the patriarch, the oligarch, and the Grand Master. His influence ruled much of the northeast quadrant of the U.S."

That truth, about Damon's grandfather, was startling.

"Oh," I finally said, accepting the weight of it. "So, here we are."

"Here we are," he repeated.

"So, am I, like, um," I stuttered, "down here now because you loved me?"

Damon almost coughed but cleared his throat instead. "If it were just about long-lost love, I would have sent you to Europe with a new identity," he said. He got closer to me again and leaned nearby. "I'm much too selfish for that."

Damon walked over to a portion of the command center that controlled levers and pushed one. The floor shifted again, and we started moving up. He came back and pulled my arms in from the window ledge. He held me suddenly, from behind, as the floor shook and rose, keeping me balanced.

He whispered in my ear. "I can't possibly win the war I was trained to win, if I let my team get taken out."

"I'm a pawn on the board," I said to myself.

"You don't know how important you are."

"Surely no better than a rook?" I joked, uncomfortably, unused to being touched, held, or wanted. My body ached from so much movement. I was hurting and uncomfortable and yet filled with too much awkwardness to stop Damon, to tend to my pain.

"At first, you were the Queen. That's how I saw you. Then, it was as if the board stopped existing, and you were the wizard who'd put the game away and gave me a moment to breathe."

What? The wizard who put the game away?

Somehow I'd expected the first part about the queen. How cliché of me. The rest really made me think. He stated it all as a fact, without emotion. I couldn't respond.

"You knew how to change it all," he reminisced. "You had these visions. We had a plan, until I stopped thinking three steps ahead, and without even realizing it, I'd stopped fully listening to you."

"I'm not that person anymore," I reminded him, bitter, unable to see his vision of me.

"You saved my soul from hell," he argued quietly, angrily.

I turned around to look at him and his hands came up to my face, holding my cheeks, pulling me toward him, as if he were going to kiss me again at any moment.

"I'm not sure I can control myself with you. I've been waiting so long to touch you again."

The floor stopped moving and there was a bright light that showed from the opposite side of the command center, through another clear wall.

Damon let go of me and walked backward to the other side, watching me as I followed him. The open window view now overlooked into some kind of contraption. We leaned over the open windows and peered down into a tall concrete area that held a prominent feature: a thirty-foot tall black-circular wall sat in the middle of the tall and narrow space.

The black walls sparkled on the inside of the cylinder shape. Inside the circular wall had a grated metal floor that reminded me of an indoor skydiving set-up. The grated floor was a step up from the ground floor which had fans below.

Above the thirty-foot circular wall, a ceiling piece, also circular and black, was hovering ten feet above the walls. It was our way to see inside it from the command center, looking between the top piece and the thirty-foot circular structure.

Looking down, I saw the black walls glittered and sparkled. It wasn't until I looked up at the screens above me that I understood why.

Although no one was inside the structure, something was showing up like a projection without a screen. Video cameras mixed with light-display lights were creating visual imageries on the screen and inside the walls, like a laser light show, which was clearly a part of the massive machine.

"What is it?" I asked Damon.

"It's a Quantum Field Reader Speculum," he said. "We call it the 'Q-Spec.'"

"What does it do?"

Behind me Caitir appeared out of nowhere with a see-through tablet and a stylus pen.

"Do you want to take her inside?" she asked.

"Not yet," Damon replied, taking the tablet from her. He tapped a bunch of different sub-files on the tablet and below us I could see lights come on and a scene come to life. The view looked much better on the large screen above my head. I stood back and watched as Damon loaded the information.

"The Q-Spec reads the energy fields of the human body and attempts to map the information so we can see how well someone's energy system works. Usually, we capture how they are depleted or broken. It's a tool to see the truth of our human energy design, to show us what has never been seen."

Inside the Q-Spec a replay of events was beginning. A woman made of light and laser-beams stood in the middle of the circular grates. One set of projection lights showed her as she was, as a holographic woman. Another set of projection lights showed the energy in and around her, lighting up in a golden stream of moving dots that created a bubble of energy swirling over her body, being fed by her body and feeding into her body from above and below her.

"The golden bubble represents the torus forcefield," Damon said.

I watched as the golden yellow moved, examining how a perpetual forcefield would be connected to its human.

Then Damon tapped another button and many streams of moving aqua blue-light-dots formed into small tornadoes that whirled both clockwise and counterclockwise. The tornadoes were many and started above her head and below her feet, then appeared individually on both the back and front of her body, seven on both sides all the way down from head to toe.

The small tornadoes existed inside the golden forcefield and came out of the woman as if they were planted up her spine and down her front, at points that correlated to important human systems. The tornadoes above her head and below her feet were tall and they fed into her forcefield too, connecting the blue lights to the yellow stream of energy and vice versa.

"These spinning energies are the chakras," Damon said.

He clicked the stylus, and a green laser shot out and started pointing to the energy systems we were looking at.

"The chakra tornadoes are rhythmic in their movement, of light-feeding-light, and they mirror one another front and back, bottom to top. The placement of each chakra coincides with other known energy constructs. For example, the two chakras at her head, coming out of her forehead and out the back of her head, represent a connection into the third-eye and help feed intuition."

Damon pointed at the connection in the front and out the back of her head, showing chakras that were vibrant and self-propelling. He motioned next to the two chakras at her throat and neck.

"These two deal with our ability to speak, or our freedom to say what we think and feel and our level of communication."

Then he pointed to the two chakras at her sternum and midback and said, "Obviously these affect the heart."

He pointed again at the next two. "Two chakras at her belly button and low back must be connected to the energy construct of the Chi. This location is considered the power chakra, so that is in alignment with the idea of Chi. We haven't been able to map the Chi energy, though we've recently discovered the variable vibration of the meridian lines. So, we think we're close."

The words Damon was saying were a lot more known to me than I first realized. Familiar because of my grandmother, whose health clinic helped my hurt body all the time, and she spoke about some of these things. Familiar because of Katherine, who mentioned it too as if it were a part of her Korean upbringing, her version of Korean Christianity with some Buddhism included.

In reality, it was always from the source first, my grandfather who'd introduced it to my grandmother then to my mother, and then to me. I wondered if it was Damon who made Katherine talk about it, since my grandmother only did so in passing, during my therapeutic sessions. To realize these things came from my grandparents, from before my injuries made them even more special. That their knowledge had been placed before me by Katherine, under Damon's instruction, was the stark reminder that my grandmother had been broken by her losses too.

Damon pointed to the woman's pelvis. "Two chakras at her sacrum, then two at her knees and feet."

I was mesmerized!

I needed to see it closer, but I suddenly didn't want to have to ask for permission from Damon, so I turned quickly for the door and skipped down the spiral staircase. At the bottom there was only one door to walk through, and it led to a short hallway which had a security hand-print pad at the side of an invisible door.

I instinctively put my hand on the reader and the doors opened, revealing a curved-ceiling tunnel to get in. On the other side I was in the machine.

The scene with the woman was playing right in front of me, life size. I walked around her as her light-form hovered above me over the metal grated floor. I stared at the millions of blue light dots that made up the tornadoes of energy.

"According to Indian philosophy," Damon said from behind me, "the chakras are considered the centers of spiritual power and energy within our bodies. The word 'chakra' means wheel, but as you can see, they are more like conjoined tornadoes, or rather, overlapping elongated tori; psychic-energy-centers connected to the body."

Damon tapped his stylus on the tablet and one of the tornadoes of energy was pulled away from the woman in mid-air. He brought it closer to us, to the edge of the grated metal floor. He turned the tornado over and stretched it and compacted it, to show how it could easily shrink from a tornado into a moving Torus, a donut shaped energy field that perpetually rotated energy in two differing directions to keep feeding itself as it spun around. When he was done showing me, he put the energy system back in place.

"These are real?" I questioned.

"Truly. Our human body has an energetic system, which we need to have intact and energized to live well here. You taught me that."

"My grandmother taught me, didn't she?" I asked, but he only smiled at me, like the question puzzled him a little. "You built this?"

"With help."

"So, you invented clones, and now this?"

Damon chuckled. "I didn't invent clones. They've been around for a long, long time. I just stole the technology so I could use it."

I wondered if that tale of theft was as dangerous as the mission at the masquerade to save me.

"And the Q-Spec?"

"Well, I collected all the latest research on the subject, of course, but there were never any big budget projects, so the rest is mine with help from Caitir and Malik, based on the ideas we got from you."

"Me?"

"You told me I should build this. You were sometimes psychic, sometimes clairvoyant, and always geometrically creative. You could see the need for new technology to make the world better. You just weren't going to build it yourself."

"I told you how to build this machine?" I whispered, truly baffled.

"Yes and no. You told me we could build it. You said what materials it would need. You could even see some of the layout. You gave me all the information you could and left it for me to figure out."

"Why build it?"

"For you to use. For others to learn."

"I'm not sure that's something I can do."

"This is how you saw the world, Gellion" he said, trying to explain. "Actually no, this is nothing. This is the first two layers of basic energy mapping. What you could see was so much more multi-dimensional. You taught me so much, but I didn't always listen back then."

"You've got to be joking. I don't know any of this," I said shaking my head.

"That's why I built it, to help you learn."

"Did I know I was going to get hurt?" I had to ask, as my symptoms pinged my body, sending shooting pain down my arm, nerves on fire from shoulder to fingertip.

"You never said so, no," Damon replied.

I took a deep breath. A permanent scowl of confusion and uncertainty was taking hold over my brow. I looked up at the woman's golden bubble and felt that if I had a forcefield too, it would surely be small. With so much suddenly on my shoulders, my body and mind felt very tired, my building pain hard to ignore.

I walked slowly to the hand-print reader inside the Q-Spec. This time, it didn't recognize my hand and made a jarring sound. Damon came near and I looked up at him, dejected.

"I'm hurting. I need out," I said, feeling faint from the sharp stabbing jolts heading up my neck, and so disappointed to be fading so fast into exhaustion that I could barely stand up.

"I didn't mean to scare you…" he said, but then I couldn't hear any more.

My eyelids drooped and I swayed and fell forward, unable to handle the pain any longer. Damon's arms caught me, and he pulled me into him and lifted me up. I leaned my head onto his chest, aware that the dizziness I felt was causing nausea, stemming from so much nerve pain untreated. The exhaustion was beyond physical. The imagery and expectations on my system were beyond my comprehension. I wanted to feel nothing, but I'd settle for anything to numb myself. My eyes stayed closed until the rhythm of Damon's feet lulled me into a relieved slumber.

4

NEVER GOING HOME

I hadn't slept long, and my head was pounding, but behind my eyes and my desperation to stay unconscious, my mind was remembering my death at the hands of Mr. Jairus, and I wanted to avoid it. It hurt still to learn the ugly truth.

In my lucid state, I chose to play for myself that kiss, the one that made contact and lasted, as it was the only spark of something beyond weird, crazy, or frightening.

The rest, I wanted to blur behind me, so I could get up.

Why can't I just sleep?

Did I need to see Damon again?

No, it was more urgent. I needed my pills, as the shooting pain crept behind my eye like a hammer to my head. I sat upright in the hospital bed, surprised to be back there. It was low-lit and quiet, but familiar.

Thank God! My purse was on the bedside table.

The pills would take time to stop the throbbing and in that silence of waiting I realized it was more than my pain that woke me.

"Brian?" I quietly cried out. It was the thought of my teenage brother, who I'd helped raise after my mom died.

"Dad!" I said more softly, like a grieving cry from deep within. I hadn't gone more than a day or two without seeing either of them since the beginning of my memory.

What time is it? What day is it? Do they already think I'm missing?

I needed to get to a computer or a phone.

I was aware, as I squinted my eyes, that I felt delirious. I didn't like where I was and very much wanted to call home. I'd heard Damon say, as I was in and out of consciousness, that he had to transport himself back to the city but would be back.

How long had I slept?

I also flashed in thought to that psychotic woman who'd killed Damon and Tombo so easily.

How much does she know?

I'd found out virtually nothing about where I was since arriving, except who was there and that the location had to be highly secure. Then there was Damon, who wanted me, needed me, and was quite frankly terrifying in many ways. The thoughts were consuming.

Waking up in the hospital bed again was weird. Though my body was screaming at me for relief, I slipped on the slippers and saw a warm white robe hanging nearby to cover my cold body. I hadn't realized how exposed I'd felt, not with the commotion of being in Damon's half-naked company. His presence made my body hot.

Now I was shivering, waiting for the thick material to comfort my cold chest and arms, while my silk dress kept my legs covered. Once I stopped shivering, I spit swallowed my pain pills and went looking for a way to reach out to my family. Beyond the sets of hospital curtains, there was a lab with some computers I'd run past following Rosie out, during Daphne's attack.

I clicked on the mouse at the first desk I saw, and the computer screen lit up but required a password. At least the date and time displayed. It was only the next morning and still fairly early. I hadn't slept long at all! Not surprising as my body throbbed too much, and

I'd craved my meds for relief.

Past the computer desks the overhead lights turned on in response to my movements, and on the other side of the glass wall were the cloning pods, in very low lighting, the liquid inside an illuminated turquoise. I was hypnotized by them and walked down the side of the wall to find the doorway to go inside.

There were rows and rows of them. Fully grown humans in liquid pods, being kept alive and built up. They were naked, though I did not focus on their nudity, but their faces, so alive, despite sleeping eyes. Eventually I came across my own clones. It was a powerful sensation seeing myself in perfection. Bodies that carried no extra weight compared to bodies that did, each version of me perfect, without scars.

I felt something else come over me at seeing them, ugly in their presence. Too many in my likeness, all naked and untarnished in ways I'd never remembered being as myself. Some had my dyed-brown hair, like now, and others had long blond hair, like how it used to be when I was younger. Damon had clearly learned to play with the DNA code, or maybe it came with the stolen technology.

There was a light at the opposite end of the cloning warehouse. It was an open area with high ceilings and several robotic looking surgical tables, with clear covers over them, and computers attached. I had seen these in movies. They were medbeds. Three of these surgical robotic medical tables sat side by side, and all of them had bodies inside that looked familiar.

On the first bed was Damon's corpse, its coloring of lifelessness clear from Daphne's inflicted wounds. It looked as if the medbeds were reading information from the wounds and preparing for surgery of some kind. Tombo's corpse was being handled in the same way.

When I saw my body in the third medbed, I felt sick again.

Is that my sacrificed clone in there?

No, wait, she wasn't covered in murderous cuts, and her flesh looked alive.

Something was happening though. The medbed was starting some sort of countdown. Then a laser lit up and hit the clone in the head. I walked quickly to see. It was cutting her open! Burning her! The robot-surgeon was using the laser to cut open my clone!

I started pressing buttons, but nothing stopped it. I could see how deep the cuts were, how much blood started to pour out of the clone before the healing laser began creating the scars. The vision of it seared pain into my own scars down my face and neck, the burn so strong I cried out.

"Ah! Stop!"

The buttons to turn it off weren't clear. In my panic and terror, I reacted. I grabbed something long and hard and started swinging at the clear cover of the medbed that kept her trapped. There was so much blood before a second laser stopped the bleeding!

It didn't take long before I finally cracked the damn thing open. Stupidly, I reached in with my left hand and got hit by the cutting laser! I was out of my mind. When I realized the burning in my hand was from actual damage, unhealed, I screamed and screamed until I couldn't make myself suffer the pain any longer, and it turned to rage.

The hot white burning in my body allowed me the strength to remove the hatch open and I toppled my clone out of the machine, and onto the ground, me beneath it. By the time I was done, I was covered in blood and breathless, and I cried out, all while holding a bleeding clone in my arms on the cold floor.

I knew I was delirious from a lack of sleep, but I also thought I was finally having the mental breakdown I'd feared. The burning of my hand and the images of my own tormented body sent me over the edge. My therapist would call it a "justified breakdown, to make a breakthrough" and sometimes she was right. I wanted to go home. I wanted to sleep in my own bed. I wanted to erase the horror show that seemed to be only just beginning.

"Gellion?" I heard a voice say, calmly.

"Don't do this!" I said, holding my bleeding hand, with the clone in front of me. "Please don't hurt her."

A voice whispered. "I told you we should have moved her to one of the studios, so she could be more comfortable," Caitir complained.

"Damon wanted her nearby." Calder argued back.

"She needs a real break," Caitir said. "Now she's cut open and bleeding."

"I want to go home." I felt drunk with exhaustion.

"Gellion," Rosie said softly, "sweetie, you can't go home right now."

"I'm not asking!" I growled at them.

"How about a hot shower and a nice big bed to sleep in?"

"I want to go home!" I sobbed.

"Are you hungry?" Calder asked, then he said quietly, "I need to treat her hand."

"MARI, locate Malik!" Caitir called out.

"Malik here," his voice sounded.

"Call Damon back. We made a mess of things."

"No! Don't call him back!" I yelled. "He's not the boss of me!" I screamed at the beautiful strangers who acted like my friends. "Where's the way out?"

I knew I was being belligerent. I didn't care. I was hysterical on the inside as the overwhelm of images: torture, sacrifice, clones, murder, technology, and now the knowing of loss, of my loved ones gone, of Dad, Brian, BB, and my friends, all gone. I was also now covered in bodily fluids that smelled of iron and turned me red.

I got up and stared at the unmoving clone, barely bleeding, and backed away. There was a stray cloth nearby, so I wrapped my hand, and started looking for a way out. It was irrational, but it was better than the current view of dead and maimed clones. I had to get out of there.

Caitir caught up to me in the hallway and walked by my side.

I was breathing too fast. Eventually I found an elevator. It required a handprint too, so I wiped my grubby hand and placed it on the reader.

It blared at me.

Of course, Damon would never allow me to leave without permission. Caitir pulled her hand out of her pocket and placed it on the reader. The elevator door opened. I went inside, and she followed. There were only two buttons to push. I pushed them both.

We stopped first at "B" and when the doors opened there was only a small room in front of us with a door and a clear storage-unit with tools.

"This is where we access the service ladder, and where we store the bomb to blow up access, to shield us from below."

"You have a bomb in there?"

She nodded and smiled.

I didn't step out.

The second stop was much lower below us. "T" opened to an underground railway-platform. There were two sets of tracks, going in different directions, and the ceiling above us was high.

"Is this the only way out?" I asked, in awe.

"Yes."

"Who drives the train?"

"It's automated."

"So, I could get on that train and leave?" I pointed at the only train there.

"Not that one. It's pointed in the wrong direction," she said, "but yes, after we turn it around."

"Can we do that now?"

"Well, I'm pretty sure the train that Damon and Tombo took is on its way back, so we should probably just wait for that one instead of causing a train crash."

"I feel trapped because I am trapped," I mumbled to myself.

"Gellion, I'm so sorry this is how you had to find out about us. You don't know how many times I wanted to call you or write or show up at your door."

"But you couldn't..."

"Evil people have no problem killing their own family members, and we are always watched," she replied, her head down. "That's how Damon's family died."

My eyes blinked rapidly, and my brain switched gears at her words,

57

and I suddenly wondered about them and their story, and what that would have done to the man who claims to have loved me.

"What do you mean?"

"In our world if you want power and money and control, you have to sacrifice someone, or a lot of someone's, to get it."

"A child?"

"Of course, or your spouse or a parent. Babies too," she said sadly. "Grandpa Jairus wanted more power and more money, and so he had to provide either a sacrifice or a new minion, someone precious to him, a relative for a ceremony to call on the dark lord to bring him more power."

"The Devil?"

"The dark powers here have many names."

"How do you know?"

"Seeing is believing, as they say."

"What did you see?"

"Evil doesn't just come from people alone. There are real forces behind it."

I could see her considering what to tell me, until words just started pouring out of her.

"Grandfather sold my mother into marriage to build an alliance with a more powerful family. She had been trained since she was a child to be what he wanted her to be. And so, she lived that life, forced to participate in the rituals and sacrifices."

I gasped! My eyes were wide with horror and curiosity, trying to envision Rosie being stuck in a life like that.

"It didn't last. She wanted to die, so she ran away and met my father. Mom never went back, so Grandfather tried to have her punished. When I was little, I was taken and forced to become a part of that world. I was stolen several times, then taken back. I saw things, was shown things, was abused, and was encouraged to hurt others. I wasn't the only one."

"Damon?" I asked.

She nodded her head.

"But my father is from an old bloodline of Scottish and British Lords, so he was able to create some protection, get me back and eventually keep me safe. His family's wealth was no longer tied into the global market share controlled by people like Grandfather."

I could only stare at Caitir, waiting for her to tell me more.

"Damon's parents left America and joined Mom in Scotland. They had four children, but when Damon turned eight everything went wrong."

"What happened?" I asked.

"Grandpa Skip couldn't control his children and that made him less powerful in the hierarchy. He needed offspring who would join him for the ceremonies and to pass down power. Since his children refused, he stole us, and offered us up as proteges, and victims. He could have our parents killed or he could bankrupt them. He gave them options, to each hand over a child, his preference being Damon and I."

"Why him and you?"

Caitir shrugged. "Firstborns."

"What do you mean?"

"We're either chosen for a greater purpose or sacrificed. Depends on the omens too?"

"My family got away. Damon's family didn't. The omens said we must live, I think. He became an orphan instead, the only survivor, left in grandfather's care. The omens didn't save grandfather from the backlash, and his station was demoted. He'd regained control of the region because of it, but his censure helped secure my freedom."

My mouth quivered in horror, and I could feel a surge of tingling move from the back of my throat up to my eyes, of hard tears formed.

"We've never spoken of what was done to him, to turn him into one of them. We all suffered some form of it and knew what future ceremonies would entail. We understood Damon, without needing to communicate."

My shivering body accepted the powerful emotion of it, a sick and twisted world they'd known. And then she said something I just couldn't wrap my head around.

"He was on an evil path, until he met you."

The cold of the underground station made the shaking of my body worse. I was so grateful for the fluffy robe, even if it was smeared with blood. A slight breeze swept over us with the noise and lights of a train coming near. It pulled right up to the station, and the door opened as the one-car train stopped.

I wanted to get in. My breathing got very heavy as I labored over my emotions, and my fear of the truth. Damon's aggression and passion and rage were a bit more understandable after listening to Caitir. It seemed I was important, yet for only one purpose, and I was inadequate for the task. I didn't really believe I was who they said I was. Too foreign.

I wanted to hug my dad, and my brother and my grandma, to smell their familiar smells and feel the warmth of their humanity.

What if I get them hurt, or killed?

Caitir's story was brief, but poignant. The stakes for them had always been death, from the beginning. What a horrible way to live. As I stared at the open door, I could feel the burning in my hand from the open wound that dripped blood to the floor, and I knew I couldn't leave, not then. I turned my head to look at Caitir, who seemed genuinely worried about me.

"Thank you for telling me," I said to her. "I don't mean to be difficult..."

"...You are not being difficult, Gellion," she reassured me. "This whole thing is crazy, I know."

"I just want to run away."

"It may not feel like it, but being down here; this is running away," she smiled slightly. "We just have to show you how nice this place is, and how comfortable you can be."

She started to reach out, maybe for a hug, maybe to check my hand, but was interrupted by the elevator doors opening. I could practically feel the anger coming from behind us. Damon was standing inside, and Caitir's face looked timid at his presence. I glanced behind me but didn't really see him. I didn't want to.

"Don't you have a job to do?" he chastised.

"I've got my comms in," Caitir said, pulling her earpiece out of her ear.

Had they all been listening to us?

"I want to talk to Gellion alone."

Caitir went to the elevator without a sound, and I finally turned around and looked at him.

I balled up my hurt hand, ready for a fight with Damon, his eyes glaring at me, at my defiance, of wanting to be close to freedom. The elevator left.

"They will kill your family."

"What if they're not watching?"

"It hasn't even been a day. Don't make me tie you up."

"I can't do it, Damon."

"Look, I told you too much, too fast...."

"...told me?"

"Ok, and also maybe what I showed you too," he added. "But there's no pressure. Just take your time."

"No pressure?!" I asked. "Well, that's just a lie."

The story from Caitir had been sobering, but it was nothing compared to the wound I'd tried to ignore that was pulsating to the point of delirium.

"No, it's not," Damon stated. "I showed you the truth, but you have all the time in the world down here."

"And what about the rest? What about all my missing memories? What about all those perfect clones?"

"I don't think you understand what they're there for," Damon argued, without elaborating.

"People have feelings Damon! People hurt when their loved ones die." I argued, as the burning from my hand intensified to the point of causing tears. "Don't you have feelings?"

"I can't tell you something I don't feel, Gellion. I feel only anger and decisiveness, most days."

"That's not it, you dummy!" I yelled at him, becoming more aware of his general defects, and how that shaped his affection and attitude toward everyone. "I can't let my dad and brother think I'm dead. It would break them!"

"Oh," Damon blinked in confusion. He looked surprised by my reasoning and changed gears, understanding my desperation to leave wasn't about getting away from him.

"Brian has lost enough, don't you think?" I pleaded with him.

Damon looked at me with pity and a bit of disdain. I couldn't compare my family experiences to the wickedness he'd suffered, but I didn't want my family to think I was dead.

"The plan was to put your body in the Potomac River."

"You did what?!" I barked at him, smacking his arm with my good hand. I was livid.

"I haven't done anything yet."

"Seriously? People go missing every day and there's never any trace of them, but your plan is to make my dad identify my dead body? There are literally sword punctures. You're a heartless bastard!"

"It's doubtful anyone would find the body. But it's still better than a dead dad."

I bent over to keep from vomiting again and breathed deeply. My reality was becoming clear, and I was sick over it.

"I'm a prisoner here. You'll never let me leave."

He looked confused, shaking his head in disagreement, and took several steps toward me, getting too close.

"Don't touch me," I said as I pushed him away with both hands, which hurt, a lot.

I winced in pain as my left hand imprinted a dark bloody mark on his white shirt.

He looked down at himself. "You're injured," he said, unable to ignore the blood any longer as it trickled down, and he immediately pulled off his shirt and reached for me.

"I'm traumatized," I jerked myself away.

"Well at least you know you're traumatized. Give me your hand."

"No."

He looked as if he would take it by force but instead threw his shirt at me. "Wrap it up better, then." He walked to the elevator and pressed the button and glanced over at my hand until we got inside. "What happened?"

"That stupid laser."

"What laser?" He said, growing angry again.

"The one being used on my clone," I said, repulsed.

"You weren't supposed to see that." He said contritely with aggravation.

As the images of violence replayed in my head, I realized that watching my body be cut open like that, cut so deep by the laser to replicate my own injuries, was almost the worst of it all. To see how bad the damage would've had to have been to my head, neck, chest, and torso to create such horrific scars, as I have, rocked me to my core. It was too much, triggering emotions so deep down that I felt unable to mentally function, and I stupidly became a threat to myself.

"I hate you," I said under my breath, completely unsure why I felt that way, or how I was brave enough to utter my current misery.

He moved away from me and rested his back against the elevator wall and hung his head.

"It's better that way," he said.

He took me back to the medical room and looked inside before taking me in. "It's all clear."

Inside, Calder was waiting. The medbed I'd attacked was gone, along with my clone, and the other medbeds were empty. Before I could figure out anything, Calder had moved closer and was unwrapping my makeshift bandage.

"Jesus!" he said, looking at my hand, as fresh blood poured from it on both the palm and backside.

I had started to feel faint from the loss of blood.

Damon immediately picked me up and tried to put me inside one of the medbeds.

"Let's do this quickly," he said to Calder, who followed his lead.

But before he could get me inside, I turned toward him and climbed up his torso and tried to get over him like a frightened cat trying to get away. He stopped me before I could get past his shoulder.

"No way! I'm not getting in there!" I screamed, struggling to get down.

"Gellion, your hand needs help right now," Calder argued.

"I'm not getting in that fucking thing!" I pounded on Damon's back, blood from my hand hitting his flesh.

"Get in the damn medbed!" He grunted, struggling to get me inside again.

"Damon, stop!" Calder said. "You'll only injure her."

"She already hates me," Damon croaked back, and for one small moment I felt bad I'd said it, but only a moment.

"Let me go!"

"Fine! Get the foam," Damon barked at Calder as he carried me to an exam table and flopped me down.

"This is gonna hurt," Calder said, "but it won't last forever."

I closed my eyes, preparing for it.

"Calder!" Damon chided. "She needs to be anesthetized!"

Calder scrunched his face, as if to say, "oops," and went back for a different bottle and sprayed that first. A numbing feeling washed over me. Then he introduced a syringe into my palm and pushed more pain relief through. The throbbing, awful pain that fueled my rage was greatly relieved. I took a deep breath, unaware of how much I needed that.

"Now for the sucky part," Damon warned.

Calder sprayed a white substance on my entire hand, which foamed up and started to seal my wound. He was right, it burned like hell despite the anesthetic, and I cried out and reached out with my right hand. Damon was the only one there to hold me in comfort and I squeezed him through the pain, and then I started to cry.

He looked into my eyes.

"Breathe," he said. "Take slow deep breaths."

I did what he said, like a pregnant woman trying to breathe through a contraction, I bared the pain and kept breathing. I thought I was through it, but then a second wave of burning sent a spike of pain up my arm and into my chest. I started losing consciousness and leaned too far off the exam table into Damon. My head was resting on his bare chest.

"She's lost blood and hasn't slept or eaten," I could vaguely hear Calder say. "She's not in good shape." He was wrapping my hand. "We'll monitor her."

"Not from here," Damon argued. "That ended badly. Caitir is right."

"Put her in one of the rooms, someplace quiet and comfortable. We can check in remotely," Calder suggested.

"Fine," Damon said, then picked me up and carried me.

"I'll get a gurney," Calder said.

"No need," Damon replied before taking me out the door and down a long hallway, as the pain in my hand felt less and less, and my eyes drooped more and more.

When we got to the door, it slid open, and Damon took me inside. The room felt large, and had a smell of incense and flowers, but I couldn't see and didn't try. It was dark when he put me gently on the bed, covered me with a blanket, and left me to sleep.

5

PURGATORY

It was so easy and yet so hard to succumb to sleep. I kept opening my eyes, a bad feeling in my stomach, of emptiness and fear. When I could sleep I would fall into it, but the visions behind my eyes just wouldn't leave. I found myself waking crying, only to lose consciousness again. Thoughts swirled over and over, trying to make sense of things.

It wasn't just the violence at the hands of familiar people, but that the world was not what I thought it was. The utter sickness and terror of understanding that Damon's world had always been there, hidden in the shadows of power. I knew the fear wouldn't leave my system anytime soon, even if the pain had gone from my hand. Other pain I felt chronically in the rest of my body taught me to fear the coming of more pain too.

It was also the shadows I feared as well. I didn't want to believe in the darkness, in pure evil, but once I saw it perpetrated on my clone, I knew it had been done to others. Others, who didn't have a billionaire trying to save them. So many times, I woke up crying that I was almost sick from it, and sick of myself. Through watered eyes, I thought I saw movement. A silhouette in the corner of the room, sitting in a chair.

"Damon?" I asked.

The silhouette didn't move at first. Then it started to shimmer like it wasn't solid or real. Its strange movement struck terror at the innate places within me. My spine tingled with goosebumps, and I shivered and held my breath, as my actions seemed to make the shadow reactive. I stared at it and questioned my clarity.

When it stood up, I gulped and started to pant. There was nowhere I could go. Inside the shadow, I thought I saw a face.

It was Damon. Relief lasted only a moment, until Damon's face was clearly not the Damon who'd carried me into this room. It looked like his clone, but younger. He moved quickly to the bed and came toward me, and before I could even speak his hands were around my throat, squeezing, and I was flat on my back.

I tried kicking and scratching his face, but I had so little energy left for the fight, I almost wanted to die.

"You shouldn't have seen that," his high-pitched voice said, menacingly. "It's your turn die, little girl."

I woke up screaming! Desperate for air.

It was a dream!

I broke down right away into fearful moans and curled myself into a ball and pulled the blanket to my face and just screamed into it, until I was spent. When I pulled the blanket away, I could see the real Damon, beard and all, staring at me. He was lying on a couch parallel to the bed, up against a wall.

"How long have you been there?" I sniffled.

"A while. I was weary," he explained. "Nightmares are normal after what you've been through."

"You tried to kill me," I explained, and he sat up slowly, his shirt still off. "It felt so real, except for how you looked. You were younger."

"I did once, yes," he said, matter-of-factly.

I started to sit up too. "You did what?"

"Tried to kill you."

"Why would you do that?" I asked, startled by his confession. "When?"

"Our first meeting, after the first day of school."

"So that wasn't a dream?"

"It's hard to say what all-of-this has triggered in you. What did I say to you?"

"You attacked me, and then you said, 'You shouldn't have seen that...'" I trailed off.

"... 'It's your turn to die, little girl?' Yes, I remember," Damon replied.

The nausea swelled in my throat. "Were you really going to kill me?"

"Yes. How far did I get in your dream?"

"I was being choked."

"That's not what happened."

"What did you do?" I wanted to know.

He was silent.

"Don't you remember?" I demanded.

"Yes, it's just, no one has ever asked me to recall it."

"I want to know."

"I threw a rock at your head and dragged you into the woods to beat you to death."

"Why?"

"I wasn't supposed to get caught being bad. You caught me."

"What could be worse than killing someone? What were you doing?"

"You didn't dream that part?" he asked quietly.

"No, we were here."

"In this room?" Damon asked and I nodded. "No wonder you screamed."

I sighed and took some slow breaths. My body aches were awful and rising again. My back felt especially sore and irritated. My knee throbbed. I'd been working so hard to ignore my pain, but it was starting to distract me.

"I killed a cat," Damon said slowly. "I was dissecting it when you found me."

"Ew!" My mind pushed my pain back, so my thoughts could focus. "Gross."

"Your dream wasn't wrong. I was a teenage monster."

"And now?"

"I'm trying to help the world, to protect it from monsters like me."

"Are you really?"

"I'm doing my part, yes."

"I don't even know what to say to that," I admitted, because I knew if I asked him for more details, I wouldn't get them, or they'd be too disturbing. "Is there a reason you're in my room?"

"Because it's my room, and I want to be near you."

"Oh," I said unsure of this new person. "Can I have a room of my own?" The thought of needing to cry without an audience suddenly felt important.

"If you wish, but I can get inside any room I want."

"Stalker," I mumbled.

"You have no idea," he said darkly.

"Have you always been this creepy?" I asked.

"I've never been normal, no, but no one is normal."

"So, what do you really want from me then, Damon?"

He stretched his arms out and yawned, then took a deep breath and looked me in the eyes.

"I want to be inside you again, Eve-Anne Gellion Greene," he said bluntly, calling me by my full name, staring into me.

I was not expecting him to say that. I blinked widely, my heartbeat sped up, and my face was flushed. It was the sudden realization that he'd experienced my body, and that I had no memory of his, that deeply embarrassed me.

"I want to be forgiven for my sins against you," he continued, contrite. "I miss a lot of things about you. Even more, I miss who I was with you by my side."

I had to gulp air, just to get my open mouth to close. Yet somehow,

69

I doubted, after all these years and all my damage, that I would "feel the same" to him.

"I've been told I'm too damaged for intimacy," I said oddly, aware I was admitting truths to a stranger I didn't want to say, so he would understand my wounds. "Though, I've never tested that assumption."

He stood up and walked toward the bed. "Your doctors are liars, but you're not ready for any of that yet. We have a lot of work to do. For now, you'll sleep here, and you'll start to dream again."

I tried to hide the sting of his rejection.

"Sleep here," I said to myself. "And dream. Is that important?"

"I believe so. Lights on," Damon said, and the lights came on softly. "You've slept fourteen hours. Your hand should be better."

He reached down to take my hand, and I unwrapped it myself and marveled at how there was only the tiniest line.

"Your wardrobe is through those doors," he said, pointing nearby. "The bathroom is adjacent. My closet is on the opposite side. We share the tub and the shower."

"My closet is in your room?"

"Yes."

"For how long?"

"Since we built it."

He walked to his closet, and I went to mine. It was a good-size walk-in with a standing mirror and a chair. There were multiple pairs of shoes and dresses and outfits for all occasions inside. I felt like I'd been transported into a mansion.

I chose something comfortable, yet designer, as all the items were designer. I thought of what Caitir and Rosie had worn and then I made my way to the bathroom door attached to the closet. I had my own private toilet and sink. Beyond that was a shared double sink, a large bathtub, and a separate shower, like he'd said.

I was starving and taking pain meds on an empty stomach had never been good for me, so I opted for a quick shower. My body was significantly chubbier than the rest of Damon's family, or their clones. Pain had made it hard to do anything, even take walks, or perform the most basic exercise. I didn't hate my body as much as I used to; I just knew I couldn't control how different I'd become or how much pain I was always enduring. In the mirror my scars were always a reminder that the pain was never far behind. At least the clothes from the closet fit well.

Damon was dressed when I came out.

"Hungry?" He asked.

For once I could think of nothing else but to feed my exhausted body and followed Damon down the hall.

"We often eat together because we work together, but it's optional."

I expected to come to a cafeteria-like setting, but it was the opposite. The room looked like a great wooden lodge in a forested wilderness. The view of trees and mountains on the far end of the wall was like something from a movie, or a magical vacation.

Before I noticed the other people in the room, I walked right up to the massive window view and touched it, only to discover that it was some kind of TV screen. It simply lined up to the trim around it to make it look like a window.

"It looks so real."

Calder chuckled and sat down at the solid wood table, next to everyone else.

"We once used a live signal, but now we use recordings," Malik said.

"From where?" I asked, surprised at its beauty and realism.

"Cambodia," Caitir chimed in. "Other places too, but this one is from Cambodia."

There was juice and tea, and silverware on the table, but there were no plates. Rosie jumped up.

"We've been waiting for you. What do you want to eat?"

"I'll have what everyone else is having."

Caitir and Rosie pulled me away from the table. The ornate kitchen off to the side of the large room did not look used at all. They escorted me to the other side of the kitchen where a machine, that vaguely looked like a massive food dispenser, was set into the wall.

The dark, flat rectangle on the side was a touchscreen and the open area next to it was closed off with glass. The system dispensed plates from below.

"We sometimes cook together, but when we have little time we use the food printer."

Caitir giggled as she lifted her wrist and placed it into a type of body reader that scanned her and lit up when it was done.

"Buttermilk pancakes with maple syrup and butter. Bacon and eggs. Avocado slices and tomato slices."

"Warning," the machine responded in a monotone voice. "Tomatoes stem from the nightshade family, and in their raw form, cause your lips to swell. Removing the skin and seeds will remove the contamination that causes this reaction."

"Please remove the seeds and skin," Caitir replied and then winked at me.

A plate arrived from below, and from above there was what looked like several different colored laser devices working together, writing the food into being on the plate, attached to a robotic arm to do so. It took no more than twenty seconds to finish. The parts that should be hot were hot, and the raw vegetables looked cool. It was like magic.

"Wow! How did it do that?"

"It's a 3D printer for food," Rosie said as she put her wrist up to be read. "Egg and spinach quiche and sliced strawberries."

Her plate was done so quickly I couldn't believe it.

"Your turn," Rosie said.

"Since you're new, you have to give it a DNA sample," Caitir said.

"What?"

Caitir pressed some buttons on the touch screen, typing in my name. She took a tiny vial from within the machine and asked me to spit into it, then she put it back into a special feature near the touchscreen. It took my sample and started analyzing.

As I waited for my results, the men arrived to order their food too. The machine could write food and compute my DNA sequence. Damon was the last before me.

"Why does it need my DNA?" I asked him.

"It can discover your food allergies and substitute ingredients, like with the tomatoes. Caitir's pancakes don't have any grains, for example, which she altered the first time she asked for them."

"I wonder what it will say about me."

"Me too," Damon replied. He held his wrist up to the reader and got scanned. "Breakfast steak, rare; hash-browns, avocado and spinach salad."

I put my wrist up to the reader after Damon signaled, and as it was breakfast, I suddenly thought of BB, who often made us brunch on the weekends. I thought of all their favorites, Dad's and Brian's and BB's.

"Be specific," Damon suggested.

"Buttermilk biscuits with white butter gravy, sliced bacon, chewy not crispy, and strawberry slices with whipped cream," I said, suddenly sad at the thought of my family, for what they were going through.

"Warning," the machine responded in a monotone voice. "MTHFR gene mutation detected. Folic acid allergy. Flour enrichment is hazardous to the methylation cycle. Ancient grain wheat substitute recommended."

I had no idea how to reply, so Damon leaned in and said, "Accepted."

"What was that?"

"You have a gene mutation. Most of the population does."

"I shouldn't have enriched flour? But that's in everything. So, is that all flour?"

"Not all flour is enriched, but most is, and now you know why most of the population is sick. Being medicated through our food with synthetic enriching has really disrupted our health."

"What does it do to me?"

"It enflames your body within, can create rashes, coughing, all kinds of gut issues."

"Is that like Celiac?"

"No, Celiac is a response to the gluten from the wheat itself. Though in Calder's opinion, he thinks a lot of people who have Celiac might also have this issue too, but getting the testing done is difficult. Your mutation makes it harder for your body to detox out the bad stuff, so you have to be more careful.

"Your body should only absorb the non-synthetic precursor to folic acid, which is folate. Actually, we should all be taking it, since our bodies make folic acid from folate, but with your gene mutation, any enrichment actually hurts you."

"More reasons to hurt all the time and not know why," I stated.

I took my plate in amazement and sat at the table. Everyone bowed their heads and reached out to each other, a circle of holding hands.

Eamon spoke, "Dear Heavenly Father, please bless this food before us, and fill it with your holy spirit, to nourish us. We thank you for all that we have and all that you give and ask for your protection over us and the abundance of our lives. We thank you for your help with our mission here, and for the moments when we succeed in doing your work.

"We thank you for Gellion's life, and for the elements of our plan working in our favor, as we've labored for years to protect and keep our family safe. Help us to be worthy of your love, to strive for better from ourselves and each other, and to make a difference here, for the betterment of this world. Guide us and keep us safe. Amen."

"Amen."

My voice joined everyone else, seeing truly what a family they were, and how I was included. It was an odd feeling, a humbling feeling, considering the lives they'd been living. It wasn't unfamiliar, as BB always said a prayer. My mother too. Between me and Dad, we left it up to Brian to find the words to bless our food, and like Mom he always did.

I ate the printed food, and it was delicious, and I wondered if it tasted any better because it had been blessed. As we sat and I listened to the chit chat, I stared at my remaining food as if something were off, like it was lacking in something.

Each bite tasted right yet missing, and I couldn't put my finger on what it was that didn't seem right, except maybe I simply remembered all the time and versions of perfection in BB's kitchen. Made by her hands and not a machine. How the flour she kept in her kitchen had always been unbleached and unenriched, as if she somehow knew without knowing what would heal and not hurt us. BB's cooking and garden vegetables always tasted wonderful, but truly this wasn't bad.

As the eating slowed down and I found my belly full, I felt my mind pose questions.

"So, it's morning for all of you?" I asked, wondering about breakfast food items in front of everyone.

"Not exactly," Calder said.

"We come back here around 1:00 or 2:00 PM in this time zone, so it's more like late lunch for us now, but it doesn't really matter."

"So where are you when you're not here."

"We live in Scotland," Eamon said, referring to he and Rosie. "Calder's clone travels back and forth."

"So, your clones are in Scotland?" I asked, unsure if I was understanding. "And then you wake up back here?"

"Exactly. We spend about eight to ten hours there each day, from about eight in the morning Scottish time, to around six or seven o'clock in the evening, and then we come back here. Though if we need to stay longer, we can."

"Doesn't your staff think it's strange you sleep so long?" I asked.

Rosie chuckled. "We don't have live-in staff. Also, our clones wake up sooner. They have a programmed system that allows us to jump in after the morning routine and leave before the bedtime routine. It's quite amazing," she said, looking lovingly at Caitir and Malik.

"We programmed that," Caitir chimed at me, her cheeks blushing at her mother's approval.

I was impressed. Their brains were exceptional, and I wondered how they'd become so mystifying.

"What about you guys? What time zone are you in?" I asked Caitir and Malik and Calder.

"Our clones are in DC, so we're in the same time zone," Caitir said.

"We're still on the east coast," I told myself.

"We wake up in Georgetown and spend about eight to ten hours a day there," Malik said.

"We do our work, see friends and employees," Caitir smiled.

"Go shopping," Malik said, leaning into Caitir.

"I'm usually gone from seven to seven, since there's much to do," Damon said, "but it's not good for our real bodies to sleep more than clones, so we have to make allowances for scheduling."

"What about you?" I asked Calder.

"I'm here full time until I'm needed in the motherland. When my body gets tired, I go to sleep and wake up as a clone, so there is always someone available to make sure everyone else is OK. Unless I'm on a mission."

"Seriously?" I asked. "Isn't that lonely?"

"I keep the same schedule as everyone else, in case my clone is needed outside."

"So, if you're all asleep," I said to Damon, "then Calder and I will be all alone for how many hours a day?"

"You'll be sleeping," Damon said, raising an eyebrow at me.

"Calder's only alone for about five hours before our parents come back," Caitir said.

"I'm not always here, but when I am, I'm on double duty," Calder corrected. "It's the only time Malik gets a break, unless Tombo isn't in the field. We've all tried to become experts here, so we can all help out, as best we can," Calder said, then got up and took his plate with him.

When he was done putting his dishes in the washer, he left without saying a word. I wanted to apologize, and started to rise to do so, but Damon stopped me.

"That was rude of me," I chastised.

"He'll get over it," Damon said, uncaringly.

"So, am I the only one who doesn't get to use a clone?"

"This is not a game, Gellion." Damon said, eager to get angry with me.

Caitir interrupted Damon and asked me, "Is there some reason you need one?"

"Does a clone's body feel less pain?" I asked, quieting everyone.

"They have no injuries," said Eamon.

"They can also be designed to feel less pain," said Malik.

"Does that translate well? For being inside one?" I asked.

"It takes a little getting used to, but yes, you can feel better," Rosie said, "or feel less."

"I think it's more important we heal this body," Damon said to everyone, ignoring my query. Then he stared at me, "You don't think so?"

"You can heal my chronic pain? How quickly?" I snapped at Damon. "Would the clone hurt as much as my real body does?"

"How much do you hurt?" Rosie asked.

"All the time."

"No," Eamon admitted. "The clone body would not hurt the same, unless your psyche takes it with you."

"I can do that?" I asked, shocked.

"The mind is a powerful tool," Eamon said. "Secondary and tertiary pain can travel with the mind."

"So, I'm doomed?"

"No, but I'd hoped we'd get you scanned before doing something so drastic."

I sighed. "In that machine you built?"

"The 'Q-Speculum,' yes," Damon said. "You've got to get suited up first."

"Whoa, hold on," Eamon said. "She needs a full exam before getting suited up. We can't take any chances. You know that, Damon."

"What kind of exam?"

"The kind that covers everything, so we don't inadvertently put you in harm's way. Those are powerful magnets in the Q-Spec."

No one argued, and so we all walked to the medical lab together where Calder had gone, except Malik. Caitir wrapped her arm around my shoulder and smiled at me, and I let her.

I didn't like the look of the clones in their pods, so they dimmed the glass walls for me. My mouth was swabbed. My vitals read. Several scanning devices were used on me from head to toe, that were non-invasive.

The group of them were wrapped around a large computer screen. I waited and they all came back.

"Gellion, we'd like to do a few more scans of your body," Rosie said.

"Is there something wrong?"

"We found metal inside you."

"Metal?"

"A lot." Damon explained.

"And that's ok with your scanners?"

"There aren't any magnetics in our medbeds."

So, I lay down in a larger scanner and closed my eyes. I'd been through this before, for all the years of my life I could remember.

The gasps that came through were audible. Their conversation got heated.

"What is that?"

"Do you see these?"

"Another set here."

"That son of a bitch."

"Rat bastard."

"Caitir, what's the protocol here?"

"MARI: Locate Malik!" Caitir said out loud.

"What's going on?" Malik replied over the loudspeaker.

"Are we safe from outgoing signals reaching the surface?" Caitir begged to know.

"We have contingencies in place, but I'm not detecting any signals."

"Malik," Damon interrupted. "Try vector vibration channels."

"Yes, I see it now," Malik replied. "It's low and not designed to move through this much ground."

"What about just before coming down here?" Damon asked.

"Can you reverse engineer to catch an echo?" Caitir continued.

"Shit! Shit! Shit! You guys. I see two satellites pinging the location where Gellion came under ground."

"What is their activity?"

"Nothing, so far. Just scanning the area for movement."

"Thank God Tombo used the wooded entrance."

"That exit must go. Malik," Damon said, "we need to rescind the tracks and cover our route. How soon?"

"There's a storm tonight. We can break it down then," Malik replied.

I just listened in horror. *How does this have anything to do with me?*

Everyone scrambled, each moving in different directions. Damon and Rosie approached me, as the scan had already finished.

"Gellion, we have to do surgery on you."

"What? I don't understand."

"You have a titanium rod in your back. It's giving out a signal, and we don't know what's inside."

"A signal?"

"And there are metal rods in your knee, hip, spine, and neck," Calder said.

"Why did no one ever tell me? That's all the places I hurt all the time."

"The problem is the rod in your spine," Eamon explained. "There's technology inside it. It's trying to respond to a satellite. We must remove all the metal from your body. You're practically a booby trap."

"Surgery?"

I sat there shocked as they all moved around me. Damon lifted me off the table and carried me. I felt like crying.

"I'm tired of being cut open," I choked out. "I'm so tired of the pain."

"I know," he said, and he gently kissed my forehead. "I'm sorry."

I saw the medbed he was walking me toward.

"If I fight this?" I asked.

"We could all die."

I just nodded and let the tears flow as he placed me on the medbed and lowered the clear cover. One robot arm found a vein and put a needle in. I started to drift off right away, the faces of these new people hovering above me, making sure their extraordinary robot did its job.

"Gellion, you're going to be okay," Damon said, and his utter confidence did make a small difference.

6

A WHOLE NEW WORLD

When I woke up something was different. I felt strange, out of place, but also, my pain was gone.

"What's happening? I'm not in pain," I called out.

I thought maybe I had been paralyzed and could no longer feel anything at all, but then I could see my arms moving at my mental command. Pain had become such a constant in my life, I didn't know what it was to not feel it. I had stopped complaining about it, but it never left me, not ever.

Suddenly, I could breathe. And being able to move, even just a little without the pushback of something stabbing me, was a miracle. I got up off the medical table and looked at myself, wondering how they could do that, how they healed me, and how long I'd been asleep.

"That was quick," Calder said as he entered the room.

"What?"

"Let me take your vitals."

"Do I have to sit?"

"Not if you don't want."

Caitir and her parents and Damon arrived too.

"How long was I asleep?"

"How do you feel?" Caitir asked.

"Amazing. What did you do to me?"

"We're still doing it," Damon replied, a scowl on his face.

"Damon," Rosie chided.

"What do you mean?"

Calder pulled out my IV and placed a band aid there. Damon took my hand and walked me to the mirror.

"Notice anything?"

I looked but didn't see anything different. Brown hair, brown eyes, scars all along my hairline and neck. Chubby for my height. I reached up into my eye, to adjust my contact lens, but felt nothing.

"What the hell?" I exclaimed. I tried again, getting closer to the mirror to see, but there was no contact to move. My eyes were just brown, instead of brown contacts to cover traumatized blue eyes. Then I ran my hands over my scars, but they stopped at the neck and did not continue down my shoulder, arm, or torso.

Oh My God! I'm inside a copy of myself!

"What is this? Where's my real body?" I asked, confused.

Was it the clone I'd toppled over and stopped from further harm?

"You've only been unconscious for forty minutes," Caitir said.

"We had you scanned during the pre-op countdown, to connect you into an avatar," Rosie said.

"So, you could experience what you said you wanted to experience," Damon explained.

"Excuse me," Calder said as he left.

"Where's my real body?" I said, wanting to follow Calder.

"You don't want to see yourself being operated on," Rosie said.

"Were you all just watching?"

"I wasn't," Caitir chimed in.

"Yes," Damon said, "but that's different."

"Why?"

"When you've seen as many brutal, torturous deaths as we have, you appreciate the beauty of a procedure designed to heal, no matter how barbaric it looks in the process."

"It's our job to make sure the medbed is doing its job," Rosie added.

"So, the whole procedure is just the robot?"

"No, it's a combination. With capabilities for human intervention, should it be needed," Rosie corrected. "Eamon hasn't left your side."

"So, if I'm not supposed to see myself getting operated on, then why are you all here?"

"For the fun part," Caitir said, bouncing up and down.

"What's that?"

"Getting you suited up."

"That machine again?" I asked, almost gasping at how intense it felt to feel so different. My heart was racing with anticipation. Could I possibly run without hurting?

I followed Caitir to the dressing room.

The outfit was like something out of a science fiction movie I'd seen except I was in white instead of black, and the suit wasn't lit up, it was covered in crystals or a crystal ribbon that ran up and down the whole suit. It was heavy too and puffed out in places.

"Why is it so heavy?"

"It's lined with magnets."

"Why?"

"The machine needs to be able to read your body, and the surrounding fields, and it can only do that if it has help."

"And the crystals?"

"You'll have to ask Damon to explain that."

After I was dressed, which included a head piece that went over my hair, Caitir walked me over to the elevators that led to the command center. I still wasn't familiar with everything there. When we got inside, she explained what would happen. I remembered the woman I'd seen in holographic form, made of laser lights, showing us energy flow. I stood inside the platform and waited. Lights came on, sounds started to whirl, and a sense of "powering-up" was realized.

Slowly I rose into the air, fully aware that the magnets in my suit were carrying the weight of me off my feet. Lights started to flicker. Little specks moved all around me, searching, looking for a place to stop and be seen. Nothing took shape, no energy around or within me.

"Look behind you," Caitir's voice said.

Behind me was a strand of energy coming from out the back of my body, going beyond where the machine could read. I knew by looking at it that it was pointing in the direction of where my real body lay in surgery or being stitched up. I wasn't sure. Without any way to look at the energy I wouldn't know if I were truly okay. That had always been my grandmother's role, to make sure my system was open and running. I didn't care to know and just let her use her gifts to help me stay alive, embracing the good feeling while dismissing the power of it.

"What does it mean when it's like that?" I asked toward the black window above me.

The window lit up and I could see them all up there, watching.

"Don't worry. We've seen it before."

I was staring at Damon, but he wasn't looking back, he was crossing his arms in front of himself, his chin resting on his hand, deep in thought. None of them answered, but I saw movement. Then Damon arrived, entering the outskirts of the Q-Spec, examining me within his reader.

"What am I missing?"

"Your energy systems are far away from this body. Do you have any memories or dreams where you created energy around you?"

Then he tapped his tablet, and my body started to lie backwards, until I was resting perpendicular to him. He looked down at me as I considered his question.

"Yes. I had a dream like that," I replied, realizing how much my dream about the ominous lover made of aether had profound meaning.

"Close your eyes. Try to go back there to that dream and recreate the energy you saw."

I closed my eyes and tried to remember. It felt like I was in a game, flying through the air, ready to fight, ready to die. Before I could even land on the ground below, someone was coming for me in the sky. It was the mysterious male, but he was just an avatar in a game too, a player on an opposing team. When his avatar reached out for me, my forcefield lit up around me, powerful, three feet out and strong. His internal darkness activated as he got close, the image of it inside his head powerful enough to destroy me.

Then his hands broke through my dwindling forcefield. When he wrapped his fingers around my neck, I saw it, the darkness inside his head that kept him from seeing me as I was, not just a faceless enemy. Like cracking a game wide open and removing the code that kept us on our chosen sides of light and dark, I removed the darkness inside his avatar head, and my forcefield returned to me, as he removed his hands from my throat.

Then the vision of my dream was over, and I wanted desperately to kiss the man of aether as he had always kissed me in my dreams. I opened my eyes and looked around. There was a small wall of yellow light around me in fine points, hovering in place. Yellow was the color of the sphere around the holographic woman I'd seen earlier. Except my sphere was small, not quite round, and too close to my body.

"That's supposed to be your forcefield," Damon said.

"How'd you do that?" Malik asked me over the intercom.

"Why's it so small?" Caitir chimed in.

"Why did it dwindle?" Rosie asked.

"And where's the rest of it?"

"Pull up the last hologram," Damon called up to them. "Gellion had her eyes closed, remembering the dream."

The magnets in my suit pulled me upright and set me down on the sidelines with Damon, to see what I'd just created played back to me.

"Your forcefield arrived strong when you first went into the memory," Damon said as we watched it appear over my body during the replay. Then the forcefield tore open and got smaller. "What happened?" Damon asked, as he pressed pause on the display.

"You broke through the field."

"Me?"

"Well, I didn't know it was you when I first started having the dreams," I admitted.

"When was this?"

"When I woke up from the accident," I said.

"Oh," he said, realizing his machine was reading energy from a surreal dream, started over a decade earlier.

Damon played the hologram again, pointing to the forcefield healing itself.

"What happened here?" he asked.

"There was darkness inside your head, and I reached in to remove it, so I'd survive," I said, feeling the heavy weight of my suit pull at me.

"I was attacking you," he surmised, chagrined.

"It stopped once the darkness was gone," I corrected. "The dream shifted."

"To what?"

It took me a moment to find the right word. "Intimacy," I explained.

"So, the forcefield healed itself but became displaced. How did that happen?"

"Your presence inside my physical space must have repositioned it?" That was my best guess.

"The end result is that you created a forcefield where one was missing, but it got contorted. Can you imagine bringing it back to its full strength?" he asked.

"I'll try."

Damon tapped on the tablet again and repositioned my body. I closed my eyes as I had before and I saw my dream again, how my forcefield lit up to protect me. I stopped my imagery there and kept myself within that moment in my mind.

"It's holding steady," Damon said. "What did you do?"

"I went back to the dream and stopped imagining anything beyond having an activated forcefield."

"Can you imagine all your other energy structures into being?"

"I'm not sure. I don't remember what they look like," I admitted, drawing a blank as I searched in my memory.

Damon brought my body back down to stand beside him and loaded a hologram into the Q-Spec playback. Again, it was the same woman I'd seen with the large spheric forcefield. Hers was three feet from her body at least.

Then the other colors lit up around her, many small and perfectly round tornadoes of shimmering energy that stuck out from her at points up and down her front and back. I stared at her for a long time as Damon paced around me, thinking.

"She is an energy worker, a light worker," he explained, as I tried to memorize the images. "We asked to scan her, and this is what we saw."

The more I stared at the woman, the more other subtleties showed through. There was a pure white cylinder-looking energy that ran up and down her pelvis, torso, and chest. It reminded me of what a battery would look like, but inside a human.

"Don't you want to ask me something?" Damon finally said.

"I'm trying to learn by seeing, that's all. What do you want me to do?" I asked.

"Jump-start your own energetic system," he said, as if I should have known. "Bring the other systems online to your current body."

My face was crumpled from frustration. "How?"

Damon jumped onto the large platform and started pointing at spots along the hologram.

"These are chakras. All of them are supposed to be working. The machine pics up nothing from your current body."

"What about my real body? Would they be there?"

"They should be," he replied, before refocusing. "Your forcefield is too small, so you need to fix that."

"How?"

"Imagine it like you did in your dream. Didn't you see how easy that was for you?"

I shook my head in disagreement. I hadn't tried to do anything. It hadn't been purposeful, it had been memory, and visceral at that. Creating it out of imagination felt like bullshit to me, but I did as he said. He put me back into the reader, and I imagined as much of it as

I could.

I closed my eyes and imagined that my chakras and forcefield looked like hers. Nothing happened, except the opposite of what they wanted to see. I tried again and again and again, and with each attempt to bring my chakras online, the forcefield I had created got smaller and closer to me. It was defeating and depressing with each attempt until I was sick of hanging in the air and dealing with Damon's frustrations.

"I want down," I demanded.

It took a moment, but I finally descended. My body felt exhausted, and my head hurt from the mental concentration of failing.

"What's wrong?" Damon asked, wanting me to keep going.

"I'm not getting it, obviously."

"You used to be able to do this," he complained.

"You don't show me how the light worker makes her own system better, only what it looks like at full operation. I need more than that."

"Maybe we should try something else."

"Like what?" I complained. "And my real body is being operated on, and my clone body is totally foreign and strange and neat, and awkward," I continued my rant.

"So, what do you want to do?" He finally asked, after I was back on my feet.

"I want you to talk to me about all of this."

"I don't know how," he threw his arms up in the air and walked out.

"What do you mean, you don't know how? You've been talking to me this whole time."

"I can't answer your questions about this stuff. Let's take a break," he called back at me.

I pulled the magnetized hood off my head and relaxed my neck for the first time since we'd started and sat down at the edge of the machine.

Still, exhausted as I was, I wasn't in pain at all, just achy. My ability to think might feel fuzzy, but my body was good, and I was in a better place because of it. But I didn't want to spend all my time in the Q-

Spec, and I didn't want to read or research. I'd done years of that. Right then I wanted to move. I followed Damon. He hadn't rejoined the others in the communication tower, as he was pacing again in the hallway. When I walked to him, he stopped.

"I want you to come with me," I said.

I'd never been so brave in my life, but I took his hand and pulled him with me. Silently we walked all the way back to the room I'd woken up in several hours ago.

As I opened the door Damon finally spoke, "What are you doing?"

"This suit is heavy. I need help getting it off."

I didn't take my eyes off him and waited. He caved and started working on getting the suit loosened.

"How did you get the crystals to bend like that?" I asked quietly as he touched me.

"They're diamonds," he said, and I gasped. "We crushed them and put them in a flexible conductor gel."

"Oh," I said, breathlessly as he removed the neck, shoulder, and arm pieces from me.

My bra was all that covered my chest as he started pulling the torso piece down. When he was done, I was standing in my underwear, without as many scars and without pain. I wanted to be touched for the first time in my life. My hand quivered as it reached for his bare forearm, pulling him closer and wrapping his long arm around my waist. Our faces were barely touching, and I reached up and kissed his lips lightly, hovering.

"What's gotten into you?" He asked, pulling away, which was easy for him at his towering height. I held onto his arm.

"You're in love with me, aren't you?" I asked.

"I'm in love with a memory," he quipped back. "I was different too."

"Did we touch? Did you like touching me? Did we ever...?" I sighed.

He knew what I was curious about. I couldn't believe I was being so bold, but I was stuck in a bunker, living in a clone body with ten years of adult memories and not one that included being with a man, or letting a man touch my damaged body. Damon held my face in his massive hands and pulled me gently by my neck, closer to him.

"We were teenagers," he replied.

"So? Answer me." I demanded shyly.

"You know the answer. Why are the details so important?" he dismissed and let me go.

"Because it is," I retorted. "You don't want me now?"

"I want...I need things to be a certain way first."

"Why?" I pulled at his arm.

"I'd rather not say."

"Fine," I huffed at him. I wanted to throw something at his head. I needed this. I needed a distraction. I needed a connection with him here. I felt like I was falling apart, my real body, my family, my reality. Damon refused to give me the closeness I could feel myself grasping for, as my mind went into survival mode. So, I thought of something that might spark in him anything.

"Is Calder out of surgery?" I asked, but didn't wait for a reply. "I should go check on my body. Maybe I'll feel welcome there. He's always so attentive and kind."

"Go ahead," he snarled at me, his chest heaving up and down, yet still controlled. "That's a great idea." He didn't walk out, like I expected. He just stared at me like he wanted to hurt me.

It hadn't worked, and I didn't really want Calder's attention, so I walked into the closet and grabbed the first covering I saw, a silk kimono bathrobe, and came back to the room. I didn't feel right, like I was sort of slipping away. Suddenly all the thoughts I hadn't wanted to acknowledge poured out of me like a liquid, crystal clear.

"Everything's terrifying and overwhelming. I can't stop thinking about dying. I can't stop thinking about how they wanted me to die, and that maybe it would be better, easier if I did. Nothing feels right, and everything feels like too much. Even in a copy, I'm never gonna be the girl you loved," I said, resolute and also disappointed at my failure to be stronger, like him.

The words were heavy but needed. It certainly wasn't the first time I'd thought of death. I kept looking at my wrists, wondering if that would be the best way to go, once I left it all behind. I held my wrists, and the skin was soft, so easy to destroy. I was keenly aware that my real body was suffering still, which made me fear waking up there.

My sightline shifted to an internal one, where what was around me no longer mattered. I'd said what I felt, that I'd no desire to go through a journey of horror and pain. I've spent twelve years in pain, wanting to die because it was endless. I wasn't strong enough for me, let alone anyone else. Well, maybe my brother Brian. But I'm nothing like the old Gellion had been, even in this clone. I began to quiver in weakness, my knees buckling under me.

Damon picked me up again and sat down on the bed with me on his lap. He wrapped his large arm around me, awkwardly cradling my stiff body, and held my chin up with his other hand. He kissed me softly on the neck, tenderly, and slowly as if to pull me from the dark thoughts. I relaxed into his mouth on mine for a while, until my body began to feel an entirely new ache I'd never felt before.

Intense pulsing came from within me, propelling me to shift my body, moving my legs to straddle him, wrapping my arms around his neck, pulling him closer until his chest was pressing against mine, and my pelvis was pressing toward him. He grabbed my hips and pulled me away from him.

"Stay," I whispered breathlessly.

He tried to stop by picking me up, but my legs wrapped around his waist, and we fell onto the bed, my back hitting the mattress, as he lay on top of me. The weight of him was nothing I'd ever experienced, like a bear hug that made the world around me disappear. His face looked bewildered as I had every limb of mine wrapped around him. Unlike all the other guys who tried to get close to me, who I rejected out of fear, I only felt desire now. I pulled at his clothes, wanting them gone. I pulled at my own too.

"Don't stop," I whispered, and gasped as he caved, pulling my robe and bra back, exposing my breast, his soft and warm mouth on me.

These new sensations brought me to a whole new thinking, one of desire and pleasure, and impending release of frustration and fear.

His shirt was off, and so was my bra and half the robe. His hands touched places never felt before, rubbing, and massaging me. He hovered over me, kissing me still, prolonging the desire. Then he puffed and started to back away, but I pulled at his neck.

"You're not ready for this," he said breathlessly.

"You don't want me?" I pleaded, looking down at his pants and the bulging that clearly said otherwise.

"I'm not ready for this," he shook his head, as he moved back.

"What is there to be ready for?" I announced.

"You don't even know me!" He barked down into my face and pulled my arms off him, shoving me down onto the bed.

"I don't care!" I roared back. "You dared to love me. That's what you said!" I reminded him.

"A lot has happened in twelve years."

"Well lucky you," I mocked. "I've had twelve years of pain and loss and misery. They should have let me die in that car, because I didn't want to live that way. I can't do it anymore."

"You don't know the meaning of pain," he said, disgusted with me.

"I don't?" I was mad, and jumped up to head toward him, ready to push him to get what I needed. Everyone was talking to me, about me, except him, the guy who knew the most. I pushed him. "Who do you live for Damon? If not me, then who?"

"I've spent twelve years trying to keep you alive."

"Exactly! For what? So, I could come down here and kill myself?!" I screamed at him.

He grabbed my arms. "You're not going to do that."

I was in his face, shoving my pain onto him.

"Have you truly examined my real body? Do you know how many surgeries I've had? How many self-inflicted wounds? The pills I had to take to survive a day, and the meds I had to take to keep the nightmares at bay. Who wants to live like that? I don't."

He grabbed my arms and shoved me back onto the bed. "And me

fucking you, that will make you want to live?"

"Maybe. How would I know? I've never been with anyone! Don't you want me?" I asked again, begging, the utter sadness of my loneliness creating tears.

The look on his face was suddenly so confused. He came back to my face, to my body on the bed and started to kiss my neck, my torso, my lips. He put his hand to my throat, and massaged my neck, then turned my head to look at the scars.

"We're both damaged goods, I think." He rubbed his thumb down the length of the scar on my cheek, and down my throat. "These scars can be fixed but healing what's hurt inside is different."

"The scars remind you I'm not the same," I accepted. "I never will be," I relented.

"Of course, I want you!" He growled at me, angrily. "I told you that."

Then he laid me down and reached for my remaining garments and pulled them away, his mouth upon me. I suddenly wasn't sure about being touched. I had wanted to be held and kissed, not to experience his mouth on my body.

"You don't have to do that," I said, trying to bring him back up to my mouth, but he just moved my arms away.

"Yes, I do," he said. "If you can't handle this, you won't be able to handle anything else. I'm not a small man, Gellion. You are tiny beneath me. If your body can't handle my mouth preparing you to receive me, then it can't handle me."

Cocky! I thought, but his bluntness made a point, I'd no discernment to debate. I took a breath and tried to relax as his large arms rested on my legs to hold them open. I felt his tongue, his lips. Delicate and slowly at first, then with more pressure and movement. My body started to shake and quiver, uncontrollably from the first touch, only intensifying.

Eyes closed, I tried to imagine us as teenagers, loving each other, but nothing came. Instead, shadows appeared in my sight, visions of fear under my eyelids; nameless, faceless shadows and they were hovering above me. The shadows laughed, and my body grew anxious and tense and suddenly my pleasure at Damon's touch turned into pain and burning.

Stabbing and shooting pains spiked through my pelvis and up and down its canal. It had never been that intense before.

"Stop!"

I screamed and opened my eyes, but when I looked up Damon had already stopped. He was sitting a few feet away from me. My body felt so confused, as I shook and jerked, laying there otherwise immobile. Damon pulled my robe back over me and rested his hand gently on my thigh.

"I told you, you aren't ready," he said.

"How do you know that?" I choked out, still feeling the surge of impeding fear and pain.

"I'm sorry I know more about you than you do."

"Stop keeping my secrets from me," I whispered.

Even though I knew it was true, it was hard to believe someone else could care so much and yet be so absent.

"What's wrong with me? Why am I like this?" I cried out, so much fear inside.

"The day you died, we all changed forever."

"Why can't I ever let anyone touch me without screaming?"

"You let me touch you," he argued.

"That's never happened before."

"Good," he said, moving closer to me, his eyes boring into me. "I don't share."

"You don't share what?" I squinted at him with a fake smile.

He moved closer to me again.

"What's mine," he said seriously.

"So, I'm yours?"

"You are. You always have been."

"And you love me?"

"That's my memory," he admitted.

"Say it," I said, as if wanting not to have to ask.

He stared at me silently, and moved slowly toward me, and put his mouth on mine. He kissed my lips and held me close to him for the longest time, until my body felt like melting, and I could hardly breathe.

We stayed that way, holding one another, half dressed, legs intertwined. As my eyelids fell, I heard Damon say, "Deeply."

7

UNSTUCK

"I didn't think people with psychopathic tendencies could be that intimate," I said softly, waking from the short nap.

He laughed and placed his lips on my forehead. "It's possible to stay calm if you learn how to control your triggers. There are different versions of me. I was conditioned to compartmentalize, as a part of my upbringing."

He got up and put new clothes on and headed to my closet to bring me mine.

"We need to eat before I depart."

"Is it time already?"

"Not quite yet. We'll have to teach you how to leave this body and wake up in your own."

He pulled me gently to my feet and took me to my dressing room, with my outfit in hand. I quickly cleaned myself up and put my clothes on, questions brewing in my mind. He was standing, at ease, ready to go, but my questions couldn't wait.

"Is my real body even ready to wake up?"

"You're out of surgery," he said with a twinge in his voice.

With the way he said it I suddenly got the feeling that being in a clone's body made it less scary for him to interact with me. He feared for that body, my real body. He wasn't as careful with me in this one.

"What happens if my real body dies?" I asked.

His face immediately became distressed by the question, and then his eyes looked away, analyzing something.

"I haven't ever tested…" he started to say, then stopped and shook his head.

"Tested what?"

"Nothing. Just something I haven't perfected," he said cryptically.

"Is it possible my body won't wake up?"

"Doubtful, your vital signs were strong," he said, "but while you're in this body, you should eat." He took my hand, and we were quickly in the hall, walking.

"Why?" I asked.

"Why what?"

"Why is it important I eat in this body?"

"Because your real body might not feel like eating as you recover, but if you're psychologically eating, your mental state for healing will be better, and you won't feel malnourished."

I followed him, speed-walking to keep up with his height. The short amount of time in his presence was filled with intensity, with my life at stake, my past more and more revealed, and my living circumstances forever changed.

Damon was rude, abrupt, and intense, but I knew he was thinking of how to keep me alive. I felt grateful for his obsession and disbelief. Those fleeting moments I'd begun losing the will to go on made me cling to him even harder than I should. Whatever oath he took toward me it was obvious he'd worked hard to keep it.

I did everything they told me to do, and I still couldn't wake up inside my post-surgery body. I visualized, meditated, and walked through the steps of commands they'd taught me to return, yet none of it worked. It was taking too long, and Damon had to go, before denying the chemical option to disconnect me from the clone.

They all left except Calder, who was still busy at work, yet now he was working in his clone body, which had thicker and darker orange hair, a clean-shaven face, and brighter blue eyes, just like Damon.

"What should I do?" I asked.

"Go take a nap," Calder shrugged, hard at work analyzing something. He was ignoring me.

I found my way back to the bedroom and laid down where I'd been with Damon not long before. I fell asleep, imagining I would wake up somewhere else soon.

When I woke up at least eight hours passed and I was still in the same body, same bed. I also hadn't had a single dream or nightmare or even whisper of an image from my time "away." That felt interesting. Maybe the day and the events had been enough to warrant an actual rest. Maybe I should visit my body.

I got up and walked back to the lab. Calder was still there.

"Is this normal?" I asked him, rubbing my eyes and stretching.

"I don't know," he admitted, but his face looked just a bit concerned. "We've never tried to use a clone to help a real body rest and heal."

"Is that what we did?"

"There were a lot of reasons to have you try. Other people usually get more time to come to terms with major surgery. It was better, I think, you didn't need to be present for that."

"But now I can't get back."

Calder sighed. "Do you really want to go back into a body that's in pain?"

"Not ever again."

"See?" he said, grimacing. "Let's give it some time."

"So, what do I do now?"

"Well, Rosie and Eamon..."

"... 'Mom and Dad'?" I asked, realizing I rudely wanted him to talk about his family in a normal way.

"We don't call them Mom and Dad in Scotland," he said abruptly, which surprisingly made me smile. "They're already back. Malik and Caitir decided to bring their clones back to base to work with you here, so they're here too. Damon will be gone for a few more hours. Maybe you could go feed yourself. Take a long shower."

"Hmmmm," I murmured to myself.

"Try to just be okay where you are." He finished, bluntly.

"Why are you alone?" I retorted, in his same abrupt communication style.

"Rephrase your question," he replied.

"I mean, sorry, it's just you're really good looking, and you seem much less homicidal," I sniggered uncomfortably, "than Damon."

Calder looked at me, took an intense breath, made real eye contact and stared at me deeply. Then he put his instruments down and came closer.

"I'm not alone. I'm just alone here, now, when it matters. But I will admit, just like Damon, I can't get someone out of my mind, someone special to me."

This revelation made me curious because I was framed within his comparison, and it was a compelling one.

"Who is she?"

"I think we've both gone mad," Calder murmured to himself, ignoring my question for a few moments before sighing. "You look like her."

"Oh," I said, stunned. "Where is she?"

"Missing."

"Oh my God, I'm so sorry. When?"

"A long time ago."

I wanted to ask more questions, but I could sense Calder's emotions changing, the mood shifted somberly.

"You all seem to have suffered a lot," I blurted out, stating something so obvious, so rudely.

"All of us, it's true but I think you get the award for the most chronic, never-ending pain."

"Me? I've never been tortured," I argued.

"This was torture, Gellion." He said as he lifted pieces of the rods that had been inserted in my body up to show me.

"Chronic pain," I corrected.

"And acute," he clarified for me, as he pulled up my physical scans. "Your scar tissue was persistent and massive. It's been removed, and there is a bit of underlying damage, but everything is in a state of shock and your whole system is weak, and filled with toxins and heavy metals, as if the tech in your body was poisoning you more than just the regular food and water supply."

I gasped because it was shocking to hear, but it made no sense to me.

"What do you mean?" I cut him off before he could continue.

"Hmmm? Which part?" he asked.

I couldn't go there, couldn't acknowledge how bad the damage was or was meant to be.

"What do you mean by being poisoned by more than just the regular food and water?"

He grimaced at my misdirection.

"Well, there are plenty of documentaries on the state of the food industry in the United States, but there are problems all over the world. Our food supply is filled with toxins at every level and is designed to kill and make us sick. The water is even worse," he said, expecting me to register this truth as if it were somehow obvious.

"Katherine showed me a couple documentaries," I said, remembering how she'd made us watch them.

"Yes, but did you change your food consumption at all after what you saw?"

My eyes went straight to the floor as I mumbled, "No, but I did start drinking bottled water."

"You and everyone else. That's just switching out the fluoride and estrogen in public water for the microplastics and leeching toxins in plastic bottles. It's all bad."

"Why don't they clean it?"

Calder typed at his keyboard and a new view of my scans popped up. It looked like a head. He zoomed in, past the skull.

"Do you see this here?" he asked, pointing to a small round area. "This is the pituitary gland. The old Gellion would have called it the third-eye."

"Wait, our third-eye is real?"

"Of course. Many spiritual scholars say that the pineal and pituitary glands, working together with the rest of the human system, connect us to God. This gland's structure can be found in many ancient drawings."

"How can that connect us to God?"

"There is a crystalline structure within the gland."

"Tiny crystals inside our heads?"

"Yes," he nodded. "The theory is that the crystals inside this gland are capable of sending and receiving signals."

"Shut up!" I said, amazed.

Calder typed again and an array of images popped up on the screen, all showing the look, structure, and dissection of the pineal gland as displayed by ancient images, statues, hieroglyphs, and jewelry that symbolized the gland too. It looked like a pineapple. This was a history I never would have pieced together. Then Calder found images of actual pineal glands, and many of them looked different from one another.

"This one over here is a child's pineal gland," he said. "Look how different it looks from the one I showed you," he said as he switched from one image to the next. The first one looked white and hard compared to the fleshy and hydrated gland of a child.

"Why are they so different?" I asked.

"If you're making the comparison, then the adult pineal gland that's been poisoned its whole life no longer works, not really," he said, carefully.

"What do you mean?"

"It's calcified," he said, waiting for me to understand. "Turned to stone, like the majority of the population, unfortunately."

"What?" I gasped. "Ew! Is that what mine looks like?"

"Yes," he replied.

"It's so evil. Do they not know?"

"It's on purpose. The toxins in the drinking water, the food and air too. The poisons calcify the glands to keep our human consciousness from reaching a higher one. It also makes the population complacent."

"So, it doesn't protect our teeth from cavities?" I asked.

Calder laughed, and stopped and looked at me, and then laughed again. He typed on his keyboard and pulled up a video of two people in hazmat suits pouring fluoride into the water supply from a container with multiple poison warning labels. I watched it in horror.

"Fluoride is a neurotoxin," Calder said softly. "The Nazi's experimented with it in the concentration camps and discovered what it could do. Then America started putting the fluoride in the water supply after World War II."

"Why would America do that?"

"The evil here has a bone to pick with the American mindset of freedom. The puppet masters do it to control us."

"Us?"

"I live in this world too. How they control the masses affects everyone."

I nodded my head, thinking, digesting. I really didn't know what else to say. My real body had calcified glands inside it, great.

"Can it be fixed?" I asked timidly.

"I believe anything can be fixed, but without the kind of tech we have here, it's not so easy. I've only ever seen detoxification reach eighty, maybe eighty-five percent with the current options on the market, which is still decent," he said. "There's hope to turn things around."

I took a deep breath at his words of hope, but I was glad he stopped talking. My brain was going in a lot of directions, and I needed a moment. He typed quietly before speaking again.

"Your current clone has no calcification. Damon wondered if you would be able to use the Q-Spec better with a toxin-free body."

"Not if I don't know any of the techniques."

Even though I was putting myself down, I felt some awe at myself. I hadn't really wanted to think about the "how" and the "why" of me feeling so different, so much better. I was significantly thinner in all the right places than I had ever been. It didn't feel like I was thin as much as less bloated, less inflamed, less bogged down. Suddenly I was thinking differently about myself.

What a gift it was to be in a body without so much trauma. The fresh scars had been treated so well that they didn't hurt. Before, it was nothing but constant pain in my back, ribs, hip, thigh, knees and head. Walking, breathing, sitting were all painful chores. If something didn't sharply stab or burn, I was otherwise in a constant state of never relaxing, never being relieved, muscles I couldn't control.

"What do you think?" I asked Calder. "Would it really make a difference to use this body?"

"I think it's just another factor to consider for the research. It's not like you've figured anything out yet within your own mind. The body is secondary, in my opinion."

"I don't miss the pain," I sighed, still amazed at how I didn't hurt. "I can't believe how much easier it is for me to think without the constant pain. Even if there's too much to think about, it's like a breath of fresh air."

"You were actively being tortured. The titanium rod in your back was capable of electronic pulses. I haven't even begun to pull apart the other ones. We have no idea exactly what you've been through. I'm still studying the technology they put inside."

"What kind of technology?"

"Top of the line. NASA probably."

I almost choked on his words. "Excuse me?"

"This is above military grade," he said with a pitying look. "It's one-of-a-kind hardware designed for your DNA, using your own body's energy against you."

"Why?" I asked again, dumbfounded, unable to comprehend that level of scheming.

"Grandfather loved games," Calder mumbled, then shrugged. "NASA has a large budget, and they have many secret programs. Someone owed him a favor, I'm sure, or needed someone to experiment on."

I had to rub my eyes at my inability to grasp that level of sadism. The sleepless nights, the burning sensations, and stabbing feelings I could never understand. A never-ending hell.

"At a certain point, you just endure it," I realized.

"How noble," he said dryly.

"How stupid, that I didn't even know, that I couldn't even sense what it was," I sighed. "I'd like to see myself."

Calder was deep in his work, but his head popped up at my words. "Are you sure?"

"Yes," I said, but he'd already pressed a button on the phone.

"Caitir, Gellion would like to see herself in the recovery room."

It was only about a minute before Caitir, Rosie and Eamon arrived and escorted me into their small hospital wing. My body was hooked up to a lot of machines.

"The incisions were healed with lasers," Eamon said. "And a lot of scar tissue was removed. The original scars were left though, as there wasn't enough time to address them."

"The trauma was deep, Gellion. Some of these items were inside you for a long time," Rosie said.

"Let's give your body some time to heal before getting worried, okay lass?" Eamon chimed in.

"Gellion, we had access to your medical records, and there was never any indication they'd done all this," Caitir said. "Someone altered your scans."

"All of that, just to make sure Damon never came near me again?"

"It worked," Caitir said. "Damon had to hire a whole team of people."

"A team?" Eamon scoffed. "He's practically got an army now."

The scowl of confusion on my face gave me away. Rosie grabbed

Eamon's arm softly and huffed at him. I sighed and re-centered my thoughts on the sleeping body before me.

"I'd love to hear about it some other time."

Eamon took Rosie's hand first, then she took Caitir's who grabbed mine. The prayer circle had formed so quickly, I felt almost confused until Rosie started speaking.

"Dear God, Almighty Divine Universe of Light, we call upon you for help and guidance. We are eternally grateful for your protection and wisdom in our lives. Gellion's body is not healing as quickly as we thought. Please watch over her body and help it to fully recover from the torment of foreign weapons within her. Help us to do what is necessary to help with her healing and give us the patience and wisdom to believe in the power of your timing here for us."

Rosie squeezed my hand and Eamon continued the prayer.

"Watch over our precious Gellion, keeping her mind safe and emotions protected as she seeks to learn about herself, make sense of our shared past, and accept the current reality of all our lives. May we walk in your guidance for a better future. Bless our family, our friends, our companions and peers, who work so hard in solidarity to save so many lives. Protect us as we do your will here on Earth. Amen."

Much of the prayer was about me, but it was clear Eamon wanted me to know there was more to their story, and maybe they meant me to be a part of it.

We stood in silence for a while, until I mustered the courage to ask for time alone. I needed to think about how to help my real body heal, given all the new information I had. Even alone I drew a blank, the only faces or thoughts on my mind most in the days that had passed were my family.

Grandma BB would age from my disappearance. I missed her the most, somehow, my substitute mom. However, I suddenly drew nothing from my memory of her and found it strange that my time with her was suddenly so hard to access. Nevertheless, she was there, my mind's eye seeing her face, until I could take the riddle no longer and felt my stomach growl.

I went for some food and found the dining room was full of people, and they were laughing. It felt exhilarating to hear them.

"You should have seen the look on his face!" Caitir cried out, poking at Malik.

"It's not my fault all our clones look the same!" Malik retorted, blushing.

"Gellion!" She saw me enter. "You must be starving!"

"Yeah," I said, sitting down and grabbing the tea carafe and pouring some.

I mostly listened again to their stories of times in Scotland and around the world. What life had been like when they were able to escape their ancestral family for a while and just be happy. They slowly talked about Damon. They shared so many kinds of stories that I got worn out from the telling and wanted to lay down again. So much happening, so much spinning in my head. The details were important I knew, but this body and brain felt foreign, and I was having trouble keeping it all in my memory.

When I woke up again, Damon was where he'd been before, laying on the couch near me.

"Why don't you sleep in the bed?" I asked.

"I'm not sleeping," he retorted.

"Oh," I said, horrified. "I'm sorry."

"It's good you're dreaming again. It's good you get to experience life without medications."

"I don't remember my dreams this time."

Damon slowly sat up and looked at me.

"I need you to start taking some vitamins. Your clone will deteriorate, but just like a human body, the right supplements help prolong the life of the suit."

Wow! I thought. *I've never heard such a clinical assessment of human flesh.*

"You'll absolutely need to do the same in your real body, but we're doing that for you now, intravenously."

I was having trouble believing a lack of vitamins was my only issue.

"You're going to knock out ten years of torture with vitamin soup?"

"No, but we are going to bring the swelling completely down with a megadose of ingredients."

"Including?"

"Hmm, well Calder and Eamon make the cocktails, but if memory serves the natural stuff is vitamin C, Boswellia, bromelain, turmeric, and fish oil. They've gotta be adding building blocks like magnesium, vitamin D and B, and zinc too. More I'm sure."

"I already take some of that stuff. BB gives it to me from her office," I said, recalling how my grandmother made me take the vitamins, even when the doctors told me it wouldn't help, and how I often would "forget" to take the vitamins over the instant relief of the pain meds.

"They'll give you several antiparasitics, antifungals and antivirals. The foreign parasites within humanity are pretty bad, and unfortunately universal and do overwhelming damage to our ability to self-heal. Eamon and Calder will decide which pharmaceuticals will help better first."

"And that will work?"

"It's already working."

"Oh," we sat in silence, eventually staring at one another. "What now?"

"I notice you're getting depressed," he stated, matter-of-factly.

"Yeah, talking about dying would be a clear indication," I said sarcastically. I'd felt embarrassed begging him to touch me earlier, I couldn't deny it.

"We had to talk about it as a family, whether or not to consider yours."

"Consider my family how?"

"The question is if our resources are strong enough to protect everyone. Psychologically, it's ideal to protect you on the whole."

"What does that mean?"

"When you died twelve years ago, it was BB who brought you back."

"What?"

I wasn't sure which thought to address first, BB's gifts, him knowing she'd fixed me in the hospital, or how my accident suddenly included him.

"Wait. Explain please."

"In the hospital. She came. Your heart stopped so many times. You were about to die again and probably not come back when BB arrived. She worked on your astral body outside the surgery room. All your energy systems were shattered. She pieced you back together. After that your vital signs never went dark again."

"Why don't I know about this?"

"Maybe she was trying to protect you," he offered. "But now we need her help. Your energetic system may be shattered again. The events at the Ball alone would be enough to shut you down, but if you include the surgeries, you're just not doing well."

"Oh. So, I might die?" I asked.

"Not even close, but you're also not healing like you should. BB can help."

"I get to see my family?" I whispered in shock.

"Just BB," he shrugged. "For now."

I could live with that, and the thought of letting her know I was okay was calming my emotional instability.

Damon explained the plan. Inside my clone I would take the train out into the world with Malik and Caitir, to where they have another Q-Spec machine. It's set up at a research facility to interact with the bigger world. We would meet my grandmother there and she would get to see that I'm alive, and then she could help me.

I couldn't believe Damon agreed to do that! I was so excited; I felt the need to reach out to him.

"Thank you!"

I moved quickly from the bed to the couch and climbed onto his lap, straddling him.

"You're not ready," he said. I put my hand to his mouth and stopped him from speaking.

"You wouldn't be here if you didn't want me."

"And I'll have you."

"You will?"

"Yes. When your real body is ready to receive me. When it matters the most that I don't scare you or hurt you." And my eyes grew wide at his expression of a darker hunger. "If I play with your clone, I might not be so nice."

He tried to push me back off him, but I just held on.

"So, you don't want to kiss me?"

He let his guard down a little, letting my lips touch his cheek and his chin.

"Why do you want to kiss me?" he said, pulling back a little, his eyes accusing me.

"I've never done this before. As terrifying as you are, being around other men who looked at me like I'm looking at you, was much scarier. You saved my life, Damon," I said softly, wondering if he understood the gratitude I felt. "I'm sorry for what you had to see happen to me. It hurt me too. Thank you for not letting me die like that."

He sat back, his legs spread, his massive body relaxed on the couch, as if I weren't right there on him.

"Is that all?" he asked.

I thought for a moment about what he might want to hear, and suddenly another thought crossed my mind. "Did you design my clone to want you?"

He smirked and then put both his hands on my straddling hips and said, "Do you want me?"

I hesitated for a moment, "Yes."

"Did you want me before you needed surgery?"

I took a deep breath and thought about it. "Yes, but not like this."

"Why is that?"

"Not being in pain has removed the fear."

"It's not the clone."

"It helps you were in love with me," I said.

"I owe you. The love was a long time ago. I may not be capable of ever getting back there. And let me be clear...there are things I want back, for you to be my Gellion again."

"Like what?"

"Like removing the darkness inside me," he said, and it sounded so ridiculous I scoffed, but he was serious. "Until then, neither of us is going to be ready."

"And what if I never see the world the way she saw it?" I asked, as I pushed myself off his lap.

"You already saw it in a dream. Give it time," he shrugged.

I sighed and rolled my eyes, even though he wasn't wrong. I had seen darkness and removed it in a dream. I just didn't know that's what I was doing.

I went to the closet to look for an outfit that my grandmother would approve of.

"When do we leave?" I asked, thinking about how lucky I felt to be considered, possibly even over their safety.

"Soon."

8

REBORN

We left for the surface shortly after eating again and took the elevator down to the underground train. I couldn't believe I was finally getting to leave their concealed vault that had been keeping me.

Malik and Caitir accompanied me as the real Damon stayed behind, and we made small talk on the train. They explained that the way they do their research is by having a second machine out in the world to work with others. What I found most intriguing, beyond riding on a one-car-train that felt like it climbed for a long time at an incredible speed, was learning where the train stopped and how short the trip was. When we finally got out, we walked down a long tunnel that forked to other tunnels. Eventually the tunnels we took led to a door.

"Did you guys build all of this?" I asked as we walked.

"Oh, no," Malik said shaking his head. "These tunnels have been here a long time."

"Like, how long?" I said, confused.

"Um, well," Caitir mutter

"Hundreds of years," Malik replied.

"Malik," Caitir muttered, followed by a grunting sound coming from Malik, and Malik stopped talking.

"It's only been two hundred since they built the Capitol." I said as we neared the end of our walk.

Eventually we reached a modern looking doorway, which opened to a long hallway in the basement of a building. At the end of the twisting hallways, we arrived at a massive elevator with an electronic key pass.

"What's the history?" I asked.

Caitir chuckled and patted my shoulder. "It's a very long conversation. Lots of conspiracies."

The elevator had two sets of doors, which both opened up for us to enter. It took us to a basement where we were forced to switch to a newer and sleeker elevator, with glass walls. As that elevator climbed higher, through the glass we could see out beyond the building. We were in DC, in a newer building on the Georgetown waterfront, and it was an incredible view of the Potomac River.

We stopped near the top of the building and then got out. There, clean shaven and blue-eyed, Damon was waiting to greet us, wearing an expensive suit.

"I like this version of you," I said, because he seemed much less aggressive.

"Don't be deceived," he said softly, looking down at me.

For a moment I thought he might take my hand or pull my arm into his, but he didn't. He put his hands in his pockets and walked, leading the way. The building floor looked empty.

"Is it just you-all here?" I asked.

"Yes," Damon said.

"We keep larger chunks of our admin personnel in the other offices farther downtown, except most of our security is here," Caitir responded.

"Because of the machine?"

"We have to offset the energy consumption," Malik said.

"For privacy," Damon replied. "Doing what we're doing here is a type of unwanted research. Any information that elevates the consciousness of humanity is considered a threat."

"The people in control won't like it," Caitir said.

"Is it that powerful?" I asked.

"It could be," Damon nodded.

"Proof that we are energetic beings who can help heal ourselves and each other from multiple issues the medical world can't seem to treat or even acknowledge?" Malik chimed in.

"I never would have thought of it that way," I replied.

By the time they were done explaining to me why their actions were so radical we had finally reached the Q-Spec housed inside the building. It was less industrial and much prettier and shinier. It looked smaller too.

"Why does it look so different?" I asked.

"It's a lot easier to make changes and add customizations here," Malik explained.

"Oh."

"And you don't want people hung-up on how it looks, so it should be as visually modern as possible," Caitir added.

Damon cleared his throat and said, "Dr. B will be here shortly."

"How did you get a message to her that no one else would notice?"

"Flower courier," he stated flatly. "With a handwritten card."

They showed me around before her arrival, to the dressing room, break room, conference room, and so on, but my mind was abuzz and overwhelmed with emotion.

Malik alerted us that BB had arrived at the building's underground parking, and security was letting her into the elevator. I could see on the monitor she hadn't changed. She was shorter and smaller than me, under five feet. Her hair was shoulder length and blond, and she wore professional attire with modest but expensive accessories, as she always did.

BB stepped out of the elevator door wearing slacks and a trendy sweater and coat, and her face was angry. She held the flower shop card in her hands and was looking hard. Her eyes landed on Damon first as he was in the middle of the foyer's floor, waiting to greet her.

"Where's my granddaughter?" she demanded as she walked straight toward him.

I stepped away from the wall I'd been leaning against and walked to her and Damon. I had a remorseful look plastered on my face.

"Gellion?" she called out to me.

"Hi BB. I'm sorry if I worried you." I went to her, and she hugged me. She was breathless and heavy with emotion, and she held back her tears and eventually looked around to see who was there.

"Your father almost reported you missing, but he found a note in your apartment saying you went to Korea? What is going on? Why are you here?"

"You know Damon," I said, reaching out for him, but he did not take my hand.

"Yes, Gellion. He's been gone, but not forgotten," BB grumbled.

"Hi Dr. B," Caitir said.

"Caitir!" BB exclaimed, surprised at seeing her. Caitir went in for a hug, and I moved out of the way. "Is Malik here? Are you still together?" BB asked.

"We're engaged," she said, as Malik appeared and bowed, a gesture which BB returned.

"Congratulations. Where's Calder?"

The way BB asked, the way she said his name made me do a double take, and I put a mental pin in my mind about her reaction.

"He couldn't be here today," Caitir said. "He asked me to give you his regards, though."

"Please do the same. I hope he is well."

Then BB looked at me and squeezed my hand.

"Could you show me to the bathroom, dear?" she asked me in her sweetest old-lady voice, and I complied.

When we were inside the dressing room, BB grabbed me by the arm and pulled me fully inside.

"What the hell is going on?" she demanded to know in a low hiss.

"Despite your note, your father thinks something happened to you!"

"I didn't write the note. I went to the masquerade," I said, and BB gasped!

"I told you not to do that! I warned you."

"Mr. Jairus is dead."

"I saw the news. What happened?"

"The coroner will say it was a heart attack," I said, not lying, "but someone blew poisonous smoke into his face."

"At the masquerade?"

"Yes."

"How were you involved, Gellion?"

"He, he...he tried to kill me, BB. Damon stopped him."

"And now the man who tried to kill you is dead."

"I'm not supposed to have survived."

"What does that mean?"

"That no one can know I'm alive, but no one can think I'm dead either. They'll be in danger for helping me, so I can't go back to my old life. I have to stay hidden for a while," I rambled.

BB sat down on the dressing room sofa, deep in shock and concentration, and finally moaned out.

"From the moment that man came into your life, danger came with him," BB said. "No one could stop it. It was like a wave of horror had arrived into our lives, a freight train of dread from his life to ours."

"I wish I could remember."

"No, you don't," she snapped at me.

"Why didn't you ever tell me?"

"He was gone, and you had a long road of recovery ahead. There was no point."

"No point?" I said angrily, raising my voice. "Then how could you let me work for Damon's grandfather?"

BB looked up at me with the saddest expression, that seemed to age her in those moments.

"I can't even begin to tell you how that happened. The layers of manipulation used to get to you. We needed the grant money for your treatment. How could I know it was coming from connected organizations who never mentioned being affiliated? By the time you'd taken the job, we realized what happened," she said shaking her head. "Knowing the truth would have only hurt you while working for that man."

I just stood there staring at her, once again letting it sink in that I'd been in a mess for a long time yet had no idea. Sure, it was weird and off-putting working for Mr. Jairus, but then I'd go over to Katherine's house for dinner, and her father was much the same. The diplomat was high-handed, insulting, and dismissive of the younger adults around him, as he spoke from a position of power. The only reaction I could muster after being around that was a shrug at the generational rift.

In turn, I'd drag Katherine to BB's house where she felt loved, embraced and well fed, and softened as a person because of it.

"So, what now?" BB asked.

"I'm forced to trust him, or risk Dad and Brian, and you."

"Is it really that bad?" she asked, having trouble believing.

I didn't know how to convince her.

"How bad did it get back then?" I asked, and it dawned on me that BB knew so much more than she wanted to say. "Was I the only one who got hurt?"

BB looked up at me like she couldn't possibly explain.

"No, you weren't."

"Who else? How many?"

"Too many!" She said, immediately choking up from the pain.

"What?" I whispered. "Who?"

She just shook her head, like she couldn't possibly relive it all.

"That's not fair," I complained, being left out of the knowledge I should have.

"What our family has suffered is not fair, but making you carry it without knowing why, would have been cruel."

"Who decided this? Why would you keep lying for so long? BB, please!"

"Your mother! Okay? That's who decided. She came over and took down all the pictures and said, 'This, this is our family now,' and not to make you carry it, and I listened."

I didn't speak; I couldn't even find the words, so I stared at the ground. Eventually BB sighed large enough for me to hear and the only thing I could think to convey was how much fear I was carrying, despite my lack of pain.

"I didn't think I'd make it out of there alive. It was so horrible."

She took my hand in hers and patted it gently.

"You have to stay by his side then," she said, vacillating her head.

"It's not just that he saved me. He took my pain away too, BB."

"Hmm," she mumbled. "What do I tell your father?"

I pulled an envelope from my jacket and gave it to her. "I wrote him a letter, explaining everything. You can't talk about me, or where I am. Pretend I'm in Korea. These people can hear what you say from a satellite if they really want to."

"But it's safe here?"

"Malik and Caitir guarantee we can talk without being overheard."

"Is that why they took my phone before I entered the building?"

I nodded.

"Why am I here?" BB finally asked.

"Two reasons," I admitted. "I couldn't stand the idea of you guys thinking I'm dead..."

"Well good," she said, reaching out for my hands to hold. "Thank you. And?"

"Damon said you brought me back to life when I was in the hospital. Is that true?"

"Oh, well, sort of," she said, sighing again. "Why, is that important?"

"So, you really heal people?"

"It's part of what I do."

"Like, what, you just include it with the bone cracking and needling?"

"Usually."

"Why didn't you ever say anything?"

"I didn't want to bombard you when you were in so much pain. So, when your system shutdown, I'd just re-energize you and get things flowing again, and you'd feel better. It's no different from what I would do for any of my patients."

"All of them?"

"Yes," she said, not understanding my confusion.

"Oh."

"These basic energy systems must be running if we are to have a good life. Otherwise, the forcefield shrinks to nothing and the body loses momentum, and functioning is hard. I always make sure to reboot whatever shuts down. Working at a deeper level depends on the patient."

"So that's why I always feel better after seeing you?"

"One of the reasons. The whole package of aligning bones, clearing meridians, and energizing energy systems helps everyone feel better."

"Can you show us?" I asked her.

Her face was confused. "What do you mean?"

As if on cue, the door to the changing room opened slightly, and Caitir's head popped through.

"Did you tell her?" Caitir asked me.

"I didn't know how," I shrugged.

Caitir skipped inside and took BB's hand.

"I can't wait to show you what we've built," she said, practically singing.

I began to follow them out when Caitir turned her head and glared at me.

"Why don't you get ready, while I give BB a tour," she lulled at me, contrary to her bossy eyes.

"I...I... I," I stammered, not wanting to admit I hadn't used anything at the DC location. "Don't we both need to get dressed?"

"Just you," she said as they walked out the door.

I was alone, so I looked around. The dressing room was more like a fancy locker room with bathrooms and seating and mirrors. It was brightly lit and warm. I started opening the large closet-like lockers.

Inside each hung a magnetic diamond Q-Suit. The fabric came in different colors, and the suits came in different sizes. I didn't know which one should be mine.

Damon walked through the door, startling me. "Yours is the white one," he said, walking to a door I hadn't yet reached.

"Why do you always put me in white? It's so revealing, and I'm the fattest one here."

"Curvy," he corrected.

He smirked and nodded his head as he pulled the suit from the hanger.

"Pig," I sighed.

"Indeed," he replied, as he waited for me to disrobe.

"I think I can handle it on my own."

"You're a danger to yourself most days," he replied. "Let's see what BB says, and get you better, and then you can refuse my help."

I removed my jacket, pants and shirt.

"Bra too," he said, reaching out his hand for more clothing items.

"I wore a bra in the last suit," I protested.

"That bra didn't have an underwire," he corrected.

"Oh," and I didn't even consider how important that detail was for the magnetic suit.

I was annoyed at having to get half naked with him there, as BB was touring the facility. I decided to move more quickly and silently started taking items off and putting items on as he handed them to me, until the pieces became too cumbersome. "I look ridiculous."

"You look like a character in one of my childhood comics," he said as he helped me into the last torso and chest diamond-piece. "Exactly what a young boy's wet dreams are made of."

"Is that your version of flirting?" I asked, trying to be cheeky.

He gruffed, "It was just a childhood memory of something normal, before dreaming was taken away. So... no."

"I wouldn't know... about childhood memories," I said, utterly befuddled by his response. I'd been fishing for his compliment to continue.

Oh well.

I snickered at the thought of my kid brother, Brian, now eighteen, experiencing comic book crushes as a kid, until he could successfully draw his own female characters to love.

"...but Brian would agree with you, I'm sure," I chuckled again.

Damon murmured a small chuckle too. He must have remembered Brian well.

We settled into silence before one another, me standing a foot taller than normal on a square platform in front of mirrors, with a man who usually towered over me. Physically face-to-face for the first time ever, I lifted my arms and rested them on his shoulders and waited to see what he would do.

"The suit is so heavy," I said demurely.

I thought he might kiss me, but he simply lifted me up from under my arms and set me down on the floor.

"You're right, it's very heavy," he said, and I felt a twinge of judgment.

"Obviously a design flaw," I retorted, since it wasn't even my real body anyway.

Except for the small platform in the suit's shoes, I was over a foot shorter than him again. Hmph! I didn't bother to look up at him, and turned for the door, moving slowly.

He just laughed and followed me out.

As he escorted me to the Q-Spec, and situated the head piece on, he handed me some glasses.

"What are these for?"

"You," he replied. Though my confused expression kept him talking. "Dr. B may not want to see the energy work as she's doing it. So, we turn the visual beams off and let it run on other frequencies. The glasses will allow you to see what the Q-Spec thinks she's doing if you want to watch."

"I wish I could see it like her," I complained.

"We've never worked with anyone who wanted to see the lights as they did the work. They needed to see it in their mind, as they always have, and not be distracted by what the machine displays. What it does or does not pick up is like an assessment and could be wrong. It helps if the person speaks about what they are doing so we can line it up with the image. Then again, not all energy workers are the same, and some are more talented than others."

I entered the fancy Q-Spec alone and I braced myself for the powerful magnets to hold and push and pull me upward into place, for the machine to read my entire field. I was floating in the air, and through the glasses I could see my own system. Not impressive. Seriously lacking.

Caitir escorted BB in, and they got on a platform that could raise and lower them to meet my floating frame. She tapped something on her clear tablet and the laser lights turned on, so I removed my glasses and tucked them into my suit. BB watched as the machine turned my barely existing energy streams into dots of light that came together through laser fields, to represent what energy systems I had, and how they looked.

BB smiled and clapped her hands together then laughed deeply and quietly. "This is wonderful."

"BB, can you tell me if it looks right?" I called down to her.

They were standing just below me, looking up. I could see BB looking at me and at the lights that made up my forcefield.

"Where's the rest of it?" she asked.

"Remember how I showed you that on a healthy person, the machine can pick up multiple layers. Well, we assume Gellion's system is shutdown," Caitir said, then looked at her. "It's why we asked you here."

"This isn't about being shut down. The systems your machine read on that other woman aren't even showing up here," BB retorted.

BB stood back and stared at me and Caitir, taking it all in, assessing, analyzing, questioning. We stayed in silence for some time.

"Will it see changes I make to the energy stream?" BB asked.

"The Q-Spec will pick up anything that changes Gellion's energy, but if you wear these gloves, it might be better," Caitir said, handing them to BB. "We'd like to take readings from the source of the energy shift too," Caitir said, as BB put on the pair of gloves with the diamond silica patterning on them. "For all of us to see it more clearly, the gloves help the machine know it's reading a second energy source," Caitir replied.

"Do the lights look right?" I asked.

"I can't tell yet. The lights are too..."

"Overwhelming?" I asked.

"More like, distracting."

I laughed. Damon was right. BB wanted to look at me without the lights, but I wanted to see her experience the Q-Spec Reader. Caitir turned the laser lights off, and I put my glasses back on.

"Can you tell us what it looks like to you or what it should be doing, so we can see if the machine reads the changes?"

She nodded and looked around, trying to figure out how she was going to reach me from all sides.

Caitir had a remote and she controlled the other parts of the Q-Spec, so she raised the other platforms up, creating a large circular platform with a smaller hole in the center for continuation of the magnetic stream. Then she lowered me down to have me laying face-up in the air, held by the magnetic fields.

BB was used to this view of me lying down, as it was how she worked on all her patients, allowing the interaction to be more comfortable.

"Your energetic core isn't here. I can't see your chakras either," BB said, confused.

She'd been making eye contact with me while she said it. Maybe it was just the energy, or a message from whoever sends her information, or seeing me in a body that didn't hurt. Her gut instinct was rarely wrong, and BB was using all her Spidey senses. I was trying to remember if the Q-Spec could even see a core. Part of me remembered that it had when we were in the bunker version. The color inside the woman that looked like a white battery, must have been the core. I wondered though if BB knew for sure.

"You mean, the machine isn't reading it?" I asked.

"Forget the machine. I mean, your core is missing," she said, somewhat stunned.

With a wave of her hand, and her intention, or her mind's eye even, she started swirling her hands off to the side of me, away from the magnetic field. It was intense how malleable the Q-Spec became in response to her. Suddenly the light trickled in from somewhere else, and a torso-long elliptical of energy emerged from beneath me.

"How'd you do that?" Caitir asked, shocked!

"What happened to my granddaughter?" BB asked Caitir in a very serious and upset tone.

I looked at what she saw, trying hard to see if the dots were displaying what she was seeing, but there was nothing there.

"What is it BB?" I asked.

"Tell me what happened to you!" BB demanded.

She wasn't going to let the machine learn anything from her until she understood why she was seeing what she was seeing. Caitir turned me upright, so I was facing them.

"I'm recovering from surgery," I said.

"What for?" BB flabbergasted.

"There were metal rods in my body. They were making me sick."

"Metal rods? From where?"

"Inserted. From all those surgeries I had."

BB put her hand to her mouth, shaken, and stumbled a step backwards. Caitir caught her.

"Why?" BB asked.

"BB, are you okay?" I wondered, dangling in the air.

"I knew something was wrong," BB said out loud, her eyes glazed over as she stared out, maybe remembering. "But your scans looked so frightening."

"They were faked," Caitir interjected. "Gellion only needed one of those surgeries. Not the other six."

"Who would do something like that?"

"Mr. Jairus," I said.

BB covered her shocked mouth with both hands.

"My grandfather was extremely evil," Caitir said.

BB's eyes were still, as her mind mulled the information over.

"Is this because of you?" BB called out above us, to Damon behind the glass panel, in the modern command center inside the building.

She just stared at the blackened window, waiting until eventually the chamber door opened, and Damon stepped inside. Caitir walked to a different platform, and pressed a button to make it go down, taking herself with it. Damon replaced Caitir inside the circular platform around me.

"He wanted to teach me a lesson," Damon said to BB, his eyes lowered, his hands behind his back. "He was malicious. Do you remember?"

"Of course, I remember," she snapped. "You were gone, and his charities were in our face with handouts for rehab and therapy and college grants. What was I supposed to do?"

"He lived for wicked games," Damon tried to explain. His stern look and stiff shoulders were tense, though his face was trying to seem timid and apologetic. "He would often play with my emotions, and those around me. Every time Gellion was hurt, or got cut open, he openly taunted me. I didn't know what he was doing, but I knew the surgeries would cause harm. She may have forgotten me, and you may want to blame me, but I've never forgotten the warmth I experienced from your family."

"My dead family?" BB asked.

Damon froze, looking for the words, unable to find them. "He's gone now. It's almost over."

"Yet, I have to think of Gellion as dead?" BB retorted, explaining her pain.

"For now."

"How much will that hurt Tony and Brian?" She asked me.

"I'm sorry," I said, remorseful for the pain it would cause my father and brother, and how separated I was from that upset. "I can't be seen alive right now," I implored. "Please, you have to let me disappear for a while."

"Can you please put her down?" BB barked at Damon in a way I'd never seen BB raise her voice. She sounded fierce.

"Can you please fix her?" he retorted, trying to get her to focus on the objective.

They stared into one another with a desire to make some shift in the stance of the other. It worked. BB started to soften under his imploring gaze.

"You've changed," she said in a deep voice, powerful but acknowledging him.

"I have a lot to redeem," he replied, with a bit of disdain, never breaking her gaze.

BB shifted to his request. "Why is her core missing? Her chakras?"

"She is far away," he said quietly, apologetically. "Can you see it from that perspective?"

I took a deep breath and closed my eyes, not even wanting to see her response. I knew it would take a while for her to acknowledge it, from shock to understanding. It was still hard for me to believe. I was still me, in most ways. I did think the same thoughts, yet without the pain I could think more clearly, yet memory wasn't so clear.

I couldn't be sure of anything absolute, as my senses of living were all new without the inflammation and burning ache. I was grateful for a body that could breathe easier, for the horror of the secret world before me, a real world for some, would be too hard to stomach in my tormented body.

I could fully live into my feelings in this new reality. Before, I couldn't even acknowledge that there was life beyond suffering. This realization allowed me to calm myself and settle in for a new kind of thinking, if only my grandmother could help me get there. BB took some breaths and finally spoke.

"So, Gellion is somewhere else."

"Recovering," Damon explained, without explaining. "But also, not wanting to wake up."

"Excuse me?" She exclaimed, her breath heavy. I wanted to reach out to her, but I was stuck.

"Gellion's body doesn't want to wake up."

"This new reality is too much for that body," she said intuitively; she knew how much I'd suffered.

"Not for me," I chimed in, truthfully, finally opening my eyes. "But in a body with that much pain, yes."

I could tell BB wanted to pace, but she just breathed in deeply through her nose.

"This Gellion can't access its battery, or life force. That's a design flaw," BB said. She kept shaking her head, like she didn't want to absorb the information. I could sympathize.

"I'm curious if you can see the same with me?" Damon asked.

BB looked him up and down and then raised her eyebrows. "Yes. What is this? You both have the same problem," she said.

Damon's eyebrows went up. "The same for the others too then," he mumbled.

"How can we fix it?" I asked.

"My best guess is to pull..." BB trailed off, "...no," she said low and serious. "No."

"What?" I asked.

"Do you deteriorate?" She continued her curiosity at Damon.

"Yes," he admitted. "Very quickly."

"Are you aware it's an energetic problem?"

"I believed so," Damon said, eager for BB's curiosity, "but this machine is the only system that ever verified it for me. I couldn't prove it without fixing the connection. I was hoping Gellion would help."

"She doesn't know how to do any of that anymore," BB argued, knowing me well.

"I didn't design this technology," he said, motioning to his body. "I only modified it. It's a design flaw, yes, and it causes problems."

BB took a step back and closed her eyes. "Are there others? Beyond you and your family, using this?"

"Yes," Damon admitted immediately.

"Good guys or bad guys?" BB asked bluntly.

"Bad guys," Damon admitted.

"They have the same problem?"

BB's mind and way of thinking was way ahead of my own.

"Same design flaw, yes."

"Can you fix it BB?" I asked, but she looked at me as if my question was offensive.

BB put up her hands, as if she were going to send me energy and closed her eyes, and after a little while, she spoke.

"I can fix it, but not here, and not for this machine to see and record."

"Why not?" Damon asked, curious.

BB stepped back and looked at all Damon had created.

"This machine was designed to read human energy. Technically, based on what I see, you're not really human. Your biggest problem has nothing to do with this machine. Yes, I can help Gellion, but I will not show this machine how to make you into humans. Understand?"

Damon nodded. BB had always been special to me, but I had no idea what she had been capable of doing.

"Can you really see what's wrong with Gellion?"

"Of course. No matter how far away, I can see my granddaughter," BB made clear to Damon. "But I will not allow that work to be recorded, to help the others make themselves stronger."

"I agree," Malik said over the intercom, reminding us they were listening. "We'll shut the Q-Spec down."

"Don't bother. I'll do the work somewhere else."

"I've got the perfect spot," Caitir said.

My body was lowered immediately after Caitir spoke and then the platform we were standing on was brought down too. The Q-Spec made a noise alerting us that it was powering down, then Caitir met us at the entrance. BB would not be playing with Damon's machine the way we all thought she would. She could see we weren't normal, not energetically the same as our originals, and that was a problem.

"I understand not showing us how to connect her, but once you've connected her, could you please show our machine how to fix the energy systems that get shut down in all humans?" Caitir pleaded with BB, taking her hand and leading her somewhere else, Damon and I behind them.

Caitir opened the door to a large office that was both lovely and lived in. Besides the array of different furniture, places to work and lounge, there was also a massage table set off to the side. It sat in front of the windows with a river view, a permanent area for body work inside the elaborate office.

"We'll leave you to connect her," Caitir said, pulling Damon away from us.

I walked to the table and laid down, and it was a relief to not have the weight of the suit to carry. BB joined me.

"I've never done this before, so just lay quietly while I try to figure it out," she commanded.

I did as she said and found I was pretty exhausted already and comforted by her taking charge somehow.

"The trick is to connect it but not fix it," BB mumbled and then went quiet.

I was enjoying the quiet of her steady breaths when she finally spoke.

"Well, that was extremely convoluted, but I'm pretty sure it's fixed."

"What do I do if I need attaching again?"

"Call me I guess," she replied.

"What about the rest of them?"

"Let's focus on you dear," she redirected.

"What's wrong with me?" I asked.

"Your systems are shattered again," BB said, looking at me. "What happened to you?"

"Beyond the surgery?" I asked as I sat up, not wanting to remember. "Learning through terror that your whole reality is basically a lie, is pretty hard on the human system."

I didn't mean to chide her, but somewhere in there was the frustration that all these relationships existed for me, and I had no idea.

"I started to give up on wanting to be here," I admitted. "Thank you for coming."

We walked back to the hallway together. Damon had been pacing outside, while Caitir stood straight and motionless, until we arrived. She was bouncing up and down at the sight of us. Damon searched my face for an answer. I nodded to them both.

Without saying anything BB walked past them and headed back to their machine. The door was opened for us and Caitir rejoined us inside. This time when my body was positioned and the Q-Spec began making the noises it made when reading energy and playing back information, I was mesmerized at the accuracy.

What we saw was both beautiful and horrifying.

The imagery was like starlight in the dark. My chakras weren't just bent or broken; they were shattered. As I stared at the particles that should be moving with vitality, all I could think of was how much my fragmented systems looked like galaxies out in the universe.

My core was dark, only a small spark of energy to tell us it even existed. Though the core battery splintered very differently from the chakras, it too was traumatized. My true force field, not the one I tried to recreate from my dreams, was filled with holes, forcing it to get smaller and smaller, closer and closer to me. It had no power, or life to it at all. Zero protection.

"Dr. B, does this look right to you?" Caitir asked my grandmother as she stared at the visions of my system and its twinkling.

"This makes it look beautiful to be broken," BB quipped to herself.

"I'm switching off the light stream now," Caitir said as she tapped the commands needed to take away the vibrant distraction.

I put my glasses back on and waited. BB stepped toward me and started moving her hands, speaking softly, as if she were digging something out of me, while putting energy in. Then she stopped and shook her head like she was chastising herself.

"BB?" I asked.

"What happened to you?" She asked again, demanding to know.

So much had happened to me in such a short amount of time. Through the glasses I could see that my energetic core had started coming together. In BB's clutching hand the place where the core was broken was pulsating. I wondered if I said the words out loud, said what the trauma was that shattered me to my very being, if BB could heal it better.

"Can I tell her?" I asked Caitir, "Please?"

Caitir sighed and bulged out her eyes as if to tell me she didn't know.

"I watched a murder, up close, knowing I would die next," I said the truth, as vaguely as I possibly could, "at the hands of someone familiar."

BB gasped!

Then she lifted her clutched hand away from me, removing the pulsating tear from my energetic core. With her other hand, she sent my core light from her palm, flowing out from her in abundance toward me. I watched in awe as the shattered construct that was my battery healed itself from the explosion, just like magic.

Once the core was whole again, BB placed her hands out, one hand hovering over my throat, the other over my pelvis. I tried to see it with my own eyes, with my own intuition, but I sensed nothing. Yet behind the glasses, the Q-Spec revealed a marvelous energetic light show, one BB was not watching as she worked.

When the energy poured from her hands, it reminded me of a battery charger, or jumper cables. Light cascaded into my core at the top and bottom of my torso, until the whole construct was not only full but propelling energy into itself as its internal structure started to run. A self-propelling unit, that needed repair, and a jump start.

I closed my eyes when I could feel it. I felt not only warmer, but calmer and more peaceful somehow. My body made me sigh with relief. The panic I didn't even know I'd been feeling was immediately discharged. Watching the work happen live, in vivid color, filled me with so much awareness so quickly that it was seared into my mind. In real time I had witnessed the whole of my system shift from broken to mended.

Then BB moved next to my chakras.

"I've only ever seen them shattered like this once before. It was one traumatic event that caused it. Is that what happened this time?"

"No," I admitted, trying to think about all the events so far, what could have been the one to shatter me the most.

That I'd watched myself be murdered?

That I could never go home, or else risk the lives of my family?

That I'd been lied to for years? My best friend was a paid spy.

That I couldn't let any man touch me without screaming?

That I'd had metal rods inside my body, torturing me?

That the rulers here were despicable and evil, and the only man who ever loved me was one of their progenies?

Would all of that be enough to shatter my chakras? Maybe.

"Finding out that your accident wasn't an accident, might be enough," BB said, as she had already sensed that the root of my deepest pain would be powerful enough to retraumatize me.

I hadn't considered that. I closed my eyes and stopped looking at the changing energy. BB worked on each chakra, bringing it back online by removing the perceived trauma there, and rebuilding the structure with intention and her channeled energy.

Since I knew the session would be recorded, I allowed myself space to receive her gifts, lying back and closing my eyes with appreciation. When she was done, my chakras were vibrant, my core strong, my forcefield growing. Even the AI inside the Q-Spec had picked up on BB's energy flowing into the unmapped Chi structure, sparking it back to life, teaching the new energy signature to the machine.

Caitir was over the moon happy to see so much information. I could tell BB was tired though, as my own energy was beyond depleted. It didn't help that all the people around us had no working energy constructs either.

When my body was lowered and BB and I walked out of the chamber, Caitir offered my grandmother a cup of tea and pastries. She knew the work could be exhausting and that I needed time to change. Caitir would, no doubt, also replay the imagery for BB, reminding her of how amazing she is and how lucky we are for her help.

I wondered if the realizations and images BB did see, channeled to her from somewhere, had worn her out. I was reminded that she was past retirement age, still working full-time, doing body healing and energy work on many patients each week. Then I felt guilty for the emotional strain I'd put BB through.

Trying to heal and survive meant I'd had to hurt my family to do it. I'm sure that any new revelations she gathered only made her concern worse. By the time I returned, it was time for BB to depart. She needed to breathe and get away from my new reality. She reached out her hand to me in the lobby area, the day's events bringing a visible fatigue.

"Walk me to my car, dear?" she asked.

"Of course," I said, moving closer to the elevator, and pushing the button down.

From behind me I could sense him, then Damon put pressure on my shoulder and said softly, "You cannot leave the elevator."

I nodded.

When the doors opened, Calder was inside.

"Calder?" BB called out to him. "It's so good to see you, young man" she said as if he were her long lost grandson. "How've you been?" she asked, opening her arms to him, as he greeted her, arms opened wide. They hugged.

"I'm living, most days, even when it's hard to feel alive," Calder said to BB.

I knew I'd missed something, something about their ease with one another in the face of BB's disdain for Damon. It caught me off guard. I looked at Damon questioningly, and he shrugged.

"I wish we had time to catch up, but I know today has been a lot," Calder said to BB. "I promise we're taking good care of her."

"You're right about that; it has been a lot. Thank you for saving my only granddaughter," she replied, which made Calder wince a little.

He hugged her again, Caitir joining in, and pulling me in too.

Calder pressed the button down for the elevator to return, and when the doors opened, BB and I made our way inside.

I held my breath until the doors closed.

"Are you ok?" I asked BB.

"No, Gellion. Are you?" she replied.

I pulled her into me and cried. "No, I'm not. I'm sorry."

"There's no choice in it," she said, pulling away from me. "Every time he comes into our lives, someone dies. Someone is tormented," she said to herself, trying to push back her upset.

"What do you mean?" I asked.

"Your mom told him never to come back, and he stayed away for a year. The day after he tried to see you, your mother was killed. I've lost so much because of him. Now I'm losing you too."

"I don't remember seeing him," I said, shaking my head.

"She stopped him before he could get to you. You'd just started walking again."

"He didn't tell me," I said quietly.

"Why would he?" she asked. She paused for a moment and looked at me. "I can see what he wants from you. He's trying to bring you back."

"I'm never gonna be the same as I was before."

"Are you in pain?"

I looked at her, growing upset over my mom, but also wanting to smile because I wasn't in pain. BB knew how much I hurt; how much I'd suffered. I was a perpetual patient of hers after my surgeries and recoveries.

"I'm not," I said, a sad smile of disgust and happiness upon me.

"You fought off the devil and won," BB said, immediately disgusted with that reality. "I don't really understand any of this, but if what you say is true, you have no choice anyway."

"So, what do I do?"

"Learn. Grow. Protect yourself, and try your best to keep in touch," she said, looking at me with so much sadness and loss.

I wanted to speak, but I couldn't, my face was so down.

"Gellion," BB said. "How could all your energy be somewhere else, yet you're here? And how did you bring your forcefield here. You were the only one with even a shadow of energy."

I wasn't sure what she was asking, but she seemed curious about that anomaly.

"They are like me. Disconnected. Can you help them too?"

"Why?"

"The stronger they are, the safer I'll be," I explained, and she couldn't disagree.

"I'll fix the problem," she said.

"For all of them?" I asked. "How?"

"Remotely," BB said without explaining further. "All of them being who, exactly?"

"Damon, Caitir, Malik, Calder, Rosie, Eamon, and someone named Tombo," I answered, resolutely.

She nodded, her gaze far off, probably wondering when she'd be energized enough to do the work remotely, from the comfort of her home. I'd been grateful for her care, and I felt so much better knowing she would be working on them too, or at least more hopeful.

"And the forcefield?" she asked again.

"I don't really know. Damon asked me if I ever imagined I'd manipulated energy around me. I remembered a dream I had when I first woke up from the coma. It was so powerful and memorable; it was easy to recall how my forcefield had appeared big and strong."

"Through memory of a dream, you brought your forcefield to this body?" BB asked me, pointing at my sternum. "If someone can do that, maybe it's not wrong that people believe you can do more."

"Maybe," I realized. "But I can't do what you can for them."

"Not yet," she mumbled. "I promise I'll connect them. Stay hidden, little one."

The elevator door dinged, and I held the open button to stop it from moving. She started to leave and then turned to me, with that look on her face she gets when she needs to say something profound.

"The Gellion I knew was turning into someone amazing because she didn't see the world like other people...you saw the world like your grandfather, and he made sure you understood what life would really be like or could be like based on your abilities and choices. You didn't care about fitting in because you had a vision. And that openness to a reality beyond the norm is what saved you from Damon's wicked intentions the first time. Trust yourself, but be mindful, be careful."

"That's a lot to live up to BB."

"He's trying to make a roadmap for you. I hope it works."

"You're the one with the amazing gifts. It should be you up there."

"But I don't want to be there, Gellion. I don't want to figure this out for you. I can't take it, being near the reason for my whole world's destruction. I want peace. It has to be you."

In that moment I realized that BB hated Damon Jairus and everything he'd brought into our lives. It had been true from the moment he arrived, and it would never change. I knew her well enough to know that.

"You're right," I replied, understanding that this path was mine alone, and that the plan Damon wanted in place meant really saying goodbye to everyone. Until when I didn't know.

"I love you, dear one," she said, hugging me again.

"I love you too BB."

I let go of her as Calder arrived to escort her to her car.

"Be safe," she said as she blew me one last belated kiss, without enthusiasm but a heavy heart.

"I will."

"Promise me."

BB was the only maternal figure I'd had to lean on since my mother died. I owed her assurance. Even though it sounded corny, the one thing my grandfather used to say to the Gellion I used to be, was:

"I swear. My word is my oath."

She nodded as if the words were enough to lessen her grief.

9

THE MONSTER REPENTS

When the elevator doors opened, they were waiting for me. I couldn't talk. It was just too much. I walked past them all and went straight to the dressing room and opened the locker doors until I found the stack of folded and categorized workout clothes for women. Once I got dressed I grabbed the music player from my jacket and walked back out.

"Gellion," Damon said first.

"There has to be a treadmill here somewhere, right?" I asked, ignoring him.

"I'll show her," Caitir said as she grabbed my hand and took me back into the elevator. Three floors down and with handprint access, the doors opened on an almost dark floor.

There was only an emergency light from the exit across the way, lighting the room. The ceilings were black and dark. Caitir said a command I barely heard, and the walls came to life. Just like the dining room in the bunker with the window-wall-view of the jungle, this backdrop was everywhere!

All the light came from the walls, covered in living scenery, floor to ceiling televisions, continuously broadcasting a living view of a panoramic forest. Like an open floor treehouse in the most awe-inspiring landscape that looked like a forest in the Pacific Northwest.

The running track around the edges of the floor forced the runner next to the forest edge view, and into a whole new reality. The center was filled with gym equipment, a boxing area, sparring mats, CrossFit, weights, cardio, Pilates and more to fill the open space.

"Caitir, this is amazing. Wow," I said breathlessly.

"Is this view okay, or would you prefer another?" Caitir asked.

"This is perfect," I said.

I put my earbuds in and started to run, and it felt so good to run without pain, to push my body without caving into endless suffering. I felt free for the first time ever, despite the extra weight. Life started in pain and just never stopped until now, well, except for the emotional pain. That was searing me.

I ran with a yearning to drive out the sadness. Being around BB and her words about my mom, and how we'd all lost her not long after almost losing me. Now they're losing me again. It just twisted the pain of that loss even more. I'd only gotten to have my mom for one year after waking up paralyzed from the car accident.

My brother lost his mother. My father lost his wife. My grandmother lost her daughter. Mom helped me learn how to walk again. She was my best friend. I miss her so much still.

How could Damon let her get killed?

I found myself asking, despite knowing that wasn't fair, but my anger needed a place to go, and everyone was telling me this was all Damon's fault somehow. As if on cue, Damon stepped out from the elevator in athletic gear and looked in my direction. I refused to even attempt eye-contact, as I was still going through my emotions, and anger was still at the top. He raised his arm as if to stop me, but I just ran past. Moments later he kept pace with me.

"Take those out," he said.

I ignored him. Finally, he yanked on my arm so hard I had to stop.

"What?!" I yelled at him.

"Take those out," he said, holding his hand out to take them from me.

"Why?" I said as I pulled the wireless earbuds from my ears and handed them to him.

"How did we even miss these?" he asked himself.

"Are they hackable?" I asked.

"Of course, but that's not the problem since we have a signal shield here. Our clones can't handle the vibration of the signal. The radiation is bad for humans, but clones deteriorate faster so you'd end up with a half-life clone that can't function because of a massive brain tumor."

He pulled a small pouch out of his pocket and handed it to me. They were wired headphones to attach to my mp3 player. I put them on while he slipped my music player into a metallic case.

"The signal from the device is harmful too," he said as he attached the case into an armband and handed it back.

This wasn't even about me as a person, but a worry over the true deterioration of cloned cells, and an investment in keeping my current body safe. I started running again, with yet another perspective shifted. It was hard to stay mad with so much changing and shifting within my psyche's reality.

Damon sat down at one of the weight machines and put his clone body to work. Eventually Caitir and Malik joined in too. Everyone was working out, sweating, and finding relief in the movement, until Calder entered, and Damon visibly shifted to irritation. I didn't want to be bothered by their issues, as I had my own, so I ignored them and kept on running. Eventually it was impossible to miss how they had made their way to the boxing ring and were fighting without gloves.

I kept on running.

Caitir joined me and waited for me to finally pull my headphones down. She was so patient, which was almost annoying.

"What is it?" I whined at her.

"They're fighting over you."

I stopped running and walked over to see how bad it had gotten.

Both men were bleeding profusely from the head and nose and had used each other as punching bags. Neither looked so good. They were both panting.

"What the hell, Damon!" I yelled at him, nudging Caitir to agree with me, but she just shrugged.

I also understood. Damon was jealous of Calder. BB didn't hate Calder. Everyone knew it, and Damon was using me as an excuse to take out his anger on his cousin. Calder didn't seem to mind. These men were large and angry, and born to tussle.

Everyone was angry. Calder, however, was not distracted by my presence and landed a final blow that sent Damon to the floor.

"Are you done?" I asked Calder, and he just smiled while bleeding from his lip.

"What now?" I asked Damon.

"I can't do business like this. I need a new body. We should all go back to the bunker."

"Mom and Dad are expecting us for dinner," Caitir said, sounding hopeful.

"How nice, you Neanderthals can beat each other up and go get new skin suits," I said disgusted. Then I added under my breath, as we made our way to the elevator, "If you'd ever suffered all the time like me, maybe you wouldn't be so pig-headed."

I was still mad. It was universal.

The train ride home was awkward but quiet. I was doubly angry at having lost my false freedom so quickly to the stark underground. When the elevator brought us back to the bunker, Damon separated from us first.

"Gotta get out of my clone," he said, waving his bloody fist, while holding a bloodied cloth to his broken nose. Calder walked in the opposite direction, and Malik glared at both of them.

"Idiots," Malik said. "Are you ok?"

Malik hadn't really engaged with me much, but we were standing in the hallway, and I suddenly wanted to ask him something.

"How do you guys all know BB?" I asked.

Malik smiled. "She demanded to meet all of us, invited us in and made us feel welcome. She was like something out of a book we would have never gotten to experience, were it not for you. Our families were not so warm."

"What about Rosie and Eamon?"

"They had to be careful. They couldn't invite all the teenagers in and be the safe place."

"Everyone knew my family?"

"We all did."

"Everyone?"

"Except Tombo. He came after, like the other security team members. Except Joseph, he knew BB too. He went to school with us. You'll meet him later."

I smiled at the revelations but couldn't think what I was supposed to do next, when Damon arrived in his real body, darkened hair, growing beard, hazel grey eyes, and his tattoos. Such distinctly different versions of Damon. His presence was much more powerful like this, for me.

"Why do you seem even scarier now?" I asked, as he grabbed my wrist and gently pulled me to follow him back to our shared room.

"I don't have a suppressed libido in this body."

"What?" I was so shocked I laughed. "You can do that?"

"I have to, to manage dealing with people."

"You mean women?"

"No, the shift in testosterone helps maintain calm on multiple levels. It's no fun if I'm spending all my time convincing myself not to kill people I know deserve it."

His blunt and bleak statements always made me pause. I had no idea how well he could justify those thoughts.

"How much different are the levels?" I wondered, visibly seeing the difference.

"On a scale of one to ten, I'm at a thirteen in this body." I rolled my eyes at his gusto. "My clone is down at a seven, comparatively."

"How about you put yourself at ten, then compare your clone to that?" I inquired, with a smirk. "So, we have a better understanding."

"Okay," he said, analyzing his own statement, and starting to smirk himself. "Six out of ten."

"Jesus," I scoffed. "Is there a clinical name for that?"

He grimaced, then squeezed and pulled on my wrist, and stopped walking then whipped me around to face him and kept my wrist in his hand. I was surprised at how gently he manhandled me.

I bit my tongue; I could tell he didn't like my tone or reference to a mental diagnosis. I'd said it trying to be mean, but he was filled to the brim with an anger I'd never experienced. He could snap at me, and I might not like him as much if he were as violent as he eluded.

"You have no idea what I'm capable of, or what I've done to survive. You don't win a war without balls of steel, or big dick energy, or machismo. Get it?"

"Huh? So, you have to get into fights?"

"Calder needed a win, so I had to let his body win."

"You're the one who got pulverized."

"It did look that way," he smirked.

"But you're the one who was rejected, while he was embraced?"

He scoffed, "You think BB's love gave Calder pride? You don't know how devastating it is to be embraced in loss."

I gasped.

I wasn't expecting him to speak so intimately about his cousin's troubles, or his leadership psychology. Or to say he let someone win on purpose. Most surprising was the effect my grandmother had had on all of them.

"I have an army of good people," Damon said, trying to explain, "but my best man is withered to nothing over the reminder of his pain. I got lucky and you survived, but it's triggered Calder's pain."

"When do I get to know? About who was lost?"

"When the people around you are ready to speak it. We aren't trying to punish you, but none of us have the energy to go there and dredge it all up."

Even though I understood his point, and appreciated their struggle,

I was still so angry inside. The little aching feeling within me that had started blaming Damon for my mother's death, wanted to poke at his pain, to see how real it was.

"You know, while you've been gone, I've been reading some of the books in your room. What if this whole thing is a mistake, and I'm just a walk-in?"

"That's not true," he snapped.

I wasn't even sure he'd recognize the term "walk-in," but it struck a nerve.

"Think about it Damon. I woke up with no memory, no ability to see energy, no gifts of any kind. Paralyzed, bedridden, broken, and scarred for life. I don't do anything like she used to do. I didn't even want to be called Gellion. I liked Eve better, but no one listened.

"And you left," I continued. "So, 'your Gellion,' the soul you fell in love with, probably left this BS life because she was never going to have you, and she was already messed up beyond repair."

My train of thought wouldn't stop.

"So, she left, and my pathetic, wretched soul jumped in, to maybe live out a couple of decades in pain. Her good Karma released her from having to live through this hell!" I started complaining. "Man, my Karma must be shit because it's just me, not your Gellion. She isn't here."

"Stop saying that," he said, trying to contain himself.

"I'm sorry, but Calder's loss is no different from yours, you've just been playing pretend all this time. I can't be her. You should never have come back for me. You got my mother killed."

I yanked my wrist away from him and walked off as his face was frozen, working through all the hurt I projected at him. The truth was, I really needed to be by myself. I was feeling suffocated and being mean worked when nothing else seemed to. Damon was so controlling, and though I tried to consider it came from fear, all I felt was rage at realizing the truth behind the loss of my mother.

It was hard to keep analyzing, when just processing was exhausting enough. I went straight to the bathroom and started the shower and took long deep breaths to calm my aching heart. Despite my upset, I needed food, so I found the softest dress in the closet, a solid grey, and brushed my long brown hair. The sheepskin slippers were calling me, so I walked to the dining room in them.

Even though it felt like I was shutting down again, I entered and assessed the activity. Everyone was already eating, except Damon who hadn't arrived. The food printer made me lasagna, which I knew would just disappoint me. It didn't taste anything like I wanted, so I put it in the trash and tried again.

"Meat lasagna. Sauce modification. Add a pinch of clove and two...hmm...morsels of maple syrup, and garlic and onion and basil."

It was better, but still not good enough.

They were all staring at me, and my frustration. I couldn't make eye contact at all. Caitir stood up from the large wooden bench she'd been on and walked around the table to where I was. First, she put her hands out, centered above my plate of food, and kept them hovering there as she sat down.

"Dear God of Light, Holy Lord of Love, please bless Gellion's food. Help it to nourish her battered soul, nourish her exhausted body and mind, and help her feel safe and loved right where she is, surrounded by all of us, her regained family."

Moisture formed in my eyes as the rest of them slowly made their way over to my portion of the table, each of them adding a hand to Caitir's, all of them calling on the same God-of-Light to help me. Tears streamed down my face as their bodies huddled closer to mine, arms and hands touching me gently, to remind me of humanity. Suddenly I was being pulled into hugs.

After all that love, Rosie gently asked, "Gellion, how can we help?"

"Why did my mom have to die?" I said, feeling so sad over the loss of her.

As if on cue, "Am I interrupting?"

I turned around and looked at Damon. He didn't seem angry, but maybe surprised, I couldn't exactly tell.

My face, I knew, was different too, from the emotion of those prayers and the release of some anger, and a need to know more. I stepped away from the group toward him, took his hand, and looked up at him. "Why'd she have to die?"

He sighed and worked hard to keep the anger from taking over, so he could answer me. "Grandfather warned me that if he didn't like my behavior that he would kill someone important. It was a no-win situation. He wanted you dead. I fought back against him."

I squeezed his hand tightly. "Why'd you do that?"

"I was out of my mind."

"You didn't care about consequences? You should have let me go."

"I cared too much! He said he was going to break me. He'd been doing it since I was a kid. He didn't know I would endure all of it just to get my revenge. He started a war, and there are always casualties."

"He's dead now," I said.

"It's not over."

Damon didn't apologize, and he didn't stick around to explain. He left, and that left me unnerved.

I turned around and looked at my new family. Calder, whose face was still bloody and bruised. Caitir and Malik, and her parents. It was enough to find company and sympathy, and I needed a different perspective.

Rosie stepped toward me. "Would you mind getting a cup of tea with me? I feel like I could be helpful here."

"Mom's a psychologist," Caitir said.

"And hypnotherapist," Rosie included.

"Sure," I said. It couldn't hurt.

Eamon opened the door for us, and I followed Rosie down one hall and then another. As she walked, I realized in all that time I'd never been given a full tour of the massive underground bunker. I decided not to ask for one just then and thought to explore on my own at some point. We eventually reached a double door, and inside was a library, like something out of a fairy tale, including the fake windows. I wondered how they could build something like this, so far down, and have so many beautiful details.

"How?" I asked in awe.

The walls and ceiling were painted in scenes from classic stories, and from the Bible. The beautiful woodwork was all whitewashed, making the room feel bright and alive. Rosie walked to a far wall, where there was a small drink station. She poured water into a boiler and pressed the button and prepared a beautiful tea set.

We sat in two large wingback chairs, with a small side table at our side, our legs meeting at a right angle. I stared at the woodwork and paintings. Nearby was an electric fireplace, which Rosie turned on with a remote.

"This is a good place to come. The collection of books is eclectic. Some are one of a kind."

"How did you...?"

"Oh, I didn't. This was all Damon."

"How did he do this?"

"With clones, of himself."

"He built all of this with just his clones?"

"Not just his, but yes, he found the base, made changes, and revamped everything. It's not the first one he's made."

"Why?"

"How else could he possibly survive?"

"I don't know. I don't know enough about any of this."

"If Damon wasn't a genius. If you hadn't been clairvoyant. None of this would have been possible and you would both be dead now."

"I want to know what happened."

"Isn't it more important to rediscover a way back to knowing yourself again?"

"Even my grandmother hid that from me."

"Gellion, my father wouldn't leave you alone. He was spying on you just as much as Damon was, to see if Damon would break down and try to contact you. This little game just kept escalating, until Damon had built his first base, perfected his clones, and could pretend to want to be a part of that world again."

"How could he convince Mr. Jairus of that?"

"Time and patience and making a name for himself in that world."

"I'd never seen Damon or even heard about him in all my time at Jairus Industries," I responded. "When did he go back to Mr. Jairus's world?"

"After your father had his stroke," she said, but in a way that emphasized something wasn't right.

And I knew her pointing out the timing wasn't a coincidence.

"That was four years ago. Wait, was my dad given a stroke?"

"If Damon made a deal to come back into the family as long as you were safely removed from the company, it's possible my father would prefer to see you reduced to a caretaker role than use your position under him as a steppingstone," Rosie said. "Damon doesn't tell us everything, even when he wants to. With you away from Jairus Industries, it was time for him to re-enter that world."

"He doesn't want me to know any of this, does he?"

"Of course not. He's terrified the details will make you hate him, and if you hate him, you'll never become the healer you were."

"What did I heal him from?"

"Oh Gellion, Damon was a monster before he met you. He was a sociopath with psychopathic tendencies. He had to have a bodyguard in school to keep him from hurting people."

I took a deep breath and rubbed my face with my hands.

"I fixed that?"

"In so many ways, yes. It was remarkable."

"What do I do?"

"I think that's what he's trying to teach you. You'll have to nag him to tell you the truth, and then decide to love him anyway, even when the truth is so ugly you want to die before hearing it again."

I gagged on my tea at her words.

"Just, love him? Even if he's a monster?"

"Well, don't you?" she looked at me as if it was already clear.

"I don't know."

"Gellion, how do you feel about Damon, after learning everything you've learned?"

"I'm upset, upset about my mother. Now my father's stroke? I feel sick inside. I'm also sad for him, for all the pain he's gone through, and completely overwhelmed by all of it, by how familiar and foreign it is."

And while all of that was true, there was another truth too.

"What about when you're next to him?"

"I'm really attracted to him," I sighed, "of course, and flattered, and um, curious. There's a feeling when I'm around him, I'm on edge and at ease, with a sort of need to blindly trust him. It's discombobulating."

"Do you desire him? To be touched by him?"

"Yes," I admitted, blushing.

"Have you ever felt that way about anyone?"

I hadn't.

Not in college. Not while working and going to clubs and parties with Katherine, loaded up on pain meds. Not while meeting up with old friends from high school, particularly Sarah, who always took me out. I kept looking in my mind through my shortened past, and while I found many handsome faces, not one belonged to a man that I wanted to be touched by or loved.

"No," I finally said, feeling that truth sink deep into me. "I always felt afraid."

"Did that feel normal to you?"

I had to think some about that too. "None of the girls I was around were afraid to flirt, so I hid my fear and pretended."

"What about Damon? Are you afraid to be alone with him?"

"I have moments, yes, but he's not really overstepping my boundaries, while I push all of his. I've already made a pass at him. Even though it ended badly, he showed my body more respect than I did."

I shook my head, a bit embarrassed.

"It's the opposite of what a normal person would feel," I continued. "I want to be alone with him, mostly, but then I find out the hard stuff. I'm having trouble knowing how to feel, how to accept and forgive, and understand. It's like I'm stuck in a nightmare, and the only thing that keeps me in my body at all is the thought of being intimate with him. He says I'm not ready, and he showed me why that's true. Just being touched made me panic, even though I wasn't afraid of him, the fear inside my body took over."

"Baby steps are important when you don't know what you can handle. Maybe that first time was frightening, but the next time won't be. Damon knows he must be patient with you, so he must learn to control his temper. How has that been?"

I didn't know why I felt so comfortable talking about intimate thoughts with Damon's aunt. She didn't seem like just an aunt, she was a lot like BB, so neutral in the therapeutic setting.

"Honestly, I see the control and rage and lust in his eyes, but he doesn't scare me the way he says he will. Even when he tries. Not yet anyway."

She smiled at me. "That's how it is with old friends."

"Friends?"

"You two were the best of friends. The never-ending conversations, and the sleepless nights of texting. It was the first time he'd acted normal since his parents died. His eyes came back to life."

"Are they alive now?"

"Since you got here, more so than I've seen in a long time, since your accident."

"So, what do I do?"

"Nag him for the truth, not all the truth, just the things you really need to know. He needs to say it out loud, and you need to hear it."

"What if I hate him after he tells me?"

"What if no matter what he's done, you love him anyway?"

"Is that what Gellion would have done?"

"You are Gellion. I know you don't believe that, considering everything we've told you. Someday your memory could come back, but it would have been impossible with that much hardware inside you. The brain cannot heal when the damage is perpetuated with new pain constantly being stimulated. Your healing has only just begun. Have faith you're in the right place."

Rosie and I continued to talk for a while, and what we focused on was the sadness of loss, and the shock of seeing my clone tormented. Those images burned into me in such a personal way that I was having trouble disconnecting what I saw from the reality that I didn't actually experience any of it. Yet it felt like I was there, that my body had been on the chopping block because the images of rape and torture were tormenting me.

After we talked, Rosie had me move to a chaise lounge near the fire and I laid down. She went through a hypnosis regression where I watched my memories of the masquerade, turning the scene black and white in my mind. From that place I watched the scene from different angles, from different proximities, and then she attempted to reprogram the meaning of it all as best she could.

By walking me through it and separating out the evil and the evildoers from me, Rosie's visuals began to help. Over and over, she moved me mentally and emotionally away from the horror of it. By seeing its power pulled off me and my energy systems, again and again until it dwindled, I could sense the power of it lessen.

The hypnosis didn't fix everything, but it did take the edge off the panic I sensed in my body. After we were done, I walked back slowly to Damon's room and almost didn't go inside. I thought it might be better to sleep somewhere else, but that was just my anxiety telling me to run away.

I opened the door, and he was there, sitting on the couch reading, waiting for me. I took off my slippers and walked over to him and sat down too.

"I wasn't sure you'd be here."

"I know you need me to be patient with you, but I need that too."

"So, you'll tell me more about why my mom died?"

"I don't know much more than what I said, just that I can't prove it wasn't an accident, but my grandfather was more than happy to hurt your family and had warned me he would."

I rubbed my hands uncomfortably together and kept going. "I mean, what was it that you did to make him so angry to kill my mom?"

He shook his head like trying to explain was futile, so I waited in silence for something real.

"Torture," he said, his chest heaving with heavy breath, "is sometimes hard to predict. I was dying inside, you see." He looked at me with resentment in his eyes. "I was dying on the outside too."

His words felt incomplete, and I wasn't sure what he was saying, and then it dawned on me.

"He killed my mom because you cried out from pain?" I asked, breathlessly.

"Not exactly."

"Then what?" I shouted at him, shocked at the vibration of my own voice, and horrified too. I smacked my hand over my mouth.

He took a deep breath. "I was given a choice; you are always given an impossible choice. If you show love or mercy, they see you as weak. So, I could let them kill you, or I could wake up every night in a copy of myself, forced to torture or be tortured."

I gasped! "What? How is that possible?"

"It didn't have a name. It was simply 'The Cloning Center.' A playground for depravity."

"Somewhere underground?"

"Probably, yes. No escape that way. Stuck with the world's most powerful and depraved."

I could feel myself wanting to cry from not understanding his words, not being able to comprehend so much evil.

"Why?"

"Those with real power are bored with daytime adventures. So, just like us, they wake up in a different version of themselves and then they want entertainment. They recruit for their entertainment, and the rest of the people stuck there have to put on a show. In a place like that they can do whatever they want, and they can do it to whoever they've enslaved."

I nodded ever so slightly, but my consciousness was disconnecting from the imagery he shared.

"Selling your soul can be a literal thing, and there are lots of pretty, talented, and hungry people who are willing to do just that. Then there are the cloned children from families who sell their own for favor. Different centers are run by different powers. Not all rulers like to share. Sometimes they watch, most times they participate to maim and torture, to rape and destroy the clones around them."

"And the victims?"

"The children are programmed to forget, so they won't tell anyone, but when they wake up in reality, it doesn't change what happened to them. Victims wake up with weakened hearts and destroyed minds. It's no fun for the rulers if the pain isn't hurting a real person."

"They tortured you every night?" I whispered.

He didn't answer.

We were silent for a while; his hand had made its way inside mine...my fingers gently rubbing his fingertips.

"Time is hard to remember. I've tucked things away so deep inside, the memories won't come, not right away."

Finally, I found the courage to ask. "How long did you suffer there?"

"Until my real body had a heart attack."

The tears were in my eyes at the horror of it all. I could tell by looking at him, that more than one part of his brain was revisiting it. His eyes looked exhausted and wide with remembering.

"This body died?" I asked, touching his chest.

"It finally caught up with me."

"How many nights were you tortured?"

"It doesn't matter."

He was avoiding it for a reason, and it automatically hurt my stomach to consider it. I was getting sick inside at all of it, and he could tell.

"Please just tell me the truth," but my jaw was shivering, and my hands were shaking.

He brought his large and warm hand to my face.

"Tell me please?" I begged as tears poured down, my throat closing with hurtful swelling.

It hurts so much! Why does it hurt so much? The sobbing I felt inside came to the surface, my own chest working hard to hold it all in.

"Take a slow breath," he said calmly. "You always wanna feel it for me, Gell, but you shouldn't."

"How many months?" I demanded, surprised by my assumption his torture had been so long. "Years?"

"No one can prepare you," he admitted.

My jaw dropped in horror. I reactively reached for his shoulders, pulling myself to him, my legs spread over his, our chests pressed together, heaving sobs into his neck, his back shoved into the couch.

"Gellion, stop."

"Don't," I cried, needing him to stay still and hold me.

"I'm alive," he said trying to remove me from his lap.

"Have you ever cried over this?" I said through the quick breaths of pain.

"I did my screaming."

I just cried louder. "I'm not okay. It hurts! My heart hurts so much!" I sobbed. "I want to remember you. I want to remember my mom!"

I realized why I couldn't stop myself. The cries and moans required physical work to manifest, to express out, and the pain I had lived with always stopped me from the deep cries necessary to mourn, to grieve, to heal. I hurt inside for Damon and myself, and crying didn't hurt to suffer, not like when I was inside my real body. At that moment, it hurt not to cry.

He finally stopped squirming, and I knew he wouldn't give me the response I wanted without some coaching, so I picked up his hands and wrapped them around me, and then I wrapped my arms around his neck and leaned back, pulling him with me away from the couch. Sitting upright, I patted his back gently, rubbing it soothingly.

When I'd done enough, I lifted his elbows, encouraging him to hold me and touch me too. He patted my back lightly.

"About your mom," Damon said, quietly, as my own weeping had started to soften. "It never should have happened. I was ready to die to stop it, but your mom died instead."

"Is that an apology?"

"I...went...I wasn't..." Damon tried to say but stopped himself.

He looked wrought with upset, sighing deeply unable to muster any more words. He kept shrugging, shaking his head. My tears dried up at his disconnect, my mind trying to let go of the visuals his story had seared into my brain. In my own torment, I thought about his different personalities.

"How can you kiss me and touch me so much more intimately than...?" I wasn't sure what to say, exactly.

"...more intimately than I can hug?" he asked simply. "My upbringing included intimacy programming. I can't cry anymore, Gellion. There aren't any tears. I'm empty inside and filled with dark thoughts."

And he wanted me to fix him? It felt so unfair. I couldn't handle anything. I suddenly had a thought.

"Will you cry when I die for real?"

In the next moment I was picked up and moved off his lap and onto the bed. He was already walking toward the bathroom, the door closing behind him.

I'd hurt his feelings, talking about my own death, not remembering he'd already seen me die. I shouldn't have spoken before thinking. I'd been mean without trying, and I wondered why he always brought that out of me.

Suddenly I liked the shared bathroom arrangement. I went through my closet and found him rinsing off in the shower. I'd never seen him naked, never alone with his naked body or any naked body. I stared, wanting to see him, to release the fear I felt about the male form, to accept that he had been my choice before I'd been damaged, and there he was, trying his best to protect me. I wanted to hold him again, and kiss him again, and be near him.

I took off my clothes and walked into the shower, turning on the second nozzle near him. He'd been rinsing soap out of his hair as I'd undressed, and only just noticed me when the extra water arrived. He turned around and stared at me, anger and longing in his face.

My lips quivered, but I reached for the body wash and grabbed the loofa sponge and turned him around, rubbing his back from top to bottom, scrubbing his shoulders and neck and arms, taking in the view of his numerous tattoos.

I thoroughly washed him, skipping his pelvic area and moved on to his legs and feet. He didn't make a sound or move except at my command. It seemed like a safe way to touch him, a buffer between us.

I eventually worked my way to his muscular butt, being gentle, making use of the soft sponge material to force him to feel my interest. He grabbed my wrist when I wanted to clean his front side and took the loofa sponge from me.

Damon turned me around and washed my body too. He was firm and sensual. The areas I couldn't touch him; he touched on me with the loofa. He was testing my threshold for what I could withstand. All I felt was desire and uncontrollable warmth pulsing within me. My breath became labored under the movement of the sponge.

As the water rinsed us clean, he dropped the sponge and came closer, pulling me into his arms. His kiss was tender, and slow and filled with attention to my emotions. Our eyes were open at first, trying to gage the reaction of the other, until it was clear we both wanted to give in, and so we did, our kissing harder, faster and more urgent.

I didn't have time to think, or panic, I just allowed the power of his pull to take me to a different place inside myself, one of longing and lust. Damon had suffered for me, sacrificed for me, gone to war with darkness just to keep me alive. There was no way I wasn't in love with him, but there hadn't been a way to love him either or be loved by him.

If what he needed was for me to become a healer, then I needed to try harder to do that. He'd become the center of my universe, and until now I mostly resented him for it, and for the nagging thoughts about my trauma and my losses being his fault.

Now I could see that it might have been me who couldn't let go of him. It might have been me who made it impossible for him to walk away. Kissing him like I did and wanting him for my own became stronger and stronger the longer I was with him. It was hard to imagine anymore that it had ever been any other way between us.

Damon reached down and with one swoop picked me up, my legs spread, wrapped around his torso, my butt held up by his hands. My back rested against the warm tiles, aware that he could penetrate me at any moment, but he just held me there and kissed me, his massive frame pressed against me.

"I'm afraid of hurting you," he said.

"I want to feel you," I responded, giving him my permission.

He started to lower my wet body, slowly down toward him. My breathing picked up again as we stared into one another, the sensation of impending contact sent my heart racing, and he hovered my body there, unsure.

"Damon," Caitir interrupted, "I'm sorry to disturb you," her voice sounding through a loudspeaker, somewhere unseen in the room, in every room.

Damon's eyes rolled back, and his mouth curled up. I moaned my irritation.

"Father Vasily has left an urgent message on the emergency line."

He wrapped one arm around my waist, holding me tightly to him so I could drop my legs down, and he slammed the bottom of his fist into the tiled wall. I held my arms around his naked torso and rested my ear to his heart. It was beating so fast, flustered but steady.

Our breathing calmed down, and his pulsating manhood softened against me.

"Who's Father Vasily?"

"An old friend," he said, kissing my forehead gently and turning off the water.

Our intimacy would obviously have to wait.

10

POSSESSION

Damon stepped out of the shower and wrapped a towel around me first, then dried himself off too.

"You need to pack a bag. We're going to be getting on a plane."

"I'm coming with you?"

"Yes," he said. "I need you there for this."

"Where are we going?" I asked.

"Rome."

"For what reason?"

"It's Halloween soon."

"Is that significant?"

"If Satan is your God, when do you think he celebrates?"

"Oh," I said, thinking of the holiday in a new way for the first time, "What do I pack?"

"Don't worry, Rosie will help you."

He was right. My closet, filled to the brim, was nothing compared to the extensive wardrobe kept near the cloning room filled with pods.

The garment room was like a versatile store with all different styles of clothes, from black-tie garments and work attire to bullet proof Kevlar suits. Caitir and Rosie were already inside, putting together suitcases for all of us, as well as cases of gear. They worked quickly and quietly as if they'd done it a hundred times before.

They noticed me just as they'd started closing the bags and suitcases, so they left mine open. I walked quietly as they worked, looking at their organization of the different garments.

On a separate massive countertop, I saw at least ten other bags of clothes and gear and wondered who they were for. There were name tags, and I recognized two. The names Tombo and Joseph were familiar, so I assumed the others were also a part of the security team that was coming.

Seeing the name "Tombo" reminded me that I hadn't seen Damon's right-hand-man at all since my first day down below. I'd barely thought to ask about him. Now I wondered what kind of emergency could bring Damon's security team, and what they planned to do. As Rosie finished up the cases that belonged to the other men, Caitir stepped up to an electric keypad in the wall.

She typed in some numbers and the whole wall opened to reveal an assortment of weapons. From the ceiling, a robotic arm dropped down, ready to lift the weapons off the wall. The floor tiles near the wall disappeared to reveal armor and artillery cases below. Caitir picked up a remote control stored within the wall and started using the game-like controller to command the robot arm.

After pulling down two large guns with the arm, Caitir turned around and winked at me. She was having fun with her toy, and I'd wondered why the weapons weren't done by one of the men.

"Do you fire them?" I asked.

"I'm proficient," Caitir said, "but these aren't exactly normal weapons."

"What are they?"

"Liquid freeze, specifically designed to freeze a human inside a liquid gel for about an hour."

"Are you serious?"

"It's bio-charged with a memory erasing drug, so they won't remember anything."

"Who created this?"

"Oh, it's definitely stolen tech, but we know how to recreate it. It's strictly protection gear designed to help us move in and out without killing anyone and without leaving any real proof we'd been there."

"Been where?"

"Oh, well, helping people," she shrugged.

"What about cameras?"

"Easy to erase or manipulate."

"Even live streams?"

"That's not something that ever happens in these places. All wireless signals are blocked."

"Really?"

"They would never allow these images to go out live. It's about blackmail, not videos they ever show the public. Those go through vendors that can and should get caught. This is different."

"What do you mean? What's the emergency? What's the mission?"

"Caitir, let Damon explain," Rosie said gently.

"It's just a rescue mission, except the timeline got shifted. We knew it was coming but weren't expecting to leave until tomorrow."

"Oh," I said, because I didn't know what else to say.

It was news to me that I wasn't the only one they rescued. Somehow, though, that bit of information felt quite significant. When the cases were all packed, and the robot arm had loaded all the gear onto the robotic rolling carts, I wondered where I was supposed to go next.

"Will you be traveling with us?" I asked Rosie.

"Our clones are in Scotland, so we will meet you in Italy," she said, grabbing my shoulders gently.

"Of course. I forgot," I said and wrapped my arm around her for a quick squeeze.

As Caitir and Rosie left with the robot bellhops trailing behind them, I stood alone in the impressive room, the weapons put away and the clothing lit up well for display. My suitcase was packed, but I hadn't looked at the contents. I was about to dive in when Damon entered the room.

"I wish I'd looked in your suitcase," I said.

"Did you pack this?" he asked about mine.

"No, it was already done when I got here."

"Ah," he said, "Rosie usually knows best."

"Will we be together the whole time?"

"No, it won't be possible."

"Where will I be?"

"You will stay with Caitir and meet Father Vasily."

"Why?"

"To jog your memory."

"Can you tell me more about what you'll be doing?"

"That's not a good idea."

I felt left in the dark about too many things, but as everything I'd learned only terrified me, I was getting used to the idea of not asking.

I sighed.

"So, there's one more thing," he said, cringing.

"What?"

"You need to change bodies before we leave."

"To a different clone?"

"Yes."

"Why?"

"There are too many eyes in Rome. If you show up there looking like this, someone might notice or remember you. Quite a few of grandfather's Italian friends were at the masquerade, and you never know where they will show up."

They put my current clone in a deep sleep to transfer me to a new one. When I woke up, I felt groggy and had little control over my muscles, at first. One round of laser treatment to activate my muscles and I was sore, but better.

Damon was in a new clone body as well, and he looked different.

159

His eyes were darker, like those of his original, dark gray, almost black, and he looked bigger, more muscular. Calder's clone and Caitir's clone were there too, and it looked like they had changed as well. Everyone looked physically tougher.

"I'm sorry that took so long," I said, joining the group, despite the delay in the departure not being my fault. The changes and necessary preparations were out of my control.

"No worries, we just got here," Damon reassured me.

"Why'd that take you so long?" I asked, surprised.

"Rosie noticed we all seemed a bit more energized, so everyone had scans done in the Q-Spec before and after we transferred bodies," Caitir replied.

"Why?"

"To check if BB connected us."

"Oh! Did she?" I asked, making sure I understood.

"Yes. She did. BB did the work," Damon replied, wide eyed.

"Mom felt different," Caitir said, "so did I, so Damon was curious. We all got suited up and checked quickly. She connected everyone to their energy structures."

"Even after you transferred?"

"She's amazing," Malik added. "The work transferred to these bodies too."

"We don't have active clones of Rosie and Eamon here, so we can only hope it will work for them too," Damon clarified.

"Even Tombo," Malik added.

"Yeah, but what if we get obliterated again?" Calder grumbled.

"We may not be back for a while," Damon said. "We'll see."

We made our way to the elevator, Calder with us on this mission, while Malik would stay behind. I had no idea why, but I also didn't feel comfortable asking. Something about the thick tension in the air made it hard to want to pull information from any of them. I leaned on Damon though, as my body still felt shaky.

When we stepped off the train in DC, Tombo and a tall black man stood waiting for us.

"Gellion, this is Joseph," Caitir said.

"Nice to meet you," I said and reached out my hand.

He looked at Damon and then shook my hand, but his expression was weird.

"What?" I asked him.

He looked at Damon and then at me. "Nice to meet you too."

"No, seriously, why are you looking at me like that?"

"He's not looking at you," Damon interrupted. "He's analyzing me."

"What? Why?"

Damon looked down at me and lifted up the strands of hair that were starting to fall into my face. I hadn't even noticed, until Damon touched me, that my hair was blonde! I backed away confused.

"I need a mirror," I said, frantically.

Caitir pulled one out of her bag and handed it to me. I looked at my eyes. They were blue, with no black scarring, no double irises, no trauma. I had never actually seen my blue eyes the way they were supposed to look and seeing them that way brought a light tear to my eyes.

My nose was a little different. My hair was long and blonde and healthy. Strangely, I could sense my shape was different. Even my chin looked sharper. I felt weird gawking at myself and tried not to touch my new features, as I realized I barely spent time touching my last face and didn't really need to compare.

"You look kinda like you did in high school," Joseph said, almost laughing. "I mean almost exactly like you looked in your cheerleading outfit," he said, ogling me. "Damn, Damon!"

"Do I look that young?" I smiled at the thought of myself in such an outfit, doing cheers.

Then I frowned. Sure, I had pain, but I hadn't started worrying about the youthfulness of my body before. Did I really look so much younger? My blond hair was naturally highlighted, and my nails, skin and teeth felt perfect. I looked down and my breasts were larger, but my legs were thinner with wider hips.

I'd been too out-of-it to notice. Everyone else had been too polite to say anything, and Damon was growing angry with Joseph.

So, I laughed.

"That's right!" I laughed again. "You knew me," I replied to Joseph. "Well, just thirty minutes ago I had brown hair, brown eyes, and horrific scars, so imagine my shock. It's actually a nice reprieve. Maybe hot, but definitely not hideous," I shrugged and elbowed Damon in jest.

Joseph smushed his lips together and turned around, silently chuckling still. I was still trying to wrap my head around it when everyone started walking. By the time we reached the private airstrip and got loaded onto the large jet, I was exhausted. I'd never really been anywhere Katherine didn't drag me, that I could remember. Why was I even on this trip if I was supposed to stay hidden?

Won't I just get in the way? I debated.

All in all, there were fourteen of us on the plane, and while I was starting to recognize more faces, I didn't know the rest of their names.

"How long have you all worked together?" I whispered to Caitir, my seat companion.

"Damon joined the military after your mother died," she whispered in my ear.

I took a deep breath.

"To get away from Mr. Jairus?" I wondered if that were even possible.

"He was suicidal until he left for basic. The nighttime torture made him want to die in college, but it made him a shrewder soldier. Yeah, I think it was to get away, in his waking hours, from anything resembling the life he'd had."

"What did you do?"

"Malik and Damon had already formed a plan, so we continued at Cambridge to help expand our tech know-how. Calder went back to Scotland to start his medical training. My parents opened a country hospital and treatment center, and it became our first home base."

"Wow. When did it all change?"

"When Damon turned twenty-one."

"Why?"

"Shush!" Calder interjected, nodding to his sister to look in a specific direction.

Damon was staring at us, possibly reading our lips.

I pulled my hoodie up and put on some headphones and laid back. Damon wanted us to turn our minds off, so we did. Everyone grew very quiet.

The cars and vans that were waiting for us were heavy, like they'd been armored. We all wore black and had our heads and eyes covered as we left the plane. The drive through the city to its border was slow and bumpy. The different vehicles split off, not everyone ending up at the same location.

The winding road to the old monastery gave an incredible view of the castle-like walls surrounding the ancient abbey. I looked around as we headed inside the gates, amazed at the grandeur of where we were. When our car arrived, it was only Calder, Caitir, and I.

Isn't this owned by the Catholic Church? I wondered.

A young priest met us outside and quietly showed us the way in. We walked through many open areas and stairwells, until we were shown into a large office with a burning fireplace. Shortly after the doors opened and a much older priest approached our familiar faces. Both Caitir and Calder greeted him warmly, but they spoke Italian.

When they were done the elderly cleric turned to me.

"Hello Gellion," he said putting his hand out to shake mine. "It's been such a long time. I'm Father Vasily."

I shook his hand and smiled.

"Father, where do we set up?" Calder asked.

"I need Caitir's help with something first. Damon wants Gellion to see something."

"What is it, Father?"

She followed him to the bookcase behind his desk. There, behind a locked cabinet door was a locked box. He brought it to the desk and opened it and showed her it was filled with memory sticks and cards.

He handed her one and she brought it to her laptop bag and started searching around inside. After only a few moments she turned around and smiled at us.

Father Vasily handed me the box.

"Your memories are inside here," he said. "Damon wanted you to have these."

"Thank you," I replied, taking the box from him, and closing the lid.

The way Calder glanced at the memory sticks, I wondered if his missing love were in the videos too.

"You cannot stay, but there is a car waiting for you, to take you to the others."

"We're grateful for your help, Father," Calder said.

Father Vasily reached out his hand to me again. "We will see each other soon. There is much work to be done, and your help will be appreciated."

"My help?" he must've been joking.

"Damon said you don't remember anything?" he asked with a smile, waiting for me to confirm.

I nodded.

"Just your kindness will matter."

The overwhelming feeling of importance he put on my presence, had a strong enough impact, to let the silence be, even though I had no idea what he was talking about. As we got ready to depart, I went to my bag to retrieve some letters I'd written, saying I was doing well and enjoying my vacation, and how much I loved and missed everyone.

"Would you mind mailing these for me?" I asked Father Vasily.

He looked at Caitir, who nodded in agreement, then took the letters with a smile and a bow. We left shortly after arriving and ended up far enough away from Rome for them to breathe without fear. We were only there to meet up with Joseph and Tombo and wait for the radio signal from Eamon and Rosie. We sat on a balcony, in the mountains, watching the water.

Caitir was on her headset and laptop. She had several devices plugged in and was typing furiously. Her laptop was attached to a satellite phone too, which was also attached to a desktop satellite dish out on the balcony.

I decided to make something to drink and asked Calder what to make. He handed me a large backpack, and inside were food supplies. One bag was labeled "tea," and I pulled that out, along with a package that said "sweetener." The condensed blocks looked like cubes of honey. I needed to keep myself busy since no one would tell me what was going on and I found what I needed to heat the water.

Caitir jumped up and grabbed a small container out of the bag and stuck it under the faucet.

"We use a compact filter. Can't afford to get hit by any kind of toxins out in the field."

"Oh, okay. Thanks." I knew it was Damon's obsession. Anything he could control he would because there was too much he couldn't.

"When do I get to know what's going on?" I whispered, before she could get away.

She looked at me, her eyes scrunched in an exhausted kind of torment and said, "I can't tell you how bad it's going to be, or even how to handle it, because everyone is different, but we're saving people from the bad guys."

Everyone appreciated the tea, except for me. The taste was some kind of blend I'd never experienced. I'd been a coffee drinker for so long that tea was just foreign. The flavor made my mouth tingle and the hair on my skin stand up.

Caitir was tracking something in the ocean, and I sat next to her to see what it was. Soon Tombo, Joseph and Calder all joined in too.

"They'll be here in a few hours," Calder said.

"Damon should have the cargo by then," Joseph said. "Right?"

"All vital signs are good," Caitir said, switching screens quickly to monitor all the men who were with Damon. "They haven't gone offline."

"Where are they though?"

"Probably underground," Tombo replied.

"Rome or Vatican City," Joseph said.

"They're rescuing people from underneath Vatican City?"

Tombo sighed and started pacing.

"No. They're rescuing them en route."

"Why aren't you with him?" I asked Tombo.

He simply turned around and motioned for me to take a good look at his face. I didn't understand at first, until I realized he would probably stand out, looking so Asian. He motioned the same at Joseph, exaggerating his movements like a dancer or a magician.

"Black," Tombo said, with a thick accent, pointing to Joseph. "Yellow," he said, pointing to himself. "We don't speak Italian. Too easy to remember our faces," he motioned over his face, exaggerating for me. "Get it?"

I nodded my head while scowling my lips. I had already gotten it. I wanted to pout for being called out for being slow to understand but didn't. Everyone was frustrated. At some point, silent movement happened, and all the supplies and gear were packed up and we were headed out. Down the mountain and out to the coast to the port where a small boat was waiting for us. That boat took us to a larger boat farther out at sea.

Damon's aunt and uncle were there to greet us and had a whole team of people with them. I could see weapons, mostly obscured, on the back deck. It looked very much like a massive luxury yacht or a miniature cruise ship, discreetly armed.

Rosie helped Caitir to the bridge, where she immediately set up her gear and got connected to their communications system. I left her and followed where I thought Calder had gone, down below the deck. It was huge below, open, and looked mostly like some kind of hospital. I found Calder, as he was reconnecting with obvious comrades, many with hugs for him. The whole group of them looked like medical staff, all wearing scrubs.

The setting seemed very off. I couldn't tell what was going on, exactly, and I was beginning to worry, so I just kept going. There were sleeping quarters, tight and impersonal, sleeping quarters with more privacy, the engine room and adjoining compartments, a kitchen and dining room, and a tiny workout room. There was very little in the way of actual luxury. Everything looked so basic on the inside that I wondered why it was so pretty on the outside, and the amount of hospital beds was unnerving.

The ship was confusing, and I got lost trying to get back upstairs. By the time I'd reached the fresh sea air, I felt sick inside. I stayed on the front deck, leaning over the side, staring into the dark waters until I noticed Caitir by my side.

"I put all the memory sticks on a thumb drive," she said. "You can use this to watch the videos. You'll probably want to wear the headphones too." She held a small bag out to me. Inside was one of the tablets she'd hooked into her laptop. There was also a charger, and a set of soft headphones, like earmuffs. Caitir had been working on the transfer for a while.

"Who's the other copy for?" I asked.

She half smirked and shrugged, daring to pretend like I didn't already know.

"Why does he need a copy?"

"To see what you see too. To know you as best he can, in his own way. I'm like that with Malik. I always need to know what he's thinking, or what truth he's uncovered."

"With Damon, it's not reciprocal," I said, without even realizing its meaning, and then letting that sink in. It hurt, to be "handled" so much by him, and be a part of the group, but separate from it.

"Damon might not remember the past so well. That time of his life with you, before his years in 'the center,'" Caitir said with her fingers in air quotes, as if saying the real words still wasn't allowed. I nodded my head, telling her I understood.

"When do I start watching the videos?"

"Now," she said. "I don't know when things are going to happen."

"You mean, when Damon gets back?"

"No, I mean when the rescued will arrive."

"Oh," I said, trying to wrap my head around it. "And Damon?"

"He may not come back. Many of Damon's soldiers leave their clone-bodies behind. They often have to sacrifice them."

My jaw dropped. I had no idea the scope of the assignment included that or could.

"Why?"

Caitir didn't want to answer my question, so she just handed me the bag with the tablet.

"The first video is from Damon," she said, as if it were an instruction. "There are several others he asked me to add that come from his files."

"Do I have to watch that one?" I whined; pretty sure his message would just hurt my feelings again.

"Nope."

Then Caitir handed me a beautiful golden keychain, covered in decorative crystals and jewels.

"The videos are on the thumb drive," she said, handing me the keychain. "Just plug it into the tablet."

The thumb drive was hidden inside the decorative part of the keychain, reminding me of its value.

Clever.

"Where can I watch?"

She took my hand and walked with me, sometimes skipping, down to a private sleeping quarter.

"You can watch in here."

It looked elegant inside, though small.

"Are you sure it's okay?"

"It's my parent's room," she said, smiling at me. She nudged me in and sat me down on the comfortable bed and went back to the door.

"I shouldn't…"

"…They're busy anyway. You know, this is Damon's boat, and all the people here are being paid with Damon's money, being provided for by him, and protected too. We are all welcome here, you most of all."

How did she know I felt so insecure? I wondered how much my

own face was betraying me these days. I was so raw from it all, and so clueless too, that I doubted I could fake my way out of anything.

I found myself on my stomach, plugging in the thumb drive and loading up the videos. The first one on the list I ignored, the one from Damon. I needed to see for myself what was going on, so I skipped ahead. The videos were all saved with a date, so I started with the first one in nineteen-ninety-nine.

The scene turned on abruptly, and a young Damon, maybe eighteen, was walking away from where the camera was placed. He joined Father Vasily and someone off to the side, out of view. The rest of the video showed a large, old, and ornate room, where a young teen girl was sitting in a chair, growling at Father Vasily.

The room reminded me of the decorative woodwork inside the Monastery where Father Vasily met us. The girl, dark circles under her eyes, was reacting to the water being splashed on her, as if it were hurting her. Father Vasily was saying prayers in what sounded like Italian, maybe Latin too.

The girl's venom and anger sounded like curse words directed at everyone in the room. It was difficult to see but the girl made me curious. Father Vasily kept praying. It was then I realized that she was struggling against ropes, tied to a chair.

Father Vasily said prayers over the girl, blessing her body with the symbol of the cross on her forehead as she squirmed. He called on the power of Christ, though he spoke in a language I didn't understand. This lasted for some time, and I felt frustrated, not knowing the language.

I started to fast-forward through the video. At no time did anything change, until near the end, when the girl seemingly calmed down and was able to come to her senses again and the video ended.

I played the next video on the list. It was dark at first, then the camera moved a lot until it was finally steadied, then the lens was covered, and eventually the dark lightened and moved away and Damon was walking toward a table, in a hotel room. My younger self sat at the table in a bathrobe, her hair wet. The quality of the image, just like the video before, was awful, not to mention dark.

Our younger selves spoke to one another with affection, familiarity, and trust.

"Gellion, what did you see?"

"Why'd he let us watch that?" she asked Damon, confused, her hand in her hair.

"Because I asked."

"You're that rich?" She was bewildered.

"No, but my mother's family is and contribute well."

"Contribute to the Catholic Church?" She asked and he nodded. "Where?"

"Here in Rome."

"You have family in Rome? Do they know you're here?"

"Not yet," he said, shrugging.

"If they didn't before, they surely do now. You should see them. Show respect."

"I'll send some flowers and a card."

"No, Damon. You request an audience and graciously ask their permission to spend time inside their city speaking to their priests. And leave me out of it."

"Oh, you're serious," he befuddled.

"Of course!" she cried out. "Stop forgetting who you come from."

He finally sat down in a chair next to her.

"You're right. I'll do it first thing tomorrow."

"Thank you."

After a moment of silence, of young Damon reaching out to young Gellion and being met with reassurance, but not intimacy, Damon spoke.

"Did his exorcism work?" he asked, changing the subject.

"No. Vasily's a fraud," young Gellion replied.

"He's just practicing. Hoping. Why can't he do it?"

"He's so filled with darkness; he's practically implanting more into others just to get it off himself."

"So, he makes them worse?"

"Yeah and steals their energy too. He's a mess."

"What else?"

"All I feel when I'm around him is guilt and fear," younger Gellion said to Damon. "It's twisting in him all the time. He did something bad or many things, and he regrets it."

"I detect that too," Damon agreed, nodding.

"What do you want me to do?" she asked Damon.

"Remove his darkness," Young Damon said, with a wicked smile.

My younger self took a deep breath at Damon's request, but before she did anything, she climbed into Damon's lap and started kissing him. He returned her kiss until he was opening her robe. For a moment he looked up in the direction of the camera before he got too far into exposing her body. Then he picked her up and moved her to the bed, out of the camera's view. The video kept playing, the noise somewhat muted by the distance, but still there.

I paused the video, stopping the moaning sounds coming from the tablet, and remembered the fluffy headphones. No wonder. Of course, Caitir must have known. I plugged them in and took a deep breath, pressing the play button and wondering how wrong it was to listen to my younger, and unfamiliar self, have sex, and moan in pleasure.

That video came from Damon's "personal files," not the videos from Father Vasily. Damon wanted me to see them, so he didn't edit any of it out. I wondered if it were a gift, a distraction, or a curse.

I couldn't watch because there was nothing to see, and I didn't want to listen. Even just the beginning sounds sent shivers to parts of my body that needed to be quiet and inactive at a time like this. Yet, these videos were precious memories of real things that had happened. They were a gift, and I wanted to experience them too.

I got up to the door and turned the lock and lay down and listened for a while to the rhythmic kissing, moaning, soft words of encouragement and affection, and deep breathing. It was such youthful affection, ending in sounds of deep satisfaction and then a release of air so swift from both bodies, as the exhausted forms collapsed from all the work.

"I love you," I heard my younger self say, quietly.

"I love you more," I heard a breathless Damon huff out.

The breathing was still labored but started to slow.

"Damon?" she asked quietly. "Do I give you as much pleasure, as you give me?"

He took a deep breath. "My nightmares have been replaced with dreams of you."

Damon started kissing her again and began their lovemaking.

Eventually the video ended on its own, as if the camera's battery had finally run out.

I cried quietly. It was just a moment in time, beautiful and encapsulated, that showed me a larger picture of the people we'd been, and the dreams we might have had together. Neither of us would ever get that back.

I wanted to get to the story and decided not to feel so strange watching myself in old "home videos." In the next video our younger selves were both dressed and seated, the chairs facing each other, except their knees were at a right angle, allowing a young Gellion space in front of herself to move her hands without interacting with Damon's body.

"Don't use the bubble babe," Damon said sweetly. "Take them out with your hands."

"Ew, really?" young Gellion asked. "Why so messy?"

"Because people like Father Vasily only understand and learn when the pain is happening to them. If he has a hard detox and gets hit with his own slime, he just might learn."

"Are you sure?"

"I know I did…"

"I never meant to hurt you," she interrupted.

"…and I deserved it."

"I didn't know what I was doing. You were my first."

"You're too damn nice Gellion. This guy needs a lesson."

"It's not that I'm nice, Damon. It's too icky to touch without the bubble. I need protection. I don't want to get hit with it either."

"Um, ok, so just imagine another layer, kind of like the bubble, except it's just around your hands, so you can pick up that piece of shit hardware and drop it down to hell...protect your hands but leave the muck and Karma back inside him."

"That's not how I clear people Damon. I try to leave them in the light."

"Not this guy!" Damon slammed his fist down on the table. "Do what I ask!" he demanded!

Gellion didn't shrink back from Damon's anger.

"Damon, sweetie, sugarplum, honey bear," she said dryly. "If we're going down this path, shouldn't I do the same to all the Bishops and Cardinals?"

Young Damon laughed. "And all the politicians and celebrities, and royalty...yes, yes, but not yet. Too soon. You'd get caught for sure."

"Nah," Gellion smiled. "I got permission."

"No, you didn't. You were told you didn't need permission, but they never said anything about repercussions. It's not safe yet."

"How do you know?"

"Because I do. Remember?"

"Rumors," she replied.

"More like a prophecy. A time when it would be safe, when a change would come. We've all heard about it vaguely."

"Rumors," Gellion stated flatly.

"A shift is coming but it isn't here yet."

"Come on," she chided.

"No really, my memory is starting to come back. The more energy work you do on me, the more my memories arrive. Is there a big astrological date coming up?"

Young Gellion was thinking.

"Y2K?"

"No, that's lame. That's a programming problem. This would be something bigger, more ancient."

"I honestly don't know. We should ask BB."

"What time is it there?" Damon asked, looking at his watch.

Gellion was counting on her fingers, and her eyes were looking up. "It's gotta be late morning. I'll call her."

They waited as the phone rang, and Gellion pressed the speaker button.

"Good morning, Gellion," BB's happy voice sounded.

"Good morning BB. How's life at home?"

"Just fine. How's life in Rome?"

"It's amazing!" Gellion squealed to her grandmother and shrugged at Damon.

"How is Damon treating you?"

"Like a princess, with kid gloves. It's kinda annoying."

Damon grimaced and squinted his eyes at her.

"Oh really?" BB asked, with sarcasm.

"No, it's nice to have a fluent Italian speaker just waiting to help me talk to people here. He's really bringing the history to life."

"Are you really doing okay?"

"Yes, but I am calling for a specific reason. I had a conversation with someone about a time in the near future when things will shift for humanity. Do you know what that could be?"

"Well, that's vague. My generation wrote a song about the Age of Aquarius. It's been a discussion for some time," BB replied. "The Age of Pisces is ending, though no one knows for sure exactly when."

"But that was in the seventies, right? So has it already happened?"

"I don't know. I don't think so. It was just the start of the end of the Old Age. No one has really said for sure when the New Age begins. Since I was a child, and at church, people spoke about the second coming of Christ or the Christ consciousness, and we're pretty sure that hasn't happened yet. Anything is possible."

"Well, is there any astrological date coming up that's supposed to be significant?"

"I'm not an astrologer, but I can ask a few of my patients."

Damon nudged Gellion.

"Damon thought maybe it could be tied to an ancient civilization."

BB laughed. "Well with the fear over Y2K, I did have one patient mention a prediction he had for the end of the world. He said it would come at the end of the Mayan calendar. Remember Gellion, we learned about that on our tour of Chichén Itzá when you were fifteen."

"Oh yeah!" young Gellion said. She and Damon looked at each other like that was something good to hear.

"Thank you for remembering that BB! We'll look into it."

I tuned out their goodbyes in the video, wondering if I should investigate what BB had just said in a twelve-year-old conversation, but young Damon was already at his laptop looking it up.

"The end of the Mayan calendar is December twenty-first, two-thousand-twelve," Damon said.

"Winter solstice?"

"Yeah."

I paused the video and looked at the corner of my tablet. The date was displayed October twenty-eighth, two-thousand-twelve. Thirteen years ago, they were talking about a date that still hadn't happened yet. I pressed play.

"What does it say will happen?" young Gellion asked.

Damon scrolled for a while. Eventually he turned around.

"Some people say it's the apocalypse. Others say it's The Rapture. Some people say it's a shift in energy. Others say it's when our poles will switch magnetically. There are contradicting theories, even ones on the return of Christ."

Young Gellion walked over to the camera.

"I need to lie down and think about this." Then her hands reached the camera button, and the video was over.

The next video on the list would have to wait. I lay back on the bed and breathed, thinking about all the information that had just come my way. Conversations from the past, that meant something for my life now too. Since I'd arrived in Damon's life, a cataclysm of information had come my way, worst of all his connection to the dark side of the world.

It was unclear just how powerful his family's circle of friends was. I didn't ask who the real power players were, assuming it was just a percentage of the elite. Some of the wealthy, powerful, political, or famous, were involved. It couldn't be all of them.

By not demanding more information or asking for more background, I had to admit my fear. I'd been unable to ask, unready to know, and too disappointed to get the details of the actual world. Now, I wanted to talk to Damon and understand more of who I was. Because in those videos all I could see, knowing what I know now about Mr. Jairus, is that the two young teenagers I was watching were very naive, and I worried greatly about them, while mourning their future losses.

11

DEMONIC HARDWARE

My weary mind succumbed to a meditative slumber until noises started reverberating in the walls of the boat, the metal of the vessel keeping no secrets. Two loud and fast boats arrived in the middle of the night. I heard banging from below us as well.

I rose and cleaned myself up, putting the tablet and headphones back in the bag, and left the small room. As I climbed the deck stairs, I heard what sounded like a slow elevator moving nearby.

When I reached the hospital floor from the stairwell, the elevator arriving brought with it a wall of energy so powerful against my chest it knocked me down. I fell backwards and landed on my butt, my back against the hallway wall.

It was fear inside that elevator, and it swirled over every emotion within and around me. I stared at the metal doors, wondering if it was my panic or theirs that was swelling within me. Had I been alone, it would have felt like death was coming for me. I curled my legs into

177

myself to get out of the way.

The ding sounded and the doors opened, and the bodies started to exit the elevator, adults with children. The hallway was filled with movement heading to the open hospital floor, which had been turned into tiny rooms with beds. The beds I could see had stuffed animals on pillows, and walls made of curtains in soft and soothing colors.

Children were being carried to bed, and as they passed by me it was clear they were young, most looked no older than ten but no younger than five. I could see from their appearance that they had not been well treated. All of them were bruised, grubby. Some had blood on their clothes.

As they walked and were carried into their new space, the wave of fear that hit me released some with a sigh. The elevator left.

"The floor?" a little voice croaked out to me. She was tiny and holding the hand of a lady in blue scrubs.

"I thought if I sat down, you would see me better, and then you wouldn't be afraid to meet me," I said, wanting to reach out and hold the little girl, sensing she was still present despite what she'd gone through.

"You don't look scary," she said softly.

"I hope you feel safe here," I smiled at her as sweetly as I could, to keep myself from crying.

When the elevator doors opened this time, and I saw the gurneys, I got up and moved out of the way. Two children were swiftly rolled in and moved through the hospital floor. The elevator left quickly again.

The faces of many of the adults were not familiar, not the ones in scrubs already. The ones changing into scrubs from nighttime SWAT gear had memorable features.

The children were all different sizes and ethnicities. Boys and girls, in dark and light skin tones. Many wide-eyed beautiful children, with horror on their faces and fear. Some of them spoke such far-off languages, no one there would understand. Most made no sound at all. I tried counting and knew there were a minimum of thirty-three children and thirteen teenage girls. From what I could see, nearly all of them had suffered. Some needed more care than others.

Caitir was having a hard time focusing on her job after the children arrived. I could tell she wanted to help them, but her job was a different kind of protection. She said she needed to spend time sweeping and checking for spies on their network. Her job was so important and required so much energy, she couldn't focus while around tormented children, so she left.

Calder and Eamon were thriving in this harsh environment, examining the patients needing care. It was up to them to find out where the trauma was and make the call for what should be done next, whether a scan or a medication. All the children needed food and water and more.

To those children who could sit up well, they were immediately served food and given a private space. Many of the children were so small they needed help being fed. I finally understood the reason for so many staff personnel. Each child needed a lot of care with consistent and kind hands.

My hands became busy with serving, while my face stayed calm and gentle and kind. But no one had warned me what was coming, how bad it was, or how much it would hurt. I found myself needing to take breaks to cry.

In the few moments Calder was attending to the children or being pulled at by the nursing staff on board, he told me the hardest thing to look for were signs of internal bleeding from the abuse. He was getting scans of all of the children, but it was taking time. Some children would require surgery to survive.

I asked what they did with the children after their bodies healed and was surprised to hear they'd try to reunite the children with their families if they were loved. If the families were good, but getting their child back would bring negative attention, they'd move the family to a new territory or country to keep them safe from whomever stole their child. Damon's non-affiliated non-profit organizations made that work possible.

Some children were from such war-torn countries that there's nothing left. So, a new family from a similar background is found to foster, with money provided to help with therapy and care. Damon's charities helped them move the children safely and implement the work quietly on the local level.

I learned a lot by being silent and taking in what others realized I hadn't been told. Caitir and I sat at a table on the ship's bridge. It was a quiet room near the satellite receiver, and all her equipment was out and being used, but for what I wasn't sure. She continued to explain some things while the crewman watched the shoreline and listened to the radio.

"If the bad guys can create fake charities and organizations to steal children, we can do the same to steal the children back and protect them," Caitir said.

She filled in a lot of the blanks that the others didn't have time to explain. I stood in awe at the measure of what they had done. They just saved the lives of forty-six human beings, and maybe even the lives of their families too.

The boat's engines were revved up, and the boat started to move.

"Where are we going?"

"As far away as we can. Someplace where it's safer to make connections and find families. Extractions and placements happen once we establish the best plan for the child's future. Sometimes just getting an interpreter is hard. We have some AI tools. This is a long process, and we have people who help with that. Our immediate team only handles the extractions, and medical care."

Caitir said it because it was the truth, but the way she said it made me aware that their system for saving children wasn't something anyone enjoyed. I'd gotten used to not asking, and it was even easier now to see why. I couldn't face it. I didn't want to know about the horrors, or the details. It hurt so much just to be in the same room with those precious lives, knowing I could do nothing for them.

She asked, "How far have you gotten in the videos?"

"Did you watch them?" I questioned.

"Not really. I checked to make sure they were intact."

"Since I'm watching by date, I'm mostly stuck in the ones with us in Italy."

She smiled so largely she almost laughed.

"Okay, those I did peruse," she said, her face turning red.

"Oh my God!" I shuddered, covering my open mouth. "I'm so embarrassed," I moaned.

"Why do you think I took you to that private room to watch them?" she asked, giving me a high-five gesture in the air. I just crossed my arms and pouted.

"Why did you look at them?" I asked, still turning red.

"Don't take this the wrong way, but Damon has had those videos under lock and key for over a decade, and suddenly he's just handing them over to me so you can see them. I'm sorry, but I had to look."

"Well, you can't really see anything," I said under my breath, and she laughed.

"No, but he wasn't ever going to erase that part of the video, and it's probably helpful for you to see why he's so devoted to you, what his memories are."

"It wasn't just sex," I said, finally understanding that young love is powerful, but what I'd once had with Damon was something different than that.

"Exactly. That's the perk of being in love, and it only complemented the devotion you showed him. It was how you changed him and brought him back to life that brought his loyalty and love. You used to say that you never would have become a healer were it not for Damon showing up all messed up in your life. That he forced you to save him...even if you were only trying to save yourself from him."

"He's doing the same thing now."

"Except being near you is hard," she tried to explain.

"Yeah, it's hard on me too," I shrugged. "I'm gonna go back to the videos, since I'm clueless with the kids, and being around them just hurts inside."

"You're not the only wimp," she nodded

"Maybe not. Your brother is incredible."

"He's got a really good team. Mom and Dad too."

"I'm in awe, watching them."

I went back to the room and plugged the tablet into an outlet and connected the headphones.

Young Gellion squirmed and got annoyed. "I'm tired," she pouted. "Do you want me to do the work or not?" she complained as Damon set up the camera again. This time the view of the hotel room included the bed.

Young Damon smiled and nodded his head. He opened a journal and took notes as she worked. Watching Gellion's hands move was like watching someone use a virtual reality gaming system. She looked like she was rearranging something as her fingertips reached for invisible objects, and then she threw them away.

She moved over and over and over, describing briefly as she went what she was doing, as Damon wrote it all down. The tally ended up at eighteen pieces of darkness she had seen and removed from Father Vasily.

"Eighteen pieces, Damon!" young Gellion said. "That level of darkness is the same as a budding serial killer."

"Damn! Did you leave the muck?" Damon asked.

"Yes. Did you hear me? This man is dangerous, Damon. Maybe it's not a good idea to leave the muck. I want to remove it," Gellion said.

"Leave it."

"But then I can't fill the space with light."

"Good."

"That's not how this is supposed to work, Damon," she complained.

"I didn't say never, I just said not yet."

"What if he pulls the darkness back in?" Gellion pleaded with Damon.

"He can do that?"

"You did," Gellion said to Damon. "I saw it go, and in your rage something else arrived, so I removed that too! Before you could pull anything else in, I blasted you with light. I didn't know I needed to fill the space until I panicked at your will to be filled with the dark."

"So, technically the darkness he would try to pull in wouldn't be as powerful as what was just removed. Right?"

Young Gellion shrugged at Damon and then did something strange with her fingers, pulling a finger from one hand through two tightened fingers from another.

"No," she said, answering his question. "It would be dark, but not as bad. Still, Damon, that could really backfire. What's the point?"

"Evildoers shouldn't get your gentle detox. Leave the muck and emptiness to show him the Karma he carries."

Gellion nodded that she would leave 'the muck,', and then she yawned largely, gathering a prolonged amount of air, like she was recovering, or stretching an exhausted system.

"You know we have class in the morning. I actually like this program, so you have to go back to your room now."

When she crawled off to the bed beside her chair, Damon gave the camera a wave and turned it off.

I wondered if he'd really left her alone to sleep or if they were sleeping next to each other at their young age. It was shocking still that I'd gotten away with such a young romance. I'd only ever known my family to be extremely cautious with new people. If they hadn't been before, it was clear they learned their lesson.

I took a deep breath and moved on to the next video.

It was young Gellion who'd turned the camera on and was recording Damon, holding his cell phone out. Father Vasily's voice was yelling at Damon in Italian through the speakerphone. Damon spoke back in Italian, sternly, but without yelling, then turned to give the camera a thumbs up and a smile.

On the other end, Father Vasily's voice could be heard making gagging and vomiting sounds. Then the yelling continued until Damon barked back, then spoke slowly and sternly. Then he hung up.

Luckily my younger self didn't speak Italian either.

"What did he say?" young Gellion exclaimed.

"He wanted to know if you cursed him."

"What?"

"I told him that's what his religion does, what his actions did. I explained that all you did was remove the demon connections inside his head. Then he wanted to know why he was so sick."

"He's sick?"

"Yeah, vomiting up black stuff, really bad, like when you did the work on me."

"I told you leaving the muck was a bad idea. I didn't know what I was doing when I cleared you."

"I told him he was sick because of all his bad deeds. That you took the demons away but didn't remove the Karma, so now he will suffer until his system detoxes out the rest of all the evil he's done."

"Are you crazy? You threatened a Bishop? Using my abilities?"

"No, I told him if he wanted to feel better and have the rest of the dark stuff removed, he needed to be helpful. People like him don't understand compassion. All they understand is aggression and coercion."

"Why are we doing this? It's not a game, Damon. Are you trying to get us killed." My younger self was scolding Damon, and she was right.

"Because he's the gatekeeper, and once upon a time he was genuinely kind to me."

"I'm listening," Young Gellion said.

"The person we really want to meet is a monk who does healing work. He is kept away from the public, unless someone pays or is already a good friend to the church. He does what he's told because they threaten his family. Father Vasily is the only way to get access to him. I've never met him, but I saw him from across the room once, at my parent's funeral, where Father Vasily had been kind, in a room full of vultures who wanted to hurt me for their own pleasure."

"Oh."

"I don't think Father Vasily is a pedophile. Maybe he's had to become one to survive the culture, but he doesn't really want to hurt people. He wouldn't be doing unsuccessful exorcisms if he only wanted to hurt people."

"I don't know Damon, an exorcism can easily end in death, when one person is tied up."

"Yes. Plenty young and beautiful have died under the supervision of a priest."

The phone rang, and Damon answered while Gellion refocused the camera. Damon listened with the phone to his ear and smiled at young Gellion. He spoke back in Italian. Then he snapped the phone shut.

"He wants to feel better. I told him it would take the rest of the night, and that he needed to vomit out the black stuff first, and then it would be over."

"Ok, I'll finish clearing the muck and debris I left," young Gellion said.

Young Damon shrugged. "Let him suffer for another hour."

"Damon, I only left the mucky tar because you asked me to."

"We only got what we wanted because he got sick."

"You only know about that reaction to the work because I learned how to do this on you, and I didn't do it right. I'm better at this now."

"Some people deserve to suffer."

"Some people don't learn unless they suffer, that's true," she said agreeing with him. "But the rule doesn't apply to everyone, and I don't want that to be me. He can always feel better and say no."

Young Damon hung his head and Gellion set down the camera but didn't turn it off. She walked over to Damon and reached a hand up to his face, gently touching his cheek. He leaned down and kissed her.

"Why are we recording this?" young Gellion asked.

He took a deep breath and let it go. "A voice inside my head told me we need to record everything we can."

"You're obsessed. Are you afraid?"

"A little," Damon admitted.

"So why do this at all?"

"I'm compelled. I know there's something we're missing, and I don't know who to turn to for help."

"I don't think this is the place to take our knowledge."

"Gellion, this is where kids get abused. When they're handed back to their parents, shattered, filled with darkness, and terrified, they go down a path that leads to an early death, or becoming a villain. This is exactly where we need to be. I want to help the ones that survive."

"You do?"

Damon looked confused. His arm was up, his hand rubbing the back of his head as he paced.

"Yeah, I guess I do."

"Damon, they kill kids."

"I know."

"Aren't we just like kids to them? Just as disposable? You're the one who told me that millions of kids go missing every year, and nobody does anything about it, because it's the people with all the power doing it."

"I know. I know. This is stupid. There's no winning against that."

Young Gellion held her hands to her chest and stared into young Damon's eyes, then she reached up and hugged him, grabbing on by using her tiptoes, pulling his massive body into hers. He lifted her up and kissed her. She wrapped her legs around his torso, and he held her up from underneath by locking his arms.

"We're in the den of the abusers. It's a bit too close for me, Damon. I'm scared."

She wrapped her arms around his neck and buried her face in him. When she pulled back, his eager lips were waiting for her, and she complied, tenderly, making him go slowly.

"I'm afraid you're going to get us killed," she said, her lips next to his.

"You're right. It was reckless."

"How many eyes are on you, and me, right now?"

He just stared at her.

"You don't know how many? How can you ever protect yourself if you don't know who is watching?"

He thought about it, while she tried to squirm away from him, but his arms were too big, and his hand was too strong as he slowly held her in place by touching the bare skin of her shoulder, beneath her shirt.

"I'll be dead soon if you don't get smarter," she whispered as she stopped fighting him. Then she looked into the camera with the saddest expression on her face.

Young Damon shook his head, disagreeing with her.

"Never," he said.

"You don't even know who your enemies are. Your grandfather has kept you in the dark about how to survive. In your world, you should have killed a lot of people by now. He should have you doing a lot of dirty work if you're ever to succeed him. You can't be a good guy with him around."

"Then I'll kill him."

"Really? Will you be able to pull it off?"

"I've been so absorbed in these new feelings with you, I stopped worrying about him."

"It's a mistake. If he sees you going soft, or sees you happy, it will be bad for both of us."

"You're worrying too much."

"Damon, when I met you, you tried to kill me. That's who he made you into. In what scenario between you and him, do I get to live?"

I sighed deeply at her knowing.

She started to push away from Damon, shoving herself backward off his chest until she toppled them both over onto the bed. They were out of view but could be heard.

"Stop Gellion," Damon said, hands moving roughly, two angry youths pushing against one another.

A loud slap sounded, and then another.

"Gellion!" Damon growled.

Several more slaps sounded, and then grunting noises commenced.

"I'm not doing this! You don't deserve my love," Gellion's voice argued.

"If we're going to die soon, I'm going to have you every moment I can."

"I'm a sitting duck," Gellion said right before a loud moan escaped her mouth. Despite her anger and fear, her breath no longer commanded anything from him except her own acceptance. Their bodies were out of view of the camera, but their noises were audible.

I shut off the video, unable to allow myself to go there again, to lean into the wanting of Damon. I could see how clearly my desire for him had remained, despite the years and time apart. Watching our younger selves together only made the feelings stronger.

I checked the date on the videos and did the math. I'd been seventeen years old. How the hell did I get free of my parent's control enough to end up in a hotel room with my boyfriend, sleeping together like we were already adults in a blooming life, in Rome? My inability to remember any of it made the shock of it all so much more intense. I was a stranger to myself, and all my best friends had truly disappeared from me.

I clicked on the next video. This one was more forward. I was sitting on the bed, my legs crossed, my hands on my knees. I looked like I was meditating.

"You need to stop wearing me out," young Gellion said, eyes still closed.

"You need to finish the work on Father Vasily."

"Yes, I know, but I'm drained. Please be quiet so I can energize myself."

"I'm recording."

"Why?"

"I want you to explain what it is you're doing, how you're doing it, and what you see."

Young Gellion opened her eyes, with a curious expression on her face.

"I'm right, aren't I, we've painted a target on our backs?"

"I'm just agreeing with Caitir, that we need to document everything."

For the next thirty minutes, my younger self explained the process of removing both the dark hardware she could see inside people, and the residual muck as well. She talked about the layers that make up the dark hardware, the Karma that brings it forth, how to clear the Karma, and how to detox it all.

As she saw it, the easiest way to remotely work on people's bodies was to shrink them down in the mind, to make the work more palatable. She couldn't really work on a person's actual body anyway since everything being exorcised from it existed inside a dimension beyond the body, or it would be seen by our human eyes.

When she saw something inside the body that wasn't supposed to be there, she would imagine her mind creating a bubble of light around that darkness, containing all of it, and all components tied into the body. Then she'd lift the bubble up and out of the body, and hand it over to the light beings she'd asked to come help.

She imagined the white light of source coming through her top chakras, and down and out her hands, a white light to fill the empty space of what was removed, so nothing dark could return.

As she spoke, I tried to imagine how her vision of it would look, how easy it was for her, and if I'd ever be able to see it like she did. Teenage Gellion said the hardware lived in the main energetic centers of the body, and when it connected into those parts of us, it could influence and assert some control. The brain-mind, the heart, the stomach-Chi-core, the pelvis, and sometimes the throat were all centers of energy that could be infected. So, there were five areas she said the hardware could be found.

Each piece of hardware had its own agenda within the body, to attract darkness like a magnet to people, to make itself larger within and play out harmful agendas. This hardware helps victims attract more abusers, and helps abusers become worse. Both abuse and abusing others help the darkness multiply within.

Most importantly, the pieces worked like hardware because they received information from those who created it. This hardware inside us didn't act alone, and like modern hardware, it too had an internal wireless signal. So, we're never actually without a negative influence over us, ever. Very few people and very few families escape the hardware curse. It is within all of us, like the apple given to Eve.

I laid back and tried to visualize what that would look like in the Q-Spec machine, how it would vibrate being represented by the machine, versus how Gellion saw it back then. No matter how horrific, I was sure the Q-Spec would make it look beautiful somehow.

Young Gellion wasn't confident in front of the camera, until she forgot it was there and simply started the work, speaking to Damon as if he were the only audience. She explained to him her process, that she simply asked a lot of yes-no questions of the light beings who arrived. This was how she found the truths she'd come to understand from loving beings she could see, who came to help her grow and learn and protected her from harm.

"What do you want to call the hardware?"

"So far, it mostly seems to be used by dark beings."

"Demons."

"I guess."

"You don't think it's demonic?"

"Yeah, you're right, it is."

"Demonic hardware," he said, using his hand to make rock-n-roll horns to his forehead to look like the devil. "Demŏnware then?" Damon asked.

She nodded in agreement. "Okay, but just between us."

I wasn't sure I was learning, but I was accepting everything I saw, because it was me, my voice and my words, and my reality. Yet asking someone else, anyone else to accept this truth would be bizarre to me. If it hadn't been me, I wouldn't accept it at all.

The most helpful tip Rosie gave me, that I'd never heard from any of my other therapists, was to see the scary things from the past like a black and white movie, as a way to remove myself from it. Lying down next to the player, I did just that, listening but not watching what was happening. Sometimes I could make it look black and white in my mind, and sometimes I could see it better than in a movie, with my imagination.

The next video was profound, and profoundly scary. No longer in the hotel room, the quality of the image had shifted again.

Young Gellion and Damon were back at the Monastery with Father Vasily. Sitting in a chair in the middle of the room was the same teen girl as before. She looked about fourteen.

She was tired, irritable and wanted to scratch her skin, but her wrists and forearms were bound to the chair. Father Vasily motioned dramatically for Gellion to approach the girl.

"Despite what you think of me, my evil deeds are nothing compared to those around me. This girl is possessed by the demons who feast in Rome."

He said something in Italian to Damon.

"He says if you are so talented, you should show him and save the girl."

"What's her name?"

"Carmella," Father Vasily responded.

"Can we cut the ropes?" Gellion asked.

Damon shook his head.

"Can she understand me?"

"There are several languages spoken, uh," Father Vasily said pensively, "where she's from. English is not one of them. However, they say demons speak every language, so who knows."

Gellion looked as if she were considering the information.

"How close can I get?"

"I wouldn't. She's already killed someone."

"Who did she kill, an abuser?"

"I don't know."

"Damon, will you ask her?"

He walked to the edge of the room, to a row of chairs against the wall and picked up two. One chair he positioned behind Carmella, and the other he put in front of her and then sat down. Damon's Italian didn't sound perfect, but it did sound correct. She cursed at him and stuck out her tongue and started heaving.

"I don't think she liked my questions," Damon said to Gellion as she walked to the chair behind Carmella and sat down on the edge of it.

Father Vasily readjusted the camera to show all three of them.

Gellion raised her hands in the air, arched her head back and breathed in deeply. Her hands came together above her in prayer then lowered to her chest. She opened her eyes and spoke.

"There is a menacing darkness in this room," she said, her voice deep and low and strange. "It does not want the girl. It wants the priest."

Carmella's eyes were facing the camera, staring at Father Vasily. She snarled at him, like an animal turned into a monster.

"It's been haunting you, hunting you, tormenting you for years," Gellion said, intrigued by the information she spoke, her eyes also focused on the priest behind the camera. Damon turned around to see Father Vasily's reaction, and what he saw surprised him.

"How do you know that?" Father Vasily's voice screeched.

"It would jump inside you, punish you and hurt you from within," Gellion continued.

Carmella screamed a high pitch tone and Damon covered his ears.

"Lui è mio!" she growled out.

"'He's mine,'" Damon translated to Gellion, then he turned to Father Vasily. "What happened?"

"He met a real disciple of God," Gellion explained, "A real remover of demons. You found a healer to help you," Gellion realized as she spoke, her voice showing curiosity and amazement.

"Did he help you?" Damon asked.

"For a time," Father Vasily said.

Carmella screamed again, at all of them, until Father Vasily stood before her, his cross in his hand, touching her forehead with it and saying another prayer. Gellion kept her gaze on Damon as Carmella shook and screamed as if she were being burned by the cross, though unlike the exorcisms in the movies, no smoke wafted from Carmella's forehead. She exhausted herself from the spasms and her body went limp.

Damon and Gellion shrugged uncomfortably at each other, waiting for the awkwardness of the possessed child's reaction to abscond. Gellion waited for the priest to remove the metal cross from her forehead and then took a deep breath.

"The exorcist couldn't keep the demon out, could he?" Gellion asked.

"No," the priest admitted. "And you? What you did to me, what you removed, can I really never be possessed again?" Father Vasily asked, moving closer to Damon and Gellion.

Gellion's eyes flickered and rolled back then her head nodded back like she was glitching. Information had to be arriving behind her sight. When her face returned to center her lip curled up in disgust.

"Tsk, tsk, tsk," she sounded, wagging her finger. "You know why you were possessed. You know exactly what you did. Did you confess to the healer, for absolution?"

"No, he would not have wanted to hear it. I confessed to..." Father Vasily trailed off, not wanting to say any more.

"...Someone who also needed absolution?" Damon whispered to Gellion.

"Am I truly free of it or not?" Father Vasily demanded.

"Father, you know you're the only one who can answer that question. Darkness can always return. Your actions and choices let it in and help it multiply."

"It's not always a choice," Father Vasily said.

"Lots of little choices are still choices."

"What's the healer's name?" Damon asked.

"Father Jerzy," Father Vasily admitted.

"We want to meet him," Damon said.

"Can you help the girl?" Father Vasily demanded as he motioned to Carmella.

"Can I ask you why you care?" Gellion responded.

"I have always cared," he replied, insulted. "Carmella is special, or she was. I want to know what happened."

"Basta!" Carmella yelled out. "Basta!"

"Can you help her or not?" Father Vasily asked.

Gellion looked at the back of Carmella and raised her hands up to feel the girl's energy and closed her eyes.

"Death by a thousand slices. Her purity was destroyed by the crimes of her abusers. She was a toy to evil."

"She was never my toy," he refuted.

"The darkness here wants to torment you. Why? Why you?"

"You wouldn't understand."

"I would," Damon argued.

"The rituals summon a presence. The way the room would change. The carnage after it arrived. There was no pleasure in it," Father Vasily said quietly. "It feeds on fear. I was unable to conceal mine."

Gellion nodded in agreement. Neither she nor Damon scoffed at the seriousness of Father Vasily's experience.

"She doesn't have any parents," Gellion said, "right?"

Young Damon looked surprised, and Father Vasily glared at her.

"How do you know that?" Father Vasily whispered.

Damon reached for her wrist.

"You brought her from someplace dark, someplace deep below, to test the healing powers of calling on Christ inside the church, but Jesus is not here."

Father Vasily put his hand to the large cross hanging around his neck and shushed Gellion.

"But you are not a believer, Father," Gellion said to him. "You can't call on Christ without first bringing him into your heart. You must know that's how it works, and your heart was already filled with too much darkness."

"Gellion?" Damon cautioned. He could see, as easily as the camera, that Father Vasily was growing angry and frightened.

"I may use the same light Jesus did to pull the dark out, but I doubt I see it the same way. I see these things in shapes, grids, fields, often two-dimensions when it should be more. I'm low-grade compared to Jesus because I can't heal wounds."

"Not yet," Damon said, signaling his flourishing confidence.

"Right now, I need a mentor more than a savior, so I can do as Jesus said, to go out and remove the demons."

"Except the darkness has changed a lot in two thousand years," Damon explained. "It's got Wi-Fi. It's got Malware. And it can clone itself. It's got all kinds of tricks and camouflage."

"This is not about faith, for every human from every faith has the right to do what Jesus and the Prophets did, but it's about sight and the true knowing that everything can be shifted, as long as you can see it, and protect yourself while you help."

"What do you see in her?" Father Vasily asked.

"Your demon wanted to use her to get to you, but the space inside her was already filled with something else, making it impossible for the demon to attach. Until…"

Gellion's face looked confused, and for a moment she stared at Carmella and then she looked down at her own body, her brow burrowed in uncertainty.

"Something changed," Gellion gasped, putting her hand over her horrified mouth. "The demon's not possessing her. Something's inside her."

Carmella's eyes shot open, as if the secret within her had heard its name. She snarled at Damon as she fought against her bindings. Something about what Gellion said triggered the insanity inside Carmella to act out, and fight and rage at those around her. She was spitting and using words that sounded filthy toward the priest and Damon.

"Gellion?" Damon asked, backing away from the growing hatred the girl was spewing toward them.

"This is wrong. This is so wrong," Gellion moaned. "She's pregnant. It's in her fetus. The darkness attached to the baby. Those men hurt her so bad, Damon," Gellion cried out to him.

Carmella was screaming at Father Vasily.

Damon translated Carmella's cursing accusations, "She said he left her there. He promised to help her, but didn't protect her. She says it's his fault. She says the demon wants to destroy him, and she does too."

"I never touched her," Father Vasily protested. "But I couldn't stop it. The demon wouldn't let me. The others wouldn't let me."

"Is she a breeder?" Damon asked.

"Damon!" Gellion chided with shock.

"She will be now," Father Vasily admitted. "Unless the possession gets worse."

Gellion gasped!

Damon's eyebrows shrugged in acknowledgement of her fate.

"Maybe it should get worse!" Gellion yelled. "If that's the only way she escapes her abusers," Gellion scoffed.

"She's only here because she's not expected to survive, the possession has become problematic enough that I'm free to experiment on her," Father Vasily confessed.

The girl began cursing again, spitting and making guttural grunting noises. The camera was far enough away that her behavior, demeanor and sounds mimicked that of the victims in horror movies and it was terrifying.

Gellion started moving her hands, as if reaching into something unseen and pulling out something equally invisible. Then she held her hands up, palms out for just a moment, seemingly sending light through prayer.

"The fetus has sixteen pieces, sixteen curses. That's not right. A baby can't handle that. The rituals keep bringing more darkness in. The energy of the demon is working so hard to reach you, Father."

Gellion did her work, moving quickly as the girl grew more violent against her bindings until the scream that emitted from her was so terrified she finally sounded like a child again.

"Gellion, she's bleeding," Damon said. "Father we have to untie her."

"That's not a good idea," Father Vasily said, fearful.

"I only have six left," Gellion called back as Damon worked to untie

Carmella's leg restraints.

Once both leg bindings were undone, Carmella fell forward on her knees, her chair lifted onto her back in the air. Carmella screamed out as if she were trying to push. Gellion stopped what she was doing to join Damon in helping, to hold the chair as he worked to free her arms from their ties.

More blood poured from Carmella onto the floor, while Damon scrambled to remove the last ropes, and Gellion held the weight of the chair above them. Carmella held her body up while she grunted and heaved her breath. Once the bindings were gone and Gellion pulled the chair away and set it down, Carmella sat upright onto her knees, and the silhouette between Carmella's skirted legs showed she was delivering, and then a thud sounded, followed by a second splatter. Father Vasily backed away, watching in horror as Carmella delivered her fetus.

The teen girl scrambled away in repulsion at what emerged from her, falling on her butt and shoving herself away from the blood and mass of flesh.

"Per favore, non farmi toccarlo," Carmella said while she cried and sobbed, the color returning to her face, her expression and body language shifted to wholly approachable.

"Nessuno ti obbligherà," Damon replied, turning back to look at the pink and lifeless body.

Then its chest moved, and they all flinched back.

"Does it still have the Demŏnware?" Damon asked Gellion.

"Yes. It needs a blanket," she said, visibly shaken.

Damon stepped away, looking in the room for something. Gellion reached in front of her to do the invisible work to clear the premature baby from the remaining darkness. She stepped closer and she moved her hands, and Damon returned with a tablecloth. Father Vasily moved closer too.

Then they all shrieked and recoiled back from it.

"It has black eyes," Damon said, alarmed.

"È un demone!" Carmella screamed.

A trail of blood had been left where Carmella had dragged herself away from the barely breathing fetus and placenta, lying on the cold floor. The cord was still attached to the sack that also vacated from Carmella during the spontaneous miscarriage.

Gellion refocused and started moving her hands again.

"Stop," Father Vasily interrupted. "The demon is still inside."

"I can clear the baby," Gellion argued.

"It won't survive," Father Vasily barked back, shaking his head, "but you can still save the girl."

"What?" Damon said.

"If you go now, you may take the girl and get her help," he said to Damon, taking the tablecloth from Damon's hands and placing it over the fetus on the ground.

Father Vasily moved swiftly to a closet within the room and removed a long black coat. He ushered Damon and Gellion to help Carmella up, wrap the coat around her and leave.

"Take her to a hospital out of the city," he instructed as he escorted them from the room.

Father Vasily returned and walked directly to the fetus on the ground, pulling the tablecloth from over it and wrapping the premature life barely breathing with the folded tablecloth as he picked it up and held it. He walked directly to the camera and paused the miniscule face before the lens. The tiny eyes opened for just a moment and they were, undeniably, completely black.

When the playback ended, I turned off the tablet and staggered to the bathroom, as flashes of images played before me as if they were suddenly burned into my eyes. Both the video I'd just watched and the images of horror movies about exorcisms flashed before me. I felt sick and disturbed and made my way to the bathroom and puked, telling myself it was seasickness and not my weak stomach at such horror.

In those moments, head hovering over the toilet, I distinctly remember walking out of a Korean movie with extremely graphic demonic possessions and miscarriage imagery, with Katherine following behind me calling me immature for making her leave. Despite the gurgling in my stomach, it was beginning to sink in how much I'd been exposed to evil, to help me understand somehow. Hollywood horror was such a frustration for me and was suddenly my greatest teacher. I couldn't imagine ever wanting to see anything else after witnessing the real thing.

I was tired, emotionally exhausted, and mentally challenged to accept truths I watched my old self blurt out, truths that hurt to hear and felt hard to swallow. Though there was some explanation for how old the dark world was, the fact it had become my reality was too much.

In the video Damon hadn't been surprised by any of it. Gellion saw it firsthand. Even when the evidence was there, over and over, it was still a shock to me now. Beyond being a lot to relive, I didn't understand things and Damon wasn't around to ask. My next option would be to talk to Caitir or Calder again, and no thanks. I had to take a break.

Maybe I could just ask the internet.

Nothing worked when I tried to use a website browser, and I saw there was no connection. Keenly aware that I still had no cell phone, something about it was driving me nuts. Caitir understood but had been given strict orders to keep it all away from me. When I explained what it was for, to learn more about the yes-no questions, and how the energy systems looked in motion, Caitir got excited and started typing.

She pulled up a list of videos with titles on the subjects I'd just mentioned and started copying them.

"What is all of this?" I asked, taking a closer look at her search. "Is that my face in those screengrabs?"

The images weren't really me, except they were, at least my eyes. The images were like a cartoon version of myself, except my form was extremely white, as if I were made of light, and the energy systems I'd been learning about looked to be viewable on my body in rainbow colors.

"It's your face. You were working on a video blog to teach people how to do energy work for themselves."

199

"You're just telling me this now? You should have shown me these sooner," I complained.

"I'm sorry Gellion, but..."

"Why is my face weird?"

"Oh, well it was the only way Damon would let you do the recordings, if he created a filter specifically for your videos, so you couldn't be recognized."

"Are these on the internet?"

"No, of course not. Damon pulled them down and kept them in our backups."

"Oh," I calmed. Then I realized I'd cut her off. "But what?" I asked.

"He didn't think you would understand any of this until being here, and seeing all of this, and the videos."

"I want to talk to him."

"He's not available right now."

"Is he still in Rome?"

"Yes."

"Why? The children are here."

"We are safe here, but the mission isn't over."

"Is that normal?"

"Yes. It just depends."

"On what?"

Caitir's face became uncomfortable.

"Come on Caitir, on what?"

"If there were any last-minute victims added to the group, or..."

"Wait, what group?" I was confused again. "The group here?"

"No. The children are replaced with copies. Like how we saved you."

"Oh!" I gasped. "All of them?" I asked and Caitir nodded.

I tried to wrap my mind around what I'd just learned. Damon and his unit had copied and replaced all those kids?

I remembered how I'd been saved the same way. My mind no longer needed anything else to comprehend how plans might change at the last minute, for such a large-scale operation.

Then I remembered the scariest part, "Wait, so, the abuse still happens?"

"Please try to understand. It's the best we can do. The bodies of the clones have microchips for brains, and memory transfers for personalities. There is no consciousness. Just programming. Programmed reactions to stimuli, while pain receptors are turned off."

I let that reality sink in.

"Why?" I asked out loud, not sure what I was asking.

"It's Halloween. All Hallows Eve is not innocent fun. It's their holy day. They must have their rituals."

I sat down, dumbfounded as I realized the extent of their undertaking. I had escaped torture and death because of a clone. My clone hadn't been connected to me, though I took her injuries personally and felt my body hurt where she'd been injured, it was still just a microchip running her brain, creating her responses to the torment. Programming capable of timing the gas poison emanating from her mouth at the end, while she died.

There was no part of that sacrifice that looked robotic or like I hadn't been one hundred percent real. That meant the children's clones would do the same, look and act real while being used and tortured. It was brilliant, but nauseating.

The computer made a chime when the video transfer was complete. I stuck out my hand and took the thumb drive and walked away, shoulders slumped, sickened by what measures would be implemented, or could not, and what Damon might be going through. And then I had to shut off that stream of consciousness.

I got lost again on the boat, meandering around, unable to focus on the path after understanding the scope of the mission, and what had been accomplished by all these people. I realized I was standing in the open hospital slowly walking past the made-up rooms, keenly aware my own chakra energy had taken a hit. I was sinking fast into a deep sort of hopeless feeling, still walking, but just barely.

"Gellion?" I heard a female voice call. "Gellion," the voice got closer, its vibration of surprise bringing me back into my body.

When I turned around to meet whoever she was, I was greeted with a hug, one of great comfort, as she reached under my arms and pulled me up and into her taller frame where she held me. When she finally pulled back she kept hold of my arms.

"I can't believe you're here," she said, her English pronounced with an accent. Her voice choking up, covering her mouth, and staring into me, starting to cry. Her emotions at seeing me were startling and brought me all the way back into my body, my eyes finally alert. I looked at her up and down and noticed a name tag over her plain green scrubs.

"Carmella?" I said, shocked, overwhelmed, overjoyed, then amazed, all in that order. "You're alive?"

Could it really be that same teenage girl?

I'd left that last video devastated for her, worried for her, sick inside over the abuse in her life, and there she was. She was tall, beautiful, spoke English, and remembered me as if she'd just watched the video too of me doing energy work on her.

"I can't believe he found you," she replied.

"Is it really you?" I asked, tears forming in my eyes.

"Yes, it's me!" She replied, bouncing up and down, then she leaned in and kissed my forehead as if I were a child beside her.

"You look amazing! You're so tall, and beautiful! Are you well?"

"Very well. I'm here, helping. Damon enlisted me."

"I was just thinking about you. Worrying."

Everyone was watching us, and it made me realize I hadn't introduced myself to anyone, I'd hidden myself away, trying to figure out how to be the Gellion they needed. It made me feel even more uncomfortable, knowing I'd been rude.

"When did Damon find you?" She asked me.

I was surprised by her question and thrown by it.

"Not long ago," I said, shaking my head. She just looked into my eyes with curious wonder, so I started to babble. "I had to be saved, and now I can't go back to my old life. I'm afraid someone will want to get rid of me in this life too," I said, sounding morbid.

"I know the feeling," she said, sympathetically.

My stomach growled and it dawned on me I hadn't eaten in a long time. "Please excuse me, I need to go lay down."

"Of course," she said reacting to my weakness. Then she reached around my waist and held me up and walked with me. As we reached the bedroom, she asked, "Is there anything I can get for you?"

"Food. Water." *And Damon*, I wanted to say but didn't.

Before the food could arrive, my eyes closed, and I drifted away.

12

THE DARKNESS WITHIN

When I woke up I was no longer on the boat but in Damon's bed, back at the underground base. I immediately looked over for Damon, who was missing from his place on the couch.

"How did I get back here?" I wondered out loud.

My eyes were no longer blue. My hair was no longer blonde. My scars had returned.

The multiple clocks, in multiple time zones, showed I'd only fallen asleep a short time ago on the boat. I headed to the command center where Malik was, working at multiple computers. He wasn't surprised to see me.

"Where is he?" I asked, and he pointed to the open window. I looked down and he was there, on the bed in his observation room. I watched him for a little while then noticed there were a lot more rooms and screens lit up. Many small observation rooms held men with familiar faces, several of their clones now on the boat.

"When will they wake up?"

"When the mission is complete."

"Really? How do they do that?"

"It's a special connection, so they can stay at the ready where they are. None of this would work if they couldn't wake up quickly in case of an emergency."

"Wow, that's amazing. Why not me?"

"Damon didn't want us to sever the connection you had with this body in case you needed to escape the boat. If you're mentally tired, you can sleep here too."

I looked back down at Damon, wondering what he was doing, or suffering from.

"Do they ever kick or move in their sleep?"

"Rarely, since they're very present in the other body."

"Can I be with him?"

Malik looked stunned to hear my request and nodded slightly. I walked down the spiral staircase and opened the door to his room. Damon's unconscious body looked so calm. His domineering presence gone, and all I could see was the face of the man who'd once been a grown boy in love with me.

After watching all those videos, I deeply wanted to just smell his skin and touch him. It felt awkward but I lay next to him, knowing I was being recorded, listening to calming music playing in the background. I pressed my lips up to his bare arm and spent time just breathing him in. Getting to know his smell again was calming.

"I have so many questions to ask you," I whispered.

Despite waking up in a rested body, my mind was exhausted. I needed to get away from the new memories, the horror of it all, but I couldn't. So, I pretended to sleep and found my mind consciously traveling to visuals inside my head, looking over and analyzing the new ideas I'd seen and absorbed.

In my mind's eye it felt like I was in a tornado, like Dorothy in "The Wizard of Oz," standing inside her house as all the objects and people flew by. Except for me it was the new energetic concepts flying by, unable to be examined as closely as I'd like. People with working chakras flew by, looking like peace and harmony because they were in tune with their energy and protected by it.

In the tornado, unconscious people like me, also flew by, and they were shutdown, sad, and unproductive. They had no life force flowing through them, and so they withered, until they could find someone to feed them, or encounter those who could energize, like BB.

Then there was a third group of people. By the grey look of them and their shadowy movements, these were the people to be feared. Not only were they shut down, but their energy systems had started working in reverse. For some reason, inside the tornado of images, this scenario stopped before me and let me look closer.

These reverse people actively feed off others, hurting them in the process. More than a need to survive, they are driven to steal energy, and the more they hurt others the more they absorb energy for backward purposes. These were the monsters who abused, raped, hurt children, destroyed people's lives, killed, and maimed. So many kinds of darkness breeders.

The tornado of images filled with only these kinds of people, and they looked like anyone and everyone, from all walks of life, no feature too different. I couldn't look at them without cringing, for all the ugliness they represented, so I tried to look deeper. Something had to be shared there among these monsters who came to their despicable lives from all different backgrounds, almost all their backgrounds just as horrible as them.

Generations of people started to fill the tornado, like staticky images from old movie screens, showing them as people from times past, connected to one another through familial blood. Like when you rub your eyes and the pressure of your hands creates new images, I let all of them, a whole world full of these monsters, become blurry within my sight and something stood out. At first it looked like a light, flickering deep within each of them, but as I stared harder and harder, finally focusing on just one nameless, faceless human, the flickering drew me in and hypnotized me.

Glued to the vision of it, and the details that emerged, slowly the understanding of it became clear. It wasn't a flickering light at all, but a churning mass of darkness that sparked light as it moved. The flecks of light were a reaction to the human system being forced to hold a conscious mass of darkness, with a layer of black goo lubricating what was hidden inside. It existed in its own dimension that lived over and within our own.

The hypnosis held me, me staring at it in a kind of growing horror, forcing me to rewire my own thoughts to escape it, and back my way out of the deep dive into the body of a human monster. I'd never visualized anything like it, except inside my own dreams, or ever tried to solve a riddle by looking into my own consciousness.

Yet the answer to the riddle had already been provided. My dream, the one I had so many times after waking from that coma, was seared into me. For a stretch, I simply had to close my eyes to see myself removing dark energy from within him. For every time I would, it began our passionate embrace, which helped me escape my pain.

My eyes blinked rapidly as I came back to myself and I gulped in the air, panicked from having held my breath for so long. I panted next to Damon's unconscious body, the body of the man inside my dreams. I felt myself calm beside him, only to realize that the vision I had of that false light actually was the true darkness, and must surely be inside Damon, as he said.

He'd spoken of it, told me I needed to see it, but if he knew about it already, why hadn't he been healed? Surely the evil Damon suffered as a child didn't continue into adulthood, right? I sighed. I was sure I still knew relatively little about his life or the lengths to which he suffered to make it this far.

I wanted to disappear into sleep, and in my half consciousness, the image that haunted me most was just how easily people with dark intentions and backwards systems could overpower and feed off others to thrive. As the images flashed again and again, it was clear they all shared a common curse, something inside them that I couldn't quite define, but had now seen, and felt disturbed by, and a chilling thought occurred.

Is the whole world really like this? I wondered.

If this was what Damon wanted me to heal, I really hoped I could recreate what I'd seen, what I dreamt, things the old Gellion could so easily do. I'd have to practice on my own, away from the machine, with real people. I wondered if Damon had intentions for me beyond personal healing. My own systems were barely functional. I had no idea how I would ever be able to fix that in me or him, but if BB's insights were right, and the old videos of myself were a roadmap, I had more than I needed to start.

The biggest encouragement also came from some recent books I was handed by Damon, that kept emphasizing the most important aspect of this work was about my intention, and my effort to connect to God and entities of light, to get me there. More and more the message had become, in covert ways, about calling on divine light sources as the only way to survive.

I tried to turn off the noise inside my head that surrounded everything, but I didn't want to fall asleep, or leave Damon, just to wake up on a boat in a tired clone. Being on that boat showed me the true nature of my "captor" Damon, and why he needed help. My life was meaningless in the face of such a mission, and its rescue of the innocent. It was also the hardest and most painful energy to absorb, too unavoidable to not feel deeply about, or be taken down by its heaviness.

I wished not to return to that just now, and for however long I could rest from it, I would. Thoughts swirled around my own awareness of ignorance, dizzying me. I'd shunned all religion after my mother died and had no interest in the history of world beliefs about God. Katherine had taken me to all kinds of Buddhist and Christian events. It was nearly ten years of her forcing me on her proper Korean mother.

I smirked at the thought of Katherine's effort to get me to church, and include me, usually with a bit of anger. It all made sense now; Katherine hadn't wanted to go either, or maybe deal with me, but was forced by Damon to try to add some religious culture into my life. She was the only one who could.

I'd had yet to hear Damon pray or mention much of God at all. He didn't talk much, actually. I imagine if I were truly looking at the real version of him, he'd be wearing a general's battle uniform, commanding the troops. Inside his mind, he was miles away, and it wasn't that he was never coming back, it's that when he returned, he wouldn't be sharing the battlefield with me, maybe ever. I didn't have the stomach for it anyway.

I had to set it all aside and focus on what was right in front of me. Damon's motivations were powerful, and overwhelming, but understandable. He was becoming my hero, and yet for what purpose? It wasn't to impress me. The videos showed he was already interested in helping children, especially seeing his spontaneous admission to it as something driving him. I'd learned a lot, yet I had more questions than ever.

Was it just about the children or something more?

He'd wanted to help me learn faster, was deeply involved in my process, and yet wasn't healed himself, at all. BB would call him a type of energy vampire, trapped in some sort of penance and torture pattern, which was hard to grasp, but at least visible to me now.

Had our safety been destroyed by reckless youth?

I appreciated how cautious Damon had become; how good he was at doing the work without getting caught. He was fighting the system by accepting it as too big to change, and working covertly within it, helping anyone he could. Maybe I inspired him, or maybe taking on a cause and seeing it through gave him a reason to live on, beyond his own dreams of happiness.

Now that I was back in his life I realized how weak I really am, and I wondered if he knew just how much the truth he'd shown me made me want to leave this world and die to escape the pain of it. I was living with the dichotomy of wanting to leave while his energy of attraction and attention kept me struggling to want to stay. How had such an energy vampire brought so much desire and anger into my system, while also draining it? All to force me to be strong enough to hold on through the horror and become something more.

No one, not in my memory, had ever needed so much from me, or wanted so badly for me to grow. I'd been saved by someone who needed a savior. In more ways than death, I'd been saved. Saved from being tortured and sacrificed or used as a plaything by the sick and demented. Most importantly, if I were still living in the pain of my real body, everything would be different.

Now I knew the power of living in a "healthy" body, a clean human-suit had allowed me to feel and see, what I couldn't muster the energy to experience over the last twelve years, except in dreams. Compelled by lust, desire, and a need for human connection, I would no longer live solely inside my head, leaving the wants of my body to the wayside. This connection with Damon was growing so powerful it was changing me, pushing me to fight through the muck.

Contradictions ran through my mind and heart, but as I kissed Damon's arm again, I knew I wanted to allow him time, even if it meant holding me in limbo for however long it took for us to heal. Whether we'd be able to hold out long enough to get there was unclear before his humanity and my survival were discovered by the real dark world.

Malik tapped my shoulder, and I stirred. I'd fallen asleep next to Damon and woke up there, dried drool on the crease of my mouth. I sat up and stretched and followed him out.

"I fell asleep, but I'm still here?" I said to him, still waking and confused.

"The music I played was for sleep, but it didn't take you deep enough. You couldn't help but succumb to it. I didn't let you stay that way, so you wouldn't end up back on the boat just yet."

"Thanks."

"Now that you've had some time to think, you should probably eat before watching more of those videos Caitir compiled for you."

"Oh. Do you have a copy?"

"Yes," he said, and pointed to a bag. "Or I could queue them up in the viewing room."

"No," I shook my head. "I'd rather grab a quick bite and get dressed, or I might lose my motivation. Can I view the energy videos inside the Q-Spec?"

"Oh!" Malik exclaimed. "What a great idea. I don't know if it can be done. That would really help you take it from watching, to repeating with verification. That's more direct learning."

"I was hoping."

"Have you seen the energy work videos from when you were younger?"

"I was about to start watching them."

"Oh, the implications. I can keep the AI's separate, but Q will learn from the imagery displayed inside the machine. Might teach more than just you, but Q as well."

"I could watch it on a smaller tablet, with headphones, if you're worried about the AI's being affected."

"No, no. I just wish I could talk to Damon about it."

"I mean, I really was just hoping for the videos as like a cheat sheet, because I keep forgetting the imagery, and the Q-Spec is waiting for me to make it happen. I just need more help."

"I agree. We all need more help."

"Maybe you should check in with Caitir, and get her option, since Damon isn't available."

"That is insightful, thank you Gellion."

"Okay, I'll go eat and get dressed."

"And I'll set up the viewing."

After ordering some food from the food printer, I quickly ate and made my way to the dressing room. The white diamond suit waited in my locker and took me some time to get on by myself.

My hand scanned and the doors opened to the Q-Spec. I climbed inside the gigantic machine and waited. Eventually Malik's voice sounded over a speaker, and I could see him in the window.

"Sorry if I kept you waiting."

"That's okay. Isn't there a way to get your attention?"

"Um, yes," he said. "We use the base's AI to locate one another, assess alarms that sound in our satellites, help automate the trains…you get the idea."

"How do you use it?"

"It's programmed to respond to voice command. We call it MARI. MARI, say hello to Gellion."

"HELLO, GELLION," it said. "HOW CAN I HELP YOU?" MARI's voice sounded.

I smiled. "Is it an acronym?"

"It stands for Moral Artificial Rational Intelligence."

"So, I just say the name, and then what?"

"It responds to simple commands, like 'contact' a certain person."

"That's great," I said, while also trying to keep the information in my mind. "I'll try that next time."

"Caitir left a list of files. I'm going to play them after I get you loaded up."

"Where?"

He ignored my question as the Q-Spec started up, and my body was positioned and moving into the air.

"Q-Spec will scan you, and once that's been recorded, you can start the videos. The videos are being run by MARI, not the Q's AI, so when you want to play or pause the video, just call MARI, and say, 'play video' or 'pause video' and it will. Call out if you need me. I'm paying attention to multiple things."

"Thanks Malik," I said with a hand wave.

Malik was shy, in his own way, and extremely focused. He seemed to understand the importance of his part in the group without anger or bitterness. Caitir must have been his reason for so much peace and tranquility in such darkness, as they were the only young couple down here. All the others, including Damon's men, seemed to be without spouses, from what I could see.

The machine let me stay upright as it scanned my energy. No longer lying down in the hopes of someone else fixing me, I was waiting to see if the trip to Italy had shut me down, and if I could fix myself.

While my body was energetically filled in all the right places, and every structure was bright, the systems didn't look full or large, or even thriving. They weren't shattered, but quite a few chakras seemed to be motionless. Those that ran moved as if they were trying to catch up with themselves.

My energetic core had energy, but the bright pulsing we saw after BB's work wasn't there. I hadn't expected my forcefield to have grown the three feet it needed to thrive, but I didn't expect it to shrink back either. I'd been exhausted by the revelations, by not understanding their mission, and by the horror it revealed.

Once the scan was done, the first video started, and it played on the window I'd seen Malik in. The clear opening had somehow been turned into a projector screen without me even noticing. The window was the only place just outside the Q-Speculum, but near enough to it to allow for outside visuals to be seen. Malik's idea of where to stream the images was quite clever.

The magnets relaxed my body back and raised me up to make viewing easier. On the screen was me, younger and chubbier in some areas, and leaner in others. I was seated in front of a green screen, and someone was working on the camera to get the best shot. Lights were moving around, and a guy with a laptop came into the screen's view to show me something.

"Do you want something like this?" the man asked.

Suddenly, their images changed. Her face didn't look like it was happy about the image. So, the man pressed another button on the keyboard and the animated images over their real selves changed. They had looked like woodland creatures before and now they were mermaids.

I could see where they were going with the imagery as it kept changing. By creating a whole world of imagery, it would be impossible to tell who I was at all. These skins were newer ideas back then and would have to be embedded to keep the real person hidden.

Teenage Gellion and the tech guy went through everything he had on his computer, and nothing was exactly as she wanted. Eventually the camera was cut and the next images looked like another day. Gellion was wearing a different outfit, with different hair. The artistic filters were very different, all of them a mutation into some form of light being. The programmer obviously took notes.

The next image was full-on filter, no Gellion at all. Just like I'd seen in the screenshots, it was my face but distorted with a smaller nose, larger eyes, and clown white shimmering skin, in shades of white, silver, and glitter. In each position on the body where the chakras were located, small, pulsing circles of color sat.

"Can I begin?" she asked.

She cleared her throat and looked into the camera and said, "If I were to ever need to teach myself, or anyone, how to do what I do, it would look like this."

The only way to describe her final look was that of a crystalline being. Crystalline Gellion pointed to the top corner of the screen, near her head, at a CGI animation playing. In view was both the crystalline Gellion and a smaller avatar of herself lying down, miniaturized before her. The chakra points of her system were present, but barely functional. The larger version of crystalline Gellion, the one who spoke to the camera, disappeared but the image of her horizontal body with chakras filled the screen.

"We all have a chakra system," her voice said over the imagery. "This system must be running well, or the rest of our life doesn't. So, this is all about intention. You see the body here; imagine it's your body. The top chakra is where life force flows into us from source, divine creation, God. If it's empty or small or barely running, it means the connection to source needs to be strengthened, and more energy needs to come into the system. That is also true of our Chi, our energetic core, the meridians, and forcefield.

"With the help of words and visuals, I will show you how to work your way through the human system, so no matter what you face, you face it energized, and ready, not depleted and defeated. First, we'll take a look at how to activate a system that is shutdown. Once we understand how it's supposed to work and what it's supposed to look like, then we can take a more in-depth journey into what happens when these systems are shattered and fragmented, making them unusable. The first step is figuring out if you're merely shutdown or much worse, shattered."

Suddenly a soothing and melodic song played, with tones that made me vibrate. My voice spoke to me.

"Close your eyes," she said, and so I did. "Now, imagine that The Divine Creator, your loving but long-lost parent, is so far away that you have to travel a great distance as a soul to reach them. And as you travel toward The Creator, you don't even realize how many systems of human control you must journey through to get there, and how many pieces of yourself get torn away, just for passing through those control grids.

"Not just control, but there are places where monsters try to thwart you, and leeches grab on to your body, a body that carries the spark of you, the spark that came directly from divinity. The Divine Creator has been so far removed from Earth that you have always felt alone. When you arrive at the edge of the universe, at the place where you notice The Divine Creator's energy, you find a spark of life no larger than your own, made of pure light.

"When you reach this tiny spark of The Divine, something happens. Instead of standing before the 'I am' to ask the questions, you arrive, and The Divine Creator immediately gives their spark-on-the-edge-of-the-universe to you, placing themself inside your dimmed consciousness, so you may feel their love directly and learn to be more whole.

"Oh! How The Creator has missed you, and how depleted you've become trying to connect to them, only to find nothing. Now you will have all the answers you need, as you've found the missing piece you've been looking for. And it's so powerful inside your body that as you turn around, turn back to Earth and to your mission there, everything looks different.

"Your once dimmed spark has turned vibrant. The Creator's spark and its love for you will work with you now, together to do something magical. In all the places where you were broken apart, stolen from, abandoned and betrayed, and lost pieces of your soul or consciousness, lost energy from your chakras or core, as you return to Earth, all those broken or stolen pieces of you, of your energy and your life force, start to return.

"They return back, like metal pieces unearthed by a powerful magnet, and when they return back to you, they are light, cleaned and cleared of the pain and darkness that tore them from you. These pieces become healed by that spark of The Divine bringing your system back to life. So that as your soul reaches your body again, your consciousness, and the mass it carries, is intelligent enough and powerful enough to energize your body in a new way, in a perpetual cycle of renewal, as The Divine's spark is a reminder of the immortality of our being."

"From that place of perpetual energetic flow, from The Divine Creator's spark first, and from the spaces where we were once abandoned ourselves, see your energy systems come to life. See the shutdown chakras start to spark at the base, near your body, initiating the energy systems to life like an ignition, arousing a new kind of fuel to be our power and vigor. Watch as the flame of illumination that is the God Spark, energizes your chakras from the top down.

"The cyclone where energy arrives at the top of your head, where The Divine first comes to us, to feed our system, to make it full and spinning. Imagine what The Creator would say to your mind and brain, knowing that you had to struggle to find the truth of yourself.

"God would be loving and encouraging, as if you were a long-lost child. The thoughts there inside that top chakra would include the wisdom of past lessons, free of Karma, and blessings from that pure spark of creation living within you.

"As the cyclone swirls in steady progression, the rejuvenated system spills its energy into the next chakra where the third eye exists, a cyclone of energy opening and growing from the connection to The Divine, as energy pours forth in front and out the back of your head."

I'd kept my eyes closed, really embracing the imagery, but when I opened my eyes, the imagery existed before me in multiple places.

"MARI, pause video," I called out.

I needed a moment to stare at what was before me.

I could see it on both my crystalline appearance on the screen, as well as through the glasses, seeing laser beams creating movement before me. The chakras, just energized in the meditation, were vibrant on me. The young crystalline Gellion had a cyclone above her head, swirling powerfully. So did I! What had been nearly shut down on me was now radiant. Through her visualization I reached out for cosmic light energy and pulled it in to jump-start me.

"MARI, start video," I said.

I visualized with her, going down each energy system. The same kind of cyclone started moving at the next energetic location, my third eye, mimicking hers. Each location down her body started embracing the energetic flow of human Mana that was filling into the chakras below the crown, flowing out the front and back of her. I saw the Q-Speculum reading my own system, and as I imagined myself becoming energized just like her, after seeing it on her, the Q-Spec showed it shift in real time.

From a trickle to a gush, my energy reading matched the one I was seeing on the screen. With my eyes closed I could see it in my mind, and when I opened my eyes without the glasses, I thought I could see it then too, if only just for a moment. The video replay of my own voice, slowly and meticulously coaching me through the work, helped me visualize each cyclone to full fruition before moving to the next.

Crystalline Gellion continued to instruct.

"Another way to help the energy move faster is to use the energy through your hands to help encourage the energetic flow, holding your hands above your head, or at the top of each chakra. Think of it like jumping the dead battery of a car, which then starts up the whole system. The battery is there but needs a bit of a kick to get going.

"Participation on multiple levels can help a healer become a better healer, and always with intention and communication."

The speaking stopped, but the visuals continued as all her chakras beautifully filled with light and color, just as she said, the energy from the working chakras flowing into the ones that had stopped working.

"Next, we move on to the energetic core. Imagine a supersize double AA battery sitting inside your body, starting at your pelvis and filling your torso all the way up to your neck. Now remove the outer casing and see the pure energy within, vibrating in infinity within you. Like the chakras, the core can take a beating but eventually shuts down when trauma happens. When we go into shock, when our lives are torn apart, the core is affected by all of this.

"The battery can no longer maintain the shape of infinity while taking so many personal hits, and so the momentum inside is lost. The system that has shutdown must be rebooted. If you don't reboot, your body will drag itself around, like a robot trying to function on lower and lower percent lifeforce.

"Your hands pulsate out energy, from your top chakra down to the bottom, then back up and out your arms and hands. See yourself send energy through the hands into the two ends of the core, like the jumper cables. Your hands' energy will be your mechanism to start the human battery, fed by Divine energy realigned with you.

"Like a charging station, pour energy from your hands into the battery until it's full, until the spark from the universe becomes energy that overflows from your chakras, and starts to overflow the battery too.

"As the core and chakras connect into your Chi system, you notice the energy of Chi as a Powerball of energy that sits in front of your gut. Chi will need to stay energized too, to have a productive life. The Chi energy also works like a torus, but on a different frequency and so its cyclone is wider and more malleable.

"Now, as the energy overflows from your core and from your chakras, see them both feed into the Chi torus, creating a powerful and stable vortex of energy that begins as a sphere in front of you, but flows out and around the body as well.

"All torus energy is designed to self-feed into infinity, but our world, the Earth system is designed to tear everyone down. Each of our energy systems must be protected, renewed, remembered and prayed over. When they are shutdown or shattered, if we stay that way too long, sickness and death will eventually follow, and flourishing is impossible.

"MARI, pause playback," I said as I stared at the images on the screen that showed what a functioning Chi structure should look like. Then I closed my eyes and imagined my hands energizing my Chi, but the Q-Spec didn't seem to see it.

"Hmm," I sighed. "MARI, continue playback."

"Before we get to the human forcefield," my enthusiastic voice said, "I'd like to briefly touch upon the meridian lines within the body. These can also be stagnated since they migrate energy through the body the same way our circulatory system moves. In order to energize those, we simply brush our energized hands along the body from the hand up, then down to the foot. On the opposite side it's up the foot and down to the hand."

She showed herself brushing her hand up her leg and torso, and down her arm. Then she switched hands and brushed up her arm and down the torso and leg. I repeated her actions, feeling a tingle in my own body but seeing nothing on the Q-Spec playback. I made a mental note that the Q-Spec hadn't reached its full potential.

"Now to the forcefield. Whatever the forcefield looks like, it is an indicator of how long someone has been shut down, or how vividly they're thriving. When we need to look at it, it is often in a state of de-energy, and if you can see or test yourself, it's helpful to know. A healthy forcefield stands three feet or farther from us, and acts as a shield to protect us from others' energy, or to warn us of energy it encounters.

"The more dynamic the personality of the individual, the larger their forcefield will be. When the field is small, like six inches to a foot away from the body, then we know there's been a shutdown of energy for a while. The smaller the field, the longer it will take to get it back to a healthy level, and forcefields can take some time to build back up, especially if the chakras are always shut down.

"The forcefield is like a giant see-through balloon, and in order to keep its correct shape and size it needs to be healthy. Sending energy into a structure that has weakened and shrunk, is just like filling the balloon with enough air, so it's the right shape, size and strength. With the intention of making the forcefield larger and stronger, we can easily visualize the energy from our hands acting like the air that expands a balloon.

"If we remember how the creator-spark of energy overflowed out of each chakra like a fountain, and into the core and overflowing still, then there is plenty of that energy left to revitalize the shrunken forcefield and have protection restored. This can take several meditations to complete, depending on how far it needs to go and how long it was shrunken.

"Take a deep breath in," the crystalline Gellion said slowly. "After having visualized for yourself and sent energy to yourself to open all these blocked or shutdown systems, you should feel rejuvenated and hopeful. If that is not the case, it could be that you need time to grow your forcefield.

"If you do this meditation multiple times over several weeks, and still feel no shift, then there are other underlying issues to address. In the next video, I will share with you what happens to a human life when it's stuck living on a shattered energetic system, or multiple ones. We will go over the steps to heal a shattered energy structure, which could include a shattered core, shattered chakras, a shattered forcefield, and even a shattered mind.

"When the shattering is severe, it's nearly impossible to selfheal. So, if you think you might be shattered, or too shutdown to do the work on your own, there are people you can seek out for help. I will share how to find those practitioners as well. Thank you for joining me today."

The screen went dark, and the video was over, but the Q-Spec visuals before me were more than miraculous. I'd been going back and forth between focusing on the video's meditation, while practicing using my hands to move energy, and then opening my eyes to see what the Q-Spec had picked up. I did my due diligence inside my mind but like Damon, I found the imagery of his Q-Spec astounding to behold. While I was imagining what the Crystalline Gellion said, the machine saw my energy becoming more vibrant.

Just because I was able to pump up my already-running energy system, didn't mean I was ready to send energy to others. Would I be able to reboot or restore the energy structures of traumatized children? I wasn't too sure.

From what I'd just seen I knew that at least energy did flow out of my hands, in my current scarred clone. I would have to watch the next video to see if her explanations of healing shattered systems made sense to me. But without a Q-Spec to help me see for sure if my attempts were working, I'd only ever be able to imagine it, and pray I'd find positive results.

BB hadn't known I would be trying to help others when we asked her to connect us. I had no way of knowing if the work would be done in a version of me that BB had never seen, a blonde Gellion without scars, reminiscent of me in my youth.

Had BB connected me to all the other versions of myself?

Or only this one?

Was her work that universal?

The only way I'd know for sure is to succumb to sleep here and go back to that pristine, blonde Gellion on the boat and see. There was so much need for lightwork and healing there.

13

THE MENTOR

When I arrived back at the boat I didn't know what to expect. The tray of food had been sitting near my immobile body for some time. I wondered if "all-grown-up" Carmella knew about the clone bodies Damon's people used. I wondered a lot about her; about all she'd seen and done and learned since I last saw her in those videos.

Falling asleep brunette and scarred, then waking up blonde and flawless was a strange transition. I felt achy from the awkward position I'd collapsed in. The water and fruit were welcome, as was the granola. I wondered if I should shower, and realized I'd never really checked this body for any smells.

Yep, I needed a shower, and the "normalness" of that sensation put my mind at ease. I didn't want to be in a body that wasn't alive enough to need a shower after multiple days without one. I realized too that Rosie and Eamon had let me stay in their suite, which had a full bathroom attached. Their patience and understanding were "next level." For them, the stakes were so high, and yet they were doing the kind of work you only do when called by something greater.

Fear kept me from walking around the boat too quickly. We had never stopped moving, I was sure, but I didn't remember where everyone would be. When I found the hallway that led to the makeshift hospital, the lights were dimmed. There was a woman at the double door entrance, sitting on a stool, reading over paperwork. She looked up when she heard my footsteps. The doors to the hospital were closed, and the windows in the doors showed a darkened room with small night lights all around.

"Only surgical personnel," she whispered. I nodded, understanding they were not to be disturbed, and continued.

Then I jumped at the sound of a muffled shriek. The squeal set off several others, as the different sounds of frightened children rose in a chorus of horror. The noises turned into cries and moans, from exhausted bodies. I didn't move until every voice had let go of its need to be heard. With my hand on my heart, I took a deep breath as the hospital wing grew silent.

As I started to walk away, the door behind me opened.

"Gellion?" I heard a strong whisper. "Gellion!"

I turned around and saw Carmella. She was smiling at me, as if she hadn't heard the cries echoing through the craft. She moved quickly toward me and pulled me gently by my elbow.

"They're sleeping," I whispered in protest.

"Father Jerzy is here," she said, pulling me through the hospital doors, as if I should know that name.

Wait. Was that the name of the healer mentioned by Father Vasily? I wondered, internally excited at the idea of meeting him.

"He's traveled from very far to be here."

I pointed to myself questioningly and she just nodded. Her enthusiastic smile was almost too much, like that of a perpetually optimistic person. I followed behind her through the double doors and we moved quietly through the darkened room of resting children. She opened a door and pulled me in. On the other side of the door was a small chapel.

It was unlike any chapel I'd ever seen, as it had large crystals inside, set in holders attached to the floor. The crystals were placed side by side, with some space between them, and had lights positioned, showing the crystals' internal details. They all varied in color and shape and were both massive and impressive.

A bearded man with sandy blonde hair stood in battered jeans and a long sleeve shirt before a large crystal with his back to us. His hands were above the crystal, hovering, as if trying to connect to the large rock. He was rugged and unexpected and turned around when he heard us.

His brown eyes grew wide with so much emotion upon seeing me. He looked at Carmella and nodded, and with just that expression she left us. I watched her leave, confused as he walked slowly toward me, his arms gently outstretched. I didn't cringe at his welcoming gesture, like I normally would while being approached by a man. It wasn't from any charm, but from his eyes which told me he was an old friend.

As he reached me, I crumpled into him from a feeling of overwhelm that swept over me. Something about this man made me feel safe. He caught me to his chest and brought me gently to the ground. I was literally in his lap, him gently kissing my forehead and patting my head.

"There. There, now. It'll be alright, dear one." His accent was European, but I didn't know where.

Something else I realized during my heavy breathing, "I don't know myself anymore. I'm nothing like I was," I blubbered.

"Your body remembered," he said kindly. "You didn't even hesitate to trust me."

"What does that mean, 'my body remembered'?" I asked.

His hands relaxed their hold, "We are old friends. You've spent time on my energetic system, healing me, and vice versa. We learned a lot from each other."

I coughed slightly and sat up, away from his body. "Right." Maneuvering out of his lap was a bit more uncomfortable. Wow, I was glad no one had seen…

…the door opened, and Eamon entered. I nearly leapt out of Father

Jerzy's lap at the sight of Damon's uncle, who chuckled as his eyes got big.

"Nice to see you're both here. Father, your robes are hanging up. There's no time to rest. She's got a lot to learn."

Then Eamon closed the door. I looked at the man before me, who was slowly standing up, as if my body upon him had left a burdened impression. He bowed, as if he was outing himself and his true intention.

"I'm you're unofficial mentor."

"Oh. Damon's request?" I asked.

"No need to request."

He smiled and pulled his hair back into a ponytail, then went to one of the pews and grabbed a large duffel bag and walked into a bathroom within the chapel room and closed the door. I assumed he was getting cleaned up, and as I'd already done that, I wondered if I should do something else.

He'd called himself my mentor. I looked around the room and thought about the way it was situated. How much symbolism there was in the room and how varied the imagery was, conveyed a worldly experience. In the silence there was a feeling too, a buzzing. I walked up to the crystal that Father Jerzy had been standing over and placed my hands above the large quartz. It gleamed bright in white and clear patches.

After a while I closed my eyes so I could focus on what I might feel. There was a frequency there, a vibration through my skin too.

What am I feeling, exactly?

I wondered if knowing that my own system was operational, according to the Q-Spec anyway, helped me acknowledge that the crystals seemed alive and full of energy. I stood there for a while, holding my hands up, embracing what energy I could accept from a stone I didn't understand. Something was happening though, and it wasn't expected. My hands started to itch and burn. It was almost uncomfortable.

I didn't notice that Father Jerzy was standing behind me as I winced and shook my hands out, but he pulled my hands away.

"Too much is too much," he chastised me gently with a smile, but my mouth had dropped open at the sight of him.

He'd shaved all his facial hair off, making himself look much younger and even more approachable. He was also wearing light blue monks' robes. The color of blue immediately put my eyes at ease.

"You changed," I stated.

"So have you," he replied cheekily.

"I'm not actually sure I'm Gellion anymore," I admitted.

"You're still Gellion, even if you're not the same."

"How can I be?"

"You're alive, and that's all any of us needs to have hope, right?"

"I guess."

"So, let's get started," he said, pulling out his prayer beads that shimmered, a long strand of small multicolored crystal balls. Then he looked at my attire and scowled. "I think someone left clothes for you in the restroom."

Inside the bathroom there was a clothing bag hanging up. I unzipped the garment bag and saw that I was to wear a type of monk's robes as well, which felt ridiculous. The color was a paler blue, but in the same family of blues, and maybe the lightness of it was to mark me as an apprentice, not on equal footing. I preferred the idea of hanging back and watching. The robes were made of silk and were extremely comfortable, demure and flattering.

"Where are you from?" I called out.

He didn't answer. I opened the door and found him on the other side.

"Poland," Father Jerzy replied. He looked me up and down and said, "I like this on you. It's tailored well."

"Caitir, I'm sure. She's brilliant and stylish," I smirked, unaware I felt a form awe for how incredible the people around me presented.

"She's one of your biggest fans. Your loss left a hole inside of them."

"I don't really feel that" I was surprised by my honesty.

"No, if anything, you would feel their trauma. It only multiplies your own."

My face scrunched up at the profound truth of his statement, and how much my brain wanted to analyze it and reject it entirely.

"Is your system set up to send through your hands?" He asked.

"I think so. I did some meditations to open my energy, but I'm not yet able to see it with the naked eye."

Father Jerzy took my hands in his and turned them over, holding my palms up. "Hmm."

He left my hands palm up then put his hands palm down, as if our palms would touch, but didn't. It reminded me of a hand-slapping game children play. I wasn't going to be slapping his hands though.

"Close your eyes," and I did. "Concentrate on the sensation in your palms."

The warm sensation in my hand didn't feel like the crystals I'd just hovered over, as it wasn't a burning feeling, but very warm.

"Feels nice," I said in a sort of hum.

"Well, the fact that you can feel it in your hands is promising. Most people can't feel anything."

"Really?"

"Absolutely. What did you feel when you put your hands over the crystals?"

"At first it tingled, but after a while it started to burn and itch."

"What did it feel like just before that?"

"Like, hmm, a buzzing feeling. Is that normal?"

"Normal is different for everyone."

"What do you feel?" I wondered.

"Nothing. I was putting energy into the crystal."

"Oh," I hadn't even considered that could be a thing. "Why?"

He smiled. "Everyone here needs a place to come, to pray, to re-energize, a place where the vibration is high. When I came into the room, the crystals were dormant. I was activating them so they could help hold a vibration of healing here."

"Crystals need to be activated?"

227

"Most crystals are entirely neutral. You activate them with energy and intention so they may do what we need them to do. For this place, the crystals must wrap everyone who walks through the doors in a feeling of safety and peace. Do you feel that?"

I closed my eyes again and tried to feel what he described.

"A little? Maybe. Not really," I said sheepishly. "The space feels, uh, hollow."

"Very good. I only had time to energize one crystal. In a room full of them, that's not enough to create any feeling."

I was surprised I was right, and even though it was hard to say it, I'd been honest.

"How did you activate the crystal?"

"You send it energy the same way you would to any of the human systems you work with, and you use your mind and its connection to God to set that intention. It's a simple transfer of pure energy, fed from an unlimited source through the body, into the hands and out. Remember, all crystals can absorb negative or positive energy. Crystals inside temples often need energetic clearing."

"Is that why my hands hurt?"

"Great question. Well, since you hovered your hands over the crystal I activated, it's probably because your hands are not used to the vibration of the energy I used. Sometimes too much is simply too much, especially for a body new to transfer energy."

The door opened again, and my hands immediately flew away from where they were, back down at my sides. Eamon called out for us.

"Jerzy, now please."

Father Jerzy walked first, and I followed. They kept a fast pace, and I tried to keep up and keep from tripping over my unfamiliar garment. The area we entered was quite dark, with low lit walkways, and white fabric dividers between the makeshift rooms. We bypassed all the beds with sleeping children and went through another set of doors, which led us to an intensive care unit, where children were in hospital beds hooked up to medical equipment, some on ventilators.

The scene around me was shocking, horrific and I wanted to stop looking, so I looked down at the back of Father Jerzy's robe, following where it went. Calder had said children had died, and he was convinced I could help him. Seeing what I was seeing hurt so deeply that I doubted I could muster any energy at all. I was so grateful it wasn't on me to do what needed to be done.

"Father Jerzy," I heard Calder's voice say, gently. "This way."

The room we entered was lit with blue lights. I found the color theme interesting as we blended into the environment in a way that made us almost disappear or walk like ghosts.

There was only one bed in the room, and it sat in the middle, wires and other lines of medicine came from machines into the human, a tiny human. I had already pulled my hood over my head, out of fear, and masks had been applied to our faces to keep it as sterile as possible.

There was no noise, except the tones of the machines as they did their work, the ventilator pumping, the heart monitor beeping. Father Jerzy walked me over to the head of the bed, and placed me three feet away, and stood between me and the child.

"Caitir tells me you've been learning the basics from your old videos," he whispered to me. "This child is recovering from surgery, but her vital signs are not good. I want you to send energy into the top chakra. Focus only on that one to start."

"What if her chakra is shattered?"

His face lit up at me under the blue lights. "Very good question. In my experience the top chakra is rarely shattered, as it's a direct link to God. The heart can be broken, the mind shattered, the power center demolished, but the link to Source is harder to break."

"If anyone should feel betrayed by God?" I asked him.

"Well, good point," he said, and he said it as if he wanted to add a "but" on the end, but he stopped. "Let's just take a look then."

When he turned away from me to assess the child, I felt a wave of anxiety and panic hit me, like when the elevator door opened, and the able-bodied children made their way toward me. This was worse.

"What do you feel?"

"Terror. Fear."

"Can you see anything?"

"Nothing. How can I? Can you?" I whispered back. I could barely handle the scene, let alone see things I'd never seen before.

"I don't see anything either. They aren't shattered; they're missing."

"How does a healer fix that?"

He looked at me as if trying to explain it would take too long and shook his head.

"Do me a favor, just stand there and see if you can feel anything at all. When you do, let me know."

I placed my hands out where her crown chakra should be and waited to feel something. Then Father Jerzy turned to the child and started moving his hands around the area. First it looked like he was lifting something out of the space. Then it looked like he was sending energy in. Then more lifting and more sending.

I couldn't feel anything watching his hands move, so I started to focus on where the long tornado should be. I stared and focused and stared and focused, and after just a little while, I could sense a great feeling of relief, and my body yawned. I felt embarrassed and despite my mask I covered my mouth.

"Yawning is good," Father Jerzy whispered. "It means you felt something release."

"I did?"

"Didn't you?"

I thought about it, and he was right, it hit me hard and swelled over my body, and then there was a great feeling of alleviation.

"As strange as it sounds," he leaned in and whispered, "the healer's body is going to need relief from the energies that hit, and if it can be without pain, then we take the more embarrassing yawns, farts, and burps for the minor inconvenience they are."

I wanted to laugh but stifled it. I couldn't believe he said that, and I quietly chuckled at the idea of doing energy work and burping through it. The yawn was certainly the most pleasant of the three and I would gladly yawn my way through the work any day over something far more embarrassing.

"Every chakra is missing," Father Jerzy said, sadly.

"Is that normal?"

"The ones this bad-off usually don't survive before I arrive. I must continue. Watch and feel and see if you can sense what is happening. If you're comfortable, try sending light into the chakra I'm working on, to help the process move faster."

The priest worked his way down the small body. I kept my eyes on him or the space where the chakra should be, because I couldn't bring myself to look at their face, beyond the ventilator and bandages. Their body was covered in blankets.

The third-eye chakra was the same as the crown. I tried to tune in, felt upheaval in my stomach and then yawned while trying to send light to the area. The throat was easier and faster, but the heart was harder to take. My stomach wanted to hurl as Father Jerzy worked on the area.

I could feel my eyes swell with tears at the overwhelming sensation that rose in me when I felt her heart chakra start again. I let the tears fall silently. And it was like that all the way down to the bottom chakra. He didn't stop there, doing all the things BB would have done, looking at the energetic core, and finding that it was shattered too.

I couldn't see the work, but I could feel it, especially as I directed myself to just keep sending light. At the end, he brought us three feet back again.

"Imagine a powerful forcefield being energized by the both of us, stretched from where it is, just a few inches from the body, to where it should be, three feet out," he said softly.

The sighs were deep and came several times until the last great yawn appeared, which I took in silence. Slow tears poured down my face and I wiped them away with my sleeve. The amount of exhaustion I felt, simply aiding Father Jerzy, was intense.

He touched my elbow to show me it was time to leave the room, and on the other side was Carmella, standing before us with a tray of waters for us to drink. Father Jerzy guzzled his glass and Carmella refilled it. I drank more slowly, as the experience had unsteadied my stomach.

Calder approached us. "I have three more critical patients, Father."

"Give us just a moment," he replied, then turned to me. "Gellion, please drink as much as you can. Carmella, after the next patient, please bring juice and crackers as well. Thank you."

I put my finished cup back on the tray and solemnly followed Father Jerzy into the next intensive care room. It was the same, the terror, the upset and fear, except now I was rawer to it. My whole system seemed to be aware of the damage to the child before me. The tears and yawns came quicker, but so did my own flow of energy, at least that's what I sensed from Father Jerzy's reactions.

As he worked, I found he was moving more quickly this time, or I could follow the pace easier. I wasn't sure exactly what I was doing to help, but he was nodding and grinning slightly at me as we moved through each energy structure. The juice was there after the second child, and then we moved on to the next.

At the end of the last intensive care child, I walked out of the room stumbling. I couldn't catch my bearings or my breath. Calder held me up under the arms. I'd had enough water so that I could keep crying, but what I really needed to do was scream out in anguish.

Of course, their chakras are missing! God has forsaken them!

I thought of all the times I had felt cursed and never loved by God. All the losses and traumas and pain. They were truly nothing compared with what I saw. It was too much, but I was trying to hold it together. I couldn't think of where to go to find relief from the burden of so much energetic information, far beyond my own understanding of torment and pain, which I had thought was bad.

Carmella reached out to help me, but Calder was already by my side and under my shoulders, his arm wrapped around my waist.

"I've got her," he said to Carmella and Father Jerzy, and he walked me swiftly out of the hospital wing and back to where his parents had let me stay and lay me down on the bed.

I curled into a ball and tried not to weep, hiding my eyes under the blue silk hood. As my face scrunched up in pain, my throat swollen and my mouth trembling, Calder squatted before me and pulled something out from the back of his pants.

Fear shot through me at the sight of the gun in his hands.

"Calm down Gellion, it's just a tranquilizer."

"What? Why?"

"You won't be able to sleep, not after what you've just seen and felt. You won't be able to meditate your way back to your other self. This will help you leave your body."

I started to cry again and nodded my head in vigorous agreement as the tears streamed down. I desperately wanted to leave that boat. It only hurt on my arm for a moment and then I was drifting away.

When I woke up back at the base, I was still in Damon's bedroom, unwatched and unattended. My mission was not dangerous and there was no worry about my safety, so I could stay in the private room, but it's not where I wanted to be. I wanted to be held by Damon, not Calder or Father Jerzy, not any of the others, but Damon. He wanted me to face all of this, but he made it seem as if he'd be standing there the whole time by my side. I felt so alone.

When I got up and relieved my body, I couldn't shake the need to scream and cry, but because this body had been well rested and so far removed from the rawness of it all, the tears and screaming didn't come to me the way I assumed they would. I felt a bit cut off from the experiences I'd just faced with enormous sensitivity, and now I felt numb.

It was so confusing. How long had they been doing this that Calder knew how much I needed to escape, to come back here just to scream? It wasn't so easy to reconnect to the full weight of it from a different body. I left my comfortable clothes on and sauntered to the command center, to see resting Damon and check in with his sleeping form.

Malik didn't say a word as he watched me drag my feet all the way down the spiral stairs to get to Damon from there. This time it wasn't enough to lie next to him. I couldn't just plop myself down and feel safe beside him. I looked around the room for a blanket and found a soft one in the corner. Once there, my forehead pressed against the side of his arm, and the images started to resurface.

The third child we went to help broke my heart. The blackened bruises around the entire eye sockets of the boy just destroyed my sense of reality.

"In the child trafficking world, they call this 'panda eyes' because the abuse was so violent that all the blood vessels broke around the eye sockets, and often the discoloration can last for years, even decades," Father Jerzy whispered.

"It's permanent?" I whispered back.

I had no other words, then or now, for the understanding of the horror I saw, only tears that finally started to pour out of my scarred-up body, as I sobbed quietly next to Damon.

After some time, my system calmed down and I found myself fading in and out of consciousness next to him, until a familiar alarm sounded, blaring out the emergency before me. Damon's heart had suddenly stopped, and the monitors were going wild with the information. I grabbed his body and started shaking him.

"Damon! Damon!" I yelled out as Malik entered the room. "What happened?"

Malik was running toward the crash cart, opening it, and looking for something, then found it and raced over.

"His clone was obliterated," Malik said, trying not to alarm me with his tone, as he pulled the tip of the giant syringe off the adrenaline needle that was to go into Damon's heart.

"What do you mean obliterated?"

Malik rammed the needle into Damon's chest, without hesitation, and Damon's body sat upright, the needle still piercing him.

"Welcome back," Malik said, a bit sourly.

The look on Damon's face was worse than mine. His scowl was powerful and frightening. He looked down at his chest and ripped the needle out, placing it on the bed. His eyeballs searched the room robotically until they landed on me, my puffy and exhausted face before him.

I reached up cautiously to touch him, and he smacked my hand away.

"Get out," he said, his breathing becoming erratic.

"Damon, it's me."

"Get out!" He screamed.

I stood up at his rage and started to head toward the door.

"Damon, you, ok?" Malik questioned, moving towards Damon.

"I didn't escape it. The program didn't take over Malik!" Damon said to his friend as I exited the room.

I sat on the spiral staircase on the other side of the door and just felt shocked. I had so many questions about his mission, and I knew I'd only get answers from him, but he was in a worse state than me. When Malik finally opened the door and saw me on the other side, I made room so he could make it back to the command center, and I gathered my strength.

"I met Father Jerzy," I said as I stood in the open doorway, unable to take a step inside.

"So?"

"We worked on some of the children in the ICU."

He didn't respond, as he rubbed his wrists and the rest of his slightly atrophied body.

"How did you save them?" I finally had the nerve to ask. "How did you guys pull this off?"

"It's not a conversation I want to have."

"But it's a conversation I want to have."

"The details aren't important."

"What didn't you escape?"

I stood in the doorway, eyes to the floor, trying not to cry, trying not to crave more information because it was probably all terrible anyway. He continued to stretch and flex, slowly, morosely.

"Can I touch you?" I let slip out of my mouth, because I wanted desperately for someone to hold me too.

"No."

"Please?"

I took a couple steps inside the room.

"Stop."

"I'm not doing well Damon," I tried to explain and took a few more steps.

He stood up and screamed, "Enough!"

I couldn't help it, I walked to him anyway, but before I could reach him, he'd already grabbed my jaw and throat and rushed me several feet away to push me up against the wall.

"I love you," I croaked out.

"You think I can just turn off the monster?" he growled at me, his body as far away from mine as his arms were long.

He was squeezing my throat so hard; he was steadily choking me. Tears streamed down my face as he held me in anger, unable to stop squeezing, until an unintentional yelp emptied out of me, from the pain. His grip didn't loosen, he simply threw his hand and my neck with it, down and away from him, until I was on the ground like a rag doll.

I coughed as he walked over to the medical cart, and Malik arrived back in the room.

"Damon, too rough," Malik said, as my coughing lightened.

"She shouldn't push buttons," he barked at the both of us, as he removed the same type of tranquilizer Calder had used on the boat, from the medical cart and walked back toward me.

"What are you doing?" Malik asked.

"Sever her connection to this body," Damon commanded, as he leaned down toward me.

"What?" I whispered, astonished, and started to back away, but he came after me, pushing me against the wall again and shoving the tranquilizer gun to my arm with way more aggression than Calder.

"Stop!" I protested. "I don't want to go back to the boat!" I cried out.

It was already too late, and I was fading fast.

I woke up on the boat and my body still felt sick to its stomach. I found the bathroom and puked, and then I puked some more. I didn't want to see anyone or do anything but find a way to actually escape. It hurt so much inside.

I was in luck; Calder had left the tranquilizer gun in the room. After I was done being sick, I climbed on the bed and held it to my leg and pulled the trigger. It was weak of me to seek escape, but I'd never pretended to be strong, and Damon's rejection was the last straw of my mental capacity. Sweet oblivion awaited.

14

THE DECOY SACRIFICE

The blaring sounds of the boat's alarm were barely enough to wake me from my daze. The flashing lights that alerted everyone to the seriousness of the issue should have pushed my body out of bed but didn't.

I was undercover this time, lying flat on my back, which was not how I'd gone into unconsciousness. After several more uses of the tranquilizer gun, it was clear someone had retrieved it, and it would be harder to escape again. I wondered how many hours or days I'd been out, but didn't actually care.

The commotion was only getting louder until the booming sound of a large gun going off, jolted me upright.

"Was that a mortar?" I exclaimed, jumping out of bed.

The closest window hole was only a few steps away, so I looked out. There was another ship, smaller than ours and not far behind us, firing a strange-looking cannon our way. Our ship jutted forward so violently, speeding up with a force I'd never experienced, that I was thrown back and hit my head on the cabin wall. Suddenly, our own boat was firing too, the pounding of guns, secured to the back deck, fired loudly.

No matter what happened, we would survive, those in Damon's inner circle, our real bodies awakening elsewhere, but the other people here... I couldn't even think that far ahead.

My cabin door flew open, and Carmella was panting and summoning me with her hand. I grabbed my shoes and pulled them on as quickly as I could as I moved toward her.

"We need to go below deck and secure the children for transport," she said as she pulled at me.

But I stopped her and took her hand from my arm and put it in mine. "I am expendable right now and you are not," I said. "I think I'm needed elsewhere."

I turned and walked the other way. Something inside me needed to see who these men were, in Damon's inner circle, and what they were capable of. If we were going to die, I wanted to see the battle. It would be my only chance to understand their world.

When I arrived on deck, everything that should have been in chaos was calm. Sure, there were large bullet holes in the cabins above deck, but there were people in military gear everywhere. The more I stared the more I realized it was Damon's family, all of them except Malik.

They were standing on the deck in full combat gear, with helmets and armor. Each stood behind a large tripod weapon bolted into the deck floor. The weapons had targeting shields, that helped them both aim and take cover. I stood in awe, in plain view and without protection, watching as their bodies shook with each trigger pulled, and how much strength it took to keep firing over and over.

"Gellion get down!" I heard Rosie scream.

Her eyes had glanced at the surroundings, probably to assess if anyone was hurt, and she saw me standing alone and unhidden. A barrage of bullets hit the metal behind me, and my body hit the deck hard, Calder on top of me, his face just inches from mine.

"I see you're finally awake," Calder said. "Welcome back to the land of the living."

239

"How long was I out?" I wondered.

Another round of bullets whizzed above our heads, and I closed my eyes out of instinctual fear.

"I took the tranq gun away after the first day, so it's been almost two since we last saw you."

Calder rolled off my body and swiveled his own toward the midway point on the deck, where an unmanned tripod gun was waiting. The shield spanned out both sides of the gun and protected more than just Calder, as it covered the entrance to the quarters below. I crouched behind Calder there and shook with each hit the shield took.

When the shock of the battle faded just slightly, I forced myself to look around and see who was manning what and where. Every face on the top deck looked familiar. I saw Damon's family, and then five distinct military faces that were definitely Damon's men. Though they wore helmets, glasses, and full armor, I tried to memorize the parts of their faces that I could, so it would get easier to tell them apart.

I was sure they all knew who I was and why I was there. None of them paid me any attention, as the gunfire continued. Then a blast hit the deck, landing directly on Calder's cannon, and we were flying, flung across the ship, our bodies slamming into the doors behind us. I'd been smashed between the door and Calder's body, and though I felt as if I'd been punched in the gut and run over with a car, I knew Calder took the brunt of the blast. When we landed on the ground, there was blood everywhere.

Calder grunted out in pain.

"Calder? What do I do?" I said as I scrambled to his body, looking for his wounds. There were too many, too many tears in his gear, too many pools of blood. "Calder!" I screamed over the chaos. "What do I do?"

He took my hand in his as he gulped his last breaths, but he did not look afraid, just pained, and angry, and riding out the moment. I wondered how long it would take to get another clone of him to the boat. Would the others not notice his disappearance? No one on deck paid any attention to their man down. They knew he was waking up alive somewhere else.

The blasts were getting too strong and too close, and I could see the vessel was gaining on us. Another blast hit the deck, and three more men went flying, their cannons destroyed, their bodies blown to pieces. The ringing in my ears was terrifying, for it pounded at my head like a hammer.

I stood up to see who was still alive, and how far away the enemy was, when something phenomenal happened. A booming explosion sounded so loud, and shone so brightly, I was pushed back again and had to shield my eyes. The attacking ship had just exploded on one side. Though they turned their cannons toward the water, before they could trigger anything their ship was hit again. This time the explosion sent the entire vessel into oblivion.

"Yay!" Were the screams from those still left alive on deck.

They stepped out from behind their cannon shields, to the very back of the ship to watch the burning wreckage sink, as our boat slowed down to a stop.

And then I stumbled backwards at the sight of a submarine as it breached the surface of the water, like a whale flying into the sky and landing back home again. It sent water splashing onto us, as it inserted itself between us and the burning enemy. The hatch opened and Damon's face appeared. I gasped at the sight of him and held my breath, as I stood at the back edge of the boat, watching.

"It's about time!" Rosie yelled at her nephew.

"I got here as fast as I could," Damon shouted. He didn't look at me, not once. "We'll hookup from underneath. Prepare to be boarded."

He closed the hatch again and the submarine disappeared. The connecting of the submarine to the bottom of the ship was a jolt, and unexpected. The boat had clearly been designed to do just that. I could barely move, but I felt female hands touching me, holding me close. The ship was moving again, quickly away from the problem.

When we made our way below deck, the movements were already quick and heavy. Everyone everywhere was hauling the equipment out, evacuating patients. Some children couldn't be moved yet, but by the time I reached Father Jerzy, he was saying goodbye to the chapel and deenergizing the crystals there. His robes were gone.

He looked at me and his face grew concerned as he pulled me in close. "You've seen war now," he said softly into my ear.

"I'm sorry I abandoned you," I said, feeling remorseful for using the tranquilizer to escape all the darkness and evil, and disappointment.

"I'm sorry that Damon can't give you the comfort you need," he said, as if he'd read my mind about what the worst pain of all could be.

I was leaning hard on Father Jerzy when the door opened, and Damon stepped inside.

"Gellion," he said softly.

I looked up at him but couldn't meet his eyes, as he hated me so much the last time we were in the same room, that I couldn't bear to see his hatred again.

"I should go get cleaned up," I mumbled as I walked past him, wondering if he would reach out. He didn't.

It was a hobbled walk back to the only familiar place on the boat, the cabin I'd stayed in. I needed to see myself. I went first to the bathroom and stared. I was a mess, bloodied and charred and bruised. Blood trickled from my head past the dried scrapes. My clothes were shredded in places and covered in blood and explosion residue. I had markings and cuts underneath my clothes.

If anyone had told me a plan, I wouldn't have heard it. There were no flashing lights suggesting I had to evacuate at that moment, and I wasn't exactly going to die for real, should my body die on the boat. So, I slowly stripped off my clothes and entered the still working shower. I ignored the bullet holes and felt the warm water cover me, blood loosening and pouring from my head and body. My wounds were superficial but still hurt like hell. The stinging pain was everywhere and constant, like I'd been raked.

I stayed for such a long time, like I was stuck in a trance. I didn't even consider whether using that much water was selfish. I must surely have a concussion, because I couldn't think straight at all, and the ringing in my ears hadn't stopped. This body was now traumatized and damaged.

I didn't consider the open shower curtain. Something about not seeing my way out felt dangerous, so I'd left it open. When Damon walked through the cabin door and looked around, he saw me clearly, naked and battered, water pouring over me. He stared hard, like he was examining each wound, and could not yet find my face. This time it was he who could not meet my gaze. He'd been responsible for the creation of my current body, and he seemed wrapped up in the realization of how much it had just suffered, because of my curiosity.

The longer he looked, the angrier he got.

I wanted to see his remorse too, his desire if possible, and his eyes connecting to mine. This time his eyes were blue, the safety of his clone self, staring at the ruin of mine.

Damon walked toward me slowly and when he got close, he put his hand out. His brow furrowed and he looked as if he wanted to speak but couldn't find the words. When his fingertips reached the water, he pulled back as if the water was fire, so I followed his retreating hand out of the shower, pushing the water handle down to stop the flow. He backed up as I walked toward him, closing the cabin door as he moved away.

"Why did you make this body, if you don't want me?" I asked, water dripping from my naked form onto the carpeted floor.

And then he snapped and started chastising me. "You're here to help these children! Not to stand out on the deck without protective gear and destroy the body that's here to help the real victims. I made your avatars," he said less loudly, "to help you survive, not put yourself in harm's way!"

He may have wanted me to explain myself, but he didn't get to be the only person who wanted to escape suffering.

"My pain is real right now," I said. "Maybe it's not as bad as yours, but I do need comfort," I said, softly, rephrasing Father Jerzy's sentiment.

Damon looked around the room and grabbed something and

handed it to me. Then he took it back, turned me around and put it on me. It was a robe, a lightweight robe that actually became see-through as it absorbed all the water off me. It was even more seductive than my naked form.

I took a deep breath and thought of my options. Jealousy had been one trigger that seemed to work.

"If you won't touch me, am I allowed to seek comfort from others?" I asked, afraid of what he might say, or not say.

"Like whom?"

The ringing in my ears made it hard to hear him, so I shook my head and rubbed my ear.

"Huh?"

"Who will you seek comfort from?" he said loudly, getting closer.

"Father Jerzy, at least?" I asked, hoping the suggestion would be seen as an innocent attempt at a need for reassurance.

"What kind of comfort?" he asked, confused, a growing upset brewing.

"I had meant hugs, maybe handholding, helping me feel safe, comforted," I said, my voice becoming frustrated, and unsure of which words would express my loneliness.

He threw up his hands. "Get dressed and do what you want," he said, heading for the door.

I stood in his way. "Maybe I'll just go like this, and he can help me," I said, bravely, and indignantly.

He grabbed my wrist and pulled me toward him, and I winced from the pain of bruises already marked, so he let go.

"I don't know what to do," he finally admitted, huffing, and sitting down on the bed.

It was more surrender than he'd given me in so long. I walked back into the bathroom and found the first aid kit and handed it to him.

"Dress my wounds?" I asked, exhausted, my voice shaky and weak, as I climbed onto the bed, my bathrobe already absorbing some blood.

Damon went to work on the back of me, and by the time he was done with all the scrapes on my backside, and I was turning over, the tears were pouring down my cheeks.

"Look," Damon said, trying not to look at me, "I was harsh the last time we saw each other."

Ignoring his non-apology, I started to blubber, "I can't imagine what living like this all the time must do to all of you. I've never experienced war."

"This is nothing."

"It's not nothing," I said harshly, "at all."

"It's an event, in a long line of events, where life and death are on the line," he mumbled. "It was just a blur," he lingered, "before."

I took a deep breath and sighed. "Before me?" I didn't let him answer. "So, it's different now?"

"Of course," he replied, placing another band aid. "I didn't, I wasn't," he stumbled, "needed by anyone before."

"Oh," I understood the implication. It was easier for him to live in war, in horror, when nobody showed up to ask for anything else from him. "Sorry."

"No, no, I just forgot what it was like, what we were like. I'm in the clown world now, playing my part. You're not the same, but you are still a woman, and those needs are pretty universal," he said, sounding disappointed. "It was a long time ago."

"This is the most normal you've ever been with me," I replied, because it was almost odd, after what I'd started getting used to.

He looked at me for a moment and analyzed my face, as his grimace grew, "It's easy like this. You've witnessed carnage now, you're battered and bruised, and you have no idea how safe we are or what is happening next. So, the last thing you're going to do is attempt to communicate with me that I need to share something with you that I don't want to revisit."

My jaw dropped, and my expression changed to one of disbelief that he could be analyzing how easy it was to avoid our last confrontation, or what created it.

"I didn't realize I made you that uncomfortable," I finally said, after a prolonged attempt to cool my frustration down.

He cleared his throat. "I'd rather stand in front of an army looking to kill me, than have any conversation where you ask me about the horrors of the past."

He'd been carefully rearranging my robe as he covered my scrapes with bandages when I decided to move away from him. What could I possibly say to someone who would rather die than share the horrible truth with me?

Lying sideways, I moved closer to the head of the bed and turned toward him. He moved closer to me and continued working on my leg wounds. When he finally finished I couldn't move and the scowl forming on my face told me I wasn't okay, to be told to just keep focusing forward, without examining everything that happened.

I'd already lost so much information about who I was, and now Damon wanted me to forget about who we were and what we'd been through, while simultaneously showing me our past. Sure, my feelings were hurt, but more than anything a moroseness fell over me. Was us talking about what I'd just been through, also considered off-limits? I was retreating again, back into myself, just like Damon.

I sighed slowly and then began to wonder why Damon would waste his precious time on me anyway.

"How soon until we die?" I asked, wondering if I was right.

Damon cocked his head to the side and looked at me strangely. Then he put his finger to his neck, activating something unseen beneath the tactical clothing.

"Auto here. How long before we uncouple?" Damon asked, then listened.

"We're ten minutes out," Damon repeated to me.

"What did you call yourself?" I whispered. "I've heard you say that before."

"Autolycus is my code name. Auto for short."

"Whose idea was that?" I wondered.

"Eamon. He taught us a lot, long before I joined the military. We all got code names from the Gods of old. Autolycus was the master of thievery in Greek mythology."

I nodded, realizing the use of real names across the airways would be unwise.

Damon looked at me from several angles, "What makes you think we're going to die?"

"Aren't we?" I asked, even more sure of my sense of it.

"The boat that attacked us was a pirate ship," he said.

"It was huge, though. So many weapons," I interjected.

"What's worth that kind of gunfight?" he asked me.

"All we have here are children and people."

"And a state-of-the-art ship. Slavery is a profitable trade. A doctor is worth a lot. So are children. So are women."

"Will there be others?" I asked.

"Possibly. Malik says a satellite is tracking us, ever since the explosions. The only way to find out which organization put the satellite into the sky is to send our own up after it."

"How?"

"We unloaded one out of the submarine. It's small, and untraceable. There's a good chance whoever it is tracking us can send another vessel, or worse."

"Worse?"

"A missile, or military grade munitions. The response we get, after we launch, will tell us who we're dealing with."

"And us dying?"

"If we plan for it, then it isn't a surprise. The sub will head north, and we will go south, after they deep dive."

I realized there wasn't much time left before everything would shift again, and Damon would be needed, so I got up and quietly got dressed and pulled back my wet hair. He led me out of the room and up to the bridge. Eamon was standing at the helm. Everyone there looked familiar again, except there were added faces I hadn't seen in some time.

Tombo was at one set of controls. Joseph was at another. And two other familiar soldiers as well as those who survived the battle on the back deck. All I'd heard were codenames though. Their silent nods told me everyone knew their plan. Caitir arrived with gear for us. It was like an LED vest, with aqua colored lights pulsing up and down over us. Everyone was wearing them.

"It's a DNA scrambler," Caitir said quietly. "If the satellite tracking us is extra smart, it will try to read our x-rays, DNA, temperature, and listen in. We have shielding on the boat, but it's best to double up. If there's smart tech watching us, we want it to read what we tell it, so when our bodies die, they think it's someone else."

I sighed, my body twinging, my ears ringing, my eyes feeling tired.

Damon took my hand. "It'll be over soon," he whispered into my ear. "Don't be afraid."

Rosie was sitting at the console, and she began the countdown for the submarine to disengage from the ship, to dive deep into the ocean, under cover of the boat.

"How long before they can turn?" I asked in a whisper.

"Start the launch countdown!" Eamon commanded. Everyone put on glasses, and Damon handed me a pair.

I realized the small satellite launchpad had been attached to the front deck, the one area of the ship undamaged. It took ten seconds and then the rocket lit up and a blast wave of heat and searing light poured into the bridge.

Eamon started barking orders and the ship abruptly turned south and started a mad dash for southern seas.

"Caitir, how's the launch looking?"

"She's passed into the geostationary orbit. She's found her target, and is redirecting her route," Caitir gave the play-by-play. "She's minutes out. No current countermeasures detected."

"Why are we going so fast?" I asked Damon.

"The only way to infiltrate the kind of satellite we think is tracking us is to physically invade it. If it has countermeasures, or alarms that can't be bypassed, the next best option is to blast it out of the sky and be the first to pick it up," Damon replied.

"Since the moment it detects trouble, it will send out a homing signal," Eamon explained.

We all held on as Eamon made the dash to reach the best trajectory.

"Your robot satellite can't just reprogram it?" I asked.

"It's not that sophisticated," Caitir said.

"She's a smash and grab model," Tombo chuckled under his breath.

"She's been programmed to explode the satellite out of orbit," Rosie said.

"And send it in our direction," Damon added.

"We've got the best shot at retrieval," Eamon stated.

I moved closer to the front, and wondered if there would be an actual view, as the sun was finally going down.

"She's made contact," Caitir called out, as the transmission relayed the instructions it was completing, and the sound of impact. "No counter measures. She's breaching the hull. Triggered an alarm. Removing enemy homing device, inserting allied tracker, and repositioning the trajectory. Propulsion explosion planted. Robot Satellite evacuation. Explosion in five, four, three, two, one."

Damon was by my side as we watched through the window, a spark in the sky lit up and something shiny started to fall. It wouldn't take us long to arrive.

Then a terrible alarm blared, and a loud pounding sound started boinging back.

"Torpedo detected!" Rosie yelled out. "Sonar contact, it's a submarine."

"From a decommissioned class," Tombo said, earmuffs on his ears.

The sonar pinged heavily.

"Thirty seconds until impact!" Rosie said.

"Deploy countermeasures."

"Deploying countermeasures."

"Okay! This is what we planned for," Eamon called out. "Everyone, take your positions."

Before I could even consider what my position should be, or what they'd planned for, Damon grabbed my hand and walked me out the side door and down a ladder to the deck. He stopped at the bottom then turned around to face me, as I stood on the rung above him. Our height difference had been remedied, and he wrapped his arms around me, one hand on my back pulling me toward him, the other at my neck and jaw.

"Are the children safe?" I asked in a panic, making double sure.

"They're long gone."

"And the other sub?"

"Didn't get here in time to track it."

I sighed, relieved they made it out safely.

The DNA scramblers were bulky between us, as his lips hovered over mine. The sonar pinging grew louder and faster, and when Damon finally kissed me, because he couldn't take it any longer, I returned his longing with eagerness and softness. My hands found his face, then they were wrapped around his neck, pulling him closer and holding him tightly.

The collision alarm sounded, and I knew we only had moments before the impact, before the explosions on our vessel coincided with the torpedoes to make sure the evidence was all gone.

He didn't stop kissing me or holding me tightly. I felt a brief moment of pain before a bright light turned my consciousness into nothingness.

15

THE STRŎNGMAN BOX

Coughing inside a clear shell, I woke up naked and cold, as liquid poured off me down a drain beneath my feet. It was obvious I was inside a cloning pod. It sat at an angle with an opening for me to get out, and my body was semi-upright so I could see around me, but the lights were blinding.

Breathing felt labored, my lungs were exhausted from the effort of each breath, and my eyes were sore at every attempt to focus. The bright lights suddenly dimmed, and the pressure in my head softened, so I started looking around. Everything was slightly blurred.

There were other cloning pods beside mine, lined up in a row to the right and left of me. These sealed pods, that started upright, were expressing liquid too, then opening up at differing angles. The way the pods came alive and moved made it feel as if the technology had been designed to spark to life the moment our consciousness connected in.

The pods were perfectly positioned to allow for slow movement, air, and a way out, all on our own. Across from the row of pods was a stark stone wall with shower heads, curtains, stacked towels, soap, and hanging robes dispersed between them.

My muscles weren't coming to life fast enough, so I began to crawl my way out, shivering from the cold. Everyone was in the same situation, none of us were able to help one another. We were each focused on reaching the warmth of a hot shower that was suddenly flowing from the wall on its own.

As I crawled, and my eyes started to focus, I could see that I had pale blonde hair again, just like I had on the boat. As my body was fresh from a pod, there were no scars, no leftover pain. I was amazed how they could change my original blonde to a Scandinavian blonde, something several shades lighter. I had wondered a lot about Damon's choice of appearance for me.

When I reached the shower, I lay there under the hot water meant for me and allowed my shaking body to absorb the heat for some time. Eventually the coolness of the floor interrupted the full experience, and I wanted to stand up. There was a vertical handrail nearby to use to pull myself up, and when I was able, I stood and reached for the shower curtain handle and closed it around me.

It was the kind of curtain used in hospitals, where you could throw it away from yourself and it would glide around in a u-shape, giving complete privacy. By the time the curtain reached the other side, I started to feel steady on my feet.

Collectively we could all hear each other sigh into the warmth, into the safety there. I peeked out of the curtain and noticed Calder standing on the other side of a glass wall, behind the pods, watching all of us while drinking from a mug. He nodded at me, in the acknowledgment that we must somehow understand each other better since our last encounter. I could feel my own sternness looking at him and remembering how I'd last seen him, his own body dying from shielding mine, dying in my arms. I was glad he was okay, that we all were.

As the showers started turning off one-by-one, I found the courage to do the same. I took my time drying my body. No one spoke, but hums and grunts, and sighs could be heard. The towels were soft, and the slippers and robe fit well enough. The cashmere robe was hooded and ankle-length. The cloth was like a thick, warm hug. Something deeply comforting existed in the choice of wellness items we were using.

I pulled back my curtain. That's when we all started looking at each other, each arousing person making eye contact with the others, and I was included. Soldiers I'd only started to see and recognize were burned into my vision now. These were now distinct faces to include in my worries and thoughts. We stepped toward Calder together, the two other women in this circle, gravitating toward me, as I was held between them. Rosie and Caitir and I moved into a walking hug, with a leaning and gratitude. They were amazing and I was so grateful they existed as such warriors, showing me my way ahead.

"If you won't be left out of the fight," Rosie said quietly, "you're going to need some training."

"It'll be a nice distraction," I said, wrapping my arm around her some, "when the energy work is too much."

"Then it's settled," Caitir chimed in, "we'll start tomorrow."

"Tonight, we celebrate," Eamon interrupted as we walked down a long corridor, touching my shoulder.

"What are we celebrating?" I asked.

"Samhain," Eamon said in a booming voice. It sounded like a Scottish word which he pronounced "Sow-in."

"What's that?"

"It's the original Halloween," Caitir complained to her father.

"It's more like All Saints Day," Rosie explained.

"That's not why we're celebrating. We're celebrating our survival," Calder said. "The submarine got away safely, and so far everyone aboard is safe."

The muted group of warriors, freshly kindled in new avatars, managed a round of howling over that news.

"Hoorah!"

I felt a startled jolt then relaxed at the joyous voices.

"Once the yacht exploded, no one even looked for the sub," Calder informed.

"They had a huge head start," Damon included.

"Malik verified no one was tracking the sub," Calder confirmed.

"Is he here?" Caitir asked, wondering where her other half was.

"Sis, he's back at base," Calder replied, as Caitir looked sad.

"Where are we?" I wondered.

"The lands of my ancestors," Eamon said. "Welcome to Scotland."

We were underground for sure, and I knew it was quite possible we wouldn't be seeing the beauty of Scotland while there, but knowing we were beneath it somewhere made me feel deeply inside that we were all safer.

"Are we needed to help with the children?" Tombo asked.

"We've got time. Right now, they estimate ten hours. Could be longer. They're taking the long way to avoid detection. We need to get these bodies primed for the coming work and then get back to our real bodies. We've been gone too long."

"So why did we all wake up here if your real bodies need to wake up?" I asked.

"It was simply protocol following a catastrophic event. We don't know what technology can track these anomalies. We assume none yet, since we can't, but it's safer to come here en masse than anywhere near homebase."

"When they arrive, the team will get the children situated, and our first reserves will jump in to give the others a break. We'll add ourselves to the rotating shifts when we get back. Everyone, report to the hospital wing then."

"We'll also be serving a big feast tonight," Rosie chimed in.

"You know the drill," Eamon called out to everyone. "Get your treatments started, then protocol out to home. Check whatever emails and correspondence you need to check, get yourself fed and exercised. We'll meet back here in nine and a half hours."

"...your copied phones are in your rooms in case you need them now, but I would wait to be safe," Caitir chimed in.

Everyone else seemed to know where they were going and walked to specific rooms down a long corridor farther away, placing their hands on scanners, and unlocking their doors. I watched and waited for Damon to arrive, and he did. He stood behind me. We were alone in the corridor.

"Are we sharing a room again?" I asked, intrigued.

"Not here. Not after the encounter we had," Damon replied.

"With your real body?" I asked, wondering if he'd made modifications to this clone too.

"With me, just me," he said morosely. "I'll get you set up."

Damon walked me to my own room, put my hand on the scanner and took me inside. In one corner of the room was a compact human-sized device, that looked like a tanning bed. He opened the top of it and showed me it was meant for my body.

"You get in naked," he said. "Then you press this button twice until it reads 'full body.' When you press start it gives you twenty seconds to get in and pull the cover down. You wear these." He handed me a pair of eye protectors. "It's energizing and draining, but every new clone needs some help getting the system going, so these bodies are running optimally."

"What does it do?" I asked before he could just leave.

"It's an infrared pad for the whole body, and it has low-lever-lasers to energize the atrophied muscles. It takes thirty minutes. You should get started."

Damon left and I got undressed, pressed the button to start, and got in my new little charge-up pod with my eye protection on.

Thirty minutes later I was completely sore and totally wired! All I wanted to do was sleep. There was a knock at the door and before I could even grunt, Caitir walked through.

"Jesus!" I yelped, jumping from the fright, and grabbing something to cover my naked form.

"Sorry! Sorry," she whined. "I just thought I'd bring you some ointment."

She pulled me over to the bed and grabbed a blanket for me to lay on, then grabbed another blanket to cover me. I did as she said and she opened a container of something and started putting it on my muscles, over my whole body. The smell was like menthol and spice, and it started to burn my eyes, which I closed. She didn't massage me for long, just long enough to apply the balm.

"This should help with the soreness."

"What is it?"

"CBD, menthol, clove, camphor, and other stuff. All the heavy hitters."

"How come I've never felt this achy before?"

"We always do the work before you arrive into the bodies. These bodies are straight from the pods and have been waiting to go for a while. You can make the body function by being in it, but if you want peak performance, you have to give the body a workout without even moving. So, we use lasers."

"I think BB had one of those. Is that the same thing?"

"Could be, but we use a whole lot more of them. Get some rest," Caitir said, before bringing something from the closet to wear.

The next thing I knew there was a knock at the door, and I was trying to get up. My body felt so much better, and the burning sting of the menthol was no longer in my eyes.

"MARI," I called out. "Lights on."

The lights turned on and when I looked around, I clearly wasn't in the Georgetown bunker. The thing that struck me the most were the multiple clocks on the wall, in different time zones, and from what I could see at least eight hours had passed, but I'd never gone back to my other body.

Damon had kept my connection to my DC clone severed!

What a jerk! I thought.

They'd all woken up in their real bodies without me. I slept while they worked. I shouldn't be hurt, but I felt left out. How could he kiss me like that on the boat, then leave me here?

I slowly walked to the chair with the outfit, and saw it was something informal, something that looked neutral but pleasant and comfortable, and I got dressed. We would be helping with the children, so the choice seemed wise.

Still another ninety minutes before everyone else got back. The small kitchenette in my room allowed me to make tea, eat some fruit and granola and spend some time alone. After about an hour of that I figured I should learn my way around.

The facility was rather large, with some parts looking very old, some built in stone with other modern areas. My handprint worked on the elevator and gave me access to the stairwells. I meandered down hallways and went up and down floors until I finally reached the brightly lit hospital wing.

When I got there I was so happy to see Father Jerzy and he wrapped me in a hug.

"You're here," he said, shocked. We heard the boat was sunk.

"We made it out," I replied as vaguely as possible, confused how he could know. "Have you had a chance to rest?" I asked, looking at his exhausted face.

"Not yet. I worried about you. I'm glad to see you safe. I wish you'd come with us," he grimaced.

"Did something happen?"

"It wasn't surprising with the pressure changes. We lost a child," he said, and my face was horrified. "The journey was hard on everyone," he tried to explain.

"I'm sorry," I said, backing away just a little. "This has been a hard transition for me."

"She was needed elsewhere," Damon said of me, touching my elbow and scaring me with his silent approach.

"Hello Damon," Father Jerzy said. "I'm surprised to see you here."

I looked at Damon to see what his expression would give away, but he said nothing.

"You aren't usually so brave," he continued, and though it came out sounding kind, it was a remark about Damon's darkness, his aura of scariness, his essence of aggression.

Damon's face tensed but he did not move. "I'm here to ask you to explain the Strŏngman box to Gellion and teach her the technique. Calder says some children aren't healing as projected."

Father Jerzy's face scrunched up, and he seemed to take the comment personally. "The pressure of the sub was hard on them."

"Agreed," Damon said, contritely.

"Well," he replied, patting Damon on the shoulder, "I'm a bit fried. You're the relief crew, so maybe you should teach Gellion. You know everything I know."

And he was right. We had been sent to relieve them, and every single nurse, doctor and crew member had earned their relief. Damon only nodded because what else could he say? Father Jerzy touched me gently on the shoulder before leaving.

"Will we be helping?" I whispered to Damon.

He was looking around the room, trying to feel at ease with all the damage being brought in and couldn't. I didn't know how these amazing people could be so strong. Damon took my hand and pulled me away with him. When we reached the other side of the exit to the hospital Damon stopped and started taking deep breaths, hunching over to calm himself.

"Are you okay?" I asked him, wanting to reach out to him, but knowing better.

Father Jerzy was the only one who challenged Damon's sense of command, or sense of morality. I couldn't be sure what buttons were pushed that had Damon so hunched over and vulnerable. When he caught his breath enough, he took my hand again and walked me somewhere new, somewhere unfamiliar.

Just like the underground base where my original body rests, this place had a library too. It was extremely calming, warm, and beautiful, with a massive collection. I felt transported in time whenever I entered a place that Rosie had spent time curating.

Damon walked to the small serving station where a tea tray sat. He opened a small fridge beneath and pulled out lemon slices and cream then pressed a button to start an electric carafe of water. I watched him by his side, noting where everything was and wondering how many others came here for tea throughout the day. The water took a short time as we stood quietly, then he brought the tray to the chairs near the fireplace and turned it on with a remote.

"Do you come here often?" I asked, sitting in one of the seats.

"Whenever we're all here," he nodded, putting the fireplace remote back on the mantle. "It reminds us of the one in Eamon's castle, somewhere up there."

"What happens when you spend all your time down here, aren't you missed up there?"

Damon ignored my question. His face was stern, as if he were irritated. He pulled the table toward his seat and poured two cups of tea. He sighed loudly, as if the act of preparing tea was grating, then he put honey in mine and added cream, while using lemon in his own. I took a sip, and it was the perfect black tea, just how BB would make it.

I didn't ask him how he knew, how BB made tea for me. Instead, I focused on his choice.

"Why lemon?"

He didn't answer, he only stared at his tea, unable to drink it suddenly.

"What's wrong? You don't know?"

"No, it's just I realized my answer wouldn't sound good."

"How could personal preferences sound bad?"

"There isn't much of a difference today between the price of lemon and cream. In some places in the world, one of those items would be much harder to get than the other, depending on where you are. No matter where we traveled, it was often our obligation to know which options were the most expensive there and choose that one."

"So, it's instinctual?"

"That's possible, but not always true."

"Lemon would be more expensive than cream in Northen Scotland, yes?"

He nodded, "Most likely, especially when I was a child."

His response made me wonder about something.

"What's your preference when you're somewhere the cost is equal?"

He drank his tea without answering, before doubling down on his aristocratic response.

"I don't have one preference over another. Sometimes there aren't any options, except the tea itself, which I've experienced being very grateful for."

"Maybe you can tell me that story sometime," I urged.

Dead silence. I sipped my tea.

Then Damon began to answer my previous question.

"Malik has programmed modified clones that play us at the office if we have to be gone for a long period of time. We call them 'true avatars' because we can technically jump in if we need to be in control of a conversation, but they have a memory chip and a protocol. They stick to a script and run the routines, so we have video evidence."

"Hmm, like NPCs?" I asked referring to video game characters who aren't playable.

"Yes, except much better. Our companies are run by all of us, and are self-sufficient enough, so no one is really watching. The bodies in the different buildings are for when one of us or all of us needs an alibi. We also have paid staff that help run things without getting in our way, as we are often working alone in our offices or in the lab, deep in research and leave our employees to run the day to day on the lower levels."

"That's very clever. So, why do you travel then?"

"When I'm doing my job as the middleman for the Cabal…"

"The Cabal?" I interrupted.

"It's the shortest, easiest name to describe the dark confederation I come from. So, when I'm working for them, I have to be at least a little bit visible. I have to get on planes even if it's not always safe. That's when the offices have to be empty."

"Sounds very complex to manage," I acknowledged.

"We have some good assistants and secretaries that help, and then AI that run the strategies and scheduling before handing out work, so it's not just our clones managing things alone. The stable image helps build a wall of resistance between those who arrive and when they get seen. Lawyers are another layer. In downtown, the lawyer's offices are located in our building. We also have multiple locations," he mumbled.

"Smoke and mirrors," I nodded back, sipping my tea, and listening.

I had so many questions I wanted to ask Damon, and I also wanted to touch him again, and be touched. The fireplace was cozy, and we were fixed there, seated in our comfort, to breathe and meditate with the dancing flames. It was distracting how much closeness Damon was allowing me to have and how present he was when I least expected him to arrive, like when I hugged Father Jerzy.

"Did it bother you that I hugged him?"

"He hugged you," Damon corrected me. "And no, it didn't. It bothers him I do my job the way I do."

"Why?"

"It's one thing to live as an immoral agent against darkness, but to do so and pull others into the danger, he disagrees with that."

I was surprised by Damon's perception of Father Jerzy.

"Does he know I got hurt?"

Damon's face frowned.

"Have you tried talking to him about what happened and how it affected you?"

"I'm not the only one who knew you. I don't have to talk to anyone about it. It's private."

- "It was private, until you brought me with you on your mission and put me on display. I'm humbled to be here, but I'd rather not cause issues with the group of you working so hard to save so many."

"I just mean others have surely clued him in. He knew you'd be there on the boat and would need his help to help them."

"Oh," I said, taking back my assumption of a lack of information.

"He's never said anything to me directly," Damon included.

"Well, you don't really stick around for the hard conversations."

Damon grumbled.

"You didn't pull me into the danger; you just couldn't ever get me out of it. You're not making me stand beside you."

"You're not standing beside me. Why? Because I won't let you, will I?" Damon said it without emotion, and it stung to hear the truth. "But he will, and that's where you belong in all this."

"As an apprentice," I clarified.

Damon gruffed.

"I'm sure he'll be happy to work with me and help me learn, but there is no way to belong with a priest."

"Can we talk about anything else besides Father Jerzy?" Damon sighed.

"You're so evasive," I complained. "Fine. Why are we here?"

"You heard me say there are some children who aren't healing right. Well, there's a technique you discovered. You'd been learning the work practicing on me and Caitir, but it really saved Carmella. She got very sick, so sick she almost died. Repairing her energy systems wasn't enough. You cleared the stored trauma in her body and mind, and she got better."

"Right after the miscarriage? When we took her away?" I asked, shocked.

Damon smirked then chewed on the side of his mouth and shook his head.

"Sneaky Vasily," he huffed.

"Was I not supposed to see that video?"

"No," he said, still shaking his head.

"I'd like to talk about it," I continued.

"I'd like us to focus on the technique."

I rolled my eyes and sighed out in frustration.

Back to business, back to the agenda, which couldn't be argued with. Damon was right about one thing, none of our feelings mattered, until all the children were healed enough to take the next step in their recovery journey. Yet being brushed aside, because it was too hard for him to examine, was getting old.

My eyebrows had taken a permanent scowl.

"Please, Gellion, it's important."

Another technique to learn? I whined inside my head.

"Okay, fine. Personal relationships aside. Explain it, and I'll do my best to learn it." Then I was confused. "Wait, what about Father Jerzy? Can't he do the work?"

"He never could," Damon shook his head. "He knows how the technique works, understands the energy of it, but can't seem to capture the method. His version of the work doesn't quite clear all the damage."

"Maybe he has it too," I mumbled.

"We found someone who could do it, a healer in South America, but he was very old and passed away last year."

"Couldn't you teach it to someone else?"

"And involve them in this? I don't think so. There's not a lot of people we can trust. Our soldiers are warriors, not healers. Our doctors and nurses and therapists can't remove evil from the body of a traumatized child."

"Okay, I get it."

"You don't, Gellion. You're trying, but you really don't get how frustrating it is to see you be such a coward," he said, disgusted. "Not when you used to be fearless."

"Whose fault is it that I'm like this?" I asked, wondering about his anger, wondering about his involvement. "Weren't you driving the car?"

"Snap out of it! This isn't about you!"

I stood up and walked to the fire. I was shaking inside, then found myself sitting in front of it, crossing my legs, which was wonderful to be able to do after so many years of pain. I felt the warmth and closed my eyes and started taking some deep breaths. Damon wasn't available for my wants, like he said, until I could be more like who I was.

What if by the time I finally get back to being his Gellion, I didn't want him anymore? His brutish demeanor was so difficult.

"Will I be learning from myself, in another video?" I finally asked.

"Malik made an animation to help you understand it easier. You were always a visual learner."

"Where's the screen?" I sighed, resigned to his demands.

Damon picked up the remote on the mantle above me and pressed a button. The artificial windows above the mantle turned into a movie screen. I stood up and backed away, into the chair I'd been sitting in.

"Evil is a vicious cycle that only begets more evil," Damon's voice began over a video animation.

I looked at Damon, recognizing his effort in the video was for me, to hear him. The video showed a cartoon of a small child with a shadow, now two, now three, no, more, so many more shadows, all hurting the silhouette child. When the shadow was done moving against the child, it became a balloon, floating above the child.

The number of shadow balloons grew so large and prominent, all attached to the child, following the child. Upon further examination it was clear the shadows all held a piece of the child. The child's mind, the child's childhood and innocence, and the child's body, all stuck inside the balloons with the shadows.

"When evil happens, a construct is made, like a balloon but more solid," Damon's voice said.

Suddenly the balloons turned into the shapes of boxes, where each different shadow had its own balloon-box to sit inside. The constructs were anchored to the child, tied tightly with a string, and as the image zoomed in, it was clear a copy of the child was stuck inside too. Every balloon-box with a bad guy shared space with a broken and petrified piece of child, permanently damaged by the harm.

"The box represents the trauma, and the trauma disassociates the person from themselves, creating a frozen piece, forever stuck in time, forever victimized. The more horrible the abuse or the more boxes created, the more the mind disassociates. If the system never heals or reassociates, sickness can enter more powerfully and bring death, or the sickness can be played out upon the next generation."

The animation showed the abused child never healing, and growing up mentally ill, broken and disconnected, their mind separated from themselves, unable to remember.

"This box can be healed," Damon's voice said. As he spoke, the visual of the steps for healing played out in the movie. "The box must be identified and brought forward. The curse of the trauma must be removed from the child and offender. Trauma, Karma, darkness, evil, pain, torment, suffering, helplessness, horror, victimization, abuse, fear, and any other encoding must be removed from the box, from the child, and the space filled with light.

"When all darkness is cleared from the child, they can be removed from the box, reassociated, and made whole again. Find the boxes, clear them, reassociate the mind, sever all ties, and then the perpetrator is left with what they did and no power over their victim anymore."

It was a short film, but it was poignant, and yet the concept felt too large to fully understand. My mind wanted to discard so much of it as too much. The visuals played over and over of what Damon perceived that a healer would see, should see, or maybe how I said I saw it long ago.

"That was very insightful," I said, impressed by how quickly the idea was presented.

"Have you been practicing your muscle testing?" Damon asked in return.

"Yes, I ask myself questions all the time when no one is looking, like you told me to do."

"Caitir's seen you working on it. Do you have any confidence yet that the answers aren't your opinion?"

"No," I said, hanging my head.

I still didn't understand how he expected my hands, pulling against each other for the answers, would help me know for sure if something was positive or negative, a yes or no. How could I tell if what I was doing was from my higher self, my lower self, or from the Divine directly?

"I don't trust it yet."

"Yet. Maybe the problem is we haven't given you enough to start the questions."

"I'd rather do it in the Q-Spec. Feels like it would be more accurate there."

Damon tilted his head a bit and tapped his finger to his bottom lip.

"We don't have one of those here. It also won't help you when you're working directly with children. Asking you to intuit information for yourself is one thing, asking you to do it on behalf of others will change how you work, maybe help you learn faster. If it isn't personal, then you can get out of your own way easier, so to speak."

I shrugged, unaware how I could get better at something that was foreign despite knowing BB had used the applied kinesiology technique to test my body for misalignments before treatment. It also seemed wacky to me when considering it as a channeling tool, especially through my confused system. How would "yes" and "no" answers help me repair so much damage?

Just then the doors opened, and Carmella walked in, a roller tray with file folders stacked on top. I was closest to her and stood, not realizing until after I'd done so it was because I was nervous to see Damon's expression toward her.

"Hi Carmella. What's this?" I asked, as nonchalantly as I could.

She smiled at me and then made eye-contact with Damon.

"I brought the files you asked for," she said to him. "Is there anything else I can get you?" Her expression was very submissive. "For either of you?" she asked, remembering me.

"Are these the children's files?" I asked.

"Yes. A full medical write-up of what we've done and any information we've been able to gather."

"Can I get some paper and a pen?" I asked, unsure if she meant her offer. "Or can I get that in here?" I added because I hadn't gotten a response yet.

"I think we have that in here," Damon said. "Thank you, Carmella. We'll see you at dinner."

He was dismissing her and her face responded in the strangest way, one of respect but maybe disappointment too. I smiled meekly at her as she left. I wanted to ask if they'd been intimate because it was all that was filling my thoughts. I felt embarrassment swell in me, my face blushing against my will, because their energy was intense and almost alarming. I didn't know how to ask without showing my own vulnerability. Currently, I wanted to run away.

My body moved for me, toward the exit. The doors to the library closed and Carmella was already gone, but my feet kept moving. When I reached for the handle, Damon's hand was already on the door, holding it shut.

"Is there something you want to ask me?" He spoke into my ear.

"Not really," I replied, unable to move, because I didn't want to ask him, I wanted to ask her. I saw so much longing in her eyes.

He took my arm and pulled it toward him, turning me around.

"Ask me what you want to know."

"She wants you," I said. I could only muster the courage to speak facts.

"She wants to be desired, that's all."

"Was she? Desired by you?"

"She doesn't really know who I am," he said, dropping my arm from his grasp.

"I don't either," I reminded him. "Did you desire her?"

He shrugged and backed away. "Most of the time I'm a good guy trying to save people. To everyone working with the children, even to Father Jerzy, that's who I am."

"And Carmella?"

"I'm a good guy to her too."

"You're her savior. I saw the video, remember?"

"You're the one who saved her. You wouldn't have let me abandon her even if that was my instinct."

"It didn't look like you were reluctant in the video."

"We'd already discussed it before we arrived, not to leave the tied-up girl there. You made it clear if I could be brave enough to make you do the energy work, I should be brave enough to help the innocent victim."

"Would you really have left her?"

"Yes. Being seen with her by the wrong people could have gotten us killed that night."

"Does she know that?"

"On some level, I'm sure."

"Are you going to answer the other question?" I asked, my stomach growing tighter from the torment growing in me. I'd never experienced the rising level of jealousy I felt.

"I don't want to talk about Carmella. She's not important. She's not in the bunker."

My brow scrunched up, realizing he had a point. Our real bodies were somewhere else. I was in the bunker with them, and currently in a cloned body, keeping me safe from death. Carmella had been in real danger on that boat and in that submarine. He hadn't kept her or any of the rest of them safe from death, just me, his kin, and his soldiers.

"So, they don't know about the cloning?"

"Of course not," he said, his eyes dropping to my hands, his hand taking mine and pulling me with him back into the library, to our lukewarm tea. "And they will stay in the dark on that. It's not their portion of the mission. They aren't built to live two lives."

"Is anyone?" I asked. "Don't you think I should know what not to say? Like when Father Jerzy said they'd heard the boat sank, I didn't know what to say because you keep forgetting to tell me what the story is for everyone else. What if I'd started talking about waking up in a clone to the rest of them? Hello?"

He blinked, surprised and shocked by the realization.

"Oh! Yeah, good point, actually. Please don't say anything about anything until Caitir and Rosie have gone over the separation of the groups. My bad."

"'My bad'?" I huffed, ready to punch him. "How come they don't know?"

"This is a choice my family and comrades are making. It's about proficiency, safety, and protection, in a never sleeping AI environment. We copy ourselves so we're double, and triple protected as we dedicate everything to this mission."

"Why doesn't that include Carmella?"

"For a lot of reasons. Carmella's history, for one. She doesn't need that level of protection, two. It's costly, three. It's confusing, four. And while I could go on and on, the biggest factor is that some people just can't handle never getting a break from the living world."

I took a deep breath. He'd expanded his thinking for me on the logistics of his inner world, and they were all things I hadn't thought about at all. I knew I should have been more impressed, but I was too emotional. Too overwhelmed to really understand that the Carmella I was seeing now was still partially that severely abused girl we helped.

"Yes, yes. But why does she look at you like she's undressing your body?" I asked, incredulously. "I'm supposed to see all of her trauma over my own fear, over my own insecurities?"

Damon's eyes grew wide then he looked up, like he was looking away to his memories.

"One of my favorite things about you when we were young, was how devastated you were for me, for all the abuse I suffered, because all you had known was love. Your life and experiences didn't trigger my trauma or suffocate me or fight with me over my truth. When I was around others traumatized like me, we became ugly and unkind as if just being in the presence of each other reignited a standard operating system from our time in Hell."

"Well yeah, consciously or unconsciously," I understood, "you rightly assumed someone was watching you, expecting you to be your worst, or you'd be punished." I said, unaware of where that thought came from, but it became clearer. "BB used to say that the God she grew up with was a mean God, a God who punished too harshly. It was even worse for you. Your God was all darkness, so if you even thought to be kind, you had to fear punishment."

"I didn't have to be unkind with you, and you wouldn't accept it if I tried," he said, his back turned to me, collecting warmth by the fireplace. "Carmella, on the other hand, would be someone who let me, no wanted me to play out my own trauma on her. She'd encourage and embrace the fiend within, then tell me I'm justified being the monster, then protect the monster all to be special, when she'd only be special to the demon inside."

Did he really just say that?

269

My mouth dropped open from the nausea I was feeling at his words.

Is he admitting to the intimacy? To harm within the intimacy?

Was he saying it was consensually abusive? My shock turned to a horrified tremble in upset and devastation.

"Is that what she wants from you?" I felt deeply disturbed by his measure of her, or the still-possible connection between them. "Is that what she got from you?"

"She doesn't know how bad it would be, what my programming was. She doesn't know how evil I've been, or what I've become in my mission to save these children. She doesn't know what she would be unleashing, and I can't trust her to keep me in the light."

"Wait, what?" I asked, confused if he was now denying the intimacy. "Just tell me!"

"I can't."

"So that's it? Not, 'she's black haired, and that's not my type'? Not, 'she's too serious, or crazy, or damaged'? Not, 'I haven't been able to think of anyone but you, Gellion'?" I started to rant. "Or she's 'dull, boring, too submissive, too high maintenance.' None of those? How about 'not pretty enough?' Huh?"

I was so hot inside over his version of events, over his ideas about life, that I was about to scream at him. He was only making me feel less wanted because I wasn't "light Gellion" anymore either, so in my current standing, I wasn't a single measure higher or even on par with Carmella.

"I would only be lying if I said those things to you."

"So, then, it's pretty obvious how you know those things about her, about her unresolved trauma, that I clearly didn't fix, or the way she would treat you as a lover."

He didn't respond.

"So, say it."

It was cruel and stupid of me to judge his relationships before I arrived back in his life, but I couldn't help it. Everyone had told me about Damon's love for me, obsession with me, making it seem so special. So, despite his very real flaws, I found myself angry to discover he was no different from any other man, who met his physical needs over the emotional and intellectual ones, with whoever was available.

While. I. Suffered.

I knew what I was doing was childish but figuring out I wasn't actually as special as I was told, stung deeper than I'd ever experienced. It hit like a poisoned dart to my chest.

"Come on Damon, you have no problem being cruel or pushing me away. Why not just do that appropriately? Here's your chance to create all the space you could possibly want from me."

"It's just a distraction from what you need to be focused on," he tried to say.

"If you didn't want me distracted with this petty drama, why did you ask her for the files and not someone else? It's clear how she looks at you, so why would my awareness be any different from the rest of the group? I think you're being purposefully cruel to me while pretending it's not premeditated."

Damon's eyebrows went up. Did my words surprise him? Did they bring a sort of understanding to his mind, that even he didn't comprehend.

"Stop punishing me for your choices," I continued.

"Maybe you're right, maybe I did this unconsciously on purpose. I don't have any interest in Carmella. I do have interest in you, but mostly for your gifts as a healer."

"Not my friendship or camaraderie?" He didn't answer. "Why the hell do you keep kissing me then?" I screamed.

"Watching children die has changed me," was the strangest answer he could give me. I just stared at him in confusion.

"Finding out about you has changed me, but I'm not trying to punish you for existing in this nightmare. So please just say it and allow it to create the space you want from me."

"I don't want to create more space."

"How long were you intimate with Carmella?" I stared at him, but he didn't answer, so I used his own words against him. "I think it's disgusting how much of a coward you are."

I got up and left. Meandering back to my bedroom, I neglected to pay attention to my route and rounded a corner where I saw Carmella in the hallway. I quickly backed up behind a wall, hoping she didn't notice me.

Shit! I said internally.

I no longer wanted answers from her. I knew I couldn't muster the strength for any more emotional pain.

"I thought you were going to get some sleep," I heard a familiar Scottish voice say in a whisper.

"I've been so worried about you," Carmella replied. "What happened?"

"They're going to miss me in the..." before she would let him finish, I could hear she was kissing him.

I peeked around the corner and saw Calder returning the kiss as Carmella put her hand on her own locked door and pulled Calder inside with her. Not that it was any of my business, but suddenly Damon's words about Carmella's trauma came back to me. She was so terribly abused as a child; it would make sense for her to seek love and attention from any and every man who would give it. In fairness, Calder was very suitable.

How odd of Carmella to be looking at Damon with seductress eyes while having a relationship with Calder. Maybe the behavior in the library was about Carmella after all, her need to be seen, to mark her territory, or relay that information. I'd seen women act that way toward Katherine, relishing the drama they stirred, but it'd never happened to me.

Well, Carmella succeeded. I had no way of knowing when she and Damon stopped being intimate, or when she started with Calder, and getting that information from someone determined to push me away was no good. At least I knew, no matter how she looked at Damon, she was being looked after. I wasn't ever going to be good at seduction games, which I'd no clue how to play anyway.

It was so distracting having desires for the first time. If I started focusing on the real mission, exactly as Damon wanted, maybe everything else really would fall into place. If I couldn't try harder for suffering children then I wasn't ever going to be someone who belonged to this group of people. If I failed to deliver, fine, but choosing not to try to help, over a flirtation, was downright juvenile.

I immediately felt ashamed of my outburst against Damon, and grateful to have stumbled upon them kissing in the hall. Had I not just seen that reason to let go of so much jealousy, it might have taken me much longer to refocus my spiraling thoughts. Damon was gone when I returned to the library, so I found a pad of paper and a pen and began looking at the files of the enduring children.

16

NO WAY OUT

Caitir arrived in the library sometime later, to tell me the dinner celebration was about to start. I didn't want to go. I'd been asking myself yes-or-no questions for a while and still felt completely lost. The animated video played on repeat and my written notes on the theory of the Strŏngman box were all over the table, but I couldn't get answers that were consistent.

"Aren't you hungry?"

"I really don't want to be around anyone right now," I said morosely.

"Anyone, or someone in particular?"

I sighed. "I'm barely able to connect with him and then I have to contend with the weirdness of..." I wanted to say past lovers, but I couldn't. "...complicated people," I finally decided to say.

She gave me this sad grin, "You know, this is such a hard and complicated life. It's scary, and lonely. Like, I really miss Malik right now, but we both agreed to this going in. We decided mutually to take this path, so we could stay alive and be together. You've been thrown into this, and the only thing keeping you sane is a promise of love from a broken man."

"He says he can't even think of me that way until I'm back to being who I was," I trailed off, "…which is just so impossible. Even with the extra hours alive, it's like there's never enough time."

"Tell me about it," she commiserated.

"It's gonna take me so much more time to figure this out than he expects," I replied glumly. "Are the children really going to die, if I don't get this right?"

"He told you that?" Caitir slackened.

I nodded my head, my brow scrunched with worry.

"Damon is such an asshole!" She chided to the air. "Gellion, that's not right. This is not on you to fix. These children were abused before we intercepted them, and many of them would not have made it regardless."

"I could see that on the ship. Oh God, Caitir, my heart has been breaking since I met you all, and it just keeps getting harder. Is it always like this?"

"Sometimes worse. It's so rare that we get a group of kids before they're hurt; we try. Many of the ones that end up where we make the handoff were on their way to annihilation."

"Wait, you buy them?"

"We procure their freedom any way we can. It's actually more effective to buy them as a part of the trafficking food chain, so we don't cause suspicion. In order to justify the buying, we also have to sell, so we sell clones. Knowing they're worth a lot of money to us keeps the real children safer from wherever they're coming from. We pay 'top dollar' for every child we receive, and we pay less for the ones malnourished or close to death.

"It's been that way long enough that handlers who know us tend to treat them better. Amazing how the normal scale for these men is severe starvation and abuse, until you pay more for better treatment. A child can only take so much before their body collapses. If our reputation proceeds us on their behalf, it's better."

I had to absorb it, the psychology of that level of power through money. While I found their dedication admirable, it wasn't enough.

"But you're only saving children, you're not even punishing these sick fucks," I trembled, starting to feel the anger swell in me.

"Well, that's not actually true," Caitir said softly, with a coyness in her voice.

I sniffled and sharpened my attention. "Really?"

"I mean, come on, we can't let them all live."

Suddenly I was leaning toward her, wiping my angry tears and pulling myself together, conspiring with them in their death dealings.

"How do they die?" I asked, so grateful for bittersweet revenge.

She started chuckling.

"Well, it's multilayered. Our soldiers go after low-level kidnappers individually. The more organized ones are different and require longer-term operations. Then there are the customers. The clones we delivery are perfect and seen as the best crop. Ours can't be the cause of any problems for The Cabal but we never provide enough for the scale needed. Damon does that on purpose, and that's where the real mission comes in.

"There are always local sources to supplement the total shipment. We have to steal the DNA of the children from the local traffickers and swap out the kids immediately before delivery. That way the traffickers are on the hook for any diseases or contagion. We implant poison into a portion of the cloned victims. Once the rapist makes contact, the poison is released, and the other traffickers are blamed."

"What poison?"

"It's always different. Damon's a genius," she shrugged, with a brazen giggle. "He uses various maladies from the region where the children are taken. Only one power player will get hit right away, always with something that terrifies all of them. Then each death beyond that is more plotted out and horrible than the one before. We make sure the deaths are staggered, so months go by before the sickness is detected, until it's too late.

"I particularly appreciated it when he used the parasite that travels

276

up the urethra. Rabies is also super brutal and hard to trace back right away. And turbo cancers easily go unsuspected."

My jaw dropped, and my eyes were alight with some sort of magical feeling inside. I shook my head as she spoke but couldn't form a smile on my face.

"Gellion," Caitir said, reaching her hand out to me in concern. "They really do deserve to die."

I laughed, and she jumped.

"Of course they do! I just didn't realize how much I needed to hear these men were being punished."

She laughed too, but tears were streaming down our faces.

"Well, not nearly enough," she shrugged.

"How many?" I wanted to know.

"Have we killed?" She asked and I nodded. "Also, not enough."

We both concurred at that sentiment.

"So, will you come to dinner now that you know we're killing bad guys?"

I chuckled and sniffled, trying to stop the sadness.

"We might be in clone bodies, but they still need to eat," she reminded me. I hadn't yet had anything in this body but fruit and granola and was feeling the weakness.

"Sure," I finally agreed.

The Scottish dining room was not like the bunker. It was a large dining hall, beautiful and majestic, if simple. The walls were made of stone and felt like an old castle. Even the arrangement of thick wood tables felt like something from hundreds of years ago, designed for many. One large and long table sat several steps up and away from the rest, on its own small peak, to be seen easier and to see.

There were no chairs on the inside-facing side, but there were eight highbacked chairs along the outside. The large and majestic table was empty and at the end of it on each wall was a large fireplace. Down the steps were two long tables with benches on both sides that sat diagonally, making the large room look like the three tables were a triangle. There were windows, with light streaming in and yet I knew they couldn't be real. It felt real. It felt almost as if everyone there were celebrating in the real world, on the topside in a Scottish castle.

The lower tables, with their informal benches were almost full, and there were many faces I didn't recognize. I hadn't yet seen Damon's face in the crowd. Everyone there was totally quiet, standing up and facing away, their heads bowed, and their glasses raised up. As we stepped inside, the rich smell of succulent food was thick in the air, the tables adorned with place settings and serving dishes.

In the center of the triangle Eamon stood with his glass held high, his head bent. He was finishing a prayer and then started to speak in Gaelic before he began to sing, and everyone in the room, holding a glass, heads bowed, was singing with him. Caitir squeezed me sideways, as we had stopped just inside the door, and she sang too. It was beautiful and I didn't understand a word.

At the end, there were no cheers, just a quiet "Amen."

It was a short and solemn song, and I'm sure it spoke of loss, and possibly redemption. No one moved, except to take a small sip of the wine within their metal goblets.

"Everyone, before we begin, we would like to introduce you to our newest member. Gellion," he called out to me. I reluctantly joined him in the center of the triangle.

Rosie walked up from behind him with a glass for me. I took it and stood next to Eamon, who was wrapping his arm around me. "She's here to apprentice with Father Jerzy. She's tiny, but mighty," he said, smiling at me, while I tried not to blush. "Please make her feel at home."

"A toast!" Calder called out. "To our new friend," he said, nodding to me. "To our wins, to the losses in our heart, and to our brethren who've all returned safely," Calder rang out in the room with his big Scottish voice.

Everyone lifted their glasses and called out, "Slainte mhath!" which sounded like "Slanj-a-va!"

I took a gulp, and the wine was flavorful, and so very different from other wines I'd had. It was light, slightly sweet, with hints of all kinds of herbs that reminded me of BB's garden.

"Let's eat!" Eamon said loudly to everyone.

They all sat down and started picking up dishes and serving themselves then passing the dish down.

Rosie directed me to the table where she and Eamon were at, a beautiful place setting with China and silverware ready to go. At our table, everyone moved in such great synchronicity that it took a relatively short time for us all to get a portion of each dish. I was so hungry that I stopped thinking about Damon long enough to appreciate the love I felt within the food. It could not have been made from a food printer. I looked at it all, and my extremely large plate, and it felt like Thanksgiving and Christmas had arrived.

"Who cooked this?" I asked Rosie.

"We did," she said, pointing to herself and Eamon. My jaw dropped and I covered my open mouth with my hand.

"Hey, I helped!" Caitir whined from down the table. "Like, a lot."

"We had a lot of helpers," Rosie said. "Calder and Carmella made the rolls."

"They're delicious," I said, grateful for them.

"Caitir peeled and cut..."

"...everything..." Caitir interrupted.

"We do have automated peeling tools," Rosie explained to me. Caitir scoffed.

"Four turkeys and two roasts and the trimmings?" I continued to be amazed.

"It's really healthy to cook and put emotion and love and appreciation into our food," Rosie replied.

At first, I could only hear those closest to me conversing, until enough people had eaten, and enough wine had been consumed that those who could project their voices, told stories for the whole room, their sounds echoing off the stone walls and the burning fires.

I'd just finished eating when I heard the first ring of a cell phone and saw that Damon was the one retrieving it from his pocket. He'd been sitting with his back to me, almost the farthest away, when I caught his face turn. Tombo and the familiar-looking soldiers sat around him. A moment later multiple other telephones started ringing, including Eamon's and Rosie's. I noticed Calder and Caitir get up too, all five of the family members and their closest security were on their feet and out the dining hall's doors.

I sat there confused and uncomfortable, and too stuffed to move. I sipped on my wine and smiled politely at the people around me, many of whom spoke other languages, and came from other countries. Their conversations were in French and Spanish and Italian, and something else I wasn't recognizing from Asia. Once Damon and their group were gone it seemed as if the English language had disappeared too. It made it easy to check out.

A woman near me passed me a bottle of wine, as new bottles were opened by the remaining diners. They were unalarmed by the early departure of the family. I remembered nurses and doctors and the new faces were mostly talking with them, so I assumed there was more than one group of medical staff that worked with the children. As I poured my second glass of wine and felt the warmth of the last gulp, Father Jerzy sat by my side and smiled at me.

We shared a weird connection, a kindness between us. He always felt familiar and safe.

"I'm sorry about earlier. I was really tired. I still am," he smirked.

"You're all pretty amazing, doing this work. So, what happens now?"

"Well, you see all the new people. They're from another security and medical team, and they just came back from reintegrating the children from the last group into healthy home situations."

"How long have they been gone?" I wondered.

"About two months," he said. "It was a group from several missions. They took the ones from South America and Asia back to their continents. You'll hear a lot of different languages here. What we can't learn, we use AI's help to get through. They've been having to speak to the children and their families, and the people in the countries they went into, to return the children."

"How many groups are there?" I asked, astounded.

"Right now, there are four."

"With soldiers for each?"

"Of course, long-term protection is needed."

"What's the process of getting the children home?"

"If we can find their families, and the children are wanted, they go home to a loving place, with support. If their origin is not so great, we place them with families willing to care for and help rehabilitate them. That can take a while. It can be traumatic for everyone."

"Are there any that don't get placed?"

"Yes, there are some who can't be fostered, that cannot move past the trauma, and so we place them in a special hospital."

"Will they ever get better?"

"We don't know, but they're someplace safe, with good care."

"Gellion?" I heard a female voice say.

"Yes?" I said instinctively, but when I turned it was Carmella.

"I'm sorry to interrupt, but I've been asked to retrieve you," she said, smiling meekly at Father Jerzy.

"Oh," I said, standing up.

I looked down at Father Jerzy and smiled and reached out my hand. He stood and hugged me. "It's always nice talking with you."

Our time was always so short, and I still had so many questions for him, but I followed Carmella out of the dining room, and down the hall to the elevators.

"Is everything okay?" I asked, but she was fidgeting in a way I'd never seen before, like she was nervous or faking being so.

"Yes, of course," she said with the lightest Italian accent.

She sounded so American before, I kept forgetting we met in Italy. Her friendly and professional face quickly turned to the fakest expression of concern, like she couldn't help but give something away.

"Is something going on?" I asked.

She dropped her head and sighed. She was doing a terrible job being coy about anything. "I just think someone should tell you."

"Oh," I said, realizing she was the one who'd decided to get me.

"They didn't ask for me?" She shook her head. "Tell me what?"

"Damon's very angry about something on the news, in the US. The family's arguing about whether to tell you about it. He said not to, that it would be harmful to you."

"How do you know this?"

"I heard them arguing in the hallway before getting into the elevator," she replied.

The elevator door opened, and we both got inside. She pressed the button for the lower level, but we didn't move. Carmella gestured to the wall, where the hand scanner was mounted, just like the ones at the bunker. I scowled. She gestured again, for me to put my hand on the scanner. I did, and we went down, deep, deep down.

"Your handprint doesn't work for the lower levels?" I asked, surprised.

Carmella didn't answer my question. So, I asked another. "Have you told me all you know?"

"No, but I'm not saying anymore," she said with a hint of indignance.

"How mad will he be when we show up?" I asked and figured she could at least consider that.

"I'm not going in," she refused.

I hated confrontation, and my stomach had already started to feel uneasy at our descent below. I couldn't believe she would create extra drama and not want to witness it play out.

"Aw," I said, partially mocking her sudden trepidation, "and miss the fireworks?"

She rolled her eyes and pursed her lips together. I didn't exactly appreciate the situation she was putting me in either. Damon was a bear I sometimes wanted to prod, not poke. Yet maybe she was doing me a favor by clueing me in. I didn't exactly agree with Damon's approach to all of this, especially the emotional stuff, and the withholding information. His temper and jealousy were confusing and overwhelming too.

The elevator was taking too long, my irritation with Carmella growing with my anxiety, as my ears felt a pressure from within.

"Did I help save your life?" I asked quietly out loud, wondering if the video wasn't just a nightmare or if it was her, as the videos I'd watched indicated.

"Yes," she said, equally as quiet, but with disdain. "And in all these years, where have you been? Did saving children get in the way of your perfect little life?"

My jaw dropped from her words and assumptions. It was so odd that she was so intimately involved, yet knew nothing about me, and had no access to the larger operation. She knew a lot, could infer a lot, but they hadn't told her I was broken and had to relearn to walk, relearn everything again.

I had to think best how to frame it for a still-healing Carmella. It wouldn't be easy to explain it and leave out the most important details, that the real Gellion was covered in deep scars from garish lacerations from a decade of torture.

"It's weird," I chuckled uncomfortably. "I thought everyone could see what a fraud I am, how ignorant and naïve, especially with Father Jerzy teaching me. You didn't seem to notice any of that."

"I saw you working together."

"No, we weren't. He was trying to teach me. I haven't seen energy or healed anyone in over ten years, and I don't remember you," I said and added bitterly, "or Damon. I was in a very bad car accident. So, I just met him a little while ago. I have no clue how many days it's been. It feels like weeks. Then I saw a video where Damon was once my boyfriend, and in the video we helped you. That's all I know."

The silence was deafening.

"Oh," she finally said, without sarcasm. "There was a video of you helping me?"

Shit! She doesn't know about the video.

"I don't remember any of it," I said, trying to downplay the horror of the images of Carmella as a teen victim.

"You just saw that?"

"I was given many hours of videos to watch. Explanations of

things, events and conversations. Stuff they don't want to tell me. Stuff they don't have time to explain. I'm sure they thought it was important I not be so naïve," I said, "about the evil."

I tried not to insinuate anything about her trauma.

"I see," she grimaced at me.

"So, yeah, I'm stuck here, and I'm clearly not up for the challenge. I have a brother and father I miss. I managed to make a couple friends," I rambled. "I'm told I'll never be allowed to see them again."

"Oh," she said again.

And though I didn't want to say the worst part out loud, I couldn't have an enemy here, so I made things clear.

"Unless I become who I was, he doesn't want me. Even if I could make that happen, I'm now so turned off by his conditions for me, I don't even want him."

"Um," was all she could muster, and it sounded confused.

The nail in the coffin needed to be said, "If he's your hero, you should be with him," I sighed.

The stopping force of the elevator lifted my stomach up inside me, like being on a roller coaster. The feeling matched perfectly the unsettling thoughts I just shared with Carmella. The door dinged and opened.

"Are you coming?" I asked.

"I like fireworks" she replied, walking out of the elevator.

I bet she does!

I followed Carmella down a short hallway and stopped at the double doors that required handprint access. I was astonished again and again that my handprint worked in these places here, as if it had been added long ago and forgotten.

Carmella walked in first, directly toward Calder, and stood behind him, whispering into his ear. I walked slowly into the room and looked around. It was another command center situation with large TV monitors, workstations, and seating. They'd all been standing around the room, facing each other.

I heard shouting as we arrived, and then silence as all eyes were on me, with controlled dagger-glances shot at Carmella.

"Sorry to interrupt," I said.

"Carmella has to leave," Damon said to Calder.

Calder nodded and promptly took Carmella by the hand. She actually resisted and said, "I want to know what's going on. Why is Calder so stressed out? What does it have to do with her?" But Calder was already dragging Carmella out the door.

The silence…oh, I could barely stand it anymore.

"Would someone please just tell me what's going on?" I demanded.

Caitir sighed, turned around and sat down, typing away. The TV screen lit up with a news broadcast.

"Welcome back. Tonight, we follow-up with new information on the unidentified bodies found in the Rock Creek National Park last week. The remains have been identified as missing teens Jeremiah Woodley and Carnegie Halifax. Mr. Woodley and Mr. Halifax are just two of three teen boys who went missing nearly twelve years ago," the female news anchor began the segment.

"That's right, Tina," the male anchor continued. "The teens, belonging to affluential families, went missing the night of their prom. Young Jeremiah and Carnegie were returning home from dropping off their dates, when they were never heard from again. A local, state, and national manhunt began for the three young men, as their disappearance rattled the prosperous Northern Virginia neighborhood of Falls Church. Though the search lasted for over two years, no trace was ever found," the male anchor concluded.

"Police speculate that the third teen's body might be found. They are continuing to search the surrounding areas for any sign he perished that night."

"Did they say what their next steps will be, Tina?" the male anchor interrupted with a pensive frown.

"Not yet, Dan. They are only just beginning to start their investigation into these heartbreaking deaths, but they will keep us updated, now that the families have been informed."

"KMLA News will be reporting on this story as the investigation unfolds."

The screen went dark.

"Who are they? What's this all about Damon?" I asked.

"Gentlemen, give us the room," Damon said to the silent Tombo and Joseph. "Don't go far."

"It was the night of your car accident," Eamon said.

I wasn't drawing a connection.

Caitir had turned her chair around and was looking at me. "We were the last ones to see them," she said.

"See who? See them?" I asked, pointing to the darkened screen.

"Damon, I can't," Caitir said, getting up, holding her hand to her mouth, not looking at me and walking out.

"Gellion," Rosie said, starting to reach out for me with concern.

"I don't understand," I replied because I was so confused.

Cell phones started ringing again, and then Malik's face appeared unexpectedly on the screen. "We don't have any more time here Damon, we have to start the protocol now if you're going to be there in time to intercept the police."

"The police?" I asked with alarm.

"Gellion, is that you?" Malik asked. "We need her too. She can stop this whole thing before it gets started."

"Out of the question!" Eamon barked back.

"They have a video, Damon," Malik said softly, with a guilty tone.

"What?" Damon screamed. "What video?"

"Of the masquerade," Malik informed him.

"Which part?" Damon asked, but Malik was looking around, trying to find someone. "Which part?" Damon demanded to know.

"Damon, I'm not asking you!" Malik said sternly. "I'm telling you, that you, Gellion, Calder and my future wife!" Malik bellowed at Damon, "need to get back here right now!"

Rosie took my hands and led me out of the room with the rest of them. Once outside the double doors I saw Caitir and Calder returning, and Damon's men waiting.

"What's wrong?" they asked together.

"You need to switch avatars into the U.S. bodies. No time to explain. Malik will debrief you," Rosie told her children and Damon's men, who scurried away, into rooms along a connected hallway.

She walked me to a room, opened the door, took me inside and had me lie down, then put an eye-mask connected to a power cord over my eyes. "Close your eyes and count to one hundred. You'll wake up soon, and Caitir will tell you what you need to do." She administered a sleep agent, and I drifted off.

I wasn't sure what time or day it was, or how I felt, but I was becoming alert to being back where I'd been, deep underground but closer to my old home in Maryland. The last time I'd been in this body, I'd been choked and discarded by Damon in a psychotic rage. I could feel the familiar scars of who I'd been, still twinging without even touching them. The skin ached, always. The brunette color that hung around my head was a welcome comfort, which surprised me too.

I got up feeling weak and found my way up to the command center. The three Jairus cousins were there, and I didn't ask where the soldiers had gone. Malik had snacks waiting, as if he knew we would all wake up famished. Even Damon went straight for the trail mix and jerky, with gulps of water in between. We even managed to smirk at each other as we ate up everything on the table.

Malik began talking as we satiated ourselves.

"It's bad," he said, pressing a flat screen controller.

A video started playing, from the night of the masquerade. I stood straight up and backed away from where everyone was. In response to my horror, Malik paused the playback before the dress was torn from my body. It was the worst possible scenario. Images taken of the ritual, torture and sacrifice of my double.

"Is this why you sent the boys to the other bunker?" Caitir asked.

"How did this get by you?" Damon demanded to know, a fury building inside.

"It's analog," Malik said, looking at Caitir, as she nodded that she saw the imaging on the corners of the video too, where he pointed to the watermark. "This is film. Not like the video recorders without Bluetooth or wireless."

Caitir shook her head, "We identified all the camcorders that were older, and magnet wiped them as they were leaving the party."

"Look at the edges," Malik said. "This is true analog. Sixteen millimeters."

The room was silent.

Damon took a breath and tried to calm himself. I took in this version of him, the real Damon with his tattoos and beard, and a whole other side to his rage.

"Someone had been prepared for the technology wipes," Damon finally said, more calculating now. "Film is easy to destroy if you know it's there. We didn't."

"You can tell the camera is hidden."

"Had all the cell phones been infiltrated and wiped clean?"

"Yes," Malik confirmed.

"Damn, these guys are good," Calder said, disturbed.

"How'd you get this?" Damon demanded.

"I made a copy off the Detective's phone," Malik replied.

"What detective?" I asked.

"It's on the detective's phone?" Caitir shrieked.

"They had it already when they questioned Damon," Malik confirmed.

"When was this?" I shocked myself with my demand. I couldn't believe how far out of the loop I was.

"Yeah, when was this?" Caitir chided, staring at Malik, who obviously hadn't told her.

"Yesterday."

"Was it encrypted?" she asked Malik.

"Yeah," he nodded. "They've requested a warrant, and the judge is about to approve it. The only way the cops don't go snooping around your grandfather's mansion, is if you all get their first, and show them Gellion is alive."

"I'll take the train in now with Calder," Damon said.

"You're going topside?" I asked, startled.

"I have to," he said. "You're not supposed to jump your consciousness into too many bodies too quickly. We don't have a choice right now," Damon replied.

Calder and Damon took off for the train, and Caitir took my hand and walked me into the dressing room. My mind felt jumbled, trying to recall exactly what I'd seen in the Scotland bunker, and if anyone had explained how it related to the video of my death.

"Caitir, I don't understand," I started to say as she opened the large female wardrobe on one side of the room. "The news report, about the missing boys…"

"…Here's the thing, you don't remember it, so it's better to just say that, if you're asked. We really need you to focus on the important part."

"Which is?"

"That you weren't murdered at the masquerade," she said, her eyebrow raised in distress.

"Right," I said, coming back to the issue. "How do I do that?"

"We'll work it out on the train. We've got to get dressed. Damon will have his lawyers there, and who knows who else."

She handed me a semi-professional outfit, like what I'd have worn working for Mr. Jairus, except this was designer and it felt like heaven on my skin. I wore slip-on boots and carried my heels. On the train we talked about what I would say and how I would say it and what I needed to avoid. I was a nervous wreck.

We arrived in Georgetown and met in the parking garage. Damon and Calder were both shaved, with fresh haircuts in place, and tailored suits. There was no trace of the covert personas. Tall, handsome, muscular men, with an aura of control.

Damon, Calder, Caitir, and I got in the armored SUV, the seats facing one another. I sat with my back to the driver, next to Caitir.

"Who's in the other cars?" I asked Damon.

"Lawyers, investigators, experts in the field," he replied nonchalantly.

Caitir reached up and touched my wrist, to indicate I should stop grasping the tip of my thumb between my teeth, like I used to do, when I first came out of the hospital. I decided to look out the window, since Damon wasn't looking at me anyway.

"Caitir, is she ready?" Calder asked.

"Yes, as agreed."

"Gellion?" Calder asked. He was directly across from me, but I didn't want to look at him. "I just wanted to say that I'm really sorry, for everything."

When I looked at him my bottom lip started to tremble against my will. Somehow the part I was supposed to play felt like the only shield I would have from the coming onslaught of confusion. The greenery and lavish homes and scenery from the city, all the way to the estate were at least captivating.

Caitir moved seats, but I barely noticed. The peacefulness of the drive, of being above ground, with just the tiniest bit of normalcy, was more important to me. The air tasted better too. I could sense Damon in the seat next to me. Eventually he placed his hand on mine, gently cupping it in the warmth and largeness of him, compared to me.

I closed my eyes and listened, for the beating of hearts, for the musings of the beings who once, supposedly, spoke to me, guided me. I listened for God himself to give me a sign, but I could hear nothing from anywhere outside me. All I felt was a slow burning inside, a raw attraction to the man beside me, from his tender touch, and the warmth that was seeping into me.

Maybe this moment, of feeling God present through Damon, was the closest I'd ever get to God. After my accident, after Mom's death, after years of suffering, this one moment, with this man, gave it all meaning. Didn't it? Maybe there could be a God for me after all. Knowing someone once loved me and wanted to protect me, was holding me up.

When we arrived at the manor, the police were already there at the gate, about to break their way in.

"We'll escort them into the sitting room," Calder said.

The gates were opened remotely, and Damon's vehicles entered the driveway first. Calder and Caitir got out and closed the door. Damon turned to look at me.

"Gellion, I want you to listen to my words now about what to say and how to behave. This is very important. You are my girlfriend. We've reconnected which means there is money and power protecting you because you have value to me. You fulfill my sexual needs in a way no fiancé can. You are my mistress. My inspiration," Damon said, his hand to my face, my chin, pulling me toward him, saying the words softly, seductively, and then he kissed me.

The bench seat made it easy to be pulled into him as he kissed me. "Can you say something for me?" he breathed into my mouth.

I nodded as best I could as he prolonged kissing me. I moaned my agreement.

"Gellion, I need you to say that you would do anything for your rich, kinky, Satanic boyfriend."

My eyes flew open and suddenly I understood the game we were playing. The word "Satanic" made me physically pull-away from Damon, but he held me close and continued to kiss me.

"That's who you need to be, for this to be believable. It's how we survive," he said, holding me a little too tightly. "You are my sex slave, my submissive, my toy, my greatest desire. You play any little game I wish, and participate in any sort of ceremony, yes?"

I nodded again, and then he unzipped the top half of my outfit and slid his hand inside, taking my mind someplace entirely different, distracting who I'd been with who he needed me to be.

"Say it," he said evenly.

"I would do anything for my rich, kinky, Satanic boyfriend."

Damon's intensity told me to take my role seriously, and his kisses and touches were designed to put me into that role more deeply. I was physically aroused. When I was intoxicated from his touch, he zippered me back up, opened the door and pulled me out with him.

At least we would face it together.

17

THE SAFE SUICIDE

We entered the manor walking past multiple police in uniforms waiting and entered the sitting room.

"Detectives, good to see you again. My lawyers have informed me that you'd like to search the property."

"We hear you have a video of our party," Calder said, "and our lawyers are requesting a withdrawal of the warrant, based on new information."

"On what grounds?" the eldest detective in the group, dressed in a suit, said.

"We were furnished with a copy of the video too. Our actress is very much alive. She was on holiday, but came back to show you she's still breathing," Damon said, reaching out his hand for me to take.

I smiled at the detectives.

"I'm very much alive, as you can see," I said.

They pulled out their phones and started tapping away, until their eyes looked back at me, and then back to their phones.

"How do we know it's really her?" the detective asked.

"We need you to come back to the police station with us," another said.

"Didn't your grandfather die at the end of the performance?" The quietest and most menacing looking of all the men there asked.

"He died of a heart attack, the ritual scene having been too exciting for him," Damon replied, stone faced.

"And the gas that emitted from your mouth?"

"Just a tiny smoke bomb, one designed for such an occasion," Caitir chimed in. "This is just one of many performances done in a year, that use such pyrotechnics."

"These pyrotechnics didn't cause any harm?"

"None at all," I said, opening my mouth to show my set of perfect clone teeth. "I'm sorry for the man who died."

"We'd like a DNA sample," the detective said to me.

"On what grounds?" Damon asked, stepping between me and the men.

"I don't think so gentlemen," a lawyer behind us said. "The warrant is no longer any good. The judge has seen our evidence and agrees with our version of events. You'll be getting the call now."

"We didn't get the victim's name," another responded.

"Whatever you want it to be," I said, playing the part, being flirty, and carefree.

"And she is under no obligation to identify herself," another lawyer chimed in.

The cell phones of the detectives started ringing, and they excused themselves. Damon smiled at me; victory written on his face.

When they were done, they ordered their men back to their cars, having been unable to get enough time there to collect any evidence. The largest and most menacing detective was the last to finish his phone call. When he was done, he returned to our group and walked straight up to me.

"Is your name Eve-Anne Gellion Greene?"

My surprised expression must have given me away, and he smiled. Damon immediately stepped forward.

"That's what I thought," the detective continued. "This investigation is not about your act in a Satanic spectacle, or Mr. Jairus's deceased grandfather. We came to collect what we thought was your DNA from the slab of rock outside, to compare it."

"Compare it to what?" I asked, confused.

"To your rape kit from twelve years ago," the detective said to me, as I stood somewhat behind Damon.

"I'm sorry, I don't know what you're talking about," and it wasn't a lie.

"Sure, you do. A girl doesn't forget her first rape."

"Detective, you're out of line." Damon's lawyer reproached.

"We have some questions, based on this new information," the detective said. "We'll be getting a warrant for your DNA as well."

"We should have it by tomorrow," his partner added, "so please come to the station first thing in the morning," a second detective said over the first.

"If you get a judge to sign your warrant, we'll be there," Damon said.

"Good, because we have some questions for you too."

And for some reason, I felt frightened by the way the detective intimidated me so easily and knew so much about me that I didn't know.

"That won't be necessary," a lawyer said, while Damon turned around and looked at me. "We have medical records and witnesses that show she has no memory of anything prior to her car accident, which happened the day before those boys disappeared."

"What is he talking about?" I said, with a huff, almost stomping my foot. I put my hands on my hips and tapped my foot at Damon, until the police were all gone. The ditsy way I approached my character seemed to need help being consistent. I didn't think my surprise was disingenuous, but I was in shock by the information.

Car accident victims with amnesia are familiar with confusion, so I was pulling from my memory of my teenage self, waking up that way, and getting mad. It was the best I could do as I started to think back to that time, to all the pain, to all the worry and upset.

I sat down the moment they were gone, and stared at the floor, my eyesight zoning out, deep back into myself, into memories I didn't have, seeking truth from my own experience and not that of others. It wasn't there, but other memories that had never made any sense were falling into place.

Fear of men, of sex, of being touched or kissed came to mind the most. Every attempt at a relationship ended in failure from the utter terror and panic of intimacy. Once the physical pain was manageable, there were other aftereffects. Just being turned-on hurt, physically hurt from within. I couldn't touch myself or even become aroused at the thought of anyone without feeling intense internal pain, a burning that sent my body into full blown panic.

It was the dreaming that told me my reality was wrong, as I felt safe to want the mysterious man there, allowed to have a sense of desire or wanting, but only there. And those dreams only lasted for a little while, like a glimmer of hope, from some far-off place. It was all making sense, here, now.

Once I'd sat down, Damon had shifted his attention to the lawyers and others there on retainer, to make all of this go away with haste. All three cousins were deep in the discussion with those who would have the judge's ear. There were many details to be covered I was sure.

It was so easy to slip outside and away.

Fall was arriving in beautiful colors at the beginning of November, but it was still somewhat warm. It always fluctuated from year to year in Maryland. The bright leaves had just started changing and were still on the trees. Reds and oranges and yellows were lit up by the slowly setting sun. I knew from experience that beyond the trees, down the small slope was the drop off into the Potomac River. I had no idea how high up the land was from the water below, but I was curious.

I made it as far as the slab of rock, the one the detectives wanted to test for my blood no longer visible upon it, before I heard Damon.

"Gellion?" he called out to me.

"I can't have children," I said, turning to look at Damon. "Did you know that?"

He made eye contact only briefly before saying, "We have a solution for that, should you wish."

My head hung back from the weight of the thoughts he was putting inside me, and I sighed. I knew he was trying in his own weird way to acknowledge the utter damage I was struggling to reconcile.

"Was there ever a car accident?" I had accepted that the car crash hadn't been an accident but never had the thought that the crash never happened at all. I needed to know if it was a lie.

"No," he shook his head and told the truth, finally.

"Whose dumb idea was it to withhold the truth, to keep me from seeking help?"

"I wasn't allowed near you after everything happened. I can't be sure who made those decisions."

It had to have been my mother, like BB said, but if she'd been alive I doubt she wouldn't have wanted me to get help for my uncontrollable fears. She hadn't been there to help me through the psychological trauma, and dying wasn't her fault.

My body felt twitchy, like I needed to scratch my head, and rub my face and I felt so hot, like my skin was reacting to something, a pain deep within. How could this copy of myself feel the same pain of my original broken body? Breathing felt harder and more labored, and I felt like I wanted to crawl out of my own skin.

"Gellion? Are you okay?" he asked, stepping toward me.

"I'm having trouble…" I tried to say, before a large yawn came out of my mouth.

"Yawning is good," he encouraged, "It helps you release the negative energy."

"I know!" I barked at him, irritated. I yawned again, as tears started to form in my eyes. Then again and again, as it was the only way to get a deep breath of air and release my tightening jaw.

Damon came closer and touched my arms to keep me from collapsing into my own chest. He tried holding me up, but as he got close, the familiarity of my memories, and the dreams that I escaped into, showed me just how much Damon was that mysterious object of affection within me, within the dreams. His absence next to me had been a hard pill in all of this, despite all the darkness he brought. Maybe now I knew why.

"Is this why you couldn't spend more time with me?" I asked him.

He was silent for a moment and then said, "Your trauma had been ignored. I triggered it. It's a bad combination."

"Was the third boy's DNA inside me too?" I asked, wanting the full truth.

Damon let go of my arms and stepped back, he didn't want to answer.

"Was it?" I asked again, broken, unable to swallow or catch my breath, as the fire I felt itching at my skin spread from one area to another.

He hung his head. Though he was with me in his original, his angriest body, I felt afraid to be near him. I didn't fear him, but I felt this sickness growing inside me, and a real fear of dragging him down too low. I wanted to say mean things to him, as the burning itch that kept getting worse made me feel vile thoughts and accusations inside myself. My mental capacity to stand my own existence was declining quickly. Then the burning started to turn into something greater, something sharper and more acute.

"What happened to me Damon?" I started to shriek at him, and then I started coughing, and the tickle in my throat wouldn't stop, until I was having a fit, and collapsing from so much shock. Damon rushed to my side.

"Water!" Damon screamed out, but no one was around.

I took a few deep breaths and whispered, "Please. Make the burning stop."

"Oh wow, your face!" he exclaimed, looking alarmed. Then Damon left, to get me what I needed, whatever that was.

I pulled myself up and took off my heeled shoes and started moving, feeling the need to escape everything, especially the red splotches and blisters starting to form all over my body and making me feel burned alive. My arms were covered quickly in expanding red sores that I could see as I pulled my jacket off. That they were everywhere and spreading told me it would only get worse. I had to escape the burning of it and started running toward the cliff's edge.

It was the very worst pain of my life, like I was on fire, and I might explode like a bioweapon filled with an infectious agent. "Triggered" didn't even begin to describe it.

I ran barefoot toward the river, barely feeling my skin pierced by sticks and rocks. The fire was consuming me. I could see the edge of the cliff coming and saw that the cliff on the Virginia side was steep and high. I wanted to fall in and die on the rocks below.

Just before I reached the edge to leap out into the cold river and find some relief to my burning and dying system, Damon grabbed me.

I hadn't heard him call for me. I imagined he would have screamed for me to stop, but I could barely recognize him, my mind was clouded by the pain and my desire to feel the chill of the Potomac.

"What are you doing?" he screamed at me, as he held me in the air, his arm wrapped around my torso, my extremities reaching beyond the hurdle.

I held up my arms in front of me and shook them. "I'm on fire!" I screamed as he pulled me from the edge. "I have to make it stop!"

He put me down, turned me around and looked at my body, my arms and face. The alarm in his eyes showed me he finally understood my reaction wasn't so insane. I screamed out in pain.

"Let me go!" I begged him, as I inched closer to the edge. "I just want to die."

"Don't go in the river, Gellion," he begged with remorse in his eyes. "That's where they dump the sacrifices."

"What?" I gasped.

I wasn't expecting to hear that, to think of the plunge in such a sinister way.

"Please, Gellion!"

I was a sacrifice. My body was always meant to go over the edge, I realized, from the moment I'd met him it was inevitable.

"You can't follow me," I said, knowing his original body needed to stay safe.

"You'll die horribly," he said as he pulled at me, pulled me from the edge.

I felt like a burn victim without any possibility of help and the pain was too much to bear. I backed myself out of his grasp and stepped to the edge of the cliff.

"If they smell any blood, they'll eat you alive," Damon screamed at me, angrily as I allowed myself to fall.

Did he say, "eat you?"

I hadn't jumped, but fell, so I scraped and mangled my body on the cliff's edge before I was in the water, face up, able to see and breathe. The pain in my body started to fade away, and the clouds and trees and scenery above me changed. I was floating away with the flow of the deep and wide river.

Then I heard a loud splash, and more splashing, until his familiar voice was beside me.

"God dammit, Gellion!" Damon said as he looked into my blinking eyes.

"You idiot!" I called out to him. "You could have died! Why couldn't you just let me go?" I said, as water got close to my mouth, as my body bobbled.

"I couldn't let you die like that. Where are you hurt?" He demanded to know.

"Nowhere," I said, grateful the pain had finally faded from me.

"Can you move your hands?"

I couldn't. "No."

"How about your legs?"

"I don't feel anything, which is what I wanted."

"You're bleeding."

"I wanted to escape the pain. Can't we just float?" I asked calmly, as my energy drained away.

Damon put his body near mine, or maybe under me, as my mouth no longer had water flowing in and out of it. The view above continued to shift and change, the beauty of the transforming leaves, moving into death and release.

"If you get pulled under, close your eyes and never open them," Damon said.

"Hmm?" I moaned back.

We floated for a time, and through it, I heard Damon's heavy breathing, his anxiety, his tugging me while swimming, his arms directing us. At one point I could swear he was thrashing his legs underneath us and then I heard the sound of something moving below.

"Shit," Damon said. "Hold on Gell," he yelled as he pushed himself away from me, and then the sounds of splashing and Damon's body going under.

"Damon?" I called out, but I quieted myself when I heard the sound of several projectiles in the water, like something out of a movie. The sounds were immediately followed by three loud pops from inside the water, then splashing and breathing as Damon resurfaced.

"Gell?" he called out.

"I'm alive," I said as he reached me. "What was that?"

"You're going to hear an explosion," Damon said. "Try not to be startled."

I felt my body move as if something were tugging on me.

The moment the sound of the shockwave hit from under the water, the tugging stopped.

I could sense Damon was pulling me hard and fast. He dragged us into what looked like a green boathouse somewhere along the river, near the city. He pulled my body out of the water and held my immobile form, my head cradled. Damon touched my face, where I could still feel, and he kissed my lips.

"You could have died," I complained and chastised as I grew cold.

"They're not used to anyone fighting back," he said softly, as if that excused his recklessness.

"How did we survive that?"

"My watch," he explained. "It's tactical with projectiles and a small explosive. I'm always armed, but especially in my real body."

"Please don't do that again."

"Don't go where I can't follow," he responded.

"You don't want me," I said. "I'm broken."

"I want to kiss and touch my girl without all the trauma getting in the way. If I do this wrong, I'll lose you forever."

"What if I don't want to come back?" I asked, unsure of how deeply my wounds were affecting my will.

"Please Gellion," Damon said, looking into my eyes. "I'll try harder, I'll be more attentive, more sensitive. Please don't give up. I can't do this without you. I need you here."

He pulled me close to him, embracing me as he held my head up to his. As I drifted away into nothingness my eyes wandered and I could have sworn I saw one of my legs half missing, blood pouring from the severed leg. Then darkness took hold.

My eyes flew open with a rush of upset and upheaval, and I looked up to see Eamon and Rosie looking down over me. I knew I was back in Scotland into the only other body they had online for me. I felt instantly guilty as they'd be scrambling now to fix my dramatic exit, a continent away.

Yet I'd never felt so grateful to be disconnected from myself. Despite the terror, there'd been no pain, and it made me wonder if I was really just losing hope, as my sense of reality was crashing down. The monitors peeled easily off my skin, and I started getting up. No one tried to stop me when I left the room and went looking for the one place where I could be alone.

I made it to the elevator when a panic started to wash over me. The eruption on my body of being on fire, that had started to develop on the clifftop lawn of the manor, had returned. I could feel it hitting me hard when I finally reached my room and let myself in. I wasn't going to be able to handle that kind of pain on my feet.

The moment my body hit the bed I started screaming, while sensing the outbreak spreading across me in a flood and dragging me back into Hell. Ablaze with unwavering pain, I had no idea why, except for the obvious trauma, and my inability to process it. I just kept screaming because I couldn't stand it anymore, and then my body passed out. When I woke up in a hospital bed, an IV drip attached to me and a numbing feeling over me, I wanted help, desperately. The burning started up again and I started to moan.

"Gellion," Rosie came closer, a mask over her mouth and nose. "Hold still," she said. "Eamon, she's awake."

"What's wrong with me?" I asked, hoping they would know.

"You're covered in some sort of hives and then your skin started blistering. What happened Gellion? Caitir and Calder said you and Damon went over the cliff."

"I couldn't stop the burning," I cried out, then I started screaming again.

Eamon stuck a syringe in the IV, and suddenly the burning turned into a warm numbing all over.

"Everything was a lie," I said, slurring my words, drunk on pain relief, sinking into the warm escape that they'd given. "Those boys did bad things to me," I garbled, "but I guess you already knew that. At least now I know why I can't have children."

Remembering again how much ugly truth had spilled out, I wanted to cry and turned over waiting for it now that the stabbing pain had been abated. Instead, I fell asleep again and when I woke up, I was back in my bedroom, alone, with an IV attached to my arm still.

The pain triggered me to wake up and seek comfort. On the bedside table were syringes, liquid medicine and a note.

> *Dearest Gellion,*
>
> *You have Chickenpox, Shingles, and Pleurisy. How your system brought through dormant viruses you once experienced, into a clean body, is quite a mystery. The DNA never forgets.*
>
> *Finding out the truth could have caused this, as a stress response. Your clone body has never had active Chickenpox, so you gave it to yourself. Here are the instructions to treat the Shingles with an antiviral, and the Pleurisy with meds, and there are painkillers to soothe what has*

already erupted.

Let us know what you need and when, and we'll wait to hear from you after you've rested. Right now, you are in quarantine from the rest of us. We're preparing another clone at the bunker, so you can wake up without this pain.

-Rosie

I had no idea what Shingles was, or Pleurisy, but I remember hearing I'd had Chickenpox as a child, and that was for the best because it was more dangerous for adults to catch it. I was in an adult body now, and I was in misery.

I utilized the pain angst to get me to the bathroom, dragging the IV line with me. It was quite difficult to freshen up while so raw before administering the meds and laying back down. In front of the mirror, I caught a glimpse of all the places where I had large bandages over the areas of my skin that burned the most. I was too afraid to look.

Once I finished the must-have syringes, I gave myself the pain relief and felt the drug wash over me like some kind of blanket of calm. There'd been many surgeries I woke up from, screaming in pain, wondering why everything hurt so much more. Morphine had been administered, and this felt similar. I drifted off again.

I woke up in the same body, same room, same everything, wondering if it was pain that was waking me again or some other primal urge. I sat up and felt the pang. I had no sense of time, no sense of reason or understanding of how long it would last. I started to groan again and looked at the nightstand to see if anyone had dared to check on me and bring me more of what I'd need when I hadn't even asked. Nothing had changed.

Except I wasn't alone, and the figure who'd been sitting in a nearby chair moved slowly toward me. He was holding vials and syringes, a bottle of water, and a bowl of some kind of fruit.

Damon sat at the edge of my bed, and placed everything down on the nightstand, and started to administer everything for me. When he was done, he brought the water to my lips, then fed me some pineapple, just before the morphine kicked in.

"Why does it hurt so much?" I asked quietly.

"You have three viruses attacking the same areas of your body along the nerve. Shingles are flared neurological torture and particularly brutal, but add the Pleurisy, which is a severe lung infection that is extremely painful, and you have unbearable agony just trying to breathe."

"Why is this happening?"

"You found out what everyone's been trying to hide from you, and it triggered your broken psyche. I'm sorry Gellion."

"Who the hell gets Pleurisy anyway?"

"You did once. Not long after we got together, you started finding out about my life and my experiences, and then I couldn't handle your unconditional love, so much so, that I did some really mean things to you, and I think it all just broke your heart, and you got sick. You kept trying to absorb darkness off me, and it was more than you could handle."

"And Shingles?"

"That happened right after we met. Your grandfather was dying, and I had scared you pretty badly, and within a couple weeks of meeting me, you got it and were gone from school for a while."

I heard him, but I was fading, wanting to escape again.

"Gellion, this is the kind of thing we wanted you to heal in the children. Many of these physical reactions are about trauma we can't process. It's the Strŏngman box."

"You fool," I garbled. "How can I heal them if I'm infected with it too?" I slurred out, confused by his reasoning.

I thought I cared enough about the children to try to learn, but nothing I tried made any sense. If the pain wouldn't go away, no matter what body I woke up inside, I was going to have to use it to motivate me to do the hardest work of all, healing myself. That felt utterly impossible, as I drifted off again.

This time when I woke up, there was no pain, and I was at the homebase bunker again, in the hospital wing. There was no IV attached to me and my body wasn't yet hurting. Damon in his real body, already sporting the shadow of a beard, with his forearm tattoos visible, was sitting in a chair nearby, his head back and his eyes closed.

There was something comforting about being near his original, who I'd suddenly remembered had jumped into the Potomac River to protect my body until I died. I cleared my throat, and he opened his eyes and looked at me.

"Are you in pain?" he asked quickly.

"Not yet," I said, taking a deep breath. "Is there a reason it hasn't started?"

"We've been at it for a while. Do you remember anything?"

"From when?"

He got up and stretched. "This time we put the antivirals in your clone before attaching your consciousness. We'll see if it works. All the other attempts failed before you even woke up."

"Oh."

"That's why you don't remember."

"What if the pain comes back?" I asked, starting to sit up.

"I'm not sure, yet. We're all working on it in our own way. I've been doing some programming on the Q-Speculum. We haven't done any work in there in a while."

"What kind of programming?" I asked, slipping my slippers on.

"Identifying the Strŏngman energy, so it's easier for you to see."

"How'd you do that?"

"I read your notes, the ones you started in Scotland. You'd never mapped it on the bone before. I had never thought to look there. Your questions made a lot of sense, and so did your guess work."

I was really surprised to hear that my thought process as the Gellion with amnesia was something that made sense enough to be useful, helpful.

"Did you find it?" I asked, of the Strŏngman energy. "Who's been scanned?"

"No one yet," he replied. "It's possible we've all got some. Especially the ones we didn't get to then. You healed a lot of our trauma. It was a great relief what you did, after what we went through."

My jaw went slack at the reminder and my eyes felt sensitive. The deepest reason for their devotion to the mission was that they'd all been victims too. I wasn't the only one who'd been brutalized, and I needed to remember whose company I was keeping.

I wasn't feeling sick at all, which worried me just a little bit, but Damon had something to show me, so we went directly to the Q-Speculum after grabbing a quick bite to eat.

I needed a lot of help getting my suit on. It had been a while, but both Damon and I got suited up. His black suit was a stark contrast to my white suit. We'd never entered the machine together, to see each other's energy or systems.

When we got inside, the magnets worked differently, more smoothly, like we were flying a bit. The fans beneath us, cooling the system, helped it feel like movement. We hovered over the scanning light display and Damon started to show me what he saw. It was obvious as the scanners displayed my entire body, internal systems, and all, that the new programming had detected something on the coccyx bone.

"I remember when we were young, and you first started seeing this darkness in me," Damon said, his body floating in the air in front of me then moving behind. "You touched me here," he said, placing his hand on my tailbone, "and I felt triggered, pained, terrified, and confused. I wanted to crawl outside of myself as you held this area of my body."

As Damon touched me there, on my bone, holding me so gently, I could see the Q-Speculum's projection of my system, and there was a pulsating light that grew brighter and dimmer within me, within that coccyx bone. So deep inside was that light that as it lit up and dimmed, I could feel it vibrating within. The desire to be held, to be healed, to be released of some heavy burden carried within me, a buried shame, throbbed deeply.

I felt a stifled moan come from within me, a longing that thudded. Desire ached in me as Damon held my tailbone, held the place where my body stored the violation.

"Will you tell me what happened to me?" I implored.

"I can't do that," he said. "I can't relive it."

"Not even if it would help me heal?"

"Those details won't help you heal. You'd only be more horrified if you knew."

"What happened that night?" I wondered, suddenly desperate for the information.

His warm hand moved away from my body, away from my rear.

"I wanted to start this session with a series of questions. I've had the Q-Spec reprogrammed to include muscle-testing. The answers will help the AI grow and work to understand the power of questioning the body directly."

"Are you going to answer the question?"

"No, this is for mapping only," he said.

"Do I need a tablet, or does the AI take voice commands?"

"Voice. You call the AI by the full name of the machine 'Quantum Speculum Field Reader' then say, 'muscle query.' What kinds of questions?"

The machine's AI responded with a female voice. "THERE ARE TWO SUITS IN THE READER. MUSCLE QUERY WHICH USER?

"Muscle Query Damon," I said.

"WHAT IS THE QUESTION?" The AI asked, as the magnets pulled Damon's arm to a ninety-degree angle. He moved quickly enough to transfer the tablet he was holding into his other hand.

"I'm not doing this," Damon said, going weak.

"If you don't then I'm leaving."

He gritted his teeth.

"Is your name Damon?" I asked. His arm remained in the air.

"THE ANSWER IS YES," the AI responded.

"Quantum-Speculum Field Reader, can the user fake a yes response?" I asked.

"I don't think you need to…" Damon said.

"NO," the AI answered. "A 'NO' RESPONSE IS SIGNIFIED BY WEAK MUSCLES, WHICH CAN BE FAKED. A 'YES' RESPONSE CAN ONLY BE ACHIEVED FROM STRONG MUSCLES, WHICH CANNOT BE FAKED."

"Quantum-Speculum Field Reader, Muscle Query Damon," I said again. "The boys who raped me, did you leave them alive?"

"THE ANSWER IS NO," the AI voice responded, as Damon's arm was pushed down, despite his attempts to hold it up.

"Thanks Q-Spec," I muttered. I looked up at the viewing window and could see Caitir, Malik and Calder all staring back at me. I was having a hard time creating honesty and intimacy with so many people watching. I wasn't going to be able to focus on systems of darkness within bones with so many questions looming within me.

"Quantum-Speculum Field Reader, lower Gellion, then release her." The AI did as I asked.

The session hadn't even gotten started, the knowledge too much, triggering more in me than I could actually process. I needed time to absorb what little I'd learned and acknowledge where the trauma was. If Damon couldn't give me what I needed then I was done giving time to his technology. I required something much more genuine.

I'd just thrown myself over a cliff, and he was still trying to be clinical with me. Clearly I hadn't been dramatic enough, and it was time to force his hand. Not knowing, not understanding, and not being allowed to get the full picture wasn't going to work for me anymore. I walked out and got out of the Q-Spec Suit as quickly as I could. But in the mirror, I became mesmerized by my clone-body that had all my original scars. I didn't know why, but seeing how red and fresh the scars looked, from my head down my face and neck and through my torso, made me feel sick inside.

The trauma that was inflicted upon me had always been horrifying to behold, but it meant something different now. My scars were made by rapists, who meant to murder me after the torture, and who died because of Damon. My trauma was intertwined with his growing darkness. That information added a layer to my history that I was having trouble processing.

18

THE FIRST TIME

Damon walked in on me staring at myself in the mirror, touching my scars, part curiosity, part horror.

"Everyone's really worried about you," he said, pulling off his head piece and undoing his suit. He stood, defeated, the top of his suit hanging off him, the rest skintight on his muscles and formidable body.

"Maybe they're worried about you. If you want me to stay, you'll help me. I need reality, not lies," I said, reaching for my robe, covering my nakedness. "If I must ask Caitir, or Calder or Malik for the truth, then it's too late for us. If you can't be vulnerable, then I can't stay."

Damon undressed too, putting his suit away before he turned around naked, with an anger in his eyes that I couldn't be sure of, and approached me. He reached for my hand and took it in his and began to force it on his skin, over his tattoos. As he traced my fingers over patches of skin beneath ink, I began to realize there were a large number of scars.

The scars got deeper and thicker and more horrible as he moved my hand around his sculpted frame. When he pulled us both down to trace my fingers across the scar along his inner thigh, I couldn't take it anymore and burst into tears.

"Why cover them? When you say your laser can heal them?"

He pulled me into him and held me in vulnerability. "How else would you know you're not alone?"

"Why? Why Damon? Tell me why!" I demanded with a cry I couldn't control anymore. I wanted to know more than anything.

"I told you, 'Because I dared to love you.' It's my fault. Love was not allowed. Love healed what they needed broken. I didn't want to play their game anymore, and that's against the rules."

"Whose rules?" I pleaded.

"The power in this world."

I pushed myself off him and nodded my head like I understood, but I still couldn't look at him.

"If you don't play their game, you are sacrificed. You saw them kill you. They enjoyed it."

The story kept getting repeated. It didn't explain why to me at all. The world couldn't be that controlled, that ruled by darkness. It felt like lies, except that I'd seen a whole crowd of people stand by and watch as I was murdered. I was, admittedly, naïve about the world, having focused on recovery and survival for so long, but this wasn't a truth anyone could easily accept.

I needed to breathe and think, so I walked out, leaving Damon naked.

He caught up with me as I entered his room, the only room I'd been given, and he followed me in. He was barefoot and shirtless.

"Why walk out when I gave you what you wanted?" He asked.

"What did you give me? So, you dared to love me, once. Now tell me something that you don't want to say. That you don't think I can handle. You can jump into a river full of monsters to keep me from being alone, but can't handle communicating to keep me from wanting to die?"

Damon's bewildered expression quickly turned to determination, and he reached for my face to try to kiss me, but I pulled away.

"Okay," he said breathlessly, "The truth is that I want you so badly I can barely stand it. I want to be inside you and make you moan with pleasure, and I want you to call out my name. I want to put my mouth on you and taste you again. I want your mouth on me, as I think of nothing else but you. My mind never stops. I want to escape into you, and let go into you, and live there forever, and keep you safe.

"I'd burn down the world for you or put out every fire for you. Whichever option lets me stay with you forever."

I gasped, and let his hands bring my lips to him, trying to catch my breath through kisses and words.

We moved to the bed, and he reached out and pulled the covers off, wrapping us in them as we lay on the mattress. My naked and fragile self filled with yearning as he put his hand on my pubic bone, cupping me between my legs as I shivered.

"Breathe Gellion," he said. "I know you want me, but you don't remember me, and your body is fearful. Just breathe, and I'll move slowly."

He touched me with his fingertip ever so gently, and it was soft and pleasurable. He moved in tiny circles, and my body began to get hotter. The sensuality that started to arrive was accompanied by a burning deep within, a pain that made no sense, but had always been there. Pleasure, or any thought of it, was always replaced with pain and fear.

I whimpered, and Damon stopped. He pulled me closer to him, wrapping his large arm around the back of me, and kissed me deeply as he rested his hand on my pubic bone and waited for my body to calm down.

His extremities discovered warmth and softness coming from within me, which showed us both that the pain had not been the only thing my body felt.

"There is a technique I read about, that I'd like to try. There is a place inside you that can trigger a release from trauma, if held correctly," he said gently into my ear. "May I hold you there?"

I nodded because I felt too much trepidation to speak, so much fear, but not of him, and I wanted to feel bliss. Damon reached slowly and gently. Palm up, he tenderly trailed the central passage to the most delicate of places. He started rocking my body with his massive hand while holding the pressure point precisely. The rocking continued ever so gently.

The motion contained my sensations at first, but then the rocking sent a shockwave through my body, and suddenly my back arched uncontrollably, as my lower half shook with each tiny caress. At first I was mute, and I instinctively held my breath until I could no longer stop my voice, and the faint moan coming from within me turned sorrowful like a long and low cry of relief.

The pain there pulsed into something different, like it wanted to change out of the stabbing pain experienced but it didn't know how on its own. Damon rocked my body into a longer caress, slowly, tenderly, and patiently, and held my quivering hips until the cries and moans started to lose their power and intensity. We spent quite some time like that. The pain I'd been feeling started to subside as I let the weeping take me.

My body never left the swaying arch it took, my head resting almost upside down. Damon's free arm was under my neck and shoulders, feeling the spasms of release seize my pelvis, unable to allow Damon access to my face. His body moved with mine, his arm for support, his hand never releasing the pressure points, until the arching of my back finally subsided sometime later, and the gentle movement of his fingers no longer brought me into trembles and tears.

I lay there breathless, then breathing deeply and heavily, unable to understand what happened and why the little he did felt like so much.

"What was that?" I asked.

"It's an emotional release technique, specific to sexual trauma. Do you feel better?" Damon asked, hovering above me.

I nodded to show that I did.

I held myself up and kissed him and smiled. "Can we try the next step?"

"Is the pain gone?" he insisted to know.

"It washed over me at the end. I feel different and I want… more…" I said, even though I wasn't sure what I wanted.

And before I could even think his body was over mine, between my legs and kissing me, bare chest to bare chest, reaching down to pull himself from his garments. He moved himself against the parts of me that were tender and receptive.

He teased me some, to acquaint my body with his warmth and size, and at first the idea of him brought more fear, until he showed me how easily my body became receptive. How appropriate it felt to understand through this contact that he was soft and tender too, his body stronger, but still of the flesh. He would bring me pleasure if I'd let him.

The burning pain was starting to return from deep within me, but this time it was echoed by a deeper aching, to be one with Damon and to feel him in place of the pain. Damon leaned into me and whispered into my ear.

"They say to distract a virgin from the initial pain, you bite down on her ear," he said and then he put my earlobe in his mouth.

Instead of biting down, he sucked for just a moment as the fervor from within me engulfed him and the burning pain that was gathering was replaced with the powerful thrill of experiencing intimate human contact. Damon had slowly pushed through my body's barriers and when he reached me, he groaned loudly from the contact, and then gradually buried himself until I could feel myself wanting to pull away.

He held instead, showing me gradually how rhythm and movement could take me someplace new. The pain deep within had been pushed back, and though his own moan of pleasure was great, Damon looked down at me with hunger in his eyes.

"Oh my God," he said, trying not to move, with a gratification that sounded long-awaited.

"What?" I asked, panting, unable to stop my expressions of experience.

But instead of answering my question, he kissed me fervently and found new momentum. Mild yet vigorous enough that I yelped without meaning to. He eased up, slowed down, only to work up to a rhythm more intensely. I feared more pain when his body consumed mine, then stopped, and I only got a breath in before he moved again.

The more momentum he gathered, the more his body's contact replaced the creeping twinges of panic and pain. A realization. The more I received, the more my body replaced what I feared with something I couldn't even describe.

Damon eased up, let me breathe, then kept going and the more he moved the more I focused on his rhythm and then the pain abated entirely. When my groans of confused discomfort turned to moans of deep pleasure, he started to shift to a rhythm that made me lose control of myself entirely.

"Breathe," Damon reminded me, unaware I'd been holding my breath as he used his hands to lift my body to meet him.

Completely naïve to the entire process, I had no idea what I was doing except I didn't have to do as much as I thought. Damon took charge, and while I tried to sustain myself up and keep my muscles tight, at one point he was holding me up too. Contact was everything, rhythm and chemistry, created by Damon's power and desire. I had not understood as a woman that I could be the vessel for both our pleasure. Receiving his powerful yearning, as the irrepressible gratification came from his body fitting into mine, was spurred on by his internal drumming.

As he moved us both, I embraced the onslaught of male energy and power that sought to dominate me into my own sensual oblivion. Love had never included this kind of understanding inside my mind, and any attempt to learn resulted in the burning that Damon had just tamed within me, by releasing my fleshly needs.

At some point I was sure I would pass out, as the new information was overwhelming what I could continue to absorb, and that's when the tempo picked up, and another new wave of satisfaction and discomfort peaked within me. My vocalization turned beyond sensual.

"Damon," I called out, confused when the places of subsided pain became hungry, like an itch that I'd never considered needed to be scratched.

That I had denied myself pleasure for so long, that any sensation good or bad felt wrong, was my adult history, that Damon was liberating from me for the first time.

"Trust me, Gellion," he replied, his voice calm and cooing, and so I did.

Relaxing down into him, giving up complete control as his powerful hands moved me to him, his eyes looking deeply into mine. I cried out as his colliding evolution sent a numbing current of decadence down my legs and feet, and then he cried out too. He was cathartic, in tune with me, his pent-up rage, sadness, and fear, all into me, in an affection that melded us together, and gained a closeness between us that only he'd experienced before.

Damon lingered over me, panting with me, kissing me with sweaty lips and making sure I hadn't been hurt. I was sore, but not in pain. Too exhausted to cry, too consumed with all of it to do anything but lie flat and attempt to breathe. I existed somewhere between comatose and hyperventilating, dissecting the whole experience while the chemicals inside me kept me in a state of mental drunkenness. My body twitched from the workout, warm and throbbing, yet numb too.

"You're crying," he said, wiping my cheeks with the sheet's edge. It was only moisture in my eyes though, as the rest of me was not sobbing.

Damon stayed there with me until I realized our bodies were still merged. He moved away from me carefully, watching me as he did. I distinctly felt different the moment his soft skin was no longer within mine, and my boggled mind lay in confusion over all the potent aftereffects that still rushed into my excited system, both wound-up and calming.

He brought water to the side table, but I couldn't move to drink, despite my thirst. He put a soft cloth between my legs, and curled up behind me, wrapping us in the covers, holding me in his arms, his warm and naked body heating mine, his hands holding me tenderly. I closed my eyes for a moment and then reconsidered sleeping, not wanting to wake up in another body with pain.

The throbbing that continued inside me was surprising, and his warmth and nakedness behind me had me curling down into him, for continued closeness. Being wanted, touched, caressed, kissed, and permeated was the most intense and releasing experience of my short life, and I was already aware I wanted more.

There was never enough time though, as a knocking on the door tapped lightly, and the intercom turned on.

"Damon, sorry to interrupt, but the police have served the warrant to examine Gellion's body," Caitir said.

I turned toward him, anxious for his expression. He nodded to me, to acknowledge my scars and how he'd already planned for the current possibility. He touched my cheek and ran his finger over the scar line nearby.

"What's the timeline?" he called out.

"I've got the law firm on hold. They have the particulars," she said.

A light started to flash on the wall, where an intercom and telephone rested. Damon got up and grabbed the phone and started pacing, naked. I watched with interest, both his tattooed body and the conversation.

"When?" he asked into the phone. Then after a moment he hummed in a questioning tone. "Our experts will be there and know what to say?" Then another moment of silence, "Good." He hung up the phone.

"When do we leave?" I asked.

"Soon."

Damon turned the shower on and cleaned me with a washcloth and let me return the favor. The shower hose could be held, so I washed away the remnants of him as he covered my body in suds. His kisses were so tender, it was like he'd become a different person, when the truth of my pain was revealed and it began to destroy me.

I'd always felt like death should be an option for so much pain, but I'd also never had anyone to stick around for, that compelled me on a carnal level. I guess he finally understood how cut off I felt from the dead reality of our youthful experience. He hadn't really shown me anything that made me want to keep fighting, until the deep pain within, the repressed need for fulfilled desire, finally found reprieve, subsided in his arms, and stripped of its horrifying power over me and my development.

I'd seen enough coming-of-age stories to understand that I fell into a cliché, a woman who finally experienced the power of the human design, and the transformation of it. Damon didn't heal my trauma, but he did strip it of its power to take all my pleasure away. With the gentle rocking of persistent fingertips from a man who understood trauma, I'd been rehabilitated by experience.

I was altered. I wasn't completely transformed, but I did feel a great relief, and a deep desire realized, which was close enough for me. What woman wouldn't want to be so carefully loved into gratification? I'd found that gift was enough to keep me going, and a future without it would no longer be acceptable.

Only special clothing would do for this meeting, so I met Caitir in the dressing room. She brought my outfit, a seductive one-piece jumper that zippered all the way down the front side to reveal the line of scarring down my body with ease, while still covering my reserved parts. It was quite brilliantly designed, and perfect for this exact occasion.

"You just happened to have this lying around?" I asked, skeptically.

"This was specifically requested months ago."

"Really?" I asked, trying to consider how much a mind would have to work to make this kind of leap, and plan it out.

She added accessories that made me look wealthy, but didn't get in the way of revealing myself, then she and Rosie did my makeup and hair. I was quite a sight to behold, in pampered perfection, even if modest, it was still designer clothes, jewels and gold. Not the plain Gellion anymore, or even the sexy version they'd turned me into last time. A beautiful costume to help me with my role.

Damon and I boarded the train out of the bunker with Tombo and

Joseph by our sides. When we reached Georgetown we took an SUV to the building where the District Attorney's offices were held, where Damon's lawyers were waiting to meet us, along with the "experts." I recognized one of the faces. He'd been my doctor at the hospital.

"Dr. Gladnick?" I asked, as I'd always remembered his name, and saying it made me smile despite how much pain I'd been in.

"Hello Miss Greene. How are you?" he asked, looking the same as when we met almost twelve years earlier.

"I'm good. I'm better. I'm surprised to see you here," I said, a bit confused. "Are you here for me?"

"Yes," he said. "Damon's lawyers called and wanted my testimony. I remember your case very well."

"Oh," was all I could say. "Yeah. I've just learned some ugly details myself, that I didn't know."

"I'm sorry if that's been upsetting."

"It has, but it's also helped me understand some things that didn't make much sense. I still don't remember anything, but I feel like maybe I see patterns between the old me and the new me."

"Well, that is a healthy way to look at it. Hopefully you can avoid the details. I'm here to talk about how it's not possible for you to even testify to what they want to ask. Also, it's best not to make you re-live it. There are other experts here for that as well."

"Thank you for coming," I said, shaking the nice doctor's hand.

The detectives convened with the lawyers and the doctors in a conference room while Damon, Tombo and I waited where we were placed. Eventually, they summoned Damon too, and then I was escorted to the same conference room. I sat between the lawyer and Damon, as most of the experts had already been dismissed.

The man asking the questions was not a detective and introduced himself as the District Attorney.

"We've been told that you have no memory of the time before your accident, is that true?"

"Yes, I only remember waking up in pain and not recognizing anyone," I answered.

"So, you have no recollection how the semen of three teenage boys ended up inside of you?"

My face grew wide and a bit horrified and befuddled.

"Asked and answered counselor," Damon's lawyer chided the D.A..

I pursed my lips and shook my head, to tell them I didn't know.

"Can you speak your answer, please?"

"The experts have already given you this information," Damon's lawyer argued.

"I don't remember anything," I said.

"And can you explain your more recent connection to the events that took place at the party where you performed a ritual?"

"I didn't perform a ritual," I said and took a deep breath, as I couldn't quite form what I knew I should say.

"Counselor, she doesn't have to answer her motivation to participate in a performance."

"The money was good," I said softly, then followed it up with, "and I knew it would please people I wanted to please, including Mr. Jairus."

"In order for us to verify that you are indeed the person in the video, we've gotten a warrant to examine your scars."

"Not my DNA?" I asked.

They all looked at each other with chagrin, but when I glanced at Damon, he was smiling.

"Again, counselor, you haven't been able to secure a warrant for her DNA, and you have pictures of the original damage and expert medical testimony to support the comparison." The lawyer argued.

"We also have a dead body that fits the description of the woman in the video!" the D.A. sneered. "The warrant stands!"

The D.A. picked up a file folder and plopped it onto the table, dramatically. There were pictures of a nude, dead and mutilated body in a wooded area. As he leaned over the table spreading out the images, I had to look away, as I was becoming visibly upset.

"Who is that?" I called out to Damon, knowing exactly who it was, my dead clone.

"She looks just like you," the D.A. announced.

When I finally looked at the pictures, it was clear that the corpse was damaged in all the places where I have scars and discernable features. I didn't know how Damon was playing this one, so I simply stayed distraught and disgusted at the violent death of the woman in the photos.

"That's disgusting," I screeched. "She's got no face! How could she look like me?" I asked, covering my own facial scars with my hands.

I stood horrified that they could compare my trauma to a half missing corpse. My eyes were glued to the horror until I felt Damon squeeze my elbow. With a big sigh I unzipped my fancy jumpsuit and opened the flaps to show them all the extent of the damage to my body. The authorities looked long enough to compare my body to the photographs from the masquerade as I stood exposed, waiting for the room of men to finish their comparison.

A doctor, hired by the state, got closer and started touching my scars to make sure they were real. Damon stood and took hold of the zipper and put it back in place.

"I think that's enough," he said to the men, who never expected me to expose myself so openly in front of all of them. "I think we've satisfied the warrant."

"She could be a fake, to keep you out of trouble. We're going to need more witnesses to prove her identity," the D.A. said.

Dr. Gladnick cleared his throat, "Gentlemen, Miss Greene is my patient. I sutured those wounds myself. I'm telling you it's her."

"Thank you Dr. Gladnick," Damon said. "Take it to the judge. I doubt he'll issue another warrant."

Damon pulled my chair back and took my hand. We walked from the conference room out of the offices without saying a word. By the time we reached the curb, Joseph had arrived with our ride. Damon's cell phone was ringing midway back to Georgetown and the lawyers informed him that the D.A. had no more questions for now.

It was a relief, but it also raised a lot of questions about what Damon had been asked that no one wanted me to hear. We were alone in the back seat.

"What did they ask you?" I asked Damon.

"About the night of the accident," he explained. "If I knew you'd been with the other boys."

"What did you say?"

"The truth, with embellishments."

"Which was?"

"We went to the prom, then we joined friends at an afterparty, where we drank and danced and partied, together and separately. We didn't leave until we sobered up, and on the way home I lost control of the car, and we crashed. Dr. Gladnick remembered I was at the hospital all night, being treated for my injuries, and waiting to see if you would survive. By the next day my grandfather knew about the accident and whisked me away to Europe, so no one would pick up the scandal."

"What did you say about the boys and me?"

"That everyone was hooking up with everyone at the party and I had no idea if you had consented or not, but I'd been too busy making out with someone else to notice how long you were gone. And that you never mentioned it at any point during the night."

"Is that true?" I said, shocked at the possibility…

"Are you insane!" Damon practically yelled at me.

"Oh, so it's not true," I mumbled.

"The fuck, it's not true."

I wondered if he would tell me the truth, or if not knowing was better than having to act like I didn't know. "Will you ever tell me?"

"Not when you're being questioned by the police and shouldn't know anything about it."

He had a valid point, and it was the first time my emotions didn't override the understanding of the importance of playing my role. Yet I wouldn't have been able to play any kind of role at all were it not for the moments we just shared, naked and together and vulnerable, and the calming it brought to the years of my untold agony.

"Is that why you didn't tell me about my dead clone found in the forest?"

322

"Ah, yes, about that."

"I asked you not to do that," I said, upset.

"We didn't have a choice. The hardware in your body was being tracked. We needed the clone to be found with the hardware inside it, near the location where the hardware sent out its last signal, so whoever was looking would assume you were dead."

"But now there are two stories. One that I'm dead," I said.

"Which is important for those watching, to confirm," he replied.

"And one that I'm alive," I said.

"Which is true," he agreed, "and saved me from getting arrested."

I nodded. He was covering all bases, yet it felt like we were being attacked from all sides. He pulled me closer and held onto me.

"Don't worry," he said.

My stomach growled and he laughed.

We met Malik, Calder, Caitir, Joseph, Tombo and two other soldiers working in the vicinity, at a posh Italian bistro in Georgetown, below ground. The lack of windows and the feeling of the stone and brick walls made the place feel like an old speakeasy, safe from the gaze of outsiders.

"Your parents didn't come?" I asked Caitir.

"They're in Scotland," she said.

"Right," I remembered.

"They wanted to give Malik some time off," She whispered in my ear. "He hasn't been out of there for a while."

It was strange to consider just how many of them were inside their original bodies, sitting and eating dinner like regular people, considering what kind of enemies they could have lurking. I worried about being defenseless close to the surface. I worried too about how long I would get to be with Damon like this, not on a mission, but together.

I wanted to take the train back to the bunker and back to our bed. Damon's hand reached for mine under the table. His silence felt impersonal until I realized how much he was touching me whenever I was nearby. It was hard to be private in such proximity to those around us, who paid close attention to everything, but he was trying.

The drinks were never-ending concoctions of delight and mystery, and the food was exquisite and perfectly timed to keep us eating and yet not get too full. We were there for hours, our small group, completely comfortable with one another. The mastery of the timing of the food and service made me realize why we were there. Damon felt safe, and so did the rest. Their group was known to this place, and the place was known to them.

As the time got late, and the unknown patrons trickled out, Damon and the others were the most loose I'd ever seen them. The men had removed their ties and jackets and unbuttoned their high collar shirts. The live music had ended, and someone was playing DJ at the PA system with some CDs. As the small dance floor emptied and the band finished packing, Caitir and Malik made their way to the floor, swaying to the beat of the music and reconnecting.

Calder and Joseph walked over to the bar and Joseph pulled out a hundred-dollar bill and placed it on the bar and looked at the female bartender.

"Kelly, I haven't danced with a beautiful woman in a long time, and you are gorgeous. The hundred is a tip for your amazing drinks, but I would be honored if you would dance with me."

"Hey!" The male bartender exclaimed as his counterpart Kelly left the cleaning duties at the bar to join Joseph on the dance floor.

Calder put two hundred-dollar bills on the bar and slid them over to the complaining bartender.

"Give my buddy a break, he works long hours and has no time to date."

The male bartender didn't say another word and went back to closing down the bar, after slipping the money into his pocket. Out of nowhere the few waitresses who'd been serving all night made their way toward Calder and the rest of Damon's men who were unaccompanied. They were dressed in street clothes, as if they'd planned to go out for fun anyway. Calder took the rest of his money and handed it to the owner, laughing about how much he loved the bistro and all the beauty there.

It was so strange to see just how comfortable these ladies were, turning their restaurant and workplace into a small party atmosphere for their best paying customers, but I could tell it was not the first time. Not everyone joined in, but the owner made sure everyone got a bonus, as he started handing Calder's hundreds to the kitchen staff. He laughed as he came to the table and took the billfold that housed a large stack of cash. The owner's largest tip came directly from Damon, for the inconvenience of the added fun.

Now that everyone else had gone, and Damon's comrades were dancing, he turned his focus on me and walked over to the PA system. He sorted through the discs there and put one in. The song started ominously, with an almost siren pulsing, and then the beat kicked in, and Damon enfolded me and pulled me in closely. I hated the heels Caitir had given me, but despite their height they weren't as uncomfortable as I thought they'd be. In Damon's arms, I found the platforms useful.

Though I felt like a potential walking disaster Damon needed to hold up, he seemed to enjoy it. His masterful control of his own body allowed him to lead me on the dance floor to the beat, while making me look good. My amazement at the swaying of my limbs brought a genuine smile to my face. I knew he wouldn't drop me, so I was free to let it be fun.

The melodic sound of the female voice reminded me of a Norwegian band that I knew well. Her voice was overshadowed by Damon, who was swaying us to the song while he sang the lyrics in my ear. It was surprising that he knew the words to any song, but that he was singing them to me was stunning.

"'Hang on to me. Don't let go. I've got you here with me. You should know. We're slowly moving closer. The feelings are right. Fly away with me, to a yearning in the night. Fly away with me, to a yearning in the night.'"

The whole evening was a first for me. To dance without pain, to trust another and be held in strong arms. To smile and laugh and be beautiful to him, even with my fully scarred body. Everything I couldn't remember or felt I missed out on was being replaced with new experiences, new realities, both good and bad, and most of all a truth that had been missing for too long, no matter how painful.

I found myself humming the song he sang to me as we walked the underground paths and waterways of Georgetown to Damon's building. When we got in the elevator, instead of going down, we went up and exited on the top floor, which housed three penthouse apartments. Damon put my thumb on the security scanner to apartment B, and the door opened. It was extravagant, lovely, and completely designed by a modern decorator. The energy was so different from Rosie's spaces in the bunker below.

"Is this your local residence?"

"We all have a suite here," he responded.

The suite included access to a large roof balcony, and I found myself making my way outside. They had planted vegetation, and it was peaceful and private. He followed me out until I reached a large round-padded swing hidden under the rooftop trees and a privacy canopy. I immediately sat down, removing all my jewelry, and putting my feet up. He sat down awkwardly until he couldn't hold himself up while we moved, and we were laying side-by-side as if the swing had become a hammock.

I rolled toward him and kissed his cheek. Though I'd dreamed of him, seen videos of our relationship, gotten close to being intimate several times, all of that anticipation culminated in us finally being together. It was still so fresh in my mind, the rapture and intensity of so much indulgence caused by the man beside me. No wonder I was still craving more attention.

We kissed and touched, until he lifted me up and walked me back inside, his hands beneath me, my arms wrapped around his neck. Damon took us into the bedroom, and when he sat me down, I screamed!

My shrill voice rang out and then my body plopped onto the carpet below. Damon began laughing at me, and that's when I saw that the unmoving body lying in his bed was just a lifeless copy of Damon. My scream was cut short when I recognized Damon's Georgetown clone, sleeping in its assigned residence.

I watched as he manhandled a large and limp version of himself, dragging the body into another room and placing him on a couch. Then he came back and pulled my mouth back to his and unzipped my jumpsuit.

"Why'd you bring me here?" I wondered.

"Because everyone else is going underground, and I wanted to be alone with you. I don't want you to hold back your voice when you're learning to be open to pleasure. There should be no witness but me to the release of your sorrow, in lustful relief."

I took a deep breath. Sometimes his words evoked too much within me.

"Wow, okay. Thank you," I was floored by his decency in working with my trauma. "How'd you become like this?"

"The good version of me, or the bad?"

"Do I know the bad version?"

"Hmph," he gruffed then shook his head. "Not really. No way."

"So, then the good version."

"You. Both sides of me were entirely inspired by everything about you. You with me, you without me, you damaged, you healed. Everything."

"Why?"

"You picked a fight, over a cat," he explained. "You could never have won in a fight against me, but you were determined to stop me. Your spirit is why I didn't just run. I wanted to destroy someone who dared look at me like I deserved punishment. I wanted to show you just how evil I could be and how sorry you'd look. Then you started moving your hands in the air, like you were pulling something out of me."

"When did I do that?"

"When I was dragging you by the ankle. I turned around and you were awake, looking at me. Instead of trying to get away, your hands were moving, like they were pulling at my head and my chest. I felt it, like my heart and mind were being tugged at in a way I'd never suffered before, so I dropped your leg.

"I still can't explain it. It was like you pulled a demon from my head and a monster from my heart, and it was so forceful I dropped to my knees. I couldn't breathe, yet a weight had been lifted from my chest. For the first time in so long, I didn't want to kill or hurt anyone anymore."

Damon couldn't look at me, but he put his lips to my bare chest through my open jumpsuit and kissed my sternum. Then he bent down and put his mouth on my breast and gently cultivated a new sensation. He hadn't done that the last time at all, and I felt my body arch back at the tenderness of it. He suckled and caressed both my breasts and the exterior throb, that didn't hurt, pulled at me to be more naked, and to want his skin against mine, so I started unbuttoning his shirt, down the front and at his wrists.

I pushed his shirt off and held his head in my hands. My fingers found his neck and shoulder muscles, and suddenly I sensed how tight and tense his body was under me. He trusted me, so I did what had been done for me when I was hurting, and I massaged Damon's weary and strong muscles. My little hands next to his large frame looked almost ridiculous to try to make an impact on his tired body.

He pulled each of my arms away from him, to remove the top half of my jumpsuit, which I slid off. He carried me to the bed and joined me under the covers with only his boxer briefs. Though he pulled me into him, his body was tensed, waiting for my hands to return to his neck, to the tension and stiffness there.

The body beneath my hands, tattooed and scarred, had followed me into a river of horrors just days before. As I touched him I also looked at him and realized Damon hadn't escaped the river unphased.

How had I missed that?

I'd been too busy losing my virginity, so late in life, to notice the marks and scrapes on his legs. He didn't wince or complain, yet I felt the injured places with my bare toes. I wanted to apologize for his pain, but instead worked my hands where I could, to relieve his tension. His hands were busy too, unable to relax under my touch, and he massaged my body too.

Kissed and held and massaged, Damon and I lay next to one another and touched. The places where we were tense and anxious. The neck and shoulders, the arms and hands, the low back and hips and buttocks too. Every place I touched on Damon's real body carried years of tension and horror. He'd walled this body off from the world, holding the weight of so many things. Yet, he leaned strongly into my hands, the need for a relief that not even sex could provide, and my unpracticed hands were just strong enough and adept enough at feeling for the right places, to bring calm to a wired system. I was remembering all the times over the last decade that I'd had healing hands on me and what I'd learned to do to massage myself.

It didn't take long before Damon fell asleep in my arms, and that was surprising. How could he possibly feel that safe while being so exposed?

I wondered which avatar he would wake up inside, as I had no idea how many he was actively connected into, or even what he used them all for. Before I could fall asleep I tried to count the ones I'd seen. There was the clone on the couch in the next room, but I heard no movement from him. There was his clone in Scotland too. Beyond that, I didn't know. So, one real Damon beneath my hands and two active copies. That seemed like enough Damons to me.

I ran my fingers through his hair over and over, dragging my short nails across his scalp as his body continued to relax on top of me. Eventually, I too started to yawn, and my eyelids dropped to closing.

19

HEALER, HEAL THYSELF

When I woke up, I was back in Scotland, in a body still sick with neurological viruses. I looked down at my skin, covered in boils, and started to scream. The pain was so intense, I lost consciousness.

When I woke up again, in the same hurting body, the pain was not as bad, but my initial scream, of utter horror, echoed in the room before it died down with the lessening of the pain.

"Gellion!" Damon sat upright from his slouched and sleeping position and came towards me, grabbing syringes and filling my IV with something.

"Why am I here?" I demanded.

"I don't know," he said, shrugging. "Even more surprising is that I woke up here first."

"Can't you disconnect me?"

"We did."

"Can you put me to sleep?"

"I'm not sure that's a good idea."

"Why not?"

"Maybe there's a reason you're here."

"To suffer?"

"Suffering is a strong motivator."

"You think this is funny?" I asked.

"It's not funny."

"Then what?"

"You tell me."

"Is it about the trauma boxes?"

"Maybe," he said, but he was holding back.

I was in too much pain to curb my temper. "What?" I screamed.

"Look Gellion, I did all I could to show you healthy intimacy," Damon said bluntly, "despite how much effort it took for me to stay completely commonplace with you. I tried to show you the possibility of love, and a way to help you do the energy work on yourself in a sterile environment, yet you woke up here. So, connecting to this body to suffer may have been a choice."

"Well, I'm telling you I don't want to suffer!"

"And I'm telling you, you're 'pain shopping' for a reason."

I glared at him, and though my conscious mind felt angry at his thoughts, at his delusions, there was a small part of me that could see his point as well. Why had I woken up there?

"So, what do I do?" I asked.

He was quiet and pacing before answering.

"Think," he finally said. "Meditate. Ask yourself questions and continue to ask. And suffer, so you'll be motivated. That's what you did the first time, because it's all you could do. It isn't any different now, unfortunately."

"Great," I mumbled under my breath.

I lay down, unable to do anything but exactly that, and that meant my mind needed to tune out everything, including Damon. My current body was too tired.

He placed a CD inside a player, and it began a melodic, sleep-inducing, tonal resonance, like something born from the New Age movement that lasted for its beauty. He brought me water, and more fruit, and then he left me alone.

A few minutes later, Caitir came in quietly, and rebandaged me.

"Am I not contagious anymore?" I asked Caitir.

"Oh, you are," she smiled. "Calder had us wake up here in clones that had been exposed to and simultaneously treated for your viruses. We'll see if it works."

"Can't he do that for me?"

"He did, but beyond the one you were just in, we didn't have any other bodies of you at this location. We've been doing substantial work on the soldiers' bodies since there've been some significant casualties lately."

"Oh," I said, obviously unaware of their larger operations.

"Hopefully by tomorrow you'll wake up for both cycles at home base, having already been treated with the antivirals."

"I understand," I said softly. "Sorry for all the fuss."

"Sorry you have to spend the day in pain. I'm gonna put some cannabinoid and manuka honey treatment on your outbreaks. It should numb you and make it easier to bear."

Some patches of skin were blistering and needed to be treated. Other areas were light and splotchy. I felt like my skin was going to fall off from a million painful pin pricks. The antiviral had barely worked. I started to think while she worked to help me heal, and in those moments I was frustrated by my continued ignorance of everything.

"Caitir?" I asked. "Don't you think I should have my own files on everything?"

She looked at me like she didn't understand.

"Damon said I need to think, to heal. Well maybe I need information from myself that I don't have, and information on all these people and situations I know nothing about where I was intimately involved. How about my medical files? You all gave me some documentation from myself, but don't you have personal files on some of this, like the teenage boys who hurt me?"

She took a deep breath.

"I'll see what I can dig up," she mumbled.

"Or maybe you can just tell me," I also added, realizing reading files in this state would be hard.

"What do you want to know?"

"What do you remember?"

"That's the thing, Gell, no one wants to remember, least of all me. It was the worst day of my life," she said, pausing, "and my childhood included torture, so that's saying something."

I felt sick inside when she said that. "Why was it worse? I don't understand."

"We've all seen your scars. Those boys were told to torture and destroy you. And they were a moment away from finishing you off when we stopped them, but you never should have survived."

"Why would that be worse than your own torture?"

Caitir hung her head and quivered for a while, almost like a Medium in a séance, and then she shook it off.

"I am a descendant of the Thirteen Families. We are all indoctrinated into our family religion, and we learn to watch people be murdered, even people we know. We learn to not form attachments. We also know that as much torture as we experience, we're always exempt from death, even without other sacrifices around, never while relatives are fulfilling their duties. Our bloodlines are to be protected, unless we're proven weak, and then we may be sacrificed too."

She took a deep breath as if she needed the air but was also giving me a moment to ask more questions. I waited for her to continue in her own words, in her own thought process.

"Those boys came from families connected to the elite circles. Their parents played the game, which included training their sons. They come from wealth and privilege but won't inherit conglomerates or great family empires, so they become corporate henchmen for the elite. Pulled into the game for a cut of power and money, the parents agree to the secret rituals and the toughening required to rise in ranks.

"It starts young with abuse and privilege, and they're abused in rituals too, just like the rest of us. I've seen them at the island parties as well, where they truly learned to become brutal. But you, Gellion, weren't just a nameless sacrifice," Caitir continued, "and the more Damon suffered, the more they prolonged your torture. Killing you may have been their initiation into something, sponsored by our grandfather."

She only took a short breather before finishing.

"Damon returned deep inside himself and embraced the psychopath he'd once been, while watching them destroy you. His monster demolished the monsters hurting you, by becoming a bigger one," she shrugged. "Except for the pig holding a gun to Damon's head, Damon killed them all. But Calder killed the cop with his long scope rifle."

I was so confused trying to rebuild the whole scenario in my mind. A guy was killed by Calder with a rifle and then Damon killed everyone else. It was too hard to believe, were it not for the outcome. I was silent, absorbing what she'd given me, powerful information in context to their lives and their experiences and my trauma.

I gagged on my tears as the wetness from my eyes poured out. I tried to breathe through it to keep still.

"The car accident was the cover, for your injuries and the forest fire that burned up the evidence, while we raced away to get you to the hospital. I'd never had to deal with the aftermath of evil before. We never had to clean up the messes. I was so ashamed."

Caitir left without saying another word and I was left to process.

I tried to sleep, but that was hard won and didn't last. I did deep breathing and tried to meditate but hadn't been so great at that in the best of situations. I cried too, just from the constant burning itch I couldn't touch, and the frustration of it all.

Three hours in and my mind started to wander into thoughts I'd been avoiding. How many of my trauma boxes came from my life with Damon, from before and after the love? Had it only been sexual trauma that created a box, or did I carry them for other traumas too?

Damon had attacked me on the first day, stalked me afterwards, I was sure, trauma dumped and played mind games. His adolescent mind had probably been abusive too, without meaning it.

Were those all trauma-boxes too?

If the Gellion I'd been was truly so awesome, why didn't she heal all those traumas? Or taught the others to do the same? Learning about Damon's own torment during my destruction triggered a feeling I'd always had about unearthing my buried history, that still very much existed within us. I had so many questions and no one to ask. What kind of trauma did Damon carry?

Then I was faced with the dreaded reality of my own torment, and how much it had taken from me. I felt stuck, unable to see it all, unable to truly process how bad it had been. I knew I hadn't prayed in a while, or thought to, but I found myself calling out to the God BB believed in, the one she said was bigger than my imaginings, to send his angels to help me.

Wishing for guidance and wanting to tune into cosmic forces was unfamiliar, but now seemed the best time to reach out, when my human suffering was at its worst. I was asking for help, asking for insight, and asking for answers, in any form I could get them. Nothing came, as I waited, listening.

And then a deep exhaustion washed over me, and I finally closed my eyes, letting images and thoughts roam around. When I first woke up to the world and spent months in the hospital, my kid brother Brian would arrive for a visit with BB, and he couldn't stand the sight of me. The only way he could handle being around me was when it was dark and we could watch a movie in my room, him sitting in the lounge chair next to my undamaged side, so he could pretend I was still the Gellion he knew.

The movies we watched taught me a lot about what the world was, and what it wasn't. I would often ask Brian if the technology or ideas inside the sci-fi movies we saw were real technology, and Brian would explain how he saw the world, and what he experienced in it as a kid. Later, I found out there were things he didn't know that existed like the movie showed, but not in a meaningful way for everyday living.

Reality then started to be defined as things that existed or didn't exist from the movies I saw. When I was released from the hospital, I found the slowness and simplicity of my bed-bound reality to be a relief. There was no need for me to move into living any faster or sooner than I could manage. It took a little time but eventually there were many programs for me to help me get back to living.

All this time later I was searching my memory for images within those movies that could help me now, help me work to heal myself without a machine showing me. The superhero movies came to mind the most. The witch who could create bubbles of energy or protection were visuals most in my awareness.

I didn't have the energy to sit up, so I laid down and put my arms up in the air, as if I were a hero who had magical powers coming from my fingertips.

"God, please help me," I said again softly aloud, "please send your angels to help me," I whispered, trying to call on whomever would give me some answers.

I closed my eyes and thought of my damage, and of the three teenage boys who'd hurt me. If what I'd learned before about healing the Strŏngman was true, then each of those boys still existed somewhere inside my own psyche. Each lived within my mind, in the box they created when they raped and tried to kill me. I vaguely recalled their news photos in my mind and then put them each in an imaginary box, so I could stop seeing their faces.

I recoiled as I put myself, visually and metaphorically, inside the box too, recognizing just how painful it was to close that lid and know I was in there with them. Similar to physically freaking out over finding a leech or tick on yourself, I wanted to remove the ick, and remove it deeply.

Just knowing the boxes were there, causing me pain, I felt awful and the growing sensation of it made me move out of bed. The boils and rashes couldn't compare to the growing sickness I felt in my tailbone. I wasn't sure how to fix it, but I was pacing, trying to calm the growing burn. It was starting to hurt inside, hurt where I'd finally felt pleasure with Damon, and the ache of the pain made me run to the bathroom.

My body emptied itself violently and I felt the grossness lift for a moment, until it returned. The shower was cold until the warmth arrived and I put myself under the water to try to wash myself clean. In front of me and for the first time, the forms of the trauma I'd imagined were dancing before my face, like when images are burned into the retina by a bright light.

The boxes were there and within them I saw myself, young and naïve, stuck there with the shadows of evil. The boxes were closed, and I reached out my hands and grabbed one of them, picking it up with a sphere of invisible light, an energy bubble, while the other two faded away.

The box floated but the bubble moved with my hands. Inside I could see something horrible in silhouette play out like a muted image on repeat. I remembered more of BB's wisdom as I watched it and felt the feelings it disturbed. I had to repair it by removing the bad stuff first.

"Remove fear," I said.

My bubble of light wrapped around the fear, and I pulled it out of the box, and sent the bubble with fear away from me. It disappeared as if there were a vortex meant for that kind of waste.

Though the bubble of fear was gone, I noticed a void of emptiness in its place. Instead of removing more bubbles filled with ick, I could no longer see what gross things existed there, because the void was so large in my vision of it.

I thought long and hard on all the times I'd been in BB's presence, when I ignored the vast wisdom coming from her. More and more words I thought had passed me by were returning to my awareness. BB's entire healing practice was a beacon of light, light being sent into those shut down, filling their sadness and empty places, as if her entire being could channel God to the world.

Thinking of her love and her wholeness and grace, I sent out light through my hands to fill the emptiness where the fear had been.

"Fill with light," I said into the void.

Where fear once existed inside my teenage self, a radiant light fortified its place. I could not explain it, as my body took in a deep breath, and I released a large yawn. The feeling reverberated off my body, down through my spine and into my tailbone, and made my knees weak.

I had to take some breaths before continuing, but the box continued to float before me, like a retinal reminder that this pain wasn't going away without looking at it. Inside the box I saw more thoughts, emotions, and feelings that needed clearing.

"Remove trauma," I said.

Grabbing the vibration of trauma within a bubble and pulling it out, then remembering the power of filling the void with light. It was all I needed to start the healing.

"Fill with light."

The intense feeling within me, as it subsided into release, was easing my body some. *Fear. Trauma.* Both gone.

So many words came to mind before me, of what words could exist within the box, and their agenda vibrations. As I saw the words that described my experience, I removed them.

Pain, Evil, Darkness, Torture, Torment, Horror, Terror...

...Filling all with Light.

These were the first energies that got bubbled up and removed from the first box. The deepening yawns after each removal, and the intensity of the pulsating release from my tailbone as the pain that had been brought forward lessened, were too powerful to ignore or dismiss. Damon had been right, of course.

Eventually I figured out that *Karma* was an energy that existed within the box, as a connection between me and my perpetrator.

I'd remembered other ideas of connection, like curses, vows, agreements, but there was no other connection between us beyond the *Karma* from the incident. Keeping bad karma was useless.

"Remove Karma," I said as I saw my hands do the work.

"Fill with light," I continued.

I put my hands up, trying to imagine light coming from my hands, and that that light would be enough to really do the job, which I hoped meant balance of some kind.

The box wasn't done being cleared and I ran out of ideas for what could be left. The shower never ran out of warm water though. Eventually I lowered the mounted seat from the wall and sat down, not understanding how the box continued to pulse with darkness when I'd removed so much already. I stared at it for a long time, and still nothing came to me.

My brain was fried. I couldn't see the way through, and I was physically irritated from the pressure of the water pouring down on my soaking bandages. The wounds felt raw. I needed rebandaging and I didn't want to do it all alone, so when I left the shower, I called out.

"MARI, locate Caitir."

"Gellion, are you okay?"

"Can you help me with my bandages?"

"I'll be right there."

I was pulling off the soaked compresses when Damon entered the room with what I needed. He immediately grabbed a garbage can and came to me to collect the waterlogged masses I was ripping off me.

I sighed in exasperation to see him, to know it would be him who would have to help me.

"Sorry," he said. "Caitir is back at base with Malik. They're working on some things and spending some time together."

"Oh, yeah, of course." It was a super normal reason for not showing up. When in times of need, most people looked to their partner for support and help, and Damon was beginning to show up for me, in the worst of pain, more and more.

As he worked to dab me dry and applied new bandages I caught a slight smile from the corner of his mouth.

"What?" I asked.

He looked up confused, "What?"

"Why were you smiling?"

"Oh," he said, "I was thinking about how much you liked to escape into water to see answers. Showers especially. You would say that it was the best way to gain enough quiet away from the energy of others, to hear answers from someplace else."

I smiled at that, at doing something the same as the girl he'd known.

"What did you see?" He asked, assuming.

"How did you know?" I hadn't said anything.

"You had a look on your face, like you were still trying to work out a vision or a half-complete vision."

"It's that obvious?"

"Only to me. I'm just glad to see the familiar."

"You're around more."

"It's been therapeutic to be present for your journey. Your healing might very well be my own."

I could see it now, how much my own destruction created Damon's current path. The ties between us were more real than I could have ever imagined.

"I saw the Strŏngman boxes," I admitted. "Once I decided I would allow myself to envision those boys, I could see them, each in a box, with me."

"What did they look like?"

"At first, like something I was imagining on purpose, then like something I couldn't stop seeing. Like when you stare into a lightbulb and the circle of it gets burned there for a while. Except they were still boxes, and they didn't go away until I decided to look inside one."

"And?"

"I saw images of feelings and the design of it, and what it needed to be 'freed from,' to start separating the pieces of it out. Like dissecting a story and getting to the root of what exists there. I saw the pain and torment and even the Karma, but I'm missing something," I said.

Damon finished with the bandage he'd been arranging on my spine and got up. When he came back, he had a clean journal sitting on a large book, with a pen.

"This was another preferred tool. It helped you to go back and see the details of everything that happened. Try to remember everything you removed out of the box, so you can reference it."

I stared at the journal for a moment, while Damon went to work on my leg, which was purple from the breakout of Shingles. He used the numbing ointment, which helped so much. I jotted down the list of what I remembered clearing from the first Strŏngman box while in the shower, which admittedly felt like a small list when I wrote it down, considering the extent of my damage.

It made me wonder about elements that were there that I couldn't see but still needed defined and removed. I handed the list of words to Damon, and he started pacing, leaving my bandage only half-taped. His face grew more worrisome, the more he paced, and then he stopped and snapped his fingers and held out his hand, as if that were my cue to hand him a writing instrument.

He looked over at me, barely able to sit upright, and softened, coming toward me for the pen.

"If that's how you treat your secretary, we need to talk about your approach," I said softly, a jibe, as he walked away and sat and started writing.

When he came back and handed me the journal, he quickly finished the work on my last open wound, then he backed away and watched me from afar.

I looked down. His handwriting was foreign, but just a brief scan of the words he wrote, and I knew it was something I no longer wanted to decipher. I was surprised how blurry my vision suddenly became in response to the new information. Eventually my eyes started to focus, and just below my handwriting I saw the first suggestions for energy that still existed inside the box.

Victimized...

Raped...

Cut-Open...

These words were accurate and obvious in their truth. I'd closed my robe and rested back, but I also felt I should continue the work I'd started in the shower. The retinal burn of the box was still present, resting like a transparency over the real world, and it was throbbing its haze. I created a bubble again and found the light-burned box inside my view.

"Remove victimized," I said, removing it, "and fill with light. Remove raped. Fill with light. Remove cut-open," I said, "and fill with light."

With each removal came the yawn and deep release coming up and off my body as my muscles stretched. I looked down at the journal again.

Helplessness…the next word. I let the word sink into my mind, and I bit my lip as I tried to stop the tears.

"Remove helplessness. Fill with light."

Sorrow…and the tears poured slowly down.

"Remove sorrow. Fill with light."

Sacrifice…and there it was, my separation from Damon and our reunion were created by the sacrifice of my body, my virtue, and my life to a dark agenda and a dark force beyond my ability to understand.

"Remove sacrifice. Fill with light."

I whimpered as I said the words and envisioned the bubbles removing the dark energy of helplessness, sorrow, and sacrifice from within me, and filled the puncture wounds with healing light.

The yawns on each were muddled with weeping, and the release from the tailbone produced small convulsions from deep inside my sacral body up along my spine, until the removals subsided. I grew weaker in my attempt to heal, as each word proved its power within that trauma, and my resulting exhaustion made me spend time catching my breath.

As I breathed, I saw Damon get up and move around. The noises he produced in the shadows of the room came from the kitchenette area. He was making tea. This would be the second time he'd done so, an act of service I considered awkward for someone like him.

I stopped seeing the words, even though I knew he'd written more. I craved rest, a break from the concentration of seeing it all step-by-step and working through it as both patient and healer. The last word especially, and what it represented, had become somehow physically heavy to lift inside that bubble, and my arms felt drained.

The tea was herbal with fruit essence and a sweetness I hadn't considered I'd taste feeling so ill. It calmed me, and we sat in the quiet of the rhythmic meditative music Damon put on in the background and drank the tea. It took a while, and a lot of deep breaths and moments of acceptance for me to be ready to face it all again. By then, the burning itch across my body had kicked back up, and suddenly the feeling of it powerfully moved my body out of bed.

"What is it?" he stood up with me.

"It hurts again," I whined as I tried to walk-off the coming pulsing burn up my back, to keep myself distracted.

Damon grabbed the journal off the bed. "The only way out, is to go through it," he said, handing me the journal, a remorseful look on his face.

I looked down to see what word or phrase had been written after *sacrifice*.

When I read the words *Involuntary Arousal,* I threw up my tea into my mouth.

I looked up at Damon, unsteady on my feet, a growing expression of disgust on my face. I shook my head from side to side as I sat down on the nearest seat. I didn't want to deal with it.

Arousal from rape? Arousal from abuse? What was he thinking?

My head didn't stop shaking. My mind disagreed.

It took a long time for the tears in my throat to subside and for the yawn of release and acceptance to be worked through, but eventually I got there.

"Remove involuntary arousal," I said with a quiver and an overwhelmed breath, without analyzing it. "Fill with light."

The next one was even worse.

Unwanted Pleasure…

That's when a realization finally sank in. The information was there but until now I hadn't understood. I stared at Damon because I finally fathomed that he knew these phrases existed within my trauma because he had been there for all of it. He wasn't just tied up somewhere as I was destroyed, he was with me through it. Despite the understanding in Damon's face at my realization, I felt completely broken by the knowledge that before they hurt me, they made Damon watch as they gave my body pleasure against my will.

"You had to watch all of it?" I asked him, trembling violently from the realization.

He nodded, stone faced, unable to look me in the eye. The following convulsion that hit the base of my spine and moved me up like a shockwave through my column, pushed me to the ground, kneeling. I had to hold myself in.

"Remove unwanted pleasure," I trembled out, sickened. "Fill with light."

I did the work while becoming internally forlorn, removing such evil brought a level of disgust I'd never experienced before, while utterly hopeless inside. Worst of all was that I had only gotten this far into understanding the complexities of my trauma because of Damon, because he knew what the boxes held.

Not even finished with the first box, with two left to go, and I could barely handle the intensity of the pain and anguish I felt. I kept myself quiet, but the tears flowed, and my arms had never felt so heavy trying to lift the energy off me. I was wrapped up in my continuous yawning and wanted to be done. I found myself looking for a way back to bed, unable to connect to Damon's presence in the room.

I sat back down.

"There's only one left," Damon said.

The journal had fallen to the floor and Damon picked it up and handed it to me, crouched down, non-threatening, looking up at me. He opened the journal and placed it in my lap.

I looked down at the last suggestion of what could still be stuck within me, inside my trauma.

Abandoned by God…

The moment I saw the words I cried, and the shift in my body was immediate and painful, as my weakened frame convulsed forward in utter desolation. My arms and forehead gently touched the ground, as

Damon caught me just in time without causing me harm. I cried open mouthed, weeping at the horror of it, into the carpet, at the truth of the depth of my despair, at what had happened to me.

God had abandoned me, for sure. My body lived through that truth.

I had been prayed for, cared for by God-loving people, while the person I'd once been had done God's work, and lived the mission of Jesus who said to go forth and cast out demons. That Gellion was abandoned for I had surely never, not ever, felt the presence of God in my miserable, short life.

The pain that swept over me, from tailbone to skull and into my eyeballs, culminated in shock, as my skin went completely on-fire, the internal pain matched by the external.

I could feel myself leaving my own body, leaving the pain most of all, and disconnecting entirely into unconsciousness.

20

THE TEMPLE OF CRYSTALS

The utter desolation of being *Abandoned by God* was still there. Like a fresh wound, a truth I'd sensed but never actually recognized, now adeptly diagnosed. I'd felt so alone for so long and never sensed a connection, not ever. So, when I woke up without any physical pain, I was shocked by how powerfully the emotional pain stayed with me, as it followed me immediately into a different body.

I woke up in Georgetown. My body was a fully scarred brunette, as close to the original Gellion as possible, and had been left asleep in the master bedroom of the waterfront penthouse. Damon's original body should have been asleep nearby but wasn't. My consciousness abandoned Damon's somewhere in Scotland. I wondered how long I had before he would reconnect to his body here, to be closer to me.

I imagined Damon's original body at homebase, in a bunker, safe and sound. I was under the covers, dressed in a nightgown. My confusion at the jarring scenario, waking up to the topside world, had me abandon the tears I brought with me from Scotland, and get up and move, discarding the healing work in search of a better escape.

The windows everywhere showed the autumn world outside that made me feel connected to living. I didn't want to be told what to do or be held back from going where I wanted to go, so I went quickly to the closet and found clothes for myself.

Wow!

Caitir put clothes for me everywhere Damon's clothes existed, as if she was always helping him to remember me too. Their perpetual care made me second-guess wanting to go out for a bit, but I needed some relief, even if I felt guilty about it.

When I saw Damon's Georgetown clone still unconscious on the couch, I felt resolved to go. I kissed his lifeless forehead and apologized for needing to be alone, like I used to be, to lick my wounds and talk myself into a stronger mental fortitude to get through the painful healing.

My existence before Damon had felt the freest driving with the windows down, through the long tree-covered parkways of Maryland and Northern Virginia. Letting the engine move me when my traumatized body couldn't, was my preferred escape. I wanted that now more than anything.

The hand scanner on the elevator gave me access to the garage floor. When I exited no one was around and the garage was sealed shut by massive doors. The security from the outside was first-rate, but inside the garage the security booth was unlocked, and there were multiple sets of key fobs hanging up. This garage level was only for Damon and his people.

The third car fob button I pressed lit up a sports car nearby, so I put the other fobs back and looked for the means to open the garage door out. It was small, and underneath the security screens, but there was a button to unlock the building's lower garage. Once I pressed it a red light flashed on a nearby wall.

I got in the car, pulled past the opening, stopped, got out and ran back to press the button to close it again. I didn't want to cause any extra trouble, just for a little freedom, and then I stepped back out of the garage before the door came fully down.

The Georgetown street ahead was familiar and I sighed deeply at having my own foot on the pedal for a change. A little speed, a cool breeze from an open window and some loud music was exactly what I needed. It wasn't long before I turned onto M Street to get to the parkway along the Potomac River, past Georgetown University and out of the city.

The perpetual parking spots along the parkway for hiking along the toe-path reminded me of my own recent journey. Leaving Katherine in DC and parking my old car at one of those locations. However, seeing the water reminded me of my plunge into the river much farther up, when I'd leapt to my death off a cliff and floated with the current into the city. The horror of the memory was so much more significant than wanting to die and succeeding only in doing it slowly.

Suddenly I wondered about a lot of things, but most of all I longed for some real memories, and some real answers. I knew more now than I ever did about my trauma and the crimes perpetuated against me. Driving the road that led out to the suburbs and the mansions there, for those who played politics outside the capital, felt like the right way to go, to try to understand it all. It was a beautiful drive as the leaves were starting to land on the ground.

Once I passed Old Anglers Inn and the Great Falls Park entrance, and then the small Potomac intersection, I started to feel a longing for home, for my dad and my brother and BB too. For quiet mornings, driving through the small town for supplies, or to go to school in a place that felt so much farther removed than just being a little way past the wealthy Potomac community.

Maryland had so many small pockets that felt like someplace else, especially when driving near horse country and the farms and vineyards. The grass was still bright green despite the coolness of early November. The beautiful houses made me feel empty inside as I raced past them.

Then I screeched to a halt before the entrance to the Jairus mansion, where too many people watched me die. Silently wishing I could burn it to the ground, for me and the others who must have died there before me, I spit the saliva building in my mouth out the window toward it then I drove on. The country road winded and continued for a long while.

I came to the familiar T-stop in the road and even though I desperately wanted to turn right, to go back home, and see my brother, I knew it was a mistake. So, I turned left instead, which I'd never remembered doing before, not really. The land was undeveloped and marshy, and there were state and federal conservation signs for land and animals, mixed with private summer camps and horse stables. I wondered how far I'd get before I'd have to turn around.

Eventually I came down a long slope and saw ahead colorful flags in solid colors. At the sight of the flags, I felt deeply inside that I had driven in that direction for a reason, beyond avoiding my family and old home. There were large multicolored banner flags outside, lining the open fence along the driveway. It was a large white house that looked like private property, but there were clear signs that said it was a Buddhist temple.

The property, which was on the riverside, had to have included the large house and the land around it. The flags welcomed the driver to enter the long driveway, and there was plenty of gravel parking. The driveway took me past the large house before reaching a parking lot on the side.

Outside, the grounds included statues and shrines for prayer and offerings, and incense burned all around. Inside there was a small gift shop. I was drawn to the house right away and noticed the signs about removing shoes and where to put them. The gift shop didn't entice me, as I was more interested in the energy I felt behind the closed glass doors beyond the large staircase, drawing me in.

The sign said to enter quietly and respect others. The prayer room was open to anyone, as there were no services in session. When I stepped inside, I saw what I felt that drew me, and I looked around amazed at the large crystals that lined the entrance into the prayer room, on both sides. The massive rocks encircled the prayer room too and surrounded the different statues of Buddha.

The crystals stood close to one another on light displays beneath them to showcase the clarity of their mass. Each crystal was different in size, shape, frequency, and color.

I took a deep breath and felt comforted at the vision of the crystals, so much more impressive than the smaller collection Father Jerzy used in the prayer room on the boat, which was now a sunken hospital ship, and I felt sad. I suddenly remembered all the children I left behind, unable to face my own fears, my own horror. I had too much to learn and I needed help, or maybe comfort.

Part of me was afraid to go back, or forward.

I'd read the sign on the wall that said not to touch the crystals, so I did what I imagined others did, just as Father Jerzy had started to show me, and hovered my hands above the first crystal. I didn't try to absorb anything, but just felt it, and checked its value to me.

The first was a yellow-tinted quartz, about three feet tall and sitting on a pedestal that raised it up another foot, and the resonance wasn't too strong, or too bright on my hands. I quickly moved on, as there were many crystals to sense, from pink rose quartz to clear quartz, to black, to green. It didn't matter the size, shape, or color, as I was looking for some kind of familiar feeling.

It was odd. I spent a little time hovering over many crystals and none of them seemed like a good fit, for what I felt like I needed, which was simply a source to help me feel connected, to feel alive within my own body. The crystals were lacking in that energy so much, I wondered if something had happened.

Was my current clone body lacking in some way?

The whole room seemed too sad, and I wondered about the state of the temple, or the monks that lived on the upper floor of the house, or in the other buildings along the grounds. Why else would all the crystals be so depleted if something wasn't wrong? Those feelings felt awful and suddenly it dawned on me that I might be intruding being there. I looked up and around and didn't know what I should do or observe.

Maybe I was projecting my own sadness onto the crystals, as I only

350

felt my own energy reverberated back to me when I tried to connect. It wasn't what I expected when I came inside. After trying to and failing to engage with the crystals, I finally gave up and wondered if I should meditate instead. There was only one other person in the prayer room, and they hadn't moved from their meditative state the whole time I moved from crystal to crystal.

When I finally sat down on the carpeted floor, behind one of the rows of the little prayer walls, I wanted to cry. I had landed here hoping for solace and energetic potential and found depletion instead. I let the tears fall and breathed it all out silently and thought again of what I was so upset by.

Acknowledging the feeling of abandonment, by the source of life, by the God I had always wanted to know, only made the wound feel that much deeper. It was nearly impossible to not sit in wonder and try with each breath to reconcile feeling utterly forsaken. But how could I reconcile being so unloved?

I couldn't stay. Nothing there made me feel any better, and I knew I needed to remove that sense of abandonment from the Strŏngman trauma box. I couldn't do that while others watched. Having witnesses to my arms moving around in the air, it wasn't so ideal, so I got up and started to leave the prayer room.

"Gellion?" I heard a female voice say. "Gellion Greene?"

I turned around to see a nearly bald, brown-skinned woman, wearing monk's robes. Despite her older age and extra weight, her mixed-race features were beautiful. I couldn't tell what race made up her features but there had to be Asian and Indian roots of some kind.

"Do I know you?" I asked.

"Do you remember me?" she asked in return, smiling. I wondered if she knew about my accident.

"No, I don't. Sorry. It's nice to meet you."

"Bhante, you can call me Bhante," she said.

"What does that mean?" I asked.

"Nun," she said, and I laughed as she took my hand and gently shook it.

"I had a sense while driving by, to stop."

"You're leaving so soon?" she asked.

And despite myself I blushed at why I wanted to leave, as the crystals had not been comforting.

"I just thought I'd feel something different," I admitted.

"Like what?"

"It feels incomplete."

"What's missing?" she asked curiously.

"Oh, well…The crystals seem so lifeless," I admitted. "They seem sad. I was hoping they would energize me."

She blinked back at me in surprise. "Wow. Are you sure you don't remember?"

"No, sorry," I shook my head.

"You used to come here and clear the crystals of all the sadness and despair they had absorbed from all the people who come seeking help. It hurt you too much to feel their energy, so you'd remove what was heavy and make the crystals feel bright and pure again."

"Me?" I gasped.

"Yes. We all know you. Your mom and grandparents too."

"Oh, I didn't know. No one told me I spent any time here."

She smiled. "And you're right, you know," she said, pointing to the crystals. "They are filled with sadness."

"Did something happen?"

"What did you feel?"

"It felt like they were weeping."

"Ah. Well, our leader passed away recently, so maybe they were."

"Oh," I said, surprised. "I'm so sorry. Maybe they've been absorbing all the sorrow."

"We knew the loss was coming, but you never know how powerful it will be until it occurs. Everyone is feeling it. When the brightest light goes out, it dims everyone for a time. Maybe you could help the crystals, and in turn help us."

"Me? How?" I asked.

"I wish I could remember how you removed their burdens."

352

"It's odd," I revealed. "I just started doing this stuff again. I could try," I said, looking around at all of the crystal, wondering if I could make a difference.

She smiled at me and motioned to the largest crystal in the room. "That was Master Lang's favorite and is likely the most depleted. You should start there."

Oddly, I felt drawn to do just that. The prayer room was empty, so I could stand there with my hands moving around in a dance, attempting to remove sadness, darkness, and energy dumping, and replace it all with light I envisioned coming through my working system. I didn't feel up to this challenge, just compelled as every time I tried to stop I'd turn and see Bhante still there, ready with a nod for me to continue on. With her encouragement, praying with me in her own way to support the work, I finished.

By the time I was done with the last crystal, I felt both exhausted and completely buzzed with energy. As if the crystals themselves couldn't help but be immediately reciprocal. I had absorbed a lot of light into me, and I was humming yet drained. We walked out slowly from the prayer room, and she sat me down on a bench, returning with water and a piece of fruit.

I sat dazed for a while, slowly sipping.

I hadn't even noticed she left. I assumed she'd been needed elsewhere, and I'd had no desire to move. But when she returned, she was holding something, outstretched in her hand. It was a sealed envelope and when I looked at it, I saw my name.

"What's this?" I asked quietly.

"Master Lang wrote us all letters when he knew he would be leaving, and included you, in case you ever came back."

"For me?"

"You came here often as a child, Gellion," she said again. "Your grandparents brought you when you were little, and you came back on your own," Bhante said then bowed to me. "It is so good to see you and thank you for energizing the crystals. It feels much better already."

Still seated, I bowed my head back at her and then she walked away, to see to other duties, as she busied herself helping someone in the eating area. I stared in awe at something so surprising to behold. I wondered if I should open the letter right away but suddenly felt the need to leave with my bounty, to walk and move.

The new buzzing inside me needed relief.

Outside there were multiple trails to take, and I knew the direction of the Potomac River, so I found a trail that headed that way. There were statues and meditation wheels along the path, and I didn't know where I should stop to read, until I found a detour off the trail that led to a spot on a hill with a large crystal in the center of it and sand all around. The sun shone brightly there, and I felt drawn to the power of the large quartz sitting in the sun.

Without thinking I removed my shoes and stepped barefoot into the sand and stood with my hands hovering over the crystal. This crystal needed no clearing, needed no energizing. The sun had kept it pure and full. With my hands above it I thought of the trauma box I'd been trying to clear with Damon by my side, yet the Strŏngman energy that was so powerful it wore me down completely.

Slowly the retinal burn image arrived, the box hovered before me like a transparent cartoon, waiting for interaction. I visualized the bubble that carried the darkness away, wrapping around the box.

"Remove abandoned by God," I said.

The words popped up into vibration and frequency within the bubble of light and containment, taking on mass. Then I lifted the bubble away from the box, pulling the energy off me. Me, abandoned by the one true power that should love me the most.

"Fill with light."

The power of the agonizing energy leaving my system, as it moved down my spine shook my knees. The massive quartz caught me when I fell forward, and I held onto it as I shook, comforted by the warmth of the smooth rock, basked-in and bathed and cleansed by the sun, before I landed onto the sand.

It took some time to let the relief move through me and to become steady again. Once I was able, I sat back on my heels and caught my breath. Staring into the sunlit quartz I could see it, the box before me as it still existed, less staticky, less heavy to view, but still present. I realized there was still work to be done, beyond clearing the detailed hurts that resulted from so much trauma. I wasn't sure how I'd get there, but I wanted to finish it.

Though Damon seemed sure that being *Abandoned by God* was the last pain or trauma within the box, I wondered if he were wrong. I'd been wrong before, and missed steps of understanding, and I didn't want to miss anything, so I sat for a while, looking into the space, asking myself through an attempt at muscle testing, if there was anything left to clear. My fingers went weak every time I tried to ask, which was supposed to mean a negative answer.

"Is my name Gellion?" I asked myself, just to make sure I could answer a question positively.

My thumb and pinky held strong together against the pressure of my index finger trying to break through the circle. I'd done it before, and had been practicing, but it was the first yes I'd gotten that felt real and solid. What could be more real than me affirming my own name? That should be the easiest to master. So, I could hold an affirmative answer using self-muscle-testing, that gave me some hope.

When I asked, "Is abandoned by God the last hurt to be removed?"

The answer was weakness, a rejection. Maybe it was right, or maybe my body was making things up to suit me. If *Abandoned by God* wasn't the last hurt on my list of what's inside the first Strŏngman box, what was left? I should be able to figure out what still existed to heal from me. It wasn't happening, so something else must be in the way, but what?

I didn't really remember the steps from the cartoon video, and where I was in the healing didn't look familiar. I wondered what to do and started asking for help, first inside my head and then out loud.

"I don't know if anyone good is listening, but if you are, God, or angels, or Jesus, or Buddha, or something, I really need help, please," I said, because prayers felt so foreign and because I wasn't sure if God would help me or not. That feeling of being abandoned had been powerful for a reason.

I stared into the crystal, and like before, when the Strŏngman box showed up in my visual cortex, it felt like a retinal burn from a lamp. This time the trauma box showed up inside the large crystal. I could see it, but as I stared at it, it didn't look like a box.

The box morphed as it glistened inside the crystal and it became bone, specifically it looked like the tailbone and the sacrum. Though I'd done nothing to be out of alignment, my pelvis and tailbone were always a mess.

The bone-shaped box kept shimmering in movement, like the bone wanted to shake the box off itself. I watched as it moved, determined to separate itself, yet without any success, and I felt the whimper of it when it failed. I understood the frustration and wondered how I should intervene.

I reached out my hands, as the retinal burn of the box-on-bone moved out of the crystal and rested before me, within reach, where I could attempt my work. I picked up the box with my bubble sphere and removed the box from the bone, by speaking it and visualizing it.

"Remove the, uh, Strŏngman box from my sacrum bone, uh, my tailbone," I said as I pulled it away from the vision of myself, using my hands.

"Fill with light."

I stretched my fingers out, working hard to visualize it, to see the light coming through me, through my palms out into the crystal visual. Then the light was being absorbed in the place where the box had just been inside my body.

Releasing the box and its weight from my tailbone, from having to carry that weight of it anymore, was powerful. Even though my body felt immensely lighter at that moment, there was still a tether, a connection between them, between the box and my bone. The tether looked like a living strand of dark matter that acted like a chain, tying my body to the trauma.

"Disconnect the Strŏngman box from the bone," I said.

This time when I moved my hands I wasn't removing or filling, but breaking something apart, severing the connection between myself and the trauma. To match the desire of my words, my hands moved like breaking a chain and disconnecting the energy of the box from my body with my intention.

"Fill with light."

It didn't take much imagination to sever the shackles binding my trauma to me. Speaking the words out loud sounded funny, but Caitir had been right that there was more power in doing so, as I could see it happening easier when I spoke it out loud. Once I filled the empty connection with light, and the space between them was no longer hollow, the deeper relief came to me, as I yawned for a long time, taking the breath of air deeper into my gut than I'd ever remembered.

My body felt lighter, euphoric almost, as the tingling in my tailbone sent soft shimmers of relaxation up my spine, and a warm, numb feeling down my legs, as if the relief was so great as to remind me of intimate pleasure, which I'd only just experienced. I quivered lightly and sat back onto the sand. It took a while to catch my breath.

Each step forward was so detailed and necessary, it felt like a long slow struggle to remove it all from me. I needed to breathe again, get back my strength. I wanted the box away from me, as I recovered. As if it read my mind, it backed away, returning to the crystal where I could more peacefully see.

Once within the crystal, the walls of the box turned translucent, exposing the players there, in a strange kind of animation. I could see myself, and I could see a teen boy and I felt a burning inside me, at the vision of him there. I wanted him to go from that place, gone from my side, gone from ever having been allowed to get that close to me.

Without-even-thinking I held my hands up, and though I knew my energetic sphere was strong, this time it grew denser, like thick glass inside my hands, weighty and solid. With my strongest energy ball, I picked up the evil teen boy from inside that box, a wave of disgust hitting me as I removed him, to some place away from me.

"Remove the evil teen from the box. Fill with light."

Even though the empty space was filled, so was the rest of the box, as if a fog of *Filth* had been left behind when he was removed.

"Remove the filth left inside the box. Fill with light."

As the fog cleared, something remained. There was a strand of connection from the box to the boy's silhouette, hovering outside it. It made me so angry that he could still be connected to me that I grabbed the energy strand with my hands and ripped it apart, as if it were real, as if the strand of it were made of dense mass.

"Disconnect the evil teen from the box. Fill with light."

The energy strand that hung in the air like a broken line of smoke dissipated entirely. That felt better, as he was no longer connected anymore, no longer an eminence. As I stared at the vision of myself, alone in the box, I started to feel bad, like I wanted to leave but couldn't. When I saw my own face, it was something too familiar, and I finally understood so much more about myself.

Yes, it was true. *Abandoned by God* was not the last of it, and not even the worst of it. No wonder I hadn't been able to figure out what was left to heal. It was beyond my compression, and there was no way I could have known that the old Gellion set inside herself the same feelings I felt my entire existence. We weren't as different as I thought, merged by our pain, before her extinction.

The girl I was, had been, the one inside that box, hadn't just been abandoned, had not just lost the will to live, she had decided that she wouldn't be coming back from the horrors of that night, not ever. Young Gellion didn't want to live after what was done to her, and in truth, she didn't. She never returned.

Eve-Anne Gellion Greene died on prom night, just like the boys who killed her.

Wanting to Die.

Dying.

"Remove wanting to die," I said, trembling. "Fill with light."

I blubbered my way through it, knowing that the next words were encapsulating her last moments and trying to reverse them.

"Remove dying, from the box, and from my body," I said, using my hands furiously, digging that energy of dying out of the box and out of me.

This Gellion wanted to live, especially after waking up without pain. I removed the energy of it from myself both then and now.

"Fill with light," I said.

I watched the light fill me, and my teenage self, filling the cracks and broken places within her, within us, with something hopeful. The knot in my throat got so tight I had to let the tears come, to open me up to breathe, before the emotions of sadness overtook me entirely.

Is my missing memory inside that box? I wondered.

The prospect of rediscovering myself, the girl who wanted to die and did, was overwhelming to the point of pain. I was choked up. I barely had the strength to continue, in my sadness and understanding, but with some drive left I made another bubble, yawned deeply to release some of the pain and reached into the box. The constant emotions were like a rollercoaster to my system, as I forced myself to inhale and sigh and even stretch out of me the pain and trauma of all the work.

I expected to be able to lift my young self out of the box, but still she was stuck.

What else could there be?

I suddenly wished Damon were with me, as he knew so much about who I was and how I healed. I was lonely doing the work. Yet, I'd been desperate to hide from him too, to have my own experience of pain and torment separated from his watchful eyes, without witness to my anguish.

I stared hard at the crystal, seeing the box within and wanting the crystal to give me insight. Watching my own teenage expressions, trying to read what she was trying to say to me, but she couldn't speak at all.

Watchful eyes? Oh my God!

Teenage Gellion's lips weren't just shut, they looked glued, then bound, no, covered entirely. I was filled with rage when I recognized the most awful truth of all, that when I was being raped, tormented, beaten, and mutilated, I was muzzled and gagged, choking on my own screams.

The sand on the ground around me would do the least damage to the pounding of my furious, clenched fist against it. I beat the earth, and this time my screams of horror were audible! I could no longer keep the emotions in my head.

"Ah!" I cried out.

And then my imagination could see it!

Even though I tried to turn it into a cartoon, the images started flooding in. Damon had been forced to watch, forced into a gag himself, tied up too. I'd wanted to say goodbye to Damon as I was dying, and call out to him, but I'd been silenced, unable to use my voice as I was being destroyed. Only our eyes could speak, and I'm sure in the end I wished he couldn't see what had been done.

Monsters! I screamed inside my head.

When I finally composed myself enough to speak, I trembled.

"Remove being muzzled. Remove being gagged," I said, because I didn't know the difference and I couldn't choose between them. I picked up the energy of my forced silence with a bubble and removed it. "Fill with light. Fill with light."

I filled my stifled-teenage self with light, giving myself back the ability to speak, and then I started to cry again, at the horrible realizations and the great relief of moving the energy off me.

"Remove the filth," I said realizing again how the *Muck* inside had mass too. "Fill with light."

It wasn't long before I realized the fog had lifted from her entirely. The box was finally unencumbered, and I could remove myself from it, so I did, in the kindest and most delicate bubble I could envision.

"Remove Gellion from the Strŏngman box," I said.

Even after I removed my teenage self from the box, the box had not yet disappeared. The act of violence and evil still existed. Removing me also left a haze of negativity behind.

"Remove the muck," I said. "Fill with light."

As the fog of muck and filth cleared, something remained. There was a strand of connection from the silhouette of my younger self to the box, just as it had been for the boy. It made me so angry that I could still be connected that I grabbed the energy strand with my hands and ripped it apart.

"Disconnect me from the box," I said. "Fill with light."

The energy strand that hung in the air like a broken line of smoke dissipated entirely after I filled the area with light. The box was now empty, and it got smaller, so small that it was floating next to my teenage self, until her arms rose to meet it, and she was holding the box in her hands. But the box didn't belong to me, or her. I didn't create that box, and I wanted nothing to do with it.

I felt a chill, and then a gust of wind kicked up sand into the air. Then the shadow of darkness that had been in front of me felt like it was floating in the breeze somewhere, ready to torment me again, from so long ago.

Deep inside the crystal the perpetrator's image returned, standing in front of the box, and the girl holding it. Once he was before her, my younger self reached out to him and handed back the Strŏngman box he had created; a box that was now forcing him to hold the repercussions of becoming a deeply rooted curse.

He didn't want to take the box, but he didn't have a choice, and when he held it, something terrifying happened. The box started to crumble, and it turned into dark dust that covered him as if it were a living flame infecting him with all its evil. Then the boy too started to crumble under the weight of it, under the weight of what he had done.

Dissipating, the layers of his existence turned to dust then suddenly came back to him, in ash and soot, and burnt coal as if the process of cremation were working in reverse. He became so whole that his face reappeared but never without cracks of darkness and fire, only for the process to start again, for him to turn to dust.

After a while of perpetual burning, he reached out to me, for help.

Mesmerized by the sight, dazed by its visual, I backed away, mystified. For a while all I could do was watch him suffer, righteous indignation within me.

It played before me like a movie, on repeat, like a "gif" file so violent you could hear inside your head a sound that wasn't playing. There I was, staring and mesmerized, wanting to see his perpetual destruction, enjoying the display of handing back the torment to the tormentor. But it didn't end, and eventually the hypnosis of it no longer held me in gratification.

I believed that eventually his torment would dissipate on its own, but it didn't. I got up and left the spectacle, eager to be free of it for a moment, and paced around the crystal, waiting for the image to dissolve into nothing, but again it just stayed. Every time I returned to look into the crystal he was there, being torn apart, as if I was watching him exist in hell somewhere, being punished for his sins. It's what he deserved, and what I thought I wanted to see, but after some time I began to want something else, for it to end.

I'd never been a punitive person before, and yet my abuser deserved punishment, but seeing a glimpse of what real Hell might look like, I suddenly couldn't bear it any longer. I began pondering if Hell really existed and if he was actually burning there all this time.

Then I had a thought.

If I set him free from the torment of it? With our Karma cleared, would I be freeing him from literal Hell?

Is that even possible?

Surely not.

If I'd learned anything from my stepfather's Catholic upbringing, it was that Jesus was the only one who could free a soul from hell.

Does this boy deserve Hell for eternity for what he did to me?

How can I possibly answer that? I argued with myself.

I have no knowledge of his life, or the other evils he might have done. What if his only evil was done to me?

Would I be helping him leave Hell behind?

No, that didn't seem right. Suddenly, neither did my most recent belief that there was no Hell at all, not when I'd finally faced real evil, purposeful evil, and understood now why there should be a Hell. Maybe also purgatory. I knew at least one thing; the souls of those boys did not belong in any Heaven my mother resided in.

It was so strange to care about things I'd never cared about before. And I had no answers, just more questions, and thoughts, and a quiet desperation to let go of controlling the narrative of another's afterlife, once the healing was done. In that moment I no longer saw Heaven as just a place between death and God, but as a place designed to protect those who died good, or mostly good, from the bowels of evil that actually existed on Earth.

Even if I cleared our Karma, and released our Strŏngman trauma from us both, only God could decide on the sinner's path ahead, in the afterlife. It wasn't on me to carry any of it. I wasn't going to burden myself with what happened to anyone else in my healing. Yet I struggled to release him still. I didn't know how long I'd stayed in the trance, watching my rapist's destruction over and over, watching him burn to ash, then come back to life, damaged and pained.

Eventually none of the thoughts mattered, as the process needed to be completed, and I'd already been there so long. I'd finally had enough. I'd seen sufficient torment of him to want relief from it too. So, I reluctantly created a bubble, one without much power or thought, yet it grabbed the black dust that had been the Strŏngman box and tried to pull it away from him, but it wouldn't go.

What had I missed? I removed everything bad I could think of and even removed the Karma of it from the boy who created the darkness on me. I was stuck staring at it still, but this time wondering what was left, what could possibly be powerful enough to torment the boy too.

After a while, I couldn't stare at him any longer, and turned my vision back to my younger self, also stuck there watching the boy be torn to bits. I stared long enough and hard enough that the look of her face morphed into a close-up view, and in the reflection of her eyes I saw what I could only describe as the vision of a curse stuck upon her, locked in darkness with it.

I didn't even think beyond that, but to make a bubble of removal, and wrap younger Gellion and the boy with it.

"Remove the Strŏngman perpetrator curse," I said, as I pulled the bubble away from them both, pulling the darkness of the dust away from the evil boy and the girl he tried to kill.

While I did send the dust away, to be gathered by who-knows-what, I couldn't bring myself to fill the boy with light. He was dead, anyway, and I was saving my light for me, sending it to myself, and I didn't care if that was selfish. I waited for him to disappear, and of course, I realized soon enough that the never-ending vision of him was a lesson I was supposed to learn.

I didn't even know how much I hated this stupid teen boy, until the work of healing it was before me. Yet hating him and carrying mercilessness toward him were just going to keep him stuck there, stuck attached to my younger self, with a hollowed out bad guy forever connected.

With just the smallest energy I could muster, I sent light to him.

"Fill them both with light," I said.

And with those words the teen boy stopped dissipating in destruction and finally disappeared. The box was gone, and the boy was gone but I was not, not my teenage self. She was still there, separated from me, not even a shared memory, waiting for me to finish helping her. I wanted to be in the crystal with her, as we shouldn't be split, but one. So, I closed my eyes and saw myself inside the crystal with her, and I made a bubble big enough for both of us, for both our minds.

She was a disassociated piece of me, like Damon had said, and I understood what needed to be healed to bring us back together.

"Remove the trauma of being separated. Fill with light," I said and watched as fissures and cracks between the two of us started to light up.

"Remove the darkness of separation," I said, taking the bubble of our separation off us, "and fill with light."

I watched as we were pulled closer together, more broken places lighting up, but we weren't yet one. I kept my eyes closed, seeing us still there, just a few steps away from one another. There were better words I could use to finish the work, and I needed to find them.

"Remove the disassociation of our minds, and fill with light," I said, as I sent us both light, and intention.

I could see the energy around our heads start to merge, wanting to pull the two of us together, but stopping just short of doing so. There was something still missing because my arms felt heavy, and my body burdened.

Can it be as simple as the intention to reassociate? I questioned.

Like when I would use my hands to fill a space with light, I held my hands out with intention.

"Reassociate our minds back together."

At once the image of my teen-self disappeared inside me, like a perfect "special effects" movie visual, our fractured selves reintegrated back together. As I yawned and breathed and released the emotion of it all off me, realizing the work was actually done, the power of the feeling grew. Whatever mass of darkness the perpetrator created in hurting me, left my body too or felt like it.

My fingertips digging into the sand, I held myself up with my hands, head hanging low, and I loudly yawned as the feeling of it melted away. Then I wept a messy weeping, from deep within me. It was the ugly kind of crying that you're grateful to do alone, for fear of misunderstanding eyes. I questioned myself and wondered if I'd truly completed the work.

Did I feel the presence of who I was return at all?

I couldn't say, but then I'd only just completed the one box. I was having trouble believing it was done, but I also couldn't quite calm my system from the relief and the perpetual yawning and need for stretching, and the tears that continued without crying.

"One box," I said to myself over and over, reminding myself it took all that work to get just the one box to go, to get a glimpse of liberation from the damage.

There were two left, two Strŏngman boxes left to face and remove, and work off me. With two gigantic constructs still housed, still taking up so much space, I wondered what it would feel like to have them all gone.

No matter how many times I asked, I only received more

confirmation that the first boy, the first offender, and the trauma stored inside me were gone. Then, I tried to remember what I'd done, what I'd learned because I'd written none of it down, but I was too exhausted to replay it.

As I thought ahead of how I would repeat the work and learn to get better at it, to help others, I felt somber. I was stuck in that stupor for a while, until I heard footsteps crackling through the forested trail. The way he stayed mostly silent made my heart race, and I half-smiled at knowing Damon had come for me.

"I've got eyes on her," Damon said into his earpiece, before pulling it out of his ear and walking toward me, his face curious. "Gellion?"

I was about to speak, to apologize, but I yawned instead, and tears dripped from my eyes. His stubble told me the real Damon had come out of the bunker to get me. He put his hands up to show me he wanted to come closer, to engage in some way with me.

"Did you get through it?" he asked me.

I nodded and yawned again, unable to control it. I was so tired.

Damon walked past me and picked up my jacket and offered his hand for me to take, to get up and steady myself as I placed my shoes back on. He continued to hold my hand as we walked quietly, me yawning and letting the tears fall on our way back up the trail.

I had to stop, to breathe deeply again, so I let myself sit on one of the benches placed along the trail and put my jacket back on. The chill felt bitter, now that I wasn't pumping adrenaline and energy through my system. The leaves were really starting to fall. I'd been gone from home long enough to make it to November.

"What's on your mind?" He asked.

"I promised Brian I'd go with him, his first time voting," I mumbled, aware again how close we were to home, and that I still had outstanding plans with people I cared about.

"Don't feel so bad," Damon said. "It's all rigged."

I sighed; his words were completely insensitive.

"Your conspiracies don't change my sisterly promises."

"I know. I miss Brian too," he said. "He was such a good kid."

I could only shake my head in agreement and rise again to walk to get out of the cold. When we arrived at the temple, Tombo was already leaving in the car I'd driven, and Joseph was waiting for us in a large transport vehicle. Damon opened the back door, and I climbed in and sat down with him beside me.

"Back to Georgetown," Damon said to Joseph as we drove away then pressed a button and a dark divider went up between us, giving us complete privacy.

"How do you know when it's not rigged?" I asked, as the topic of it was bugging me.

"The election?"

"Yeah."

"Oh, it's always rigged."

"How?"

"The candidates," he said, as if I should have guessed.

"What do you mean?"

"Both candidates work for the bad guys."

"Always?"

"Always," he said, as if it was common knowledge. "Or they're blackmailed into it."

"But different candidates wouldn't do the same things in office, so how is that possible?"

"The stuff that makes the candidates look like they are different is just culture and theatre. The things that really matter, never really change, or they change to what the rulers really want."

"Like what?"

"Biggest example? The number of children that go missing," he clarified.

"What do you mean? They're in on it?" I asked, incredulously.

"Of course. It's big money and big business, and they have to keep their friends happy, and their puppet masters satisfied, while keeping the bribes coming."

"Are there never any good guys?"

"No."

"Seriously?"

"A leader who would help the children?" He asked, rhetorically. "No, no way. The imperators here would never allow an outsider to fix their war machine system. They can't afford to. The child-trafficking numbers have only gotten higher and higher in the last seventy years. War too. It helps lose track of children. Orphans are easy to collect."

"All of that just for sex?"

"Oh, no, Gellion. This is more than that. Organ harvesting, blackmail on all levels of society, religious occult, and beyond."

"Is that why you do what you do?"

"Helping children is a very dangerous business. If you do it openly, like some law enforcement try to do on a state level, you become a target of the cartel, or even the CIA and FBI. The alphabet agencies are just as corrupt and vindictive if you mess with their flow of currency."

"Children are not currency," I shook my head and tried to sniff back more tears. It wasn't a topic I'd meant to peak again while lamenting over lost time with my baby brother. "I'm sorry I asked," I grouched. "It's so depressing."

"The only way your vote will matter is if someone with a proven track record of stopping traffickers, and saving kids instead of losing them, shows up to lead. Should that man exist, he probably won't for long. They'll kill him before they let him stop their flow of sex slaves."

"Okay, I get it," I grumbled.

"Or clone him and turn him into a monster."

"Okay!"

I didn't want to think of the world through his lens. These people he was talking about were power players that Damon hobnobbed with, sold clone children to, and had to be sociable with, and I was sick from it. The details felt abusive in the telling. At least he finally stopped talking.

The tears I'd experienced had mostly subsided and I'd already found a bottle of water to help me rehydrate. Though I was still focused on my breathing, and wanted to avoid any more conversations, Damon moved abruptly, pulling me into his lap.

"That wasn't very tactful of me," he said to my turned-away face. "I forgot how little you know; how new you are to this." He kissed me softly on the cheek, pulling me closer into a tender hug.

"I hate this world," I said, as he rested his lips on my forehead.

"You, leaving like that," he said gently in my ear, "it upset me."

"Scared you," I corrected.

"Offended me," he corrected.

I heard the words but didn't acknowledge any wrongdoing. I kept my breathing strong, to help me with all the tremendous feelings and sensations, as I responded to his body's actions.

"I know you needed space," Damon finally breathed out, as he broke away from me.

I stayed present, aware his fear had been real and yet my need for space had been understood.

"I want you too," I said, suddenly feeling something more powerful than exhaustion.

He sighed deeply, grabbed my body, and turned us both around, me straddling his lap instead of resting on it. He was reaching up for my face, trying to pull it down to his, but also wanting to look at me, his longing and confusion seemed to be mixed.

"What did I miss?" he asked, clearly wanting to know what I'd done to finish the work on my own.

I sighed too, and sat back on his lap, his body ready beneath me.

"I'm starting to see things," I said quietly.

It was odd admitting that whatever I'd just done at the temple wasn't done by my imaginings alone. There were visuals that directed me. Wherever they'd come from they helped me to work through the healing process. Damon brought his hand to my chin, to force me to look at him, as he examined my eyes.

"Seeing the work? Visions?"

I nodded as he stared in wonder and even some confusion at me, as if he were trying to find the old Gellion within the eyes of the new

Gellion and was successful. He smiled a strange smirk then pulled me into him, kissing me gently, and holding my weakened body inside his strength. I softened, letting my body rest completely on him, yawning again.

Recognizing my weariness, Damon repositioned me next to him so I could lean on him on the way back. He spent the rest of the ride holding my hand in his.

21

DISASSOCIATION

We arrived at the Georgetown building and I assumed we would head back into the bunker but went upstairs instead. I'd already forgotten how nice, modern and underutilized the Q-Speculum was in that location. Despite the short amount of time I'd been with Damon it felt like years had passed since I was there, seeing BB and learning what little I could from her while asking so much.

When we reached the research floor, lunch had been catered and delivered. Malik was scanning it with a device, and he smiled at me. Caitir also joined in to get lunch set-up. Multiple familiar male faces arrived.

The men in uniforms, on the boat!

Men who'd put themselves in harm's way for those children! They were all alive and breathing and ready to eat. I hadn't noticed them in Scotland, or maybe they hadn't been there. My heart felt lighter seeing their faces again.

Damon tried to usher me away, but I just sat down at the table and waited for the food to reach me. I started salivating and that's when I could sense I was in alignment with the men around me for the first time. Our appetites were all gearing up for something delicious. It's amazing how good food can immediately put a smile on your face.

Caitir led a quick prayer to bless the food, and everyone's heads were bowed but mine as the entire group held hands. It hit me as she took my hand in hers, that all these people acting as one for the same mission and its high stakes were quite incredible.

I didn't talk but listened to others talk as the eating slowed down. I didn't want to be pulled away from the people who meant the most to Damon just because I was fragile. If I were to be an ingredient in their work, and do my part, I needed to know them and be known. The least I could give was some eye contact and face time.

"You didn't have to stay," Damon whispered.

"I still don't know them well at all, and that's just wrong," I chided back, quietly, "considering how much you ask of them on my behalf."

"I ask on my behalf," he corrected me.

"Damsel in distress, without personality," I replied. "How disappointing."

"You don't have to have personality to be worthy of saving."

"What does someone have-to-have then?"

Caitir leaned in and interrupted us. "There is no need to ask any of us when we're here for the children too. Besides, you're family."

"Yeah, but why?" I leaned back toward her.

"Because there would be no family without you. Damon was lost to us until you came along, then we all started making plans for a different life. We also had a great time, for once. The best memories of friendship and laughter." She squeezed my hand.

"Oh," I said, not realizing just how much they were all involved in our relationship. I was trying to imagine how that worked. "Did we all go to high school together?"

The soldier men shook their heads. "We served with Damon," one of the men replied.

"Which branch?" I asked, hoping my query was vague enough to get some responses.

"Raiders," one guy responded.

"Delta," said a second.

"SEALs," another added.

"No way! Shut up!" I guffawed and smacked Damon on the arm. "You?" I laughed. "You, taking orders?"

I laughed again, with a full belly, trying not to snort or spit up my food. The thought of Damon choosing to serve and taking commands was ridiculous. And surprisingly, the other men laughed with me. They got it. Damon was trying not to respond, but his raised eyebrows said he was feeling something about us laughing at his expense. I hadn't seen him play a submissive role yet, so I felt confident in my shock at his military accolades. I also considered how Damon didn't start recruiting until we were already apart.

"Who was Calder with back then?" I asked, realizing I still didn't know about his girlfriend, except for the cryptic information I'd received.

"She disappeared the night you got hurt," Damon said to me, and then he glared at Caitir. She shrugged.

"What? Seriously?" I asked, looking at Caitir, Malik and Damon. Their faces were dejected, unable to respond. "Were we good friends?"

"Like sisters," Caitir mumbled.

"Oh," I said, deeply saddened to hear it. It was odd to finish eating in so much silence.

"Do you need to rest?" Damon asked me.

I shook my head. Sure, I felt tired and more than a little bewildered by the new information, yet they were all there, counting on me. Waiting for me to be ready to continue their research, to map the human system and its steps toward healing.

I took a breath, "No, I'm okay."

The best part about going into the Q-Spec machine was the added intimacy when dressing, as Damon helped me put on the magnetic suit. He touched me gently as I moved in front of him, working to slide the bottom half of the suit up me. His attention was giving me just the amount of adrenaline I needed to stay focused, to want to do the work again, and see it mapped in his machine.

He too got undressed and I felt a desire to touch him. His tattoos made me curious, and his wounded skin made me wonder; a stark reminder that I was with the real Damon's body. It was so much more interesting to touch him like this than his perfect clone. This body had a story I wanted to know better.

Damon's excitement at what he thought I'd already done was electrifying, clearing that first trauma box, and hoping his quantum field reader would work with me to see the next one. I hadn't really seen Damon's geek side until now; his new programming algorithm was a mystery. His pride in doing the work was invisible, until we made our way inside, me in my white suit, him in his dark suit.

When I stepped into the center of the machine with Damon, he carried a see-through screen in his hand. I prepared for the exhilaration of becoming weightless. The magnets throughout the newly improved suit worked smoothly to make my whole body feel equally lifted and cradled.

"When did you have time to do all this?" I asked, my eyes denoting the changes to the bodysuit.

"I have staff, remember? We saw what wasn't working from the last round and had new ones made."

"Right," I shrugged, incredulous. I was still having a hard time remembering the wealth and resources Damon had to pull from. "Has it gotten easier since your grandfather died?" I blurted out.

"What brought up that question?"

"I don't know. You don't talk much about it. Not the publicity, the funeral, the reading of the Will. All these events I assume are happening, but you don't say anything. I'm not dumb, and if you know that, then why shut me out? You seem to hide a lot from me, and maybe I just want to know what everyone else knows. Which would help me feel safe right now."

"I will always keep you safe," Damon scowled.

"Can you protect my heart from your constant rejection?" I

retorted, reminding him how important mental health was in our survival.

I was centered into the machine, while Damon floated closer to the edge, just outside the laser scanners. The lasers mapped my information and when they were done, I was copied into a light displayed version of myself, miniaturized, for easier reading.

"I'm not hiding anything," Damon replied quietly as both of our bodies hovered closely together, "but I don't want to scare you, so I don't tell you things I don't have answers for yet. As far as your question is concerned: yes and no. Any gains I made within Grandfather's group were lost. It's possible I will have new enemies, but I have allies, especially ones who appreciate the smuggling I do.

"As far as I'm aware, with my family lineage and the knowledge that I serve the required requests to stay active in the rituals, I imagine I'm not allowed to be touched, for now."

I hadn't put it all together in my head quite like that, but it made sense and was a completely terrifying answer. "What about the discovery of those boys' bodies?"

"It's quite possible that grandfather set that up, in case he died mysteriously, or maybe just in case he died, we don't know. I do know he never truly trusted me. You were the last test, the final acceptance between us, and I don't know how many he talked to about that. He found my insolence against his authority quite humiliating, so it's possible he told no one I was warring with him over a commoner. We're monitoring it as best we can and will be responding when needed."

Commoner. Me. Why does it bother me so much the way he uses uppity words to describe the differences between us? It sucks.

"Wasn't your grandfather a commoner too?" I asked, trying not to give away my annoyance.

"Yes and no. Grandfather Skip…Clarence was born without wealth from an upper middle-class family. His father's father was disgraced by failure in finance and society despite being a distant relation to one of the thirteen families. It was Clarence's mother's bloodline connection to French royalty that helped grandfather rise to the top of the social circles at university. From there he connected to other ambitious inheritors and grew his mini empire."

Damon tapped on the clear tablet and the single-color version of myself suddenly had color inside the body, in the tailbone. It displayed exactly as I'd seen my trauma on the bone. He'd mapped the energetic foundation of the Strŏngman construct.

"You found it? Wow, so where does it exist?" I asked, wondering.

"As far as we know, everything we're seeing in the speculum exists in the multiple dimensions of our world, where only energy and vibration can touch it. Does each construct belong to its own respective dimension? It's possible. Things we found seemed to vacillate. It's still unclear, but once we discovered the places where the positive energy systems were housed…" Damon said while showing me with the laser lights, how he'd taken others' research and used it to help him discover how to tap into the human's positive energy structure.

"We hypothesized by a process of reflection, opposition, and elimination, where the negative constructs should be transposed. With trial and error, I finally found this," he motioned, pointing to the mass sitting on the bone, "by reaching a frequency and vibration that existed where you said it did. I would say the quantum speculum has gained access to several connected dimensions, but only specifically tied to this construct, and not universally."

I mostly understood every word he said, despite it being more ambiguous than I'd hoped. I wondered who was more intelligent in the discovery, Damon, Caitir, Malik or the AI assisting them. Incredible either way, especially since the perfection of the lights showed two of the brightly colored designs existing on my bone, over top each other. Was that a guess or Damon's programming?

If there were only two, then the one I'd cleared or neutralized outside the temple today wasn't showing up as existing on me anymore. How odd, and amazing. The ones that still existed, their energy throbbed, pulsed and illuminated further the more we looked at them.

"Can you turn them into the shape of a box?" I asked.

Damon's eyebrows scrunched, but he started typing swiftly with one hand.

"A box?" He asked me.

"It looks daunting in this disheveled cluster," I replied, repulsed by the vision of it as the shape of the bone, like a colored clump of tumor. "Besides, you've all called it a box, so that's what I imagined. Now I'd prefer it that way."

"Alright."

"You can make it a manly box," I joked, and shrugged but he didn't make a sound.

I was confused that Damon seemed to be mourning the switch I was making from my current hypothesis of the bone back to that of the original box.

"Having a hard time letting go of the bone?" I queried gently.

He looked up and his brow, which had been stern, relaxed at the realization that he was holding onto something that made no sense.

"No," he quipped back.

Eventually, the different colored lights changed from embodying the coccyx and sacrum bone structures and became a box of the same magenta color but stacked flat like a picture instead of three-dimensionally.

The box was the right design because it was impersonal. I thought about how well that had worked for me in the shower in Scotland, and even better within the crystal at the temple grounds. How neutral the box felt helped my current thinking, reminding me of what I needed to do first.

"It's easier to remove the trauma from the bone if it's recognized as separate from it. The box accomplishes that," I said, explaining.

I reached out my hands, wrapped in diamond and silica open-tipped gloves, and carried an imaginary bubble to capture one of the boxes. When I reached the box, the bubble I'd made in my mind arrived in the Q-Spec's visuals, in real time. I felt a tingle down my spine at the symbiosis.

"That's new," Damon said. "Caitir, you seeing this? Capture the code."

I realized I was changing the steps of healing, that instead of starting by removing the words, I wanted to remove the box itself and get it away from me. Maybe then I wouldn't have to feel the nastiness of it so strongly.

"Remove the Strŏngman box from the sacrum," I said.

I dragged the captured construct of the Strŏngman from off my sacrum bones and pulled it away from my avatar with my intention.

"Fill with light," I persisted.

Holding out one hand to send light while the other hand stayed with the bubble, not wanting to release it, afraid of what it would do. I watched in awe that the light I sent actually came from me, still surprised to see it visually fill an empty space in a tiny version of myself. When I finally let my hand down, the box hovered, still wrapped in the energy bubble.

Then a visual appeared without warning. A strand of connection materialized in bright magenta and pulsed like a lightning bolt from the box to the bone, reminding me the Strŏngman had been removed but was still connected to me.

"Disconnect the Strŏngman box from my bone," I said, "from my body," I added, reaching out with my hands, breaking the strand.

"How did you do that?" Damon asked.

"Well, the word 'disconnect' definitely means something different from 'remove,' but both seem to be necessary," I responded, trying to explain.

"Well, yes, that makes sense. I meant the strand and the sphere."

"This is your quantum machine, Damon. I only imagined the energy bubble and it arrived, and I didn't even remember the strand of connection until I saw it, until your machine saw it," I exclaimed. "But how did the machine see my imaginary orb?" I countered, remembering the machine had never shown the bubble before.

"It's clearly not imaginary," Damon shrugged back.

"Did you change the code?" I asked, wondering if it was just me or if he'd been inspired too, by my pain maybe.

Damon got quiet, staring at how the Q-Spec had matched its visuals to the imaginary tools I used to do the healing work. My energy had been represented by the machine without my saying a word, as my intention through my hands was to be able to remove the box, to pull it from the body and bone, and disconnect it.

"Being with you again has inspired new code, yes. I changed the gloves too, to amplify the signal," he said, and I blushed.

The gloves I wore created reception between the box and my attempt to affect it. When I let go of the bubble, it had hung in the air before a whisp of empty space from my astral body to the box vibrated. I hadn't finished the work.

"Fill with light," I said, sending energy to the broken connection.

The laser lights showed the broken strand between me and my trauma dissipated by the incoming energy. The remaining energy that once made up the connection quickly disappeared.

The box hovered with ease, separated from my avatar entirely, allowing my hands to move it away from the miniature version of myself. I felt lighter seeing it detached, but I wondered if the amazing feeling of that light show was simply psychological.

Sure, I felt a lot of emotion as I came to realizations about my assault. Did that mean something really happened to me when I finished the work at the temple grounds? Maybe the need to feel something was simply that.

What if I'm fooling myself?

What if my captor is just insane?

I shook off the feeling of being a fraud or falling for one. If I were being honest though I never had any faith in me, not without doubting myself on every level first.

"Hey, Gell," Damon said.

"Yeah?" I asked.

"You look distraught," he stated.

I stopped and recognized my facial expression was indeed not good.

I was distressed and couldn't bring myself to look at Damon. So, I took a deep breath and started to yawn and stretch, pushing myself against the magnetic suit until it let me have full control of my arms and torso. He wanted my input, but I wouldn't give it, as I was too interested in containing it, so Damon spoke.

"This is all new code. It could have mistakes. The quantum AI needs time to learn, and this is its first time reading this energetic construct. There's no pressure," Damon said as he floated closer to me. He took my hand in his. "This is just a toy, for us to play around. Experimenting to see if you can recreate the healing work here, and have the Q-Spec read the exchange, and the changes in the energy as it occurs. I built it for you, only you. This is yours."

Damon then removed my glasses, and the light show disappeared, and when I saw no more lights as energy I calmed and sighed. The visuals had been too much! My anxiety had gotten the best of me, so I slowed down.

I didn't need the laser light show to sense the trauma box before me. Even when the light show disappeared, I could still detect it there. It was my own trauma, after all, and I had been shown it before without the machine. Though I knew I could do the work, I was having trouble starting.

After a quick command of his hand, an image of the list Damon wrote for me in Scotland projected before me, to help with the Strŏngman removal, as he had done with the first. The set of words on the list in my handwriting, of what I'd figured out while suffering in the shower were the easiest to look at. It created memories of what I started to learn and what I would need to remove again, and to fill with light.

The first round of healing included deep breaths and yawning through clearing the energy of *Fear, Trauma, Pain, Evil, Darkness, Torture, Torment, Horror, Terror,* and *Karma,* and the filling of the empty spaces with light.

Karma felt particularly heavy, eliminated with tired arms.

I could see beyond my vague vision of the work that Damon was watching the Q-Spec's version of the events as I labored. His usually stern face had expressions of awe that made him look boyish. I knew at some point I'd need to put the glasses back on to help the system learn, but I was glad Damon was getting to see it.

Then Damon's list began, words that would hopefully feel less raw this time.

The second round of healing included clearing again the energies of *Helplessness, Sorrow, Sacrifice, Involuntary Arousal, Unwanted Pleasure,* and being *Victimized, Raped,* and *Cut-open,* and *Abandoned by God.* Then filling the empty space with light followed by deep breaths and yawning.

I felt a great release at the last one and my body shook. It was the end of Damon's list, so I tried to remember my own list of what I'd removed from the box at the temple, with the help of the crystal. When I remembered what I'd done at the temple, that I'd removed the teen perp and his ick from the box next, it didn't feel right this time. The words I'd been able to see after I'd removed the boy last time were brutal, but I didn't need to remove him to know the energies were still there. I'd get to him next.

The next steps brought trembling and even tears, but not the deep breaths and yawning from release that helped so much. My body was carrying the extra stress and anxiety of seeing Damon's reaction to each new word I was forced to add, in order to clear the full darkness from me.

I cleared the energy of *Wanting to Die, Dying, Being Muzzled,* and *Being Gagged.*

Damon's face had contorted during the work on the words I said beyond his list, beyond being *Abandoned by God.* He was staring at me, his ears pulled back, and his features raised. His face was flush and his cheeks aflame.

He looked physically pained at the words *Wanting to Die* and *Being Muzzled.* Then he removed himself from my view, floating around the periphery of the Q-Spec, stopping behind me. I knew the truth, that the words I said weren't in my memories, but had always been with Damon. When the vibration took shape inside the box, I turned my head and looked behind me, a foreign thought arising.

"I had wanted to say goodbye to you before I died, but I couldn't," I croaked out, my throat tight and hurting, "right?"

The welling-up hit my throat, my body rocking faintly, shaking slightly but uncontrollably as he stayed silent. If releasing the trauma off me were cathartic for me, would it be the same for him? As the only living witness to so much pain? I imagined it would be.

Damon put his hand gently on my back, behind me for support, not to distract me with his own emotions. I remembered wanting him with me earlier, while I stood barefoot in the sand and finished removing the darkness. Though it had been arduous, each instance of negative vibration I removed from the box made it seem lighter and more pliable.

I put the glasses back on and stared at the lit-up structure for a while and let the changing feelings release from me. I knew the next step was removing the boy, the perpetrator from the box, from being by my teenage side. I wasn't sure how to show that.

"Remove the perpetrator," I finally said.

I stared, glasses on as my energy bubble started to pull the energy of something from the box.

"Wait," Damon said. "Give me a second, the Q-Spec is struggling to define it."

"Why?"

"Sorry," he scowled. "I didn't program in the actual Strŏng-Man. Just one moment," he said as his hand typed furiously and then his body moved, floating down until he reached the platform and the computer console there.

After several minutes of coding he called out, "See anything?"

I watched a shadow form inside the box.

"Try it now!"

I said it again, "Remove the perpetrator from the Strŏngman box," as I held my energy bubble in my mind around the shadow in the box.

When I lifted my hands a convoluted light moved with it, representing light and dark, creating the outline of a silhouette.

"What did you tell it to do?" I asked.

"I had the AI look for the signature of a 'foreign' energy inside the structure."

I had it in front of me, between my hands and it moved. Unlike seeing it only in my mind where it was imagined, something about this image really caught my attention. It wasn't a dust cloud of energetic debris, no, the energy that represented the teenage rapist was moving, like liquid glass trying to become solid, almost alive. When I finally let go, the churning energy floated away from me but stayed inside the bubble.

"Fill with light," I said instinctually.

I hadn't noticed but Damon had returned, the magnetic suit lifting him toward me, his body suddenly blocking the churning light of the perpetrator who hadn't disappeared.

"What's next?" he asked, refocusing me.

"The filth he left behind, it needs to be removed," I said softly, my eyes leaving their trance, returning to the box. "Remove the filth left by the perpetrator," I said, and lifted the light-pretending-to-be-dust particles away from the box. "Fill with light."

Sure enough, the strand of connection existed between the perpetrator and the box he created. It was his only lifeline left to the living world, I imagined. My own personal ghost, hidden within my psyche.

"Disconnect the perpetrator from the box. Fill with light," I said, breaking the strand and filling the space.

I could hear Damon typing, tapping away trying to help the Q-Spec keep up with my steps for clearing. I breathed erratically but deeply, as the overwhelm of the images and feelings were hitting my torso, like cramps. The tapping stopped, and I felt his hand touch me, holding me steady. I reached out my hands with the intention of pulling my young self away from the trauma box.

"Remove myself…" I started to say.

"Shit!" Damon interrupted, as he lowered himself back down to the platform to put in more code.

"Try it now," he commanded after he'd finished.

"Remove me, at age…" I tried to recall, but the age of my trauma and awakening eluded me.

"Eighteen," Damon answered as he returned.

I held my hands out and watched a tiny version of a person form, their age regressed before us in light.

"Remove my eighteen-year-old self from the box. Fill with light." I said, as I picked her up in my sphere.

That strand of connection arrived again, and it was becoming familiar enough to give me comfort.

"Disconnect my eighteen-year-old self from the Strŏngman box. Fill with light."

The machine's reader was either becoming more accurate or the AI was growing cleverer, as the gloom I'd seen before had arrived in the Q-Spec's laser light visuals.

"Remove muck. Fill with light."

And then something happened. The box, which hadn't moved or changed in all that time, became smaller, all on its own, and moved closer to the eighteen-year-old version of me, floating. This was familiar from the last time, but not this powerfully visual, and though I remembered what was supposed to happen next, the others had never seen this before.

"Give it back to the perpetrator," I said, giving my younger self permission to get rid of the box she'd been forced to keep.

Damon shook his head like he hadn't programmed any of that into the Q-Spec, but after a long pause it happened anyway. As it all played out before us, like a play writing itself, it started to become even more dramatic and intense.

Eighteen-year-old Gellion, miniaturized and made of laser-light, handed the box back to the teen boy before her; a perpetrator who'd floated away, but was pulled back into the boundaries of the Q-Spec. The little box of trauma floated from her to him then turned into a dark dust that infiltrated the teen boy with a roiling Strŏngman energy. Angry sparks flew at the union of a perpetrator colliding with the vibration of his crimes. The laser display looked like fireworks going off.

Once the dust reached the perpetrator, he started to disintegrate as it entered his energy field, as it crumbled him from within. This was the part that felt both sick and powerful, and just as it had happened in the crystal before my naked eyes, it was happening here. As the Strŏngman perpetrator received back his box, his disintegration continued in a loop until all who watched began to understand the horror.

Damon was mesmerized by it, circling around it to see it from all angles. I looked up at the command level above to see who was watching and the window was filled with so many faces. The imagery I saw in the crystal matched well with the Q-Spec's version. What the machine was scanning and displaying for us to see and record was even more detailed than my own visualization.

What we saw only strengthened my growing confidence that I hadn't made it all up, that the visions were real, and the work I'd done to heal myself would make an impact. When I went to wrap a bubble around the disintegrating Strŏngman, Damon pulled my hands back, as if he wanted to continue to watch my pain and torment become the torment of the boy. Somehow, a young man who no longer existed to receive the energy exchange, looked real still.

If this was for me, and me alone, I wanted to see it no more and end the cycle of destruction. I gently removed Damon's hand from mine.

"I'm tired," I said. "And I need to be done with this one, so I can get to the last one."

"Remove the curse of Strŏngman off him," I said.

As I pulled the black dust from the ashen boy, I moved slowly, letting Damon absorb the powerful imagery of it. Vengeance rolled off Damon, toward the silhouette of someone already long gone, so I was giving Damon time to discover the truth.

Just like before, the boy stopped dissipating but remained before us charred, broken, cracked and hollow. I waited to fill the empty space with light, to show Damon that the cycle would not heal without that light, as darkness is bound to return to an emptiness not reprogrammed. I tried to leave the space empty at the temple, and learned it was not the way.

"Fill with light," I finally said, and when it was done, my silhouette was all that was left, as everything else had faded away.

Repeating what I'd done before, I knew that what was left was the reintegration of self, of the piece of me that broke apart to survive the damage. The last round of healing, for reintegrating my current and past selves, included clearing the energy of *Separated by Trauma, Darkness of Separation,* and *Disassociation of our Minds* and the filling of the empty space with light.

I watched as the fissures and cracks between the two of us, me and my silhouette in lasers, started to light up. With the Q-Spec glasses on, watching she and I being pulled together, the broken places sparking as I sent us energy and intention. We could see the energy around our heads start to merge, wanting to pull the two of us together, but stopping just short of doing so, as the image of my younger self grew larger to integrate with me.

I held my hands out with intention and said, "Reassociating our minds."

In a flicker my younger self disappeared inside me, our fractured identities reintegrated together.

The silence around it was deafening, and I didn't know how to feel. Tears had formed in my eyes but had not fallen. I held myself together, but my body was exhausted, and I was having trouble keeping my eyes focused from the fatigue, as I yawned and yawned and yawned.

"That was visually stunning," I finally heard Caitir's voice say.

I muttered, "I'm so worn out."

The next moment I was floating down to the platform with Damon by my side, and when I got there, the weight of the suit was crushing as the magnets released. Damon pulled my head piece off gently, then picked me up before I fell back or collapsed under its weight. The dressing room wasn't too far, and Caitir entered right after us with snack bars.

"Chocolate?" I asked.

"A chocolate protein bar," she smiled hard. "Your blood sugar is crashing," she said as she handed us both the treat, already open and ready to eat. "It's good. Try it. It'll help."

She didn't say anything else even though there was so much within the expression on her face, and I took a bite, surprised by how incredibly good it was, and how needed. Damon left me to eat bites as I slowly started removing my suite. I was gaining a bit of manufactured energy to get me dressed. I wondered how much energy I would have after this for time with Damon.

I still barely knew him.

When we left, everyone else did too. We took the elevator down to the underground railway. I didn't recognize the path we were taking this time. When we reached the doors to the platform, Caitir moaned as we got to the other side.

"Who forgot?" she asked, looking around at the men with an accusatory face.

"My bad," said Tombo.

Instead of a train waiting for us, there was a moving platform on wheels that looked quite terrifying.

"Who wants to wait?" Malik asked.

"Wait for what?" I asked.

Everyone started getting on. There were two large metal poles on the front and back that came up from one side, like a guard rail, and attached to the other sides. Large straps had been connected to these guard rails. They'd obviously hauled some large pieces of equipment. Caitir grabbed a strap and began to wrap it around her body as if she were recreating a five-point harness used by race car drivers.

"This train would have to leave and dock at base before the other one could be sent," Damon explained. "Takes too long."

I wasn't sure the treat I'd devoured was enough to get me through a seatless roller coaster. Damon strapped us in, then fastened me to him. He took my hand and smirked at me with a raised eyebrow. We started on our way, Tombo at the controls. When he turned everything on, it was the first time I noticed the technology being used for the trains underground. I'd always been inside, but now I could see that there was a buzzing noise that accompanied the rest of it. There were train tracks, but there was also something else, something quieter and more fluid.

"How do the trains work?" I asked, as we made a noiseless descent.

Damon was checking my straps when he replied, "It's a combination of tracks and magnets."

"Is that why it always feels different?" I had noticed.

"The magnets are faster and quieter but can create a signal that's traceable. The train tracks are harder to track from farther away but make noise. We ride based on what the satellites are doing."

The ride was smooth, but without the protection of the train, the inertia was quite powerful. Though the front of the platform had a shield, and we all had protective glasses, I'd closed my eyes. It was much more intense than a rollercoaster that was designed for thrills, and I imagined as our stomachs dropped that we seemed to be at a freefall at some point.

The adrenaline rushing through me woke me up, it also gave me a new perspective on just how much they'd worked to secure some form of survival and protection, deep down into the earth. I felt myself lean back, held up by both the straps and Damon's massive body behind me. He held onto me tightly as some of us squealed, while Tombo laughed.

I felt like I was in an adventure film where they end up on a mining rail that turns 'roller coaster' while trying to escape, except I was not escaping. When we reached the bunker station, my legs were shaking. I smacked Tombo's arm on the way off the platform train.

"Was that really necessary?"

He chuckled and shrugged as he held my other hand.

While in the elevator, Tombo mumbled, "You know that was fun."

There was a collective chuckle, including my own, but I was yawning from the exertion.

I thought of the car ride back to Georgetown from the temple, how I'd alarmed Damon by running away, and how much he'd needed to touch and kiss me. I was so drained, but I wanted him by my side, and I could sense the need had never left him as his hand stroked mine over and over. His desires had been postponed by circumstance and the timing of working all together to map something unique.

I didn't have to say a word, as we broke away from the group, Damon's hand was pulling mine until we reached the door to our room. He was lifting me up into his arms before we were even through the door, my arms around his neck, returning his fervor. When we made it to bed he was trying to help me with my clothes as I pulled him closer.

"Gell, you were amazing," he said, removing his shirt and reaching again for me. "The Q-Spec has never lit up like that before or been so reactive to the work."

"Yeah, that was something," I mumbled, his mouth on mine.

"Did it look the same as what you saw at the temple?" he asked, pulling back from devouring me, but holding onto me still.

"Not exactly," I said, wondering how much of a distraction his curiosity would create.

"How far off?" he queried.

"Not off, just nondescript versus extremely descriptive," I tried to say.

"Which one was more descriptive?"

The questions he asked took me back to the two instances of pure exhaustion I'd just experienced, exhaustion and relief, and I sat back.

"It played more like a fuzzy movie within the crystal. The feeling of being abandoned by God, for example, was, um," I yawned, just like I'd done throughout the healings, "really heavy and ominous within the box, and the lightness of healing it was maybe more profound, and also more revealing."

"How so?" he asked as he loosened his grip around me.

Our eye contact was intense as he looked eager for information, and I had a lot more words than I thought I would.

"Well, once I healed the girl in the box of being left-to-torment by the almighty, I had to stare at it for a while to get the next clue. The crystal at the temple, or whatever helped me see, showed the box was free of all the energy that held the perpetrator to me, except it left my own discomfort to see him so close to myself, to be close enough to touch me still.

"Removing him looked so different, and when she gave the box back to him, to watch him dissipate into dust repeatedly, it was quite stunning and taught me a lot about what it means to be a healer. That I couldn't leave the curse within him, because it also meant leaving it in myself. Even though it was an evil he created, leaving it unfinished would keep our Karma alive, so it changed what I could choose to hold onto anymore. Those details didn't quite show up in the Q-Spec, not the same."

Damon's eyes were down, and he lifted his fingers up and moved them a little, like he was writing or counting, "Yes, those discrepancies make complete sense," he agreed, without anger or irritation. "The rest followed the same energetic patterns?"

"Definitely," I said, because they had.

The programming or the AI understood.

I could tell he had more questions, but he just grinned before staring at my lips and leaning closer into me.

"I did feel like I had a memory though," I managed to say before he reached me

"What memory?"

"What I told you, about wanting to say goodbye."

"Right," he grumbled, trying not to take my words personally. "Did you remember?"

"Not exactly. It was like a 'knowing' that an inevitable part of the story might include something I couldn't let go of. It took me such a long time to realize what was left to clear. Like, part of the reason our memory should participate in healing is because trauma is so specific. Then, I finally had the sense that I'd been gagged, because she wanted to communicate but her mouth wouldn't move."

I waited for his eyes to confirm my suspicions, but his face was controlled.

"In that moment I thought I remembered looking at you but not being able to say anything and how much pain that caused," I said, not really understanding how I knew it was true without a true memory.

Damon's face had frozen, like he was unsure which direction his mind should go in.

"What do you remember?" I asked.

"Like I said, you died."

He tried to move back from me and his hands flew up to his forehead and he slowly pulled back on his hair, clenching his head in his hands, his face pained. He massaged his temples. I wanted to reach out to him but knew better. He stood up and started pacing as he rubbed his head and eyes and cheeks, and as he worked his way down, past his mouth and over his throat, his hands clenched himself there and he finally looked at me.

"Yes, they gagged you. Me as well," he said, anger forming in his eyes. "I was tied up, neck in a noose, on my tiptoes."

And then he broke down, falling to his knees, his hands intertwined, clasped together, held above him, his head bowed down. He was trying to hold back the rage. He looked so agonized I couldn't help but go to him, down to the ground, beneath him, reaching up to his cheeks and seeing the wetness as I wiped away the few drips my thumbs caught.

"I'm sorry," I said, not realizing how much pain it caused him to relive any of it.

He had not forgotten. The horror had been burned into him.

I kissed him gently, as slow tears rolled down my cheeks too. "I forgive you," I told him, as he looked wracked with guilt in his prayerful position. "I'm so sorry you had to watch me die."

I wrapped my arms around his neck and held onto him, wanting his chest to meet my chest, and to be held deeply.

"Twice," I corrected, remembering that he hadn't just seen me die once, but at the masquerade too, in gruesome fashion.

"I'm wrathful," he dropped his praying hands and pulled me into him, and held me tightly, on our knees, on the floor.

"I love you," I said into his ear, and he pulled me from our hug, and kissed me as if we'd finally found each other, getting up and picking me up, to take me back to the bed.

This time, no thoughts could distract him from removing our clothes and kissing me until my back arched, and my legs stretched, without any ability to be coy. I responded to him with trust, as he already knew what had gratified me before. I wasn't having any issues with silhouette monsters, or panicky thoughts, at all, but instead was focused solely on him and how he wanted us to move.

He had no patience to tease me or prepare me. Though it was still so new being with Damon, my body responded immediately to his want. He moved himself into me slowly at first but rapidly progressed to a rhythm shared by familiar and hungry lovers. It felt overwhelming and painful for just a moment before his purposeful cadence coached my body to accept more.

Damon had been tender, but I could tell he was getting frustrated trying to be gentle. He kissed me intensely, so I bit down on his lower lip and held on, trying to match his passion. He lifted my hips into the air and drove himself harder into me, my body so vulnerable, so pliable to his size and strength. He set the tempo with his profound need for our bodies to merge. I embraced him clashing into me, his positioning just right to maximize contact, and I muffled my sounds. He made it impossible to be demure. My moans were deep and throaty at the intensity of our mutual lust.

His amalgamation didn't last as long as our first time, but it was enough for us to find the release we needed with one another. He groaned out in fulfillment as I convulsed. Slumped over, he kissed my neck and collapsed beside me, pulling me closer.

I couldn't move. When he covered us with a blanket he held me, one arm under my neck, the other wrapped around me, resting on my bare sternum. I fell asleep almost immediately while securely in his arms, though I knew he was uneasy behind me.

22

THE DEMON INSIDE

I woke with a start and a sense of dread, before clutching at myself to see if I was naked, as the setting was not where I just was. The hospital gown and robe were lightweight but warm, and the bright lights were enough to remind me I was somewhere being treated.

As I moved myself I felt no achiness or weakened muscles and wondered how long they'd been working on this copy of me, to get her ready. I had never been inside this body before. I had brown hair, not blonde, but the scars I'd just had, while naked with the real Damon, were gone. I hadn't woken up in Scotland, so when I got up and found my way out of the curtain maze, I was surprised to find Rosie and Eamon in the lab next to the hospital ward, seemingly flirting, from what I could tell.

"Good morning," I said.

"It's evening," Rosie said back. "You weren't gone long. Good to see you."

Eamon chimed in. "Damon tells us you've been making some real progress, lass."

"We just watched the playback of the work," Rosie chimed in.
"We're proud of yuh."

My mouth curled up and the top of my head arched away from itself, the skin stretching in a kind of embarrassing stress at the compliment I wasn't prepared to receive.

"Thanks. It's strange. Foreign to put myself through it, but the visuals were quite magnificent. Will Damon be joining us?"

"His clone schedule is off after being with you in Scotland. So, Damon's clone is waking up in Georgetown now," Rosie said.

"He had to wait to see which body you'd wake up in before re-ordering a connection," Eamon explained. "He'll take the train and be here soon."

I hadn't realized Damn had messed up his real body's sleep cycle to show up for me, and I smiled. "I'll get dressed."

"Gellion?" Rosie called. "The dressing room has some new clothes in it for you. I've added your handprint to the access point. You should check it out."

"Thank you," I replied, but then felt curious. "Hey Rosie, how come this clone of me doesn't have any scars?" I asked.

"Well lass, you melted down," Eamon pointed out succinctly.

"I think what Eamon means to say is that Damon wants to heal your trauma, not trigger it. We won't scar anymore versions of you unless it's absolutely necessary."

"And your eyes are blue this time, like when you were young," Eamon added, as Rosie walked to a drawer and grabbed a mirror compact and handed it to me.

I took the mirror and nodded with a grin, knowing they were trying to protect me and heal me. They all were.

I walked to the room where they equipped everyone with weapons and clothing, all the gear they needed for their different missions. My handprint worked and inside there were mirrors everywhere, so I stopped to look at myself. I stared at what looked like the younger version of my image in family photos at home, from before.

My eyes were so foreign to me in such a bright and perfect blue. I barely looked at my original eyes anymore, only long enough to clean and replace my brown contacts. Once the novelty of my old eyes wore off, I used my handprint again on a new screen that asked me to identify myself. Large closet doors opened, and I saw that indeed, many new items were hung up for me. I wondered if Caitir and Rosie had spent time shopping, as at least a fourth of my walk-in closet showed gowns and suits and high heels.

Eventually I found an outfit and went down to the train platform to wait for Damon's clone. I chose something revealing but comfortable. I wanted to be touched again, held and be open to feeling Damon's hands on my skin.

When the train stopped, he was already standing behind the doors, smiling to see me.

"I wasn't sure where you'd wake up," he said, stepping forward. "Glad to see your choice was to stay here."

I was on my tiptoes, waiting to receive him.

"I don't like pain," I reminded him.

My current clone body didn't have any scars at all, and neither did Damon's, so there were no aches, just feeling young and healthy. I walked into his arms, and he picked me up. I wrapped my legs around him and just started kissing him. He cradled my butt and walked us to the elevator and kissed me and held me up as we rode up. Once in the hallway he tilted me over his shoulder and slapped me on the butt as he walked. I was laughing and squirming until we were inside the room.

"Ah," I screamed as he sat me down on the bed, and we both realized the place was already occupied. "Stop doing that!" I complained, smacking Damon's arm.

We started laughing as I rolled onto the floor, into arms that didn't have tattoos, away from myself, and away from Damon's original body, covered in ink and sleeping so soundly, curled together, naked. Surprised by the creepiness factor, but I also felt concerned.

"Why didn't we wake you up?"

Damon laughed even harder. "I'm too connected to this body right now, being awake with you. I'm used to deep dormancy so I can be fully present somewhere else," he said and then he chuckled. "And we were both so tired."

He offered me a hand to help me off the floor, and I got up, still mesmerized by the sight of our bodies post-coital. Once outside the room, I no longer needed to touch Damon. I had already taken a step away from him, unintentionally.

"Are you okay?" he asked me, seriously.

"I got away from reality a bit. We both have," I said, not realizing I felt that way. We'd been having fun and now I felt serious.

"Distractions, especially normal ones, could be good for us," Damon countered.

"I could have died several times now, were it not for you being focused. My real body is in a coma. Maybe I shouldn't get lost in the fun."

"That's valid. Truthfully, I haven't spent a single moment in over a decade having fun," Damon said, looking down at the floor. "Not then, not until just now."

"Oh," I replied, realizing I was chastising him for enjoying me, when we'd both suffered the exact same amount of time, while apart.

He got very serious as he held my arms.

"Being inside you again, letting my guard down, laughing. I didn't think I'd ever get that back."

I walked into him and wrapped my arms around his waist, resting my head on his chest, squeezing him. He enfolded me and rested his cheek on the top of my head. I arched my neck and stretched on the tips of my toes and waited for his mouth to find mine. He kissed me sweetly, gently and with sadness.

"I promise to be here," I said, seriously. Then I smiled at the paradox of my promise. "Even if you're completely psychotic," I chuckled.

"Me? Have you seen the circle I was born to?"

I nodded, as old and awful memories started to surface, of my time working for Damon's grandfather. My job there had never made any sense to me, until just recently, and so I'd allowed my mind to sometimes wander back there and revisit the awkward situations from this new lens. Before I could say anything, share any bizarre memory like normal couples do, my stomach growled.

"Yeah, I feel it too. Let's eat," Damon said, taking my hand and pulling me gently to a healthier place to be.

The dining room wasn't empty. Tombo and Joseph sat at the table, each with a hot drink. Tombo was reading a book, and Joseph was reading something on a tablet. Damon sat me down and went to order food.

"So, what's the story with you two? How'd you guys end up here?" I asked, interrupting their thinking time.

They looked at each other, as if wondering whether to even speak.

Damon returned with the 3D printed food and placed my plate before me. It was an open-faced turkey sandwich with gravy over mashed potatoes, cranberry jelly and broccoli on the side.

"Yum!" I almost squealed. "Comfort food!" I exclaimed.

"Just like late nights with Katherine," Damon replied.

I started remembering the local after-club diner in DC that served the same meal when I'd been out all night with Katherine.

"Ew! Why'd you have to ruin my favorite drunk-girl meal with your creepy stalker vibes?" I said, sneering at him sarcastically with a full mouth of food.

I was famished, shoveling the good-memory food into my mouth way too quickly while I looked at the men with my eyebrows raised. Joseph put his tablet down and took a sip of tea while looking from me to Damon. He sat back and crossed one leg over the other.

"You may not remember me," he said with the tiniest of unidentifiable accents, his brown skin so dark it was entrancing to look at. "But I remember you."

I felt drawn to Joseph's face and leaned forward, like his dark features were mesmerizing yet foreign. My only other friend besides Katherine was Sarah, who hadn't left our small town after high school and still lived at home. Sarah was almost as dark as Joseph, but there were shades and undertones of yellow in her skin that I didn't see in

Joseph's. My stepdad's skin tone was something I'd observed over the years, as his mixed Caribbean features made him very dark during the summer months, and as pale as a tan, white man in the winter.

Tony's loose and soft curls, when he grew his hair out, made him look more Latin, while his short haircuts made his features so universal that many of his Arabic customers mistook him for Middle Eastern. I'd always envied my half-brother Brian's perfect brown hair with lots of body, and his ability to tan, like Dad, without burning. They also shared Dad's tough skin, and how little he seemed to care when getting bruised up by his hobbies.

He was just "Dad" though, after the accident, when I couldn't remember anything before.

Sarah was a dancer and a licensed beautician, and her adoptive parents built her an apartment in their basement, so she would always have a home while trying to be an artist. She lived down the road from my parents and I saw her all the time after the accident.

"Where are you from?" I asked Joseph, wondering.

"I'm from Ghana. My family came here when I was young. My father was a diplomat. I attended the same school as Damon, and he was an asshole," he said with great gusto and a chuckle. "When they finally kicked him out of prep school and his grandfather sent him out to the boonies to torment all the hicks, we threw a party. No, seriously."

I had to look over at Damon to see his reaction to Joseph's words. He was not amused, and I had to work hard to keep my building smile from becoming a toothy grin.

"A couple months later Calder and Caitir showed up at our school. I didn't know they were related to Damon, so when I ended up on a camping trip with him I was shocked," he said, and Damon chuckled at Joseph's words.

"What?" I asked, interrupting the story to make Damon explain.

"The look on your face," Damon said to Joseph.

Joseph started laughing, "Yah, man. I was terrified. I thought it would be the worst trip, and it was the worst trip, but also life changing.

Both because of Damon, and not at all. I had really hated his guts before then. On the trip, not only was he completely different, like a complete one-eighty, but he saved our lives. You both did."

"Me?" I asked and Joseph nodded.

"I'm pretty sure it was you who saved us," Damon said to Joseph.

"Well, maybe at the end there," Joseph agreed, "but every time before that, it was you guys who got us out of the worst of it."

I took a breath, wanting to know more, but I could see the two men were locked in each other's stare, in a long-ago remembrance. Damon was smirking with a look in his eye toward Joseph that told him the story was one he didn't want him to tell.

"I don't want to ruin it, as it'll make a good campfire story," Joseph said to me, "but that was the beginning of me being here. You don't forget the first time you survive a truly fatal environment, or who had your back."

"I never would have guessed you'd have mine," Damon agreed.

"Me and my Glock," Joseph said, pretending to pull a handgun out a jacket pocket.

"You mean Sarah's Glock," Damon blurted out, then looked at me liked he'd said something he hadn't meant to say.

"Oh yeah! That's right! Oh man!" Joseph said shaking his head with a smirk on his face. "Like I said, best and worst weekend."

"Sarah who?"

"Your Sarah," Damon said.

"My Sarah? She was there?" I asked.

"Yeah. It was supposed to be a couples' camping trip, but Sarah didn't trust me and convinced your mom she needed to be there. So, Calder thought Joseph would be a great distraction and get her to back-off a bit."

"Yeah, but I didn't know that!" Joseph said, shaking his head. "Turns out she and I had a lot in common. Her distrust of you saved all our lives," Joseph laughed and laughed.

"Wow, she never said anything about any of this."

"How is she?" Joseph asked.

I had to think about it, about what Sarah's life had been like after high school, and realized we had such separate lives, even if we were close.

"Busy, always dating and looking for love. Always switching jobs, working gigs. Dancing, making people beautiful. Different but the same," I said, smiling a sad smile, one filled with a longing for my friend.

Joseph's eyes looked like they wanted to spend some time staring out into space, remembering the vivacious Sarah, with her beautiful face, her warm brown skin and her tall body with amazing curves. She always filled the room with radiance whenever she entered.. He got up and took his tablet and his tea, and bowed his head, and I realized he also left out of respect for Damon.

Damon may not have said anything to all of them about how to behave around me, but everyone kept their distance, respected Damon's need for me to be cloistered, and not allowed information at will. After everything I'd been told so far, I didn't feel the need to prod for anything extra, unless it was something I needed from Damon on my own.

I couldn't help but look at Tombo and wondered if he would speak, if he wanted to, if he cared, or if he'd already been told what he could and could not say. He was a stern and quiet enigma to me, one who instantly made me feel safer when he was there. I wondered where that feeling came from, and why it was so intense.

"Did you know me too?" I asked Tombo.

"No," he shook his head, "but my brother did."

Then he looked up at Damon, almost glared at him, pushed his chair back, and took his book with him out the door.

"Oh," I said to Damon, "Definitely not a campfire story, then?"

Damon chuckled but the humor wasn't there.

"Are you two, okay?" I asked.

"He thinks you're a distraction," Damon replied, with a shrug.

"Am I?"

"Of course you are. You're new, and I'm, well, different with you here. What he doesn't understand is that you're so much more than a distraction, you're the end goal. Saving you and planning for a possible outcome with you was how all this started. My only real plan, all along, was for you to survive."

"I'm honored," I muttered, despite feeling speechless.

"Tombo just didn't know any of that until you got here. He didn't know us together, not the way Joseph did, or the way my family knew. It was too painful to talk about with anyone."

"Yet he's loyal."

"Some are here because of the trauma that happened to someone they love. That's Tombo."

"He reminds me of Katherine. They're both stern and broody yet sarcastic and solid. I miss her," I said, then smacked Damon on the arm. "Still mad at you about that one."

"What? I needed an insider."

"You bought me a best friend."

"I'm sorry, but Sarah wasn't up for the amount of work needed to keep you from killing yourself," he argued.

"My mom would have," I lamented.

"I know, and when she was gone, I couldn't let you wither away."

"Katherine did convince me to quit working for your grandfather," I said. "She convinced me to stop getting the surgeries too."

"She took you out and showed you some of the world. She always looked out for you, even though that wasn't her nature."

"I'm kinda heartbroken over it."

"Lose a poser, gain a lover," he said, shrugging. "I don't see how that's so bad."

I smacked him on the arm again, and again, and again until I was exhausted, and he pulled me into his arms and squeezed me, planting a kiss on my cheek. "A loyal lover, at that," he said, in a self-congratulatory display, "And you can smack me as much as you want. I know you're angry. If anyone deserves to be smacked, it's me by you. You've lost so much because of me."

I leaned into him, glad for his acknowledgment, until he added,

"Besides, I barely feel them. They're like little kitten paws patting at me without any claws."

My love and losses weren't a joke, and I felt hurt, so calling my anger endearing just irritated me. Instead of smacking him with my pathetic kitten taps, I decided on something else instead and got up and went for dessert, requesting several complex concoctions from the food printer, and devouring the sweet concoction while Damon sat beside me.

"You're going to crash," Damon murmured as I moaned over the decadent tiramisu.

"You know, I couldn't really handle alcohol because of all the pills I was on, so I used sugar and treats as a way to dampen my emotional pain and sadness. When I'd gained and gained in the process and was crying to my therapist about how fat I'd gotten, she asked me a profound question.

"She said, 'Gellion, how much sweetness do you have in your life?' And I was honest and said 'None.' And she said something like, 'Maybe don't beat yourself up so much about using sugar to supplement for actual sweetness you should have in your life. When your life is filled with sweet moments of love in friendship and partnership, then you can chastise yourself for what you eat. Until then, be kind to yourself, because we can't survive here without any sweetness.' Or something like that. And she was right.'"

"You're really not that fat."

"Can you shut up?" I moaned through another bite of peach pie.

Damon was more like sweet candy with a sour shell, which could be daunting, and I needed actual sweetness while reminiscing my lost friends. It would take real work to get real sweetness from Damon without being naked.

"You were doing the best you could," Damon agreed.

"Well, I worked really hard to get the weight down in the last couple years. Here," I said, scooping a bite of the dessert and hovering it before his mouth. "It's so good."

"I don't need treats," Damon rejected.

"That's a lie."

"I don't eat sugar. It dulls the mind."

"I'm not a treat?" I asked, contradicting him.

"You're a complex situation that requires work to contain and protect."

"You might as well call me a gorilla."

I put the bite in my mouth and moved the plate away, climbing onto the edge of the massive table before Damon.

"So, ask me why I need to eat sugar right now."

"Why do you…"

"…because my boyfriend thinks it hasn't been a treat to be naked with me, to be inside me," I said, annoyed.

"There is a vast difference between a simple treat and a drug so addictive you'd chop off your arm to have it again. You are the latter."

"Ew!"

While I tried to feel flattered being compared to a powerfully addictive drug that could lead to amputation, I found it intimidating and disturbing to be thought of in that way. Now I wanted even more sugar, or maybe to throw up the last sugar I ate since it felt so tainted inside my gut.

"That is not the complement you think it is," I quietly chided, my expression perplexed. I had been trying to flirt and keep it light between us, despite missing my friends and gorging on dessert.

"This life is pretty ugly. Do you want the real me?"

"Is there a real you? If so, does he not change when the people around him do? Maybe consider me worth the same effort as the psychopaths you have to charm."

Damon's vision left his body at my wounding words, and it was the first time I could stare at him and know his mind was truly somewhere else. I hadn't thought my statement was that profound, though. I was simply repeating the questions I'd been asked by BB when I was lamenting my miserable existence and needed to see a view that included others.

"I'm sorry," I said, inching toward him, my hand outreached, touching his forehead with my fingertips, trying to return his consciousness back to himself.

"I do not charm Satanists," he growled as his eyes refocused, and he returned back to himself.

I wanted to be vulgar and say something demeaning to Damon, to dig for answers about what he actually does around those sick people, but I knew it would be going too far. I'd never been triggered to feel the need to be so mean until meeting Damon, and it was maddening.

Then, as I tried to separate out my upset at all I didn't know and couldn't ask about, I decided to redirect to what I could control. I needed to stop looking for answers outside myself and couldn't help but think about that last trauma box, the last Strŏngman inside me, poisoning me, and how much my system still needed relief.

Since everyone seemed worried that I'd wake up in Scotland in a still-sick body, it meant I really wasn't done healing. Despite the new body and new energy of waking up refreshed, or a driving force of a perpetual reconnection of affection between Damon and I, I couldn't keep melting into him. It wasn't enough to keep me coming back for more when I carried something so gross inside me.

I'd satiated myself on multiple levels and felt solid enough to exhaust myself again.

"We should get to work," I said, squeezing Damon's hand.

I got up, put my dishes away and headed to the dressing room to get dressed for the Q-Spec, to remove the third Strŏngman box.

The steps to identify and remove concepts and vibrations, while AI scanned the work, were stunning again and easier to see, as we went through it all for a second time in the machine. This time we could work without having to pause adding new code, as those missing pieces were addressed in the last round.

I remembered the importance of starting the work by removing the Strŏngman construct from the bone and then disconnecting it. Without that removal and disconnection, seeing inside the box would be more difficult.

Oddly, despite my rest and reset, the energy bubbles I visualized to remove the negativity were very heavy, as with each execution of elimination my body shook as if the removal itself were trying to hurt me. The relief of the light I could provide myself, from whatever source I pulled from, which I envisioned as a universal light energy, lessened the severity of the effect of the removals, but not the need to recover each time.

The first round of work was the same as before. I recalled the themes, and made a bubble for each, working through them quickly.

Remove Fear, Trauma, Pain, Evil, Darkness, Torture, Torment, Horror, Terror, Karma.

"Fill with light," I'd said with intention after each removal.

I needed a break before even reaching the really hard words, especially after removing *Karma,* as I shook so violently that I felt pained by the contorting muscles in my system, and how the spasm felt too close to a seizure to ignore.

Even stranger was that I looked quite like a parishioner having an evangelical response to being touched by the Holy Spirit, and I wondered greatly at that correlation. Damon lowered us and ran up to the command center and brought back water. I drank it as I slunk to the ground, decimated by something I thought I'd been through the worst of already.

"Why's it so hard to do this time?" I asked him, once I'd sated my thirst.

"The tiramisu?" he said, seriously, and I laughed!

"Oh, shut up!" I cackled and leaned into him with a shove.

He was smiling at his successful attempt at humor. He sat down next to me and pulled off his head piece.

"The worst is usually avoided until the very end. Not surprising it's the hardest."

"Tell me about the worst one," I said.

"The ringleader?"

"So, there was one?" I nodded.

"He was brutal."

"How did you know him?" I asked.

Damon sighed.

"He was the child of one of the subordinate families' included in our inner circle. He was a peer in the torment, of lesser status, but we had no friends in that place," Damon said. "It was harder for him because he was more expendable than some of us. I was always going to be rewarded with privileges because of my family, but also because I'd learned to take a lot of pain. I'd already been through torture and knew what to expect. Everyone around quivered, which just egged the elders on. I gained favor for my ability to withstand the suffering.

"My mother comes from the most powerful family in Italy. I was ignored by them after her death, but everyone knew who I was, and nobody knew who the ringleader was, or cared. He thought he was tough, but he wasn't prepared. I was warned what would happen to us, and I was mentored on how to make it through. Several of them didn't know what was coming, or how it was designed to break the psyche."

"Jesus," I mumbled, horrified by such an intimate connection.

"I don't even want to say his name," he said, shaking his head. Damon removed himself from his trance and looked at me. "Yeah, there's quite a few of these assholes walking the Earth. Each willing to do whatever is asked of them to take another step-up in the ladder of power. The sadists are related and work together to protect other sadists. Lots of henchmen."

"It's still so hard to wrap my head around, even though I saw it with my own eyes."

"Not many people get to see. The club is small but always recruiting and sacrificing."

My body took a deep breath at the thought of an enemy so large and powerful that they never stopped gaining in numbers. I felt very small and insignificant, just another victim of their evil, and yet I was doing something. I put my hand on Damon's bent knee and pushed myself off the floor and headed back into the Q-Speculum.

The second round of words was the same again. Deep breaths and held-back tears.

Remove Victimized, Raped, Cut-open, Helplessness, Sorrow, Sacrifice,

Involuntary Arousal, Unwanted Pleasure, and *Abandoned by God.*

I said them and as I did each materialized into bubbles.

"Fill with light," I said after each clearing.

When I finally got through clearing *Abandoned by God*, I was shaking again.

The third round included trembling and crying to get through.

Remove Wanting to Die, Dying, Being Muzzled, Being Gagged.

"Fill with light," I said again for each.

The next step somehow felt the hardest, I would have to remove the ringleader from the box and get him away from me.

I kept envisioning the thickest energy bubble I could think of, one that started out with layers made by me, but got the extra strength treatment from the light-forces around, or maybe angels that might be watching. I was thinking more and more about the idea of light beings as I witnessed more of the dark. Either way, I didn't want to feel the boy's essence or evil when I reached in to remove him.

"Remove the perpetrator," I said, but it didn't work.

He became a silhouette, but wouldn't move, not at all. This was the first time in the whole process where a removal bubble didn't work for me. I looked at Damon, confused.

"It's not working. I can't remove him."

Damon floated down and started looking through the code.

Something was left inside the box, something I hadn't needed to clear from the other boxes, I was sure of it. I looked at Damon and remembered his words about the last clearing, when he said I'd been gagged. I felt my throat close up and wondered if I'd been choked too.

"Remove being choked," I said, making another bubble and seeing the energy of the words form into mass, allowing me to remove it. "I guess this is the worst of it. Fill with light."

"Caitir," Damon called out. "I need another set of eyes on this."

Within moments, both she and Malik had entered the Q-Spec in their regular clothes, and were looking at the screen Damon had been working on. The space of the box felt lighter, and I wondered if the last one I'd done completed it, so I tried again.

"Remove the perpetrator," I said, again, trying to pull him out.

Again, it wasn't working, except this time, something else was there. I couldn't help but stare at the laser-light show that represented him, my rapist, and how violently it churned on itself when I tried to remove him. I hadn't even handed anything back yet, but so much was happening visually.

As the moving lights churned, flashes of activity sped up and became more violent. The sparks of light created an image of a tiny black hole that sat in the center of the boy, inside the silhouette of him. The churning hole started to grow bigger until it had sucked up the entire silhouette of the boy into itself, and was spitting the silhouette of darkness back out, creating what looked like a self-feeding sphere of blackness, a blackhole with a tiny lit-up dot of sparking light at the center.

That tiny hole started moving around like the pupil of an eyeball, looking around the room, forming a shadowy iris; the black pupil getting larger and smaller, as if it were trying to focus. It was unsettling watching it as it seemed to analyze the Q-Speculum. It looked around, assessing the room. My flesh shivered.

The energized ball of dark matter was building in personality. I stared at it, unnerved. Then its gaze landed on Damon, Caitir, and Malik below us. It watched them intently as I watched it in a growing internal horror. I was mute though, as I couldn't express the fear that was swelling inside me.

Then the blackhole energy-eye slowly moved its gaze to me.

"Damon?" I trembled out, but he didn't seem to hear me.

"Damon!" I screamed, as the mutated perpetrator had started to get bigger inside the box, forcing the size of the box to get bigger, while I tried to back away.

"Get me down!" I screamed, and my body was finally lowered, away from the lit-up sphere.

"What the hell is that?" I asked, exasperated.

They were all looking up at it. "What is it doing?

"What did you see?"

"It came alive," I said, trying to explain it.

It had stopped growing and stopped watching us.

"I swear," I said.

Malik typed on the keyboard and pulled up the video playback from multiple camera angles. They watched it, as the energy turned in on itself and became the blackhole inside the silhouette of the boy. That it behaved like a sentient eye, looking for visuals and information made them gasp.

"Ew!" They collectively shrieked at the playback, in the same horror I felt, only verbalized.

"I tried removing the boy from the box, and that's when it changed."

"Are you sure that was the next step?" Caitir asked.

"There wasn't anything left to clear, so yeah, I should have been able to remove him like I did the others."

Damon looked at me with deep concern. "I think we should step outside," he said to me, then looked at Malik, "but don't turn it off."

"Don't turn it off?"

"The work isn't done," he tried to explain. "If we stop before it's done, it might not return to what it's become."

I didn't know how the machine worked, or if his assessment was right, but I knew it wasn't his only line of thinking, and his face told me several possible truths existed. My mind was wild with fear and curiosity. We all seemed to need to walk away from it, to collect our own thoughts on what had just occurred.

Damon and I undressed in silence, and then we went to the dining hall and collected our food and returned to the command center. While we'd been gone, the new sentience seemingly slept, but once we returned and started to look at it again, it awakened, the pupil of attention returning to stare back at us. Malik remarked on how the sphere was adhering to one of the rules of physics, that which is paid attention to can be changed by that attention, or something along those lines. It was accurate.

As time passed, one by one, more of Damon's men arrived, from where I didn't know, to see what we had seen and begin their own process of considering the ramifications of it. These were men I'd never seen in the bunker before, only out on mission, or viewed their clones in the pods. Their presence with us, below the world, added to my mind the true scale of Damon's fiefdom.

Tombo sat at one of the consoles and read over Damon's code, asking quiet questions about Damon's work and conferring with Malik in other languages, over what had been written. Joseph was watching the replay of the video with Eamon and Rosie. Even Calder arrived, returning to his real body from the prolonged trip to Scotland. He stood there with them, also mesmerized by it, and became the most vocal about the whole thing being wrong.

I'd been sitting at a console myself, ignoring the chatter and journaling in a notebook, when I noticed the lack of voices. Damon and his cousins slipped away while no one was looking. I looked over to Malik and waited until he returned my gaze.

"Did they leave?" I asked quietly. He nodded. "Should I know what they're saying?"

"Not yet," he replied, then went back to his work.

I'd been sketching the energy inside the box, the eyeball, and I spent a lot of time considering why it was so different from the last one. It felt like something else was doing all the looking, not the boy. If it was true that Damon had judged and dished out his punishment almost immediately, then there was no perpetrator to arrest. If the boy really was dead, then all he could be now would be a ghost of himself, or a memory, unless his ghost wasn't alone in there.

I made a list of ideas of what else could be connected to this but was not confident in any of the muscle testing I'd been doing. I had to consider a lot of options, and all of them were from my imaginings. I realized that I had a lot of visual vocabulary to pull from, a long list of science fiction and fantasy movies, and horror movies with demonic themes, of possessions and sacrifice.

The one true gift of Katherine was her eagerness to drag me, sometimes kicking and screaming, to all the movies in the theatres, most of them filled with unspeakable horror. She seemed to need to take me. And while I could see now that Damon had been behind a lot of that, I was sure Katherine enjoyed that part of our time together.

I often hid behind her large fluffy coats and cried during especially brutal horror movies, even covering my ears, and pulling a hood over my eyes. Katherine watched, wide eyed at the horror, and I could never understand why. And while I avoided a lot of the darkest moments, I still had plenty of nightmare fuel and moments of sleepless dread. Without all those years of visual conditioning, I'm not sure I ever would have been able to survive the last few weeks with Damon.

The movies had desensitized me, and I wondered if that was on purpose, to desensitize the whole world of decent people to the evil here. Maybe even more nefarious, to condition humans to accept evil and eventually plunge us into living that way ourselves. I had so many questions now that eluded me before.

Did the world of entertainment exist to tell us the truth? Knowing what I knew now put an entirely different spin on my understanding of the movies I'd seen and how much truth was in them. Suddenly my mind was back in time, back in the movie theatre. Instead of remembering Katherine sitting by my side, I was imagining Damon, holding my hand, and smiling at me. I was scared and horrified, and he was smiling, just like Katherine had, and this time I asked why.

I could hear his words as if the scene were real, as if he and I were there together right now.

"Because I had to prepare you for the truth, and the stories here are made for that, to tell us convoluted truths about this world. There is so much evil and so much darkness, and you must remember that it's real somewhere, so you know how to protect yourself. When we were young, I let you live in the light, and we ignored the darkness. Being that unprepared destroyed us."

I got up from my seat, took my notebook with me and nodded at Malik before I went looking for Damon and his cousins. Eventually I found them in the library, huddled near the fireplace, talking lowly amongst themselves.

"Why not include Malik in your discussion?" I asked them, catching them off guard. Even though I'd entered quietly, I didn't want to spy on them.

They were silent for a while before answering. "Malik doesn't want to talk about that night," Caitir said.

"And suddenly you three do? Why? And why not include me?"

"Because we're not talking about just that night, not solely," Calder grumbled.

"That's only a piece of what we're discussing," Damon corrected.

"Is it about what you think is embedded in that boy, the one in the box with me?" I asked, assuming that was the right answer.

"Yes, and no," Damon replied.

"Then what is it that I don't know, and Malik doesn't care to remember?"

"We're trying to figure that out now, Gellion," Calder griped at me, annoyed at my presence.

"I'm the one who has to do the removal work, so help ME figure it out, by telling me what you're talking about."

Damon looked at his cousins, asking them silently with his facial expressions. Calder just shook his head and walked out without saying a word. Caitir had never looked so sad, or so unable to meet my gaze before, and she left too.

"What is going on?" I demanded to know from Damon.

"We've all reached a certain age where our brains have started to show us truths we couldn't remember before. I've read about it, from other victims, that the stored trauma from childhood would start bubbling up around age twenty-seven to thirty. We've been having those memories too. Strŏngman boxes you never healed because they were buried, so they stayed hidden.

"From what we've pieced together, the trauma happened when we were young, during a ritual. It's possible we're all filled with demonic programming, not normal Strŏngman stuff. Maybe even worse than the one that seems trapped under layers of your broken psyche, being dislodged from inside you."

My eyes squinted at the confusion I felt, trying to understand his words. The information I understood, I was having a hard time accepting. My entire body filled with a sort of jolt of rage and astonishment to hear a realized truth of another horror.

"So, you think the energy connected to him, inside the Strŏngman box, is demonic?"

"That's our best guess, yes."

"A real demon?"

"Yes."

I ran my hands through my long and unruly hair and sighed in dread and then I yawned.

"Sorry. Is the Q-Spec designed to contain any of that energy, or protect itself from it?"

"No. There's been no way to know how to create that programming without a trial attempt, which has never presented itself. We can't even attempt to implement anything without help from the AI. I haven't been able to figure out the code. We don't know if it can do anything more than it's doing. This is new to us."

"Maybe you should warn your AI."

"If it's not already too late," he shrugged.

"How do I remove something that's seemingly sentient?" I asked myself in his presence. I had so many thoughts I hadn't said out loud.

"How can it be sentient inside my machine?" Damon countered.

"It's almost as if the darkness is behaving like it's captured a part of your AI and made it its own. Why else would the AI allow the shape of the box to change, or the shape of the perpetrator to dissolve? That's too much conjecture for your AI's level of sophistication, right?" I asked, while trying to explain my thinking.

Damon's eyebrow-ridge creased, and he looked up and tilted his head. "That makes me think of the code in a new way," he said, his chin crumpled. "I bet if we looked at the changing code in the interior portion, we'd see something."

He looked at me and stepped closer, putting his thumb on my chin, he squeezed me there slightly, as if telling me I'd done a good job. I hadn't even meant to be helpful and wasn't sure I had been. I was still thinking about it, on multiple levels.

Yet something much more important was lingering in the background. I'd only addressed the problem with the machine, and not the possibility of Damon's similar trauma housing this kind of energy inside it. If so, wouldn't it be eviler and more alive than the "sentient" energy sitting inside a decade's old trauma?

Even though he had my chin in his grasp, and I was looking up at him, it still surprised me when his lips met mine, and the intimacy of his kiss. At first, delicate and loving then voracious as he picked me up and sat me down on his lap, leaned into a wingback chair, entangled fingers in the hair above my neck, and cradling my head to meet him.

We were entwined until we both felt satiated at the connection, like innocuous teenagers who could kiss until exhausted, without needing more. Yet my brain never quite left the questions arisen and unanswered, and I wondered if Damon's mind were the same.

23

BREAKING THE PARADIGM

Resting on Damon, like a high school sweetheart, I held his hand in mine. I knew he wasn't interested in more than just a warm body to hold, that he was invested in the way my brain worked and in the visions I once had and was having anew, from a version of me I never knew existed. He wanted more than anything for us to be rid of the trauma we still carried, and whatever else might be attached to it. We were beginning to become one mind on these things, even if the rest of us were worlds apart.

"We should head back," I said, aware of his distraction to solve a problem and continue the work within his tech, in a documented way, that allowed him to see it too.

He kissed my forehead, as if to thank me silently for understanding his need to continue the effort and work out the fixation. I resumed my location in the command center, as a spectator to all those who could read and analyze code, as they moved in and out of the machine and labored for hours at the workstations. This time I sat with reading materials to help enlighten me.

Eventually, despite the food and fascinating information, my body grew weary and tired, and I found myself yawning. Surely, laying down must be better than sitting still for hours. I longed to stretch out on something soft and wiggle my toes in privacy. So, I cleared my throat and Damon turned around and looked at me. I pouted my lips and silently yawned in exaggeration. I didn't have a place to rest, as our room was full, so I needed his help.

When Damon came and took my hand and walked me out, it made me think of the few times I saw Caitir and Malik leave together and return, within a different version of themselves. If we went to sleep together and woke up together, we'd be on the same schedule.

We went into our room, saw ourselves again and grabbed some clothes for sleeping.

"Is this room any different?" I asked, as we arrived at another secure door, needing a hand at the scanner to open it.

"It's not as nice," he said, and when we entered, I realized just how much they'd put into the other rooms.

It felt like a metal box. Despite the furniture, the walls resembled an old submarine or navy vessel, something metal and large. The bed was nice enough, and there was other furniture in the room, but it felt cold and desolate. The linens were stacked on the bed, and we went to work making the bed together and climbing in after taking our slippers off.

The coziness of our warm bodies together helped a lot. I could tell he wanted me, but before I could even figure out how to move toward him, Damon had gone under the covers and down my body to my torso and lifted me up and removed my pants. I thought of how different I already was in response to intimacy, yet we'd only cherished each other just twice. It was still so new to me.

His mouth was on me and the sensations that shot up and down my legs and into my stomach made me unable to do anything but react to his movement. He lightly, yet powerfully, teased at the deeply exposed and sensual essence of my womanhood. So vulnerable, yet warm and welcoming when trust and adoration are present. I had felt so out of control yet did not fight his holding my arms and hands, to keep me from stopping him.

"You don't have to…" I lamented.

He was not bashful about foreplay, while I closed my eyes and existed between part embarrassment and rapture. Being sensually loved was still so new to my senses. He knew it too, as he seemingly knew everything about me. What surprised me most was how much effort he put in to making me feel deeply wanted.

How much of this sensation was obligation, and how much was from gaining pleasure from watching my own? It was still so different to be so thought of, so loved, or obsessed over. To be venerated while I'd only ever felt repulsion toward the opposite sex before, was so foreign.

Damon warned me of his darkness, hinted at his masochism and sadism, and insinuated he had kinks, none of which I'd seen. He didn't say how deeply moved I would be though, to be so desired. Despite my own internal loathing at past flirtations, or any kind of attention, it was confusing after years of disinterest to find myself eager now. It was a lot to get used to, but I was quite willing.

If only the new and good feeling could last, but the pleasure of his attention suddenly poured into me a deep internal mourning. So powerful was the feeling, I relaxed into the sadness, no longer responding in spasm to pleasure. I touched Damon's hair lightly and began to cry.

This time it wasn't just the trauma I'd been working so hard to heal that brought the tears, but also the time we had lost together, and how much love I went without. Damon's love was too strong, too overwhelming, too pleasurable. For a system so depleted, it was like overdosing on the most powerful drug, the way he was making me feel. The sadness of realizing all the time I lost with him, was sending my body into a kind of shock.

My cries turned to sobs, and that's when Damon released my legs, and brought his face up to meet mine. He didn't say a word but pulled me into his fully clothed self and wrapped his arms around me and held me tightly, chest to chest. Within the flexibility of his understanding, and the patience of his presence, I continued to heave, to mourn, and to release the sorrow, over and over and over. As he held me, Damon took slow steady breaths, acting as a conduit for me to find my own ability to breathe, to be reminded to breathe, to work my way through the pain by coming back to center.

"All those years without you," I finally whimpered out.

Eventually after the ugly tears had poured their way out of me, my body found the sensual need for touch once more and I pulled at Damon and pressed my lips to him. My half-naked body was vulnerable, swollen with anticipation and pressed against him where he couldn't disguise his desire.

I backed away just enough to pull up my shirt, while I tugged at him. He was naked quickly, but immediately back to holding me, the skin of our chests touching, keeping one another warm and safe in each other's arms. He kissed me slowly, intentionally, eyes open, looking for my facial expressions, eager to see my emotions, as I worked to stabilize them.

When I calmed down, and my body was more ravenous than sad, Damon moved himself slowly between me, into me, aware of my body's newness still, of that initial shock when joining.

"You feel like home," Damon said, kissing my neck and ears and chest, as he deliberately moved. "This is where I always want to be," he whispered.

Being wanted so intensely, and wanting so intensely hadn't existed, and now suddenly I was beyond my dream's comprehension. Damon's ability to maintain the movement lasted much longer than mine. My body went limp multiple times as he continued to fill me with breathless bliss. When he was spent loving me and exhausting us both in the effort, I drifted off.

This time when I woke up, I was just next door, in a body closest to my original self, brown haired with scars all over. I was naked, next to the real Damon, who hadn't woken up yet, because he probably hadn't fallen asleep yet. His tattoos were visible, and his fresh stubble reminded me of how much more real he was to me like that, more intimidating too.

I sat up and yawned and walked to the bathroom to get cleaned up. When I was done showering I looked at the bed and he was still sleeping. Even after I got dressed, he was still under. I wondered if he was having a hard time falling asleep, or if he was working something out inside his head and needed the time apart.

I took the opportunity of being alone to seek out Caitir for some questions I'd been working on. She was dressed in different clothes when I returned to the command center, and since Malik was freshly changed, I asked if she would get some tea with me.

She smiled with an expression of relief to have something else to do and got up with a bubbly step. In the hallway she pulled out her cellphone and put her arm in mine.

"I'm taking a selfie, so smile."

I complied and while we walked, arm in arm, she put on some upbeat music that had no lyrics but made us feel the need to walk down the hallway half dancing. It was silly and fun and relaxing to move our bodies in a rhythmic fashion, and by the time we reached the library, we were smiling at each other in an awkward, childish way.

"MARI, please Bluetooth my music," Caitir said, and the music moved from her phone to a speaker system in the walls somewhere. She continued to dance around the room as she started the water for the tea, turned on the fireplace, dimmed the lights, and pulled out candles and lit them. After the room was filled with ambient living light, she came back with the tea on a rolling cart and handed me a small box.

The music changed, and the beat was good, but much slower. I opened the box and saw bound sage inside and pulled it out. Caitir handed me a lighter.

"I thought you might need that. I feel like we need to remind you of your tools and what you used to do to clear a space."

"You think the Q-Spec could use a sage cleanse?" I asked, cynically.

She laughed and nodded while smirking, "Maybe. Maybe. But that wasn't my thought process. I meant you and Damon and anything in between. Lots of stuff is coming up to heal, and there are more tools than this, and they're all over this place, so we need to get them back to you."

"Well, I didn't ask you to tea to get my stuff back. I want you to help me look at the code in a different way."

"Really. What way?" Caitir gasped.

"You've all stopped interacting with the Q-Spec's AI, because you think it's corrupted."

"I don't," she corrected. "Didn't I just Bluetooth my tunes to MARI?"

"You know I mean the AI in the Quantum-Speculum," I reminded her, aware she was trying to evade my questions.

"Okay, you're right, we don't even consider it a self-growing system since its given so many limitations, and it was made separately and completely cut off from the rest of the facility."

"I think that's a mistake."

"Why?"

"Because if it has decent programming, it won't want an anomaly to take over, and it might be able to help us find the anomaly, if it had a bit more brain power."

"Damon won't agree to integrate it into MARI because it could corrupt her. So, the only way to communicate with the Q-Spec's AI is within the way she was designed, directly."

"What if you made a copy of MARI to give the Q-Spec's AI someone to communicate with, to problem solve with? At least MARI could tell us if the AI has been corrupted or simply shut out. Will you help me?" I asked.

"Why not ask Damon?" Caitir wanted to know.

"Well, something tells me he's not going to listen to this."

"He built the Q-Spec. He knows it inside and out and he wants to help you. He built it for you."

"Except that he doesn't even want me inside the machine anymore, because of the anomaly."

"I see your point, but I see his point too."

"Damon says the work can't be done by anyone but a healer, and the work has to be captured in the machine, yet he won't let me enter."

"Did you ask him why?"

"I assume he's worried about danger. It's not like it could kill me, right? And this body isn't me, so there's no real threat of permanent harm."

"Hmm," she grumbled, unable to answer. "Where is Damon, actually?"

"I fell asleep quicker. I figured he had some thoughts he needed to be alone with. So do I."

"Like what?"

"Is the AI in Georgetown connected to the one here?"

"No. All the Quantum-Spec machines have standalone AIs."

"Do you share files between them?"

"Of course, but we manually import sessions that we want shared."

"And which Q-Spec is easier to repair?"

"Repair?"

"Which one?"

"Gellion…?"

"Hear me out. This 'thing' isn't normal. No one can find it in the code. The AIs don't talk, but if they did, would they be able to help? Well, what if this 'thing' did take over? We still need to know how, and if it's done some damage. I say we take a copy of the original file of the work and a copy of MARI and boot them into the Q-Spec above ground and let me in there."

"It's already contained down here, though."

"Yeah, with someone who wants me to be fearless, but forces me to stay afraid until he says so."

Caitir sighed, knowing the complexities of being heard while surrounded by exceptional and formidable men, all protectors. So, I drove my point home.

"If it's really that dangerous to use the Q-Spec, I'd rather go back to the Buddhist temple and finish my work away from here. Besides, if I do the work and that 'thing' gets released into your machine, something bad could happen."

"What?" Caitir asked, almost insulted. "You're not even a little curious to document not only trauma, but possible entities that exist in other dimensions that can cause us harm? Who cares about the machine," she said, throwing her hands in the air. "We can build another, and we have. We're talking about proof of demonic forces, which is even more fascinating than the energy systems that keep us alive and thriving.

"I mean, haven't you felt cursed and haunted, almost? If it's real and it exists somewhere, it means it can also be removed. We need that, and we need light. Life got so much better when you came into our world. You did all kinds of work on us, and we felt alive and hopeful and happy."

It was then I realized just how invested Caitir was as well, how many hours she had given with her own brilliance to support Damon's work. I took a deep breath. I didn't truly understand her passion, and I wondered, even if I could do what they all wanted, and make it happen inside their machine, and help the machine learn to see it all, would it be enough?

Would me, becoming their Gellion, ever be enough to make even the smallest dent in the powerful sadness and darkness in the world? It would be a nonstop effort against forces so large and abundant, there was no way to win. I felt beyond discouraged.

Caitir was waiting for me to decide, to have a response, and it wasn't going to be what she thought. I leaned in and pinched her.

"Ouch," she squealed. "What was that for?"

"Which body are you in right now?"

"Clone," she replied.

"Yeah, me too."

"So?"

While everything I'd said to Caitir had been on my mind, I had to admit my greatest fear.

"Damon's about to wake up in his real body, and something about that doesn't feel right, about him going into the machine with his real body and this demonic eyeball that's taken over. I came to you because when I'm with him, I can't think as well, or I shrink back in his presence. I can't do this work in front of him when I'm that easily distracted. He's beautiful and intimidating and that makes me feel weak."

"Oh, well yeah. I can see that. He's new. You'll get used to him, and then you won't shrink back. Right now? I get it. You want us to try this on our own."

"Just the girls. Please?" I begged.

"It is a betrayal," she whined, but just slightly.

"The work will be documented," I reminded.

"True. Better than you leaving again. You're not going to take 'no' for an answer, are you?" she questioned me, wondering how far I would go, to get some distance from the watchful eye of all those eager men.

"I'd prefer they all watch the playback, over a need to be right there, analyzing it their way," I shrugged, feeling like my brain didn't work like theirs, maybe not as quickly, but also not as analytically, and I feared a lack of patience for my learning curve.

Caitir silently agreed and gathered her things from her room before we headed for the train below and left without saying goodbye. The night view from the elevator in Georgetown reminded me that Damon's copy acted as his daytime eyes, and that Caitir and Malik were on the opposite schedule as Damon since they split their time between here and Scotland.

"Why are you helping me if you know he'll be pissed?"

"Because you asked. He can join us when he wants. Nobody is stopping him, but I don't need his permission to spend time helping my only sister."

I smiled, the way she said "sister" tugged at something deep inside.

"At the very least, cousin-in-law," she added. "Besides, this is exactly what we did in high school when we were all together. We'd often run off, go have our girl time. He shouldn't be jealous, but he

423

always was. He never wanted to be away from you. And when the boys weren't on an adventure, they were always pining a bit when we got to talking and laughing."

I couldn't say anything because I desperately wanted to remember. It was nostalgia I wish I had, a really meaningful experience for all of them, and I couldn't remember any of it.

We both suited up for the Q-Spec work, and I'd never seen Caitir in a Q-suit. I hadn't realized everyone's custom suits looked so different from one another. When she pulled out the red material, covered in strips of clear embedded diamond dust and sewn-in magnets, it was like something on an Olympic athlete. I didn't realize how incredibly fit her figure was, at least her clone's.

"Are you always this hot?" I asked.

"Oh," she laughed. "The real me is way more out of shape. And my Q-suit hasn't had the latest updates."

"Well, this clone is a bit flabby," I complained.

"Um, unlike you, my clones don't have to look like the real me for legal purposes, so I tweak her for Malik. We both do. It's fun," she giggled in embarrassment. "I mean, you didn't really ask me anything about the busty, bodacious blonde version of yourself when we were in Italy or Scotland."

Now I was blushing. She was right, I had enjoyed the younger skin and flawless body I'd been given, without any of the effort at the gym. It was more than that too as I had never seen my naturally colored blue eyes without their damage. Only in pictures did I recognize the blue-eyed girl they said was me. And I knew the busty version stirred something more in Damon too.

"Yeah, why did he do that?"

"He didn't. Calder did, to fuck with Damon," she said, and it was the crassest thing I'd ever heard her say, which caught me off guard.

"Oh," I laughed.

"We didn't like the way he was treating you, and I knew he wouldn't be able to keep up his shitty behavior once he saw the way the other men were looking at you. By exaggerating your features, in an almost cartoon like way, he was forced to take a position of protection and claim on you. He had to choose, either embrace his own desire, or let you go for someone else to treat kindly," Caitir continued, explaining her reasoning in such a way as to be irrefutable. "Your blue eyes coming alive must have also brought it all back for him. It was easier for him to keep away from your traumatized copy, that reminded him of his guilt."

I could see she was right, except that in the end it was the traumatized copy that was getting to be intimate the most. Scarred and healed skin and brown eyes and hair, but still a body without pain. It hadn't taken my mom long to order the colored contacts to cover my damage, so my little brother could look at me again.

Caitir tried to twirl in the red Q-suit but almost fell over.

"It's so heavy," she moaned then laughed.

"Why red?" I asked, since she had a color when no one else did.

"It's Malik's favorite, and Damon spent some time experimenting with colored suits to see which would work best. Red, not so much."

"What color is the best?" I asked, surprised.

"It depends. To read the energy coming from someone doing the energy work? White, of course, is the easiest for the lasers to see through," she said reaching out to touch my suit.

"And for someone receiving the work?" I asked.

"Didn't seem to matter as much. We'd only found that it was better they weren't wearing white, to help distinguish them from the healer."

Caitir was adorable, more petite than me, almost pixie except for the long auburn hair, that looked like it wanted always to be more of one color or the other, not orange, not red, not brown, yet all three. I could tell that she had naturally more copper hair mixed between the red and brown highlights. She resembled a darker version of her twin brother, and shades closer to her mother, Rosie.

"Was your hair always that color?" I asked, as I closed the back of her suit, wondering if she had looked different when we were friends.

"It's changed a lot," she said, closing my suit too, returning the favor. "It was much more orange when I was younger, and then I dyed it with henna. I was trying to look different from Calder yet also still match him too."

We walked into the beautifully designed and executed Q-Spec machine. I could tell from Caitir's comfort level, she had participated in its creation, in a large way. She didn't brag, ever, about how hard she worked, and how relentlessly she sought to learn. I didn't know how she became so amazing, but I figured it was Malik, the two of them together.

With a clear tablet in her arm, we were swiftly floating, being scanned together by the Q-Spec's AI. Caitir loaded information with what looked like a tiny thumb drive and within moments the information from the other machine, isolated far below us, was being recreated before us.

"How'd you get it?" I asked, shocked she could bring us right back to where we were, instead of me trying to recreate it energetically.

"Malik," she said, nonchalantly.

"Gosh, he's loyal."

"And super bored with the fear. We all appreciate how much you've rattled Damon again. He's not completely unhinged, but he's much more preoccupied, so he can back off a little bit from reminding us how careful we must always be. We already know."

"Wow," I sighed deeply. "You know, I thought I had such a simple life and then all this happened, and it's so much more than I ever thought I could handle. I do need to finish this work, so I can regain myself, right?"

"And then you can help the rest of us too. You'd only just begun to see and understand this stuff, on many levels. We appeared in your life and challenged you with our pain, and you never stopped showing up for us. Then we all got hit so hard. The punishment was too severe. All our fun was over. Lives shattered." She spoke as if she was remembering and then she got still.

I didn't want to admit the quiet ruminations I'd been having, small visions, leftover dreams while moving from one body to the next. Fulfilling the consciousness-jumping was doing things to my mind, with involuntary invasions of visions and possible memories, and lessons within, none of which I knew how to process. I didn't say anything because I figured I'd eventually get there, to some form of understanding.

Though I wanted to see this work through before addressing anything else, I was afraid of how much darkness I was meddling in.

I watched for a time as the playback of what the "thing" had become ended its loop, and then the strange consciousness that moved on its own took over from where we were. The recorded information was now the current energy, and when the demonic-looking eyeball realized reality, it looked right at me. I tried to jump away from it, as the Q-suit held me, so Caitir instinctively moved us away.

"Caitir, do you think Damon will be very mad we're doing this without him?"

"Probably, but sometimes we need to separate ourselves from the other injured party, so we can help ourselves first. He's a bit of a disruption, isn't he?"

"Sometimes, and other times I'm so afraid of moving forward without him."

"So why take-off with me this time?"

"Honestly?" I asked, my floating body paralyzed, my eyes unable to move from staring at this machine's version of a dark, demonic eye. "I keep seeing things when I jump bodies, like the start of a dream or a vision. Maybe it's a warning, but I see Damon hurt, and it's not during a mission."

"Fair enough," she said, satisfied with my answer. "So, before Damon can get here and shut you down, maybe you should get to it."

I sighed. "Okay. Can you move the eyeball back and make the box smaller?"

"I can't. The 'thing' is the box," Caitir said, suggesting I might not realize.

"You can't make it so he's smaller. I'm just trying to make it more malleable."

"It took control," she smirked. "It's not working."

Caitir was tapping away at the clear tablet keyboard and then lowered herself to the bottom where the computer workstation could be accessed.

"I can't make it smaller, I already tried. The AI is not responding."

"What about my suggestion, about integrating MARI?"

Caitir pulled out another thumb drive and sighed while staring at it. Had MARI really fit inside a thumb drive? I had second thoughts on merging the AIs.

"Integrating now," Caitir called up to me.

'Did you give it a directive?"

"Yes, analyzing the code and keeping user control over the construct," she said, in a nervous voice.

I listened to the clack of Caitir typing it all out ferociously, her version of commands for integrating one system into another. Then unexpectedly it was all there, all of what I needed to do the work, before me. My own body laid out in light but turned small enough for me to hold with the length of my arching arms.

"How'd you do that?" I asked, in astonishment.

"I told the AI to invert the sections of code that carried your energy signature, to separate out from it, for us to see. I'm just trying to protect the machine from getting overrun."

My light avatar was turned upside-down, the Strŏngman box hovering over her, disconnected from the bone, but not from her as a whole. The dimension of where the demonic-eye was housed was still on top of her, living side-by-side, always. I still didn't have the answers I needed, to know what was next, so I stayed quiet and realized I needed to start guessing.

"Caitir, did Damon migrate his code for the Kinesiology, um, the muscle-testing protocol?" I asked.

"We keep them updated. I'm sure it's here."

"I need to ask some questions."

"Quantum-Speculum Field Reader, Muscle Query Gellion's suit," she said to the AI inside the Georgetown Quantum-Speculum.

My arm moved slowly into position, for whatever questions I could ask myself, using the magnetic system to help me determine my own body's answers.

"Are the boy and the demon connected?" I asked myself and then I squeezed my arm muscles as strong as I could, as the magnets tried to pull my arm down. My arm held strong.

"THE ANSWER IS YES," the AI responded, and when Caitir and I heard the sound of MARI's voice speaking, instead of the original AI voice, our shocked faces stared at one another?

"MARI?" Caitir asked. "Nice to hear you."

I shook my head at Caitir, annoyed she was interrupting my questions.

"MARI IS FULLY INTEGRATED. THE REQUEST PROTOCAL HELD. THE ENTITY SIGNATURE IS CURRENTLY CONTAINED," MARI replied.

"MARI, Can I pull the Demon and Boy apart?" I asked, and my arm immediately went weak.

"THE ANSWER IS NO," MARI's voice sounded.

"MARI, are you speaking for the Quantum-Speculum?" Caitir asked, and by her facial expression and tone, I feared I didn't have much time to get my answers.

"MARI IS FAMILIAR WITH VOICE COMMANDS AND PRACTICED WITH COMMUNICATIONS."

"MARI, Can I remove them from the box?" I asked.

"THE ANSWER IS NO," MARI said, as my arm went weak.

"MARI, is the next step in the process to remove them?" I asked, wondering if I was even on the right track anymore.

"THE ANSWER IS YES," MARI said.

So, I wracked my brain for ideas of how I could do that.

What am I missing?

"MARI, does Gellion need help?" Caitir asked.

I thought Caitir was asking me, but she was asking my body, and so the suit pushed down on my arm, and I almost missed it, holding my muscles steady, showing me her question was the right one.

"THE ANSWER IS YES," MARI said.

"I need help? From?" I wondered, then considered just how little I'd looked for a source of light when I was working within Damon's technology. At the Buddhist temple, I went searching for the divine and found it within the crystals. This time, the crystals were adornments attached to me, surrounding me, but not inspiring me to see godly visions or messages, like I had with the crystal on the mound off the trail.

"God?"

"THE ANSWER IS NO," MARI said.

"Help from the angels?"

"THE ANSWER IS NO," MARI said.

"Help from a different healer?"

"THE ANSWER IS NO," MARI said.

"From a light being?"

"THE ANSWER IS NO," MARI said.

"From a dark being?"

"THE ANSWER IS NO," MARI said.

"From the demon?"

"THE ANSWER IS NO," MARI said.

"From the teen boy?"

"THE ANSWER IS NO," MARI said.

All "No's." And then I could only consider that I was hitting a real roadblock.

"Is there something in the way?" I asked.

"THE ANSWER IS YES," MARI said as my arm stayed strong. Finally, a "Yes."

"Is it a curse?" Caitir said abruptly, then looked away.

"THE ANSWER IS NO," MARI said.

"I removed the curse of the Strŏngman from the last two boys, and none of this happened."

"It's not that kind of curse," she corrected.

I wasn't sure I agreed with her, so I asked.

"Is there a curse standing in the way?"

"THE ANSWER IS NO," MARI said.

Caitir just shook her head as if she was sure she was right.

"Maybe that's just the wrong word," I said, looking for the answer inside my imagination.

"Possession?" she choked out.

My face immediately sulked and smirked, "Damon said that. Said you all thought it could actually be demonic."

"I used to lie to myself," Caitir admitted, "that what I'd seen was because of the trauma, or because I was told over and over it was real, like conditioning someone for a magic trick. I didn't need to be convinced. I never disbelieved my eyes."

As Caitir spoke, a vision played before me like shadows burnt into the iris.

"I see children in an empty pool," I said, trembling.

When the words came out of my mouth, the demonic-eye, that had gone dormant during our failed questioning, came back to life and stared at us, expanding and contracting its black-hole pupil, churning the dark energy.

"Can you let me down," I whined in response to the energy ball staring at us.

"Sure."

We walked out and pulled off the head gear of our suits, Caitir following me as I went looking for some water, and a window with some sunlight, which only existed on the exercise floor, as the real windows only showed a night sky. Caitir joined me and played for us a sunny mountain-top view of Switzerland.

We rehydrated in the filtered sunlight, staring out at a recorded video feed of a beautiful river below, feeling as if I were truly there in all the beauty and life.

"So, it was more than just a possession," I stated, feeling the power of it hit my chest. "It's the ritual Damon mentioned."

"An incantation. An oath. An induction into the order and a binding agreement with a demonic entity," Caitir said, quietly, trying to make me understand, to trigger a deeper comprehension of what I was working with.

"You've done this ritual?" I asked, concerned.

"A long time ago," she said, her head hung low.

"How long ago?"

"I was twelve," she whispered.

"How do you know the boy inside the Strŏngman box did it too?"

"He was there," she confessed.

"With you?" I asked, shocked.

"Mm-hmm," she nodded. "Damon too," she said.

"Please explain."

"They group us by age, the children in the families within each quadrant of territory, needing a specific number for the rituals. It binds us to other families in the same region and at the same financial level, or close to it. You must be exclusive, to keep it all secret and safe, but calculated to ensnare other rising families to get roped in."

"Why not just tell me?"

"We haven't needed to look back, just kept moving forward. For a long time, I didn't remember. Then I worked hard to forget. Forget what happened. Forget how I got away. Forget how Damon never got away," she said.

"Why?"

She sighed, like the burden of telling it was too much.

"Once we were inducted, we were to become progenies to a specific master within the region, each master with their own function and requirements. Once assigned, we had a lifetime ahead of us to look forward to, where, as we aged, we'd be required to turn from victim to abuser."

"But you got away?" I asked.

"I escaped."

"And he didn't?" I asked, wondering if that was why he was so desensitized to violence, but she didn't answer. "Damon had to pretend to agree with what happened to me at the masquerade. Why?" I asked, needing clarity he didn't want to give. "How did he get pulled back in, but you didn't?"

"To protect you," she said, then admitted, "and me. Mom too."

"So, he sacrificed himself to make your grandfather happy?"

"Every time he had to, he did. I barely made it through that ritual, and though Damon couldn't help me during it, he got me out and back to Mom."

"What do you mean? How did he get you out?"

"I was a prisoner. Grandfather had taken me from Scotland the year before."

"Oh my God!"

"He needed to present heirs in order to continue gaining power. Calder got away, but I couldn't fight them off."

"He sent people to steal you?" I asked, shocked.

"My mother ran from the family before I was born and refused to return. Taking me was his revenge for her turning her back on that life."

It was horrifying, and I felt the hurt of it, of the torment and pain they experienced, burning me from within.

Wasn't Damon also just a kid?

"Wait, how did Damon get you out?"

"We separated from the group, during the hunt, after the ritual, and he took me to the property line where there was a wall. He told me where we were and what direction to walk and then gave me his shirt and hoisted me up. He was the tallest of all the group. I stood on his shoulders and used his shirt to get over the barbed wire before I slid my way down the other side.

"I did everything Damon told me to do," she said, visibly shaking, her voice shimmering, "I hid myself off the road, but followed it all the way to town, then out past town and beyond, eventually stopping at a farm, at a house with children and loving parents. I watched them, to make sure they weren't participating in any occult celebrations. They opened the door for me, and I calmly explained that if I could use their phone and stay the night, my parents would gladly pay them a million dollars in cash for my safe return."

I covered my mouth. "That was Damon's plan?"

"It worked, I was home within forty-eight hours, back to Scotland,

and into therapy, before they were able to find me and take me back," she chuckled briefly as she continued to shake, telling the story. "He saved me and probably got in a lot of trouble."

My face couldn't disguise my disgust at every new detail that emerged, disgust and horror and sadness. I was curious though. "Did he ever tell you, if he got in trouble?"

"Damon's parents were dead, and Grandfather was his guardian, so Damon had nowhere to run, and for a time he became one with the demon."

I felt so sad for Caitir, for what she'd experienced, and how I'd been spared so much of my own trauma, while she relived hers. The tears I felt down my cheeks were for Damon, though, and for the years of suffering he experienced before our meeting, at the hands of someone so evil.

"He won't speak of those times. Not to me, but I would never ask."

"Because of your own trauma?" I wondered.

"Because I can imagine what might have happened to him next, and it's all bad."

"So how did you get here, in all this chaos and subversion?"

"It's organized chaos," she sighed. "I think Damon had a lot of time stuck in torment to hatch a lot of plans. He's a natural strategist, with a photographic memory, using all his wits and charms to survive, and get away with things others would have been crumpled by. He's a survivor, and they rarely self-reflect when they must keep moving forward. This war never ends," she lamented. "You know, this is the first time in years he's stepped away at all from the warfare and focused solely on the idea of healing."

I sighed.

"I'll figure this out," I said. "It's just so obscene what you lived, and heartbreaking."

We both sniffled a bit as Caitir pulled me into her, and we held each other in consolation. The understanding of it was far from transparent, of demons and rituals, but clear enough for me to get just how much more powerful such things were with so many voices working together for a specific sacrament.

24

UNLEASHING THE CURSE

Caitir and I didn't have a lot of time before Damon would realize we were top-side, working in the fancier Q-Spec. The workout floor had been the perfect reprieve, but it was time to get back to work. We took the elevator back to the observatory command center.

"So, how do I remove a demon? One brought in with a curse, created during a ritual?" I asked Caitir.

She ignored me and pulled up the other energy readings the machine had noticed but had been overlooked by the massive eyeball in the room.

"Well, it would have to come off the boy or out of him, the demonic entity, which means you would have to think of the demon as the curse. No personality, no sentience, just a curse, to be lifted and removed."

"That simple, huh?" I said, skeptically.

"I read your journals," she shook her head at me, maybe in embarrassment, and shrugged, "and you always quoted your grandparents, and the wisdom of their experiences."

"I did?" I had no memory of my grandfather, who I'd been told I was close to.

"And one of the things you wrote that stuck with me was that, if there is darkness that does not belong to us, then the law of the universe says it can be removed even without permission. Curses never belong to the victim, so energetically, it's only a weak imagination that can stop you from removing it."

"Thanks," I said but scowled at the way she made it sound so easy, like only lazy people couldn't do it, then thought about her argument. "What if it's not that kind of curse?"

"What do you mean?"

"Well, he agreed to the oath," I stated, trying to figure out why something so simple, was seemingly more complex.

"Gellion?!" Caitir chastised.

"Under duress, obviously," I corrected, knowing no child could ever consent to such evil, so what else could it be? It was a challenge to imagine life through the lens of devil worship, but I tried. "Did he take the oath with his own blood?"

Caitir's mouth dropped before she nodded her head, "We all did," she said, as if she forgot that a blood oath could carry more energetic power. Blood seemed to be at the center of so many things.

"I don't know much about the world you come from, but I imagine that if these people truly rule the world, then they know the rules of energy, vibration, rituals and blood magic very well, much better than we do."

"They speak everything into being," she said. "Literally and offer sacrifices and suffering to appease the dark entities who give them information and attack their enemies."

"So, sacrifices and oaths," I quipped. "Did they use the blood to summon the demon?"

"No, the cuts were made when the entity arrived."

I stared out into space, waiting for my old Gellion mind to start working, to do better at piecing it all together. I'd made some real progress and didn't want to stop until I understood at a deeper level. And I thought of how it would look, in a movie, in front of me.

"How many children?" I asked.

"Nine?"

"Total?"

"Twelve," she said, her voice turning to a tremble, and she started to sniffle.

"Jesus," I mumbled.

I closed my eyes and saw a fuzzy background, where I focused only on locating the incoming demon, but then I saw there were three demons. Demonic shadows circling the ritual, waiting for the silhouette sacrifice to bind them into the oath-takers. The complexity of the ritual, the sacrifices required, the number participating, and the death of three "unimportant" children, made it easier to consider that the level of people involved meant the demonic entities would also be uncommon.

"Did you believe in it when you were doing it?" I asked her.

"Yes."

"Did you truly give yourself to the power of the entity?"

Caitir stayed stuck in her head for a bit before answering. "No, I wanted to go home. I hated every second of it and I wanted all the bad men to die."

"Did Damon give himself over to it?"

Caitir scoffed. "You know Damon. I, at least, had enough humility to fear what was showing up."

"Did that boy give himself over to it?"

"Oh, I see!" She exclaimed, like my line of questioning was finally making sense. "Yeah, even under coercion, I never submitted inside myself, inside my head, I never gave in. I never wanted the demon inside me. I get it now. Yeah, the boy took the oath and meant it. He was just as angry and scared as we were after the abuse, but proud when he enthusiastically made the first kill. His eagerness was scary. Does that truly make a difference?"

"It means he might have wanted the demon, and if he liked the darkness, he would have used it to gain power, instead of fighting it," I concluded.

"So, you can't separate them?"

"Maybe," I replied, but felt there was more. "If we go back to the universal law, even if he wants that darkness, if he used it to hurt me, and it's still hurting me, I have the right to remove it, don't I?"

"You tell me?" she questioned back.

I looked at the box made of laser lights and stared at the demon inside it, and the deep disgust that sat within me grew into a powerful anger. The damage I'd suffered, the torment of so much sickness, the endless anguish was a hell I didn't deserve.

I suddenly believed that if there was a God in this world, and he was my maker, he did not want my soul-in-human-body to live through such darkness, to be abused for their fun, without rebuke. I couldn't fight their collective evil, but I should be able to save myself and remove anything foreign and unwanted from me. I had so many questions.

Is this the same darkness Damon spoke of when he said I'd removed it from him all those years ago? No, he said it was a piece of something, like hardware.

They would have told me if I removed an actual demon from him when we were teens, right?

So, if this is the same demon from their ritual then it accomplished its wickedness, and I'm done being plagued by it any longer.

"Yeah, I have the right to remove it from me," I said, and I knew it was true as I spoke it, but I just didn't yet know how to do it.

When we were back in the Q-Spec machine, as I stared at the angry demon inside the Strŏngman box, I realized it was an immovable energy I couldn't release from my own broken system. So, I pondered how to separate its mass from the structure that was holding the trauma to me.

No energy bubble I could imagine was strong enough to hold a shadow of a demon, not yet. I didn't know how to get it out, and I was starting to get frustrated.

"Caitir, can you put me in a relaxing position and float me around this thing so I can look at it from different angles?" I asked, knowing Caitir had been waiting for me to say something. She nodded in agreement and my magnetized suit pulled me back to a floating position. I rested in the air, able to stare at the Q-Spec's light replication abilities while gently horizontal.

The most practical viewpoint from that position was looking at it from underneath, and it took a very short amount of time from that angle for me to realize something. I didn't have control over a demon, but I did have a right to the structure that was holding him to me. That box might have been made by someone else, but it actually belonged to me. It was my box, attached to my body. That trauma was my trauma, and only I could own that.

I reached up, my desire to get closer to it, and I was surprised when my body moved with me, with my thoughts and arm gestures to move closer. I felt like MARI was responding to my movements against the magnets in a way the original AI hadn't even considered. I was air-swimming, or virtual climbing, and no longer on my back. I turned vertically as I pulled my way up to the top of the invisible box.

"How did you do that?" Caitir called.

"I didn't," I called back, "I just tried to, and the resistance responded. I think it's MARI."

"That's new."

"Awesome!" I was enthused.

Reaching high enough, I found the edge of the box, and there was an invisible lid that lit up in the display when I touched it. The edge, where the box lid should be accessible, wouldn't budge, no matter what I tried. Eventually, I became enraged at its stubbornness, at all I endured and the insanity of it defying me.

So, I did what any brute would do and started pounding on it. It was shocking how accurate the magnetic resistance was with the laser light display, as they worked together to provide me with a fully kinesthetic experience. The more I pounded, the more the lid lit up and became unstable as I manhandled the box's invisible edge, all while the demonic eye watched me. Seeing it glare at me maddened me even more and I felt unencumbered to climb the see-through walls of the sphere's enclosure.

"Remove myself from the box," I said, as I yanked.

The resistance didn't last as I pulled harder and harder, until the edge of the lid ripped open and separated. I pulled the entire top of the box off and threw it away.

"Fill with light," I said, my mantra over and over.

It took a lot of effort, but it was worth it. I smiled at Caitir watching, then I tore one of the box's walls off, the one holding me up, before climbing to reach another.

The size of the box, of its pieces, began to shrink as I pulled them away from the demon eye they were housing. When I yanked the base of the box out from underneath the demonic sphere, I felt my magnets slip for a moment, startling me, as all the floating pieces of the box disappeared.

Then the structure reappeared on its own, a small black box in front of me and my reemerging teenage self. The demon wasn't gone, and neither was the boy, who'd been absorbed by the demonic eye, but once the walls were gone and the Strŏngman construct was broken up, my younger self was finally free.

"Wow," I could hear Caitir say, and I felt the same astonishment.

The demonic eye had watched me rip its walls off, but it only just noticed the little black box. As I reached out for it, aware of it as the archetype of my harm by a demonic perpetrator, the eye focused closely on it. The box was mesmerizing as I held it in my hands, the inverted lights moving in connection to the magnets inside my gloves, showing I had energetic dominion over it. How connected I was, was apparent as I held it between my hands.

The box needed to be returned, but when I tried to hand it to my younger self, she didn't move. When I examined her more closely, she was bound, unable to accept the box. I guess dealing with a demon wasn't something I could expect that long-lost part of me to handle. So, it was on me to give it back. I started to move the cube construct, to direct it from where it was to where it should be, but it was heavy and moving slowly.

"Why isn't it moving?" Caitir called out.

"It's moving, but I'm having to push hard to get it to go."

I looked back at Caitir, and didn't know why, but I had the sense that her awe was not the only amazement, and that her eyes were not alone in watching. When I looked up, to where Caitir would usually be behind the glass and inside the command center, I saw Damon. His eyes were wide with shock and confusion.

Despite our eyes meeting I didn't stop and like a child trying to drag something heavy they have no business moving, I slowly shoved and heaved the Strŏngman box to return it to its maker. If I couldn't separate the demon from the boy, then they'd both have to take the evil back and own it together.

By the time the box was close enough to reach them, I was running out of stamina. The magnets held me and let me move forward at a crawl as I pushed the see-through box, heavy as a boulder. The presence of opposition against me was very real.

"Gellion," Damon called out from below me, having entered the Q-Spec, his stubble and tattoos my reminder of his original form.

He was dressed in street clothes, simply a bystander.

"Pull yourself back once you've made contact," he said, as a warning.

I nodded, only half a foot away from the demonic eye, and gave one last shove into the Strŏngman box and watched as it made contact and disappeared into a cloud of black dust. The cloud spun around the demon, in a tornado of energy engulfing them, and oddly, beginning to separate them from one another.

The structures changed from the large eyeball orb into two different beings. One was made of mostly muddled light, and the other was almost entirely dark, and muddled too. When they were completely separated, the black dust particles that were once the Strŏngman box infected the muddled boy, turning him so dark that he started to turn inside out, into a ravenous tornado inside his loosened body structure.

As it slowly took him over, it caused damage, trauma, and pain, and he looked agonized. When the agony made him no longer recognizable, the demon in laser-light structure, turned and looked at me, watching.

In my memory, when I couldn't watch the dark dust tear my abuser apart anymore, I'd made peace with having to free him. It was impossible for me to do the work when the demon and boy were one, but now that they were separated, I felt emboldened.

"Can you make them smaller," I called to Caitir, but Damon was already at the console and began typing, and the boy and his demon got smaller before me…

…until the demon stopped shrinking and started regrowing itself against the programming command.

"COMMAND PROGRAMMING INFILTRATED," MARI blared out.

"Oh shit," I said, realizing something had shifted again.

The gigantic fans at the top and bottom of the Q-Spec started spinning faster, pushing against us as the magnets held us in place. It was beginning to feel like a tornado inside the machine. I made an energetic bubble as quickly as I could and wrapped it around the inverted boy, being torn apart over and over, and pulled all the dust from him, that had once been my Strŏngman box trauma.

"Remove the Strŏngman curse," I said loudly, over the sound of the spinning fans.

I pulled the dust away from him, holding it inside my energy bubble.

The boy was free of the darkness, and when I sent him light from my unoccupied hand, he bowed to his demon and disappeared. The demon turned and moved toward the dark dust still inside the sphere but stopped when I put my hand up in defense of myself.

"Gellion," Damon yelled. "Let it go!"

I knew I could drop the dark energy, but I didn't know if the demon could take it or use it. What would happen then? I couldn't let go, but I couldn't stay like that either.

"Let it go!" Caitir yelled at me too.

The fan blowing beneath us started speeding up even more, and the gust of wind wobbled me as the demon launched itself forward, toward us. The magnets in my suit held me steady, but the feeling that hit when the demon flew through me was sickening and terrifying, like all sense of gravity and space had disappeared, then reappeared to repel me.

I dropped the energetic bubble holding the Strŏngman dust, and it fell to the bottom and beyond the Q-Speculum's ability to scan, as the demon eye dove for it then hit a magnetic wall, an invisible barrier with Damon standing just beneath.

The Q-Spec contained the demon!

With the boy gone and the box gone, the demon was alone and pushing against the edge of the Q-Speculum, its spheroid structure just two inches from Damon standing at the bottom of the structure complex, bound by an intangible prison.

"Damon, get us down!" I yelled, but he could only seem to stare at the entity as it focused its attention on him, until it realized there would be no way to reach him.

Caitir typed on her tablet, but nothing happened.

In an ever-growing frenzied state, the demonic sphere looked around the room and its eye landed on Caitir and came speeding toward her at an incredible rate. Still frantically typing on her tablet, I watched her suit slowly lower her as if it were fighting against another command.

She screamed as the demon stopped just before her and a dark cloud shot out from the center of the demonic eye and flew inside Caitir. Her screams turned hysterical.

"Damon, get us down!" I screamed again. "MARI!" I yelled. "Save Caitir! Get us down safely!" I commanded, but nothing happened, no one was moving.

Then the demon looked at Damon, and something even more horrifying happened as sparks lit up in the center of the demon's false iris. Like a chainsaw splitting open a door at its center, the demonic orb started to splinter itself from within, ripping itself apart, becoming two clouds of dark gloom.

The first cloud of demonic gloom imploded in a fog, like a fast-moving smoke bomb deploying in reverse, it gathered itself up and slung itself directly into the center of Caitir. As she screamed and protested, the laser lights displayed that the demonic energy had fully absorbed into her, and then Caitir went limp.

The second half of the imploded entity went flying toward Damon, who was still outside the Q-Spec, protected by the magnetic wall.

Caitir lost all control of her body, dropping her clear tablet as her eyes rolled back. She contorted inside her suit then convulsed as if having a seizure, dangling in the air, moaning.

"Damon, what do I do!" I yelled.

There was no one to send the command to help me get down to her, so I used my arms, and pushed against the magnets, and the AI didn't fight me. MARI might not answer my commands, but she wasn't stopping my resistance. I pulled my way toward Caitir, pushing myself through the magnets power with both arms and legs, moving until I found resistance, to get to her while also watching in horror at the scene below me.

At the bottom of the Q-Spec's perimeter, the demon had reached the edge of the Speculum's sphere, as it had when it tried to chase after the Strŏngman dust. At the edge, it pushed its branching energy against the field, banging itself as it raged against the domain walls, trying to reach Damon on the other side. Damon just stared at the shadow-being, until its banging limbs started sending sparks into the laser-fields.

"Damon!" I called out, from high above him, as the sparks of light were going off like fireworks inside the machine. "Get us down!"

I'd reached Caitir, who was still convulsing, and grabbed her by the ankle. Moving my arms to pull us down I got her below me and started shoving her toward the ground, pushing farther, faster. That's when the lights flickered, and Caitir and I dropped at least a foot before the magnets caught us again.

We dropped downward in the air, in the short time between when the flickering power went off and on, as the Q-Spec seemed bombarded by the demon's thunder. The flickering continued, dropping us by inches from up high, too high for the fall not to injure. Damon looked up at me and winked, and I realized too late that he meant to stop the demon the wrong way.

"Don't!" I yelled. "Not your real body!" I screamed!

Damon walked inside the bounds of the Q-Speculum Field. The demon turned into inverted lighting and swam into Damon's body, like an eager parasite.

"No!" I screamed, disgusted.

The flickering stopped as Damon fell to his knees and lurched forward, holding himself up by his arms, heaving like he might retch.

"MARI! Take us down!" I screamed, and she finally listened, lowering us down quickly but safely.

When we got to the ground, I dragged myself over to the emergency power button and shut the machine down. Caitir, whose body was shaking and trembling, lay unable to move past her shock, then sounds came from her mouth.

"It was in there all along," she mumbled. "It was in there all along."

And she kept saying it to herself quietly, over and over, in a soft and disturbed murmur. She was staring out into nothing in a daze.

"Damon, are you okay?" I asked, reaching out to his back, but he winced at my touch.

My eyes got foggy when I tried to get closer to him, like everything was blurred the closer I got, and I couldn't really see who he was.

"I'd forgotten," Damon said, also in a daze. "Caitir never forgot, not really. I did. I'd forgotten how bad it was."

His body started to convulse, his torso looking like it wanted to spasm, and I stood by, helpless, his reaction blurry for me still. As he fought the tugging from within him, before stopping it and trying to stand, he managed to hold himself steady long enough to let some of it pass. He got to his feet but was wavering and unable to look at me.

I moved over to Caitir and crouched down beside her, my focus returning.

"How do we get in touch with Malik?" I asked, realizing how little I knew, but Caitir wasn't even present before me either. She was somewhere else, deep within her own trauma.

"MARI-G," Damon called out in a quivering voice, "Contact Malik, call for help."

"CONTACTING MALIK," MARI-G said, sounding almost like the other one, but with an accent I couldn't place.

I'd shut down the Q-Spec, but clearly the emergency power button had not disconnected the whole building's AI.

"This building has its own MARI?" I asked.

Damon nodded his head.

"Is there anything I can get you?" I asked Caitir, feeling helpless.

Caitir couldn't respond, so I touched her shoulder gently, wondering how long it would take for them to come. I looked back over to Damon, who was standing inside the inactive Q-Speculum, looking up into it.

Instead of seeing just Damon, I could see something else too, something vivid and throbbing, something that burned in my sight like the retinal burned images I'd seen at the temple. These burned images never moved from their positions inside Damon, even as I tried to change my point of view.

I stood and walked toward Damon, watching what I saw inside him churning, as it burned my eyes. I stared at the purple and black blobs I saw, as they swirled over themselves like sparks of violet light trying to break through a layer of hot tar. They were small at first, but by the way they moved they looked alive. Like a dark-energy virus, sitting inside Damon's systems of human energy, infecting them.

In Damon's head, his heart, his torso, and his pelvis. In all his major body systems he was contaminated with dark energy. All this time, just like my dream, but more vivid, the dark hardware Damon spoke of was there. What it manipulated inside him I didn't know. He turned and looked at me staring at him, but he couldn't speak.

"I can see it," I whispered, unsure of what it was exactly.

He looked queasy or drunk, swaying slightly.

"See what?" he said looking down at himself. "The demon?"

"No. Something lit up after it went inside you. The more I stare at it, the more it looks like, um, like an orb of hardware wrapped in slime. It's solid and alive but not living."

"Is it purple?"

"Yes, and black," I said, lightly, quietly, like I'd finally discovered a secret. "Like tar, with black magic sparking inside it."

"Where do you see it?" He whispered as he wavered.

"In your head, chest, stomach and pelvis," I admitted.

"Can you see my face, or just the hardware?"

"Both. I see it behind your face, inside your brain, linked into your mind."

Suddenly, the human Torus fields that I'd tried to understand were all showing up before me, their donut shaped energy emanating from each area where Damon also carried the dark hardware.

"And Caitir?" he asked, and I turned to look at her, and I could see it in her too.

I went back to her and took her hand. She was staring into space, twitching.

"I only see it in her pelvis," I said, whispering.

The doors opened and Malik entered with Tombo and Joseph behind him. He came straight to Caitir and waved his hand in front of her face, but she didn't respond.

"What about them?" Damon asked.

I only shook my head. I saw nothing. Either these warrior men, who I knew had to have killed people, seemingly carried no darkness, or it was buried too deep for me to see. Maybe the demon that entered Damon and Caitir removed a kind-of camouflage that would normally cover the dark hardware, concealing it.

Malik whispered into Caitir's ear then looked at me.

"I hope you're prepared for what you've started," Malik said to me. "They need you now more than ever."

Malik picked up Caitir, in her heavy magnetic suit, while Damon stumbled toward his comrades, who wrapped his arms around their shoulders, carrying him out. Joseph and Tombo both looked at me, and then at Damon in confusion, as he went limp during their assistance.

"We're a lot more connected than I thought we were," I quipped quietly, my inner thoughts getting the better of me, as I followed them out of the Q-Spec and into the elevator.

The suit was so heavy, and I wanted to pull some of it off me, but the elevator was full. I couldn't complain while Caitir was being carried, and Damon was leaning hard.

The cousins were put on medical transit beds on the train. We were back in our underground bunker quickly. Caitir and Damon were taken to the small hospital, both shuddering and fading in and out of consciousness. I was surprised how quickly Damon deteriorated once he knew it was safe to do so. Both had fevers.

Tombo placed the intravenous lines, while Malik pulled out a vial and placed a syringe to fill.

"What are you doing?" I asked.

Malik ignored me and pushed the medicine through, into Caitir's body, which relaxed after he was done.

"She called out for her mother," Malik explained. "Her parents are in Scotland right now, and so is Calder. She doesn't want to be here."

"I thought you said she needed me?" I asked.

"She's afraid to wake up in her real body without her parents. Maybe everyone needs a break, I think."

"Maybe she needs you," I argued.

"She winced at my touch. She's reverting to a childlike state, back to when the trauma happened, I think."

"And Damon?" I asked, as I watched him fill the syringe for Damon.

"He doesn't have parents who were there, who helped save him. He will probably seek solitude. He's connected to a clone here and one in Scotland. His consciousness will decide where to go."

"What should I do?"

"First of all, are you okay?" Malik asked.

I almost cried, "I don't know. Caitir told me they went through a ritual with the boy who hurt me, but I didn't think they shared a demon with him or each other, or that the small piece of it inside me would be strong enough to hurt them."

"No one would ever think that was possible," he said, sighing. "They don't speak of it. They claimed not to remember for a long time. I'm surprised she told you. As we can all see, it's not completely healed. Children repress so much to survive a dissociative event."

"If it was in there all along, how come they aren't evil?"

"I don't think we can quantify how hard they've fought against the dark thoughts inside their heads, thinking it was all from themselves, all from who they were, instead of the truth, that the darkness that plagued them was always demonic, and never belonged to them."

"What now?" I asked.

"Well, you can wait here to see where Damon wakes up and decide then what to do."

"Anything else?" I asked him, because I could see he was irritated with me and wanted to add something else.

"What were you two thinking?"

"I'm sorry. It's my fault."

"I know it's your fault," Malik chastised. "Caitir would never have gone against Damon's wishes concerning the Q-Spec, and he knew it wasn't safe. Why didn't you?"

I looked down at Damon and didn't want to say the words out loud.

"Well?" Malik barked at me, demanding an answer.

"Aren't you sedating him?"

"I think he should hear what you have to say."

"It can be hard to concentrate around Damon," I admitted. "I feel things around him that are so overwhelming. His energy is brilliant but obsessive, and really aggressive, and I'm, um, I'm…" I wasn't sure how to describe myself, to convey just how different I knew my perspective was, so I settled on the word, "…I'm simple. It's intimidating to be around him. I fear failing in his presence."

"Oh," Malik replied, as his eyes blinked rapidly, and he cleared his throat, and then he looked down at Damon.

I reached out to convey my sincerity, and Damon did, indeed, flinch at my touch, again.

"I'm sorry," I said as the sedative went into the line, and Damon's tattooed body stopped twitching.

Then I walked to the dressing room to drop off the suit I'd been wearing and get clothes. When I got back to the hospital bed, Tombo was the only one still there.

"He hasn't checked in from anywhere," Tombo informed me.

I sat on an adjacent bed and looked up at Tombo. "What do I do?"

"When the time is right? An exorcism," he said seriously.

My mouth dropped and I finally choked out an exasperated huff, then stopped myself and breathed in, yawning in reaction to the terror of what happened, and how real it looked.

"You're serious?" I asked, confused about what he meant.

"Are you blind? You saw it. I watched the playback. Damon didn't program that in."

"Yeah," was all I could say.

Then Tombo bowed before me and held out an envelope.

"Damon asked me to remind you of this, should a free moment present itself."

It was the letter from the Buddhist monk, to the Gellion he'd known, before he died.

"Thank you," I said.

Damon and Caitir's bodies were separated by curtains. When I looked over at Damon, I no longer saw the purple and black blobs of darkness. I wondered if they were missing because Damon's consciousness had gone elsewhere, or if I was selectively clairvoyant. I also wasn't sure if my emerging visions were consistent enough to see under all circumstances or only under the right setting, at minimum.

My eyes saw nothing, despite his stubble and tattoos reminding me of his original body. He must be conscious somewhere, though I could understand the need to flee. I'd done the same.

The envelope had already been cut open, so I pulled the letter out and read the cursive that felt like it came from long ago.

Dearest Gellion,

There was a time when it was easy to believe you might recover and return to our temple. God teaches, however, that the phenomena of a miracle will arrive only on their cosmic timing. The journey often makes no sense to our mortal minds because our life here is short, but memory exists beyond the contingency of our time, so your lessons may never be forgotten.

The way you saw the world, and your hope to heal it amazes me still. Healing others is a duty beyond prayer, and it grew in me from your presence. We shared a desire for dialogue and for participants in the collective light journey.

Were you still the same Gellion, I would have felt the healing hand of God upon me by now, or an understanding of why it was my time to go. How brutal, that the world would do so much damage to you and all the gifts you had to give your fellow man. How sad for me that I will miss your awakening, without bestowing a helpful voice on your way ahead.

The row against sickness has been long, but now it's time to work on letting go; letting go of fearing death and worries that should not go with me. Unfortunately, our paths will never cross again in this life. I've run out of time. My prayers now are for a peaceful passing, and to see your grandfather among my loved ones in the afterlife.

May this letter serve as a form of celebration, that who you were was never forgotten, that these words are a reminder of what we shared, a mutual love for the flawed people of Earth, ourselves included. We held hope, and a belief in the greater laws of the universe that want us to heal and be healed.

We are not alone, but we suffer without God's tools to repair, and you must share yours with the rest of the world when the time is right.

Blessings for a beautiful journey,

Brother Poe Lang

The letter read like something from an old friend to a person I just discovered and desperately wanted to be. However, the letter didn't resonate the way I thought it would and all I felt was doubtful.

I'd been someone naïve and without proper fear, not once, but many times. I was no longer stupid or curious, and more than anything

I'd developed a great desire to never live in torturous pain again. Beyond that, experiencing union and fulfillment with Damon, and seeing if love could be viable with someone so overtaken, was newly important, even with a great fear of mortality.

Brother Poe Lang reassured me that those around me were not deluded or overexaggerating, but that only made the weight of the obligation much heavier. I wanted to be near Damon, to gage his emotions, but I was already drained. I put the letter back in the envelope and lay down on the hospital bed near Damon's and let myself fall asleep with ease.

When I woke up, after what felt like a long dream elsewhere, I was shocked at first to discover I was naked in bed with Damon, his body warm and curled up behind me. He was quivering, inaudibly, as if trying to stay perfectly still.

How long has he been like this? I wondered.

He moaned out quietly while I tried to appear outwardly unconscious. He'd been there for a while, processing grief alone. I feared he might stop his tears, to shield me, so I stayed still.

Eventually I worried he'd been waiting for me and decided a soft hum, like the beginning of a wake-up yawn, would be the least-scary way to alert him to my consciousness. Damon tried to back away, but I turned around quickly and pulled him into me, his bare chest against mine, our skin becoming warmer together.

When he tried to put space between us, I pressed my hands to his shoulder blades, to keep him close to me and vulnerable, then I wrapped one arm around him and cradled his head with the other. Damon eventually stopped fighting me and enfolded me into his arms and rested his face against my breasts and cried quietly. I gently massaged his head and touched his back, and as he started to calm, I wiped the tears from his eyes.

"I'm so sorry," I said, holding him tightly to me.

"You don't ever apologize to me," he replied, almost angry, trying to figure out how to pull me away from him, to look at me. I held on tightly.

"I'm sorry for what happened to you," I moaned out sadly.

"I blocked so much of it out. It's all come pouring back in. I can't escape it. Too many memories. No!" He yelled out, then broke into a sob. "I stopped believing in the demons. I told myself I'd been drugged into what I saw. It's all coming back. I can't control the pain. Oh my God! Those children!" He screamed.

"I'm so sorry, Damon. I'm here for you. I'm not going anywhere," I said, tears coming to me as he screamed into my chest, banging his fists on the mattress and pillows beneath us, me safely feeling his rage. "You can tell me anything."

"I don't want to tell you this. I can't. It's too ugly. It's burned into me. You can't unsee this!"

"Caitir told me," I admitted to Damon.

"She paraphrased! I can't, Gellion. It's making me sick. I feel infected."

"What do I do?"

"Let me go," he moaned.

"I can't!" I argued, holding onto him harder, kissing his head while massaging his tense neck muscles.

"I have to get away from you. I'm seeing depraved things. I can't control it. I feel violent," he confessed with a growl.

Suddenly, Damon grabbed my shoulders and pulled me toward him, his face no longer at my chest, but eye to eye, his hands pulling my legs apart, and he was gripping me hard, tugging my form down to him, as he hurriedly penetrated my naked body with tremendous force.

"Uh!" I shrieked, followed by an, "Ah!" that I repeated, as I was too shocked to do anything but embrace for the impact of his entreaty.

Damon hadn't asked my permission or given me any warning, yet my current body had been naked and still sodden from our lovemaking earlier. The initial jolt was immense and even painful at first, until I reminded myself that I wanted this, to be trusted with Damon's pain and vulnerability, to be a part of his healing, even if it came with some aggression.

Unlike the last several times in his embrace, the shadows that had plagued me were no longer knocking at my consciousness while with him. This onslaught was what Damon's impulses told him to do, to distract him from the pain or help him lean away from the memories of it, so I tried to relax and embrace the shock of it, of something so primal and new coming from someone I wanted deeply to love. When my mind relaxed at his aggression, so did my body. Unable to keep up with his pace, or his strength, I went limp enough within his embrace to accept him, while holding parts of my body taut. In helping Damon's body to access mine, organically my breathing turned to murmurs and gasping under his vigor.

He didn't make a sound, but kept the potency of his movement rhythmic, like a machine working at its optimum to achieve a goal. The duration and need for sensation was unending. I couldn't stop him, and I didn't even try. He was over a foot taller than me, with upper body mass at more than twice my own. I was soft and breakable beneath him. I knew I'd passed out, and stirred aroused over and over, until time was unknown and irrelevant.

Eventually I couldn't ignore the prickly sensations that his body was provoking within me, that made me cry out from the tension and need for relief from the exhaustion.

"Damon!" I called, breathless.

When I reached up for his face, stroking his cheeks with my hands, his eyes blinked rapidly before they came back to reality, and he looked down to see me beneath him.

"Gellion?" he asked, as if he hadn't known I was there.

"It's too much."

My face was filled with sensuality and fatigue, as I stared up at his recognition. He slowed his pace to a stop, leaned down closer to my face and pulled my chest to his, taking the stress off my hips, and started kissing me.

"You're back," I puffed out between kisses.

"Did I hurt you?" he asked, starting to worry, looking down at my body, checking my neck and face.

"No," I assured him, kissing him back then panting into his ear. "I'm okay."

And as he kissed me, his lips grew soft and supple, making my own body melt and crave him once more. All the friction was replaced with desire.

"I should stop," he said, pulling away.

I held on as he tried to draw back.

"We should finish," I wheezed out, catching my breath.

His mouth was back on mine, our intimacy gained with connection and care and short lived before he was spent, our limbs intertwined as we lay down, recovering. It was mesmerizing to not know how to analyze an experience, overtaken by its power and enigma. My body laid muddled and confused, unable to process, only able to throb.

The silence lasted too long, listening to each other breathe.

I finally said, "Tombo told me to perform an exorcism."

"Do you know how?" he countered.

I shook my head on his chest.

"Do you see the hardware in me?" he asked.

I pulled my head away and looked at him. "I did, but not now. I need help to focus and I'm not sure if it lives inside every version of you, or just your real body."

"I do feel less homicidal in my clones, but we tweak them to help me with that. You said you saw it in Caitir's clone," he argued.

"I only saw it light up in one area for her, but in you it was everywhere."

"Maybe she has less," he countered. "What about the demon?"

"You mean the thing from the Q-Spec? That took your body down?" I asked.

"Yeah, do you see it?"

"I don't. I can try," I said my eyes glazing over as I started to consider the two as connected. "I don't think I can remove the demon without removing the other stuff too, so I've gotta figure out the layers."

"Do you have to remove the hardware first?" he asked, but my brain was mush.

"Sorry Damon, I'm not seeing much while naked and wrecked," I said, looking down at myself.

"Oh," he reacted, sounding disappointed. "I wasn't too aggressive, was I?"

"I'm pretty sure you left your body and went on autopilot. Like something you've done before?"

Damon looked over at the lowly lit clock on the wall, and asked, "How long?"

I blushed. I didn't want to admit I'd noticed when we'd started and when we finally stopped, as the whole thing had been so impulsive. I did the math in my head.

"Thirty-eight minutes, I think, before you recognized me."

"I'm pitiful," he sighed. "I'd been doing really well to be normal with you. I thought I could maintain it. Are you sure I didn't hurt you?"

"No. You were in a state of shock. It's passed now."

"How can I keep everyone I love safe, glitching like this? I've got no control over myself right now. I need your help."

"I don't think the speculum is a good idea."

"Agreed."

I sighed, unsure how I was going to get the help I needed to be the one to fix this, then I thought about all he had done and all he was capable of.

"I'm having trouble believing you don't have a secretly hidden quantum-something down here somewhere, with a bunch of crystals and tech, that might inspire me."

Damon's face changed and he smirked, "Well, not down here, but nearby."

I shook my head and chuckled at the brilliance of his mind, and the obsessive traits that got him here.

"So, where to?" I asked Damon, aware I wasn't ready for what was next, yet willing to follow him anywhere, to try anything, to help him, as much as he'd been helping me.

25

EXORCISM

The tunnel-entrance to Damon's first quantum speculum build couldn't be opened alone. We would need help to re-enter the site of the experiment he'd closed up but now wanted us to use. The first readings on his research came from deep underground. Since the other two quantum machines had been compromised by the remnants of a demon, we only had one option left for recording the work.

On the platform to the train, I was very surprised to see Calder again.

"Hey!" I called out, internally wondering how Calder and his parents had been. "Good to see you again. Thanks for coming."

Everyone else was quiet. Damon grimaced at me, like I'd broken some social code.

"What? Was I supposed to be quiet?"

Tombo snorted. He got it.

"Sorry," I continued, "everyone's always so serious."

Calder turned around. "Your boyfriend's real body is on a gurney, that we now have to carry into the deep underground, just so you can figure out how to do an exorcism. Come on Gellion, you're exhausting."

"Aren't we all?" I asked, suddenly less overwhelmed by his demeanor. "I mean I get so sleepy watching you brood, but I don't say anything."

This time Damon snorted.

"Har har," Calder muttered.

I took it a step further, "I mean, it's me, right? I bet if I weren't here, you'd all find something to laugh about, some joke, some show, right?"

My attempt to get them to lighten up reminded me of how I would act when working for my dad, at his garage, trying to lighten the mood after a grueling day of men working manual labor.

Joseph sighed while Tombo rolled his eyes, but neither would look at me. The cousins shook their heads as the train rolled into the station, for us to board.

"What? Never? Not even reminiscing?" I was genuinely curious about what they discussed when alone. "Come on Calder, you're Scottish, you've got to have some good stories."

"My sister was nearly catatonic," Calder replied, and my mood dropped. That shut me up.

We got into the train with Damon's unconscious body while the men loaded bags, then each stood near a pole after securing the gurney. I found a seat and sighed before settling. It was the first time I'd been on the train when it went in a different direction. This time it didn't climb at the beginning but stayed level. The ride was fast and quiet which meant the train must be gliding on powerful magnets so far down.

The task of an exorcism sounded like a cosmic joke, and when I looked behind me, at the militarized men, at least one actively inside a copy of himself, I had to stifle a laugh before the overwhelm hit me, then I immediately started to yawn. Yawning meant release, so I tried not to be noisy about it, as I kept covering my stretching mouth, to hide that the energy was battering me.

The answers and vision had just arrived for me at the temple, and I hoped the same would happen here. However, the deeper we went the more I wished I'd asked to go back to the temple. It was Caitir's words that stopped me. Getting proof had meant so much to her that I wondered if it meant the same to Damon too.

"Where exactly are we going?" I asked.

"It's hard to describe," Damon replied.

"No, it's not," Calder disagreed.

"Yeah, it's not," Tombo agreed.

"So, describe it," I said.

"I know," Joseph replied. "I've got the perfect example."

"Of where we're going?" I asked, feeling a blip of enthusiasm.

"Yes!" Joseph exclaimed. "Have you ever seen the first 'Superman' movie?"

I nodded about the movie, while scowling about Damon's set-up being compared to it, but before I could say the words, Calder was laughing so loudly, everyone else suddenly burst into cackles too.

"The Fortress of Solitude!" Tombo exclaimed, adding to the joke.

"Is that what it's called?" Calder asked.

"You remembered that?" Joseph asked.

"What?" I said, as I clearly couldn't remember that part.

"The crystal fortress in the arctic," Damon said directly to me, "where Superman speaks to his father using the crystals."

"Oh, yeah!" I remembered. "Wait, you built something like that?"

"Not even close," Damon said.

"A little close," Tombo corrected, and the guys chuckled again.

"The non-superhero version," Calder added.

It was nice to see them smile, to allow themselves to be just a little playful, even if it was at Damon's expense. As we left our dive and started an ascent, it wasn't nearly as steep as I thought it would be, and only a short distance after we leveled out.

We came to a stop before a set of double metal doors and the train doors did not open at first. Laser lights sitting outside the train did a scan of the area in the dark before the men got out, opened the sealed doors, and the train moved on. The magnets were de-energized as the train car docked into the sealed off station.

"NO SIGN OF MOVEMENT. RADAR INFARED SCAN CLEAR," MARI said again as the second scan was done.

The doors opened at the platform and Damon stepped out into the dark. It felt creepy and ominous. He carried a flashlight as he walked toward the corner of the large L-shaped platform.

Against the wall was a security screen, which required a number pin, which gained him physical access to a control panel. He manually turned on the power by lifting a lever, and then the small train station lit up. The whole thing was only a little bit longer and wider than the train.

It was a stopping place, and in front of the head of the stopped train, where you'd have to walk around on the platform from the side of the train to get to, there were doors with small signs for bathrooms and food. Beyond the train's entrance, Damon walked up a small set of stairs to double doors along the same wall as the electricity panel. He used his palm print to open the double doors.

Tombo, Joseph and Calder went to work, taking the bags through the double doors as well as Damon's unconscious body.

"There are restrooms and a kitchen around the corner," Damon said, as I walked out behind them.

"I saw. That's impressive."

"Obsessive," Damon corrected. "I spent a lot of time down here, and then I wanted others to join me. It's not much, but behind those doors is my first attempt at something original."

"You know I looked it up, and a speculum seems pretty specific to the female body, to medically look inside. Kinda makes your machine sound kinky."

"You're a woman. You're the only woman I want to look inside. The only one I want looking inside me. It's a pretty personal device, don't you think?" He said bluntly, seductively, using his power over my newly sparked sensuality. I had to gulp while nodding in agreement.

"Did you design all this?" I asked, wondering about the rest.

"No, the train tech is all copied designs," he corrected.

"Why were we able to travel magnetically this time?" I asked, aware he'd said something once, but wondering if there was something I didn't know about the train scanning for movement when we arrived.

"There are satellites that track magnetic signatures, and there is tech that tracks vibrations happening underground too. If one is on and in our vicinity, we can usually use the other tech. We switch how the train works based on the movements of the watchers of the world."

Tombo, Calder and Joseph returned with empty bags and an empty gurney and placed everything off to the side.

"What are they gonna do?" I asked.

"Loiter," Calder quipped.

"I could eat," Tombo interjected.

"Is there anything edible down here?" Joseph asked.

"Hmm, survival food," Calder replied.

"Noodles and Soju!" Tombo shouted.

"We'll be around," Calder said, following the others around the corner to the entrance for the bathrooms and food.

Damon gestured for us to walk into his first creation, the first Q-Speculum. Up the stairs and beyond the door was a rounded wall of white, that was illuminated from the other side through an opaque, almost see-through material. It was massive, and continued upward beyond the rocks it sat inside, high above us and below.

The entrance in was like the awkward moment when stepping from the gate onto an airplane through a large oval door, where you can see the space at the edge of the platform as you step over it. I looked up and around to see what we were inside, and it looked like an oval sphere, a perfect ovum.

"What is this?" I asked, touching the walls. "It looks like a huge egg."

"The walls are diamond and crystal dust."

"You made walls out of it?"

"There are natural crystals behind the wall and underneath, but I needed a smooth surface to perfect the readings. It had to be created in such a way that it could adhere to the quartz in the ground as it wrapped around the sensors and magnets inside. Essentially holding the structure together. It clung much better than I thought."

The platform inside was also made of the same substance, and it bridged into the center platform, held up by four pillars, made from cut crystal.

"I feel a bit underdressed," I said, looking down at my rugged athletic wear.

"I'm so glad you said that!" Damon replied, smirking, as he bent down and opened the remaining bags that hadn't been unpacked and removed something from inside. It looked like a glimmery space suit that was missing pieces, as if seeing exposed flesh were the style, like something from a 1970s sci-fi movie.

"What is that?" I asked, not happy at the thought of wearing it.

Damon walked to the crystal slab in the middle of everything where his sleeping, stubbled and tattooed body lay and pulled back the thick white covering from him. Damon's body was wearing something similar, except it seemed to have full coverage, like the other suits I'd worn. Whereas mine was missing most of the fabric.

"Why does his look so much warmer than mine?"

"I built one for myself first and then I started this suit but gave up before finishing them."

"Why?"

"I decided to reinvent everything. I changed the Speculum design, so I could see it in real time. The new laser-light version wouldn't work like this. I shut everything down and started fresh."

"When was the last time you used this place?"

"Last year. It's just too hard to get to. No one wants to come all the way down here."

"I'm here," I argued.

"Because the other two Q-Specs are corrupted."

"Right," I said remorsefully, frustrated with my participation in the damage, but unable to apologize.

"The demonic energy changed both the machines even though you completed your Strŏngman work. Now one machine is unstable and the other is frozen."

"I didn't though," I started to say about not actually finishing the work on the last Strŏngman, because of what happened with the machine.

"It's peaceful down here, and easily energized, and I still wanted a reading on the work you need to do. You just won't be able to see it, not from inside. I'd rather not distract you with AI conjecture."

"Your body did not overreact to an AI interpretation."

"I'm not sure what it was."

"Liar," I challenged. "You're now doubting your machine could read information inside another dimension, when you've been asking it to read information inside multiple other human dimensions already?"

"I'm not saying it was wrong, but it gave-way to the power of it, did it not?"

"Did you ever program the Q-Spec to protect itself or the human from what might be discovered? If you had thought that far ahead maybe it would be different, but how could you? I think you need to give your artificial intelligence more credit, considering how far you've come."

"Your thoughts surprise me."

"You're too quick to take all the blame. I was reckless. My thoughts surprise me too."

He held the body wrap made of bendable diamonds up for me to step in, and I wondered what boyhood fantasies helped design it. Katherine had taken me to a midnight showing of a sci-fi flick with a similar outfit. We joked they'd made her costume out of band aids. Like straps of glittered and lacquered leather, covering only the important bits, but not much else, I feared its ridiculousness.

Fortunately, I'd dressed in athletic wear, knowing it would be cold below. Damon and I had been naked together, but I felt bashful dressing and was grateful for my choice of underwear. The material was thick and covered me well. Like mini biker shorts and a full coverage sports bra, but not as thick as a bathing suit, the plain white undies were newly crisp, matching the room, so I tried not to feel too exposed.

I stripped down before working to get inside the malleable suit that seemed to strap itself to me as it laid its crystal-diamond design onto my skin. Damon helped secure me to the rest of it and when we were finally done, it felt much lighter and more comfortable than the suits that required magnets. I could move much more easily.

It came with sensors for the hands as well, like bendable jewelry instead of gloves, and as he put the malleable gems in place, sliding them up my fingers to secure them, he held the piece connected to my left ring finger a bit longer. I got the distinct impression he had thoughts he wanted to share, but they were fleeting.

In the last duffle bag was a white leather cloak with a real fur lining, and he wrapped it around me.

"This is polar bear," he said of my cloak, that had clearly been treated and bleached, and softened, making it feel heavenly and shiny on both sides.

My mouth dropped in awe, but also in concern.

"Don't worry it wasn't killed but found dead. It can get really cold down here before the speculum gets warmed up."

I'd only been half naked for a few moments and he was right; the chill had started to take hold until he wrapped me up. Then he took the empty bags and our clothes and walked them out of the oval speculum.

"Now what?" I asked.

"It's warming up, the system takes a while to get to the right frequency, since it's working its way through so much mass. I suggest you do whatever you think would help you see the next steps, while it gets ready. I need to check the gauges, and make sure it's still taking accurate readings," Damon said before he left through the entrance.

"Should I wait to start the work?"

"Yes. I'll let you know when it's fully operational."

I noticed there were large and fluffy white pillows that were placed around the crystal slab where Damon's tattooed body lay. So, I went to touch his bearded face and felt worried for him, for his mental health, and for the trauma he'd been forced to relive and remember. His real body was in shock and his consciousness within his clone was pretending none of this was serious. It felt serious and painful, and I didn't really understand any of it.

"Hey Damon, you got any old videos of me talking about exorcisms?"

He poked his head back in. "I thought you saw the one with Carmella. I'm pretty sure that was an exorcism."

"Ew! No! That was just gross!"

"Look at you? Arguing with me like you used to. So, what were you doing in the video then?"

"Ugh! Can we just not? I can't talk about that girl."

"Oh, I haven't had a chance to watch it yet. I'm sorry, some of those were Father Vasily's videos."

"There was clearly hardware removal, but no explanation about what happened, just me saying that the demon had never been possessing Carmella, only her baby. Then…" And I really just couldn't relive it.

He shrugged. "I know you see better when I'm not around, so take your time." Then he disappeared.

I sighed and touched the cheek of the dormant Damon before me, and tried to see inside him, but I couldn't, so I plopped down on the massive white pillows.

Instead of looking at him, I looked at the slab of perfectly cut crystal beneath him, real crystal, not something powdered and set. Its opaqueness drew me in, a blank canvas to my mind's eye and the desired visions, even more pristine than the crystal outside the Buddhist temple where I removed that first Strŏngman box.

As I stared, my eyesight separated from myself, getting blurry to the reality before me, and in that space of distortion I could see Damon inside the crystal, not on top of it, but an astral version of him within.

He was see-through inside the crystal, so I could view his energy inside, and what I saw was what I'd been looking for.

Within Damon a dark shadow glimmered, and as I stared at it, the astral version of him looked back at me, darkness in his eyes. It was too reminiscent of the dreams I had with the dark stranger. It was easy to be the hero there, after my grandmother had told me how to fight back in my dream.

This was too real and the darkness of it was scary. I suddenly felt vulnerable, like the part of him that had wanted to hurt me, and probably had to fight that feeling still, came from something older and much more sinister than I could comprehend. I grew more afraid the longer it stared back at me.

So visceral was the fear that it could only be compared to childhood terror, when monsters were easy to believe in. Unlike then, when we could close our eyes and escape into sleep, that wasn't going to work now. In that place of adolescent fear, it became easy to realize I needed help.

"God," I called out in a whisper, "or angels? Guides?"

Is this why people call out for Jesus? Would Buddha help?

I felt so foolish. I questioned out loud who should be showing up to help me, as I truly didn't know.

"I need help, please. Give me the sight to see what to do."

And behind my tightly shut eyes, in that darkened sight, the bright lights of my temporal illumination started to send colors into my view. Like moving neon lights against a black night sky, I was stuck inside the moving lines inside my vision, waiting for the information to turn into something useful.

"You can start the work at any time," Damon said, popping his head into the opening, startling me.

By the time I opened my eyes to look his way, his presence was already gone. The opening where I entered slowly started to close, an opaque door dropping down from within itself, and sealing me in. Once shut, the low-level lights dimmed around me while the lights below the crystal slab turned up to help me see inside.

"Damon?" I called out, a little panicked to be locked in.

"I'm here," his voice said through a speaker. "I can see and hear you. Take your time, there's some cleanup that needs to be done in the system that doesn't affect what you're doing. I'll work on that while you meditate. The guys found some Korean junk food in the storehouse, so they're fine."

"Okay, thanks," I said, because everything he told me made me feel safer, less rushed, and less of a burden.

"Is it okay if I play some music?" Damon asked, and the music began before I could even answer.

"Sure," were the words that came out of my mouth as the long tones, that sounded like singing bowls or meditation chimes, played all around me and I could feel the vibration within the oval speculum shift.

I felt lighter, like a weight was lifting from my body, and I found myself inhaling deeply and calming.

"What is that?"

"Vibrational music, for healing and resetting the body and mind," I heard Damon say through the speaker.

"Who made the music?" I asked, half expecting Damon to be the composer.

"Created by Dr. Thompson."

"It sounds familiar," I realized.

"BB went to school with him. She used to play his CDs decades ago when he was starting to get them out there. We used them to help us meditate."

"Does everything go back to BB?" I asked, in awe of my grandmother's effect on others.

"All your gifts come from them, your grandmother, grandfather, and your mom. Their ability to see and feel more than just what our eyes and ears tell us, colored your perception of everything. They had different gifts though."

"I wish I could remember my grandfather."

Damon didn't say anything at first, like the topic itself was too far back to go, and we had such a powerful problem before us.

"I wish I could forget mine," he finally replied.

I laughed because he was right, forgetting Mr. Jairus would be better for all of us. I couldn't compare forgetting one evil man over remembering beloved Grandpa Greene, but the ick Clarence Jairus left on all of us was impossible to shake. The level of evil, so enormous.

"I second that," I said.

I focused on the music, the tones and especially the vibration coming through and realized the speaker system had been designed to broadcast the frequency at its zenith. My entire body began to feel like it was floating, and my consciousness moved away from my body, merging with the canvas my mind had already created inside the crystal slab.

I didn't know or understand how others might see it or even how the old Gellion would have walked through the steps. I doubted those trained to remove demons would try it my way. I was beginning to believe that I couldn't remove the demon from Damon without first removing the Strŏngman boxes created to bring the demon in. Caitir made it clear that the abuse happened first, before the demon arrived.

The Strŏngman clearing was the one technique I'd had any practice in, so I had to start there. Damon's astral miniature was inside the crystal block, floating, and the retinal burn of my visual awakening showed me the edges of the trauma inside him. My consciousness went deeper within Damon, as if I were inside the version of him that I saw within the crystal.

There was more than one Strŏngman box, all with shadows attached. I could see them on his bone but vaguely. I closed my eyes as my mind dove deeper into Damon's body system. The tears would have to wait until I was done flying on a vision quest through him to see the layers of darkness. It was shocking what was there.

The number of abuse boxes, layered over top of one another, were too many to count. So much so that I felt lost within it, overcome with the dread of so much damage.

The vision didn't end though, as the propulsion dragged me ahead, where a sight of red hues stuck out in a sea of dark shadows. Three revolving connections into the bone pulsed in crimson, like a warning light that twirled around a dark circle center.

The meditation showed three boxes deep within Damon that looked the darkest and most marred and connected. The static of the spinning shadows within were violent and imbalanced. The center of these connected traumas created a dark core that looked almost alive, as if it were widening and shrinking over and over in response to the Strŏngman constructs swirling around. The vision was reminiscent of the spherical eye, whose pupil attacked Damon and Caitir.

The longer I stared at the spinning vortex the more the whole structure looked connected as one machine, alive and feeding off something. While the demon only left a tiny remnant within me, bound to just one of my abusers inside one of my traumas, this was not the same.

Here the demon energy seemed equally connected into the three spinning boxes and the dark core, that looked like both an eye and a portal. The whole thing looked active and alive, as if it were a solid mechanism housing a demon, forced fully into the child-size Damon.

Like leaving one conception to climb into another, next I saw something I didn't want to see, but it was too late to back out, so I turned it all into shadows and silhouettes, and avoided the details. The perpetrators chosen to both abuse and mentor Damon, stuck out in a sea of other monster perpetrators, pulsing and alive within the demonic trinity.

The perverse thrill that vibrated within the mentors' expressions told me what I needed to know, that the demon came through them, as it was meant to do, to bind Damon to his own possession. The abuses solidified the opening of his childhood-body to absolute darkness pouring in, the portal creation and demonic gateway. The human devils who moved with purpose and ceremony to see it done were maintaining rituals to protect their hierarchy and uphold their power.

It was a perpetual cycle of narcissistic violence to maintain hedonism, through trauma and abuse, of children programmed to keep their own succession going.

"I'm going to give you back your evil," I whispered to the blank faces of the evil perpetrators, whose human carnage created in Damon many a dissociative event.

I grabbed the first Strŏngman box. Inside it, along with Damon's childhood self, was the evil mentor and his demon. Then my mind backed me away and I dragged the box out with me. As I began all the work to clear his body of the same kind of trauma I'd pulled out of mine, I recalled the steps. Removing and disconnecting the box from Damon's bone. Digging out all the negative vibrations, experiences and feelings. Removing Karma and curses, oaths and agreements too.

The problem began when I realized my ability to see had grown, and the details I'd kept in black and white were suddenly assaulting me. I looked away from Damon just then, unwilling to allow myself to see any of it, avoiding details. My mind was smart enough to protect me, even if I could sense the specifics. Seeing that level of evil was unacceptable to me. I consciously fought against knowing too much.

"Please don't," I whined, putting my hands in front of my face to stop the details from developing further. The imagery abated, and I sighed.

"Gellion?" I heard Damon say over the intercom.

"I'm okay," I said back.

So, I saw it as I could handle seeing it, back again in black and white, playing like a slow-moving shadow puppet show from long ago, characters moving indistinctly. The removals of Damon's Strŏngman boxes included the need to heal terms like *Ritual Sacrifice*, *Possession*, and *Being Forced to Agree to Rape*. The words weren't hard to understand, knowing the story, yet I was surprised how quickly I accomplished the work once it became silhouettes, not details.

I said it all out loud so Damon could hear the work and connect it to the images he was getting. It felt different doing the work inside the crystal egg, safer, less infiltrated. Maybe that wasn't about the machine, but about the subject. No longer working on myself gave me great relief, to feel the horror of my own story behind me and healed, so I could face this one.

When I was able to remove Damon's child-self from the box construct, I wondered how Damon was feeling on the other side. My healing and experiences were recorded and on display. Damon was outside the eggshell, experiencing my words of healing without witness. As the box started to shrink for the childhood Damon to hold and return to his abusers, I hoped we were close to the end.

"Return the curse back to them," I said, encouraging my vision of the work to continue, and letting Damon know where we were in the process.

When little Damon handed the boxes back to his perpetrator mentors, the vision of it played for me like a movie inside the crystal slab. The box turned to black dust; the men and their own demons were overtaken by the tornado and separated from one another. It was then that I saw what I didn't even know I was looking for.

"Are you seeing any of this?" I asked, aware the visions before me were about what my mind was envisioning, or at best, channeling.

"Not really Gell, what do you see?"

But I couldn't say out loud what I was seeing. I didn't want to, and it was happening so fast before me that I didn't have the wherewithal to translate.

The point of entry for Damon's very own demon was created at the end of the third dissociative event. The portal in the center becoming large enough for its own demon to enter, the events connected. It looked like a small black disc or hole in the middle of a fire, but the way it reflected was like a cartoon portal that let the cartoon rabbit escape its hunter. The portal had been connected to the Strŏngman traumas inside Damon's sacrum.

I thought by removing the Strŏngman curse off him and his abusers, it would remove the connection. I thought that traumas connected, and removed all at once, would be enough to affect it. The portal showing up but being immovable made it clear I'd have to work harder to figure it all out.

As I considered the process of trying to separate Damon from his abusers and their demons, or how to remove his own demon, the silhouette shadows that moved within the crystal multiplied to tell a larger, older story. A shadow puppet show continued in my mind's eye.

In order to bring true power to the rituals, under the watchful eye of satanic priests, it was necessary for the abusers to already be possessed themselves, in order for the ritual possession of the children to be successful. The transfer of energy from aggressor to victim saw the creation of the boxes, but unlike my trauma which was designed to kill, Damon's abuse was different. The demons inside the perpetrators activated during the ceremony, inviting both themselves and another of their kind into the abused boy. The portal insertion was only possible during the act of trauma.

Children cannot choose, are not old enough to submit to such power and knowledge, so this first ceremony forced it upon them. Childhood innocence sacrificed, provided by their own families, to continue a long line of power and control on the world, and within their inner circles. A longstanding cycle, a tradition passed down.

This was not just any ceremony; it was an ancestral ritual to bind these children to the hierarchy of darkness, helping the dark agenda, in exchange for power. Their ruling family children needed to be programmed with powerful rituals, given freely to become future culprits and servants of the dark. It taught them all to take their loyalties seriously.

The abuse was the vessel through which the demon was able to enter, and beyond the ritual and the bloodletting, the trauma was the last step to make that possession permanent, with an implanting of a portal. The whole system was about creating demonic vessels on Earth, controlled vessels, in the most powerful families, to keep consciousness from ever succeeding to bring any light.

The human system working at its best wasn't designed to be embracing so much evil. So, the demonic energy was actually about making it easier for a human to participate in it, separating their daily living from it, and disassociate them enough to spend a lifetime there, while still thinking they were human. A demon is entirely narcissistic and entitled, and so the child given over to it becomes the same, taking on those patterns and other dark personalities to survive.

Damon was forced to withstand the creation of a trinity of trauma within him, for the exclusive purpose of installing a demon.

So why didn't it work?

Why didn't he continue to live with the sacrifice of innocence?

If I freed him, why hadn't I ever delivered him of it entirely?

The visual of the portal before me, underneath the vision of those Strŏngman boxes, made my mouth water with nausea. It was the most foreign concept of all, something so separate, so purposeful, so evil. How could I even touch it?

I'd gotten all three boxes to the same place, near the end of the work to remove the disassociation. All three demonic perpetrators staring at me. Their power to even frighten me was gone because I knew I could remove them, but beyond the boxes I feared what I would find.

"Remove and disconnect the curse of the Strŏngman from all the perpetrators," I said.

In my vision of the work, I included the strands of connection to the generations back whose silhouettes were collecting inside my energetic bubble.

"Remove and disconnect the ancestors who created the Strŏngman from off Damon's bloodline," I said, feeling deeply the need to add such an ancestral separation, to stop the curse from inherently repeating itself out of habit.

"Fill with light," I finished and sighed.

"I'm seeing something now," Damon's voice said through the intercom.

The dust from the dissolved boxes came off Damon's perpetrators. With the connection gone and the humans disappearing, their demons had nowhere to go, no human to connect into, no shared strand of consciousness, unlike Damon's demon whose fragment was once inside me. The three demonic energies that belonged to the old, maybe dead men, far away from here, started to dissolve with nothing left to hold onto to stay. With the perpetrators' connections gone, the demons' eyes slowly disappeared, along with their human hosts.

"Remove the portal," I said, attempting to wrap my imaginary bubble around it, but it didn't move from within Damon.

"You finished all three at once?" I heard Damon's voice over the intercom.

"Yes, I was hoping that would remove the portal too. It didn't work."

"We never mapped a portal before.."

"What do you see?" I asked.

"Quite a bit actually, but not as much as you. The portal opening is resonating."

I could sigh some relief with the abuser boxes and their demons gone from Damon, but my eyes never left the portal within him. The demon that lived within Damon still had not made an appearance. Then again, I would hide too, if I were being rooted out. I feared it still had power within him, and I knew it did. It disturbed me, knowing the entity was using the portal I couldn't remove, probably hiding behind it.

"I added the code for the Strŏngman steps before you started, so the quantum reader saw the work on the boxes. It also shows something where you see the portal, but it's only highlighting or capturing signatures after you find them first. It can't see the demon inside."

If I ignored the portal or the supposed demon inside him, then the last step to healing the boxes was to reassociate the broken mind, integrating the severed pieces of Damon's childhood with the current consciousness. Somehow I doubted that was what was needed to deal with the portal, and I muscle-tested my fingers to be sure.

"Can I reassociate Damon before removing the demon?" I asked out loud for him to hear.

"Nope," I said as I pulled one finger through the others.

My legs ached from sitting cross-legged and my eyes were sore from trying to use them to analyze the information within the visions. I decided I'd been planted too long.

I paced a bit while shaking out my body and went to sit next to Damon's unconscious form on the crystal slab, stroking his cheek, trying to help myself remember the importance of the work. The body I touched was cursed, abused, and toughened by hardship. His life had not been one of leisure, but of fear and torment and pain.

Something was keeping this portal here, and I couldn't help remembering the concepts I'd gone over with Caitir about blood magic within the ritual.

"Remove the blood magic curse that created the portal," I said, "and fill with light."

And that's when things visually shifted in a way that told me I'd made a real impact. A visible shadow appeared, covering Damon, then it sort-of quivered and separated from his body, breaking apart as it started to shrink within him.

"Holy shit!" I called out to Damon.

"What was that?"

"The demon," I guessed.

It was the blood magic curse that intertwined the demon to Damon, so removing it was forcing the entity to make an appearance as it became disentangled. I wondered if it was the first time. The demon's connection to Damon and Caitir was evident in how the remnant of it, left in me by a boy with the same demon, disappeared into them. I'd never removed it from them, only just separated the minor demon portion from myself.

What would have happened if I hadn't removed it from myself within the Q-Spec? We never would have known it was actually still living within them, always there, no matter how dormant, to continue its damage.

As the shadow shrank down, a glowing light appeared, a newly familiar vision. The purple orbs of demonic hardware vacillated within Damon's chest, stomach, pelvis and head. The shadow of the demon had released itself from Damon's blood and moved into the multiples of throbbing matter within him.

"Oh my God," I said, watching the demon shadow meld into the muddled spheres.

I could finally see in brilliant clarity the hardware as it connected to the demon that once took up residence inside my trauma. I understood why they'd named it long ago, Demŏnware.

"What's happening?" Damon asked.

I wasn't sure where to begin. I had so many questions.

"I saw it. It moved. It looked like it got disconnected from your blood, so it broke apart and then," I said but couldn't finish.

"Then what?"

"Is your machine reading any of this?"

"Yes, but I don't know what I'm seeing."

"It shrank itself down into the demon hardware," I explained, then thought out loud, "I wonder if the reason I can't remove the portal is because the whole thing is attached to this Demŏnware."

"You did tell us a long time ago that the Demŏnware multiplies itself during acts of evil, whether you're the perpetrator or victim."

"So, which act of evil is it attached to?" I asked without expecting an answer.

"Damn, that's why they made us kill the kid," Damon said softly.

"Jesus, Damon," I said.

To hear him admit the truth was shocking, despite it being revealed to me as kindly as possible. I was exasperated at his ability to disconnect from it. Maybe he could say it out loud because I couldn't see him; not so brave, after all.

"Well, I imagine it would make for a distinct piece," he lamented.

"If they're made like that. I guess that's what I'll look for," I said, trying not to snap at him from how anxious I felt.

Damon was right; it wasn't hard to see them. The Demŏnware orbs hadn't left my vision, but as Damon and I spoke about the specific piece of hardware connected to the demon's portal, I saw the shadow reemerge out of the orbs. It was trying to get back into Damon's body fully, trying to reconnect to his blood.

The crystal block allowed me to move my visions to someplace safe. Inside the crystal I saw Damon and I saw my healing hands reaching into him, energetically moving the pieces of Demŏnware around, to analyze. As my astral hands moved, I caught glimpses of the structures, agendas and memory attached to the pieces of hardware as I pulled them away from one another.

In Damon's head I waded through brief glimpses of horror as I searched but none of them resonated as the demon's specific piece. There were five pieces of hardware in Damon's head, another five in his heart, six in his gut, and I counted six more in his pelvis before I began to look deeper.

There in his sacrum, hiding behind all the other pieces was one that was different. The shadow of the demon had wrapped itself protectively around the hardware, trying to camouflage and shelter itself from being seen. My astral hands reached for the dark orb, and it lit up with information when I touched it. Images of brutality flashed before me, telling me it was the piece I needed to remove.

But I'd never removed this energy structure. When my hands made contact, the outer layer turned into a black slime that was goopy and slippery, as if it were trying to force my hands away and make it impossible to grasp. The feeling of the sludge made my skin crawl and my innards turn gross. I realized it was the muck and ick Damon had once asked Gellion to leave inside the priest, to punish him.

Ew!

"I found it," I called out.

My astral hands backed away and started making a protective bubble for capturing the dark hardware. The orb tried to avoid it, so I made the sphere larger, until the dark orb was within my control. When my astral hands backed away and pulled the Demŏnware out of Damon, his real body on the crystal slab started to convulse.

"It's out, but you're shaking!" I shouted. "What do I do with it now?"

"Say the work out loud," Damon reminded me.

"Right," I said breathlessly, feeling awkward about what I was doing and how it suddenly felt scary to be doing it. "Remove the demon hardware and fill with light."

When I used one of my hands to fill the empty space with light so the hardware couldn't return, my energetic bubble slipped. The demon hardware fell, and that's when I saw the most terrifying vision. What I saw I doubted his machine could read. At my feet, a black hand with long sharp nails rose up out of the ground, held its fingers out, and caught the slimy orb of black and purple hardware, that had fallen.

"Ah!" I screamed briefly in shock.

The demonic orb pulsed beams of purple and black light into the palm of the demonic hand, and the lines of pulsing color made the energetic exchange look like a download of information and a reconnection. Then the hand recoiled back from where it came, disappearing with the orb.

"Oh my God, I did it," I said.

But I knew it wasn't over. I needed to see if I was right. Was the demonic portal free of what anchored it into Damon, now that the hardware was gone? I refocused on Damon's astral image inside the crystal slab, looking for the portal again.

This time when I reached for it and wrapped it in a bubble, my grip took hold, and the portal came out too.

"Remove the portal and fill with light."

The portal couldn't return to where it was, for I had already filled the space with light. I held my breath and waited as I let go of it inside my energy bubble, but there was no demonic hand surfacing to retrieve the portal, which was a bit of a relief. Nothing I'd ever removed so far had ever had a demonic owner appear to repossess it, except the Demŏnware.

"Damon, I did it. The anchor hardware is gone, and so is the portal. Did you pick up anything?"

"There were readings for the ones you said, but nothing else has shown up," Damon replied.

Maybe I had to remove all the Demŏnware. I refreshed my memory of the numerous pieces of hardware I'd seen inside Damon. Six plus six plus five plus five, minus the one I'd just removed and that was still twenty-one pieces left!

Oh malarkey!

It was going to be an even longer day and had already felt like an eternity trying to figure it all out.

26

KILLER CLONES

Twenty-one hardware pieces still inside Damon, which meant twenty-one stories of awful to try to avoid. I'd already done so much to try to get that damn demon out of Damon and realizing it might take me twenty-one more tries made me want to cry out in frustration. Gosh, my mouth was so dry!

"Could I get some water, please?" I said, feeling my throat grow hoarse.

The door opened and Damon came in with a blue glass bottle of water. It was cool and soothing, and tasted amazing.

"What is this?"

"Japanese water, from under the mountain," he shrugged.

"Of course it is," I chuckled under my breath. "Thank you."

"Money can buy so many things."

"I wouldn't know," I replied.

"But it can't buy anything that actually matters," he said, as he sat down next to me, on a large fluffy white pillow.

"It can buy cures, and medicine. That stuff matters."

"It can't buy a soul."

"What if we don't have souls?"

"Then there would be nothing divine here to fight against the darkness from taking over completely. Maybe I don't have a soul, but you certainly do."

"What? That's ridiculous. The guy who fights the hardest against evil doesn't have a soul? What's the prerequisite? Innocence and naivety do not equal spirit," I argued. "Whatever I am, at least I'm not hurting. What a wonderful gift that's been, to have some memories of living without pain. Your money bought that."

"I never meant…" Damon tried to say.

"Don't worry about it," I dismissed.

"Do you want to talk about it?" He asked.

I took a deep breath.

"No, do you?"

"No," he chuckled.

"Besides, I'm so close to getting through this, so I think, well maybe I should just keep going."

"That's my girl," he said, jumping back up and patting me on the head, before walking through the door and sealing it.

It felt painful seeing what Damon lived through, but in a way I was trying to save him from it, at least some of it, while helping him through it. That was the working theory.

In the crystal slab, inside Damon's astral body, the hardware was present but dimmed. The shadow of the demon was trying to cover the sparking light emanating from the hardware as it churned, but it couldn't hide from me.

My touch activated the visual playback of the moment of creation in each hardware as I touched them. I didn't look while moving them out of the way of each other, so I could get a clue for which one to do next. Just like the first piece I removed, I found what I was looking for last. The hardest one to see was inside Damon's gut, and the shadow of the demon swirled all its mass around the hardware, trying to make it invisible, the most protected.

The moment I touched it with my astral hands, a vision appeared before my eyes.

I'm getting better at this!

It felt staggering to tap into the ability to just let the images come when I needed to see, to play like a movie before me, without my having to think. The vision showed a ritual sacrifice; a woman tied to a slab of rock that jutted out of the ground at a forty-five-degree angle. Farther back, the rock formation looked like it was a part of an outdoor stage, surrounded by trees, deep in the forest. Three boys with knives stood before the woman, a crowd of eager spectators behind them.

The faces of the boys appeared next, and I fell backwards from the shock of it, from the shock of seeing Malik's young face as one of the three boys. Skinny and small, standing next to young Damon, they were barely teens and persuaded into a public human sacrifice.

I didn't want to go any further, so what was already there played over and over again, two of the three boys paralyzed by their fear. The third boy, who would grow up to be the ringleader of my rape, was the only boy looking forward to the slaughter. The scene was so visceral, so overwhelming as it took over all my senses, as if I were there with them. Yet all of us existed as sketched images, my mind having turned us shades of gray to save myself from the horror. I heard them talk, like faded echoes in space and time.

"Isn't that your nanny?" the childlike-faced Malik asked Damon.

"She was," was all the scrawny teen Damon could reply.

"This is gonna be fun," the third boy said.

I stopped it again, not wanting to see the moment of murder, so it played over and over before my eyes like it wanted to infect me with its evil. The shock, the acceptance, the shift from boy to predator. Without ever having a choice, Damon was made to kill his own caretaker.

Of course, the demon's bound itself to this darkness!

This was an intense level of evil. From the look of it, the event happened not long after the installation of the demon. This hardware was another anchor, keeping the demon within.

Then from the corner of my eye I saw a shift, and the rest of the Demǒnware that had been trying to find somewhere to hide within Damon, started moving. The unshaven man lying on the crystal slab contorted as if he were coughing without making a sound. I realized I was out of time.

"Remove the Demǒnware and fill with light," I said of the hardware I held in my hands.

"Ah!" I screamed.

Dammit!

I forgot about the demonic hand coming out of the ground to retrieve its hardware. I jumped back at the terror of it arriving in front of me. But it was only a distraction, as the real show was much more frightening. I could see the shadow demon trying to jump out Damon's body, trying to crawl outside him, its shadow tugging and pulling at the hardware still left inside Damon, loosening their grip from within Damon.

As the demon tugged and yanked at its connection to the hardware, I wanted to help remove it too.

"Disconnect the demon from Damon. Fill with light."

Suddenly the remaining hardware pieces all broke free of Damon, vacating onto the floor, like a prisoner escaping in iron chains.

How did it do that?

"Something's wrong!" I called out.

Detached from Damon's blood, the body's hardware anchors just removed twice, this demon was on the run and had taken possession of Damon's hardware. Unlike the demonic hand that arrived to collect what I removed, nothing came to claim the pieces from the demon dragging them.

"Are you seeing this?" I called out.

I could see the masses of hardware floating all together, twenty pieces left, giving the shadow depth and dimension, making up a sort of figure with their mass. The shadow got darker, losing its transparency, and stood upright, pulling the churning pieces of hardware strategically into place, to help it take the silhouette of a human form.

"Oh my God," I said, not because it was coming toward me, but because it was backing away, and though I could see it, I knew no one else could.

"What's going on?" Damon called out.

"The demon's out, but it took your hardware with it," I said, panting. "It's backing away from me."

"I see it."

"What do I do?"

"Can you detach it from the hardware?"

"There's still twenty pieces!"

"As quickly as you can."

I took a step forward and reached out in my mind for another piece of Demŏnware, but instead of the shadow backing away it came at me, trying to jump into my body. It felt sickening and I backed away until I could see it had no hold over me as I moved.

"Oh gross," I said feeling nausea sweep over me, until I yawned it out.

When I reached out again, the demon's shadow turned and moved in the other direction, toward the door.

Oh shit!

Through the door!

"Damon it's coming toward you!" I yelled. "Open the door!"

I heard the screaming through the intercom then the sound cut off. There was a thud on the other side. I started banging on the door.

"Damon!"

The door was closed with no way out. I couldn't hear anything, so I just kept banging on the door. When it finally opened, I heard Damon scream again. As I got through the entry, Calder, Joseph and Tombo were trying to help Damon, who was writhing around in pain, clutching his body, and seizing.

"What the hell is going on?" Calder yelled at me.

I couldn't answer, as I stared at Damon, trying to think, trying to figure out what was happening, why it was able to jump back in.

What had I done wrong?

I dropped to my knees to be near him, to see it all better, but when he saw me, he lunged at me, wrapping his hands around my throat, both of us landing hard to the floor, him still convulsing. Three sets of hands were pulling us apart. It was so hard to see past the chaos of the hardware pieces piercing my sight with the brightness of their churning, attaching into a new body.

A new body!

Wait! This clone was created with blood from Damon's body before removing the blood curse!

That had to be it.

"Remove the blood curse of the demon off Damon and fill with light," I said, making the hand movements, trusting my bubble to be there for me.

Then it happened again, the shadow shivered, shook and disconnected from the blood pumping through Damon's clone, and his body stopped seizing and relaxed for a moment. I looked but didn't see a portal, just the twenty hardware pieces, wondering which hardware he'd used to anchor into this clone.

I didn't have time to find it.

"Show me the anchor," I said quietly, and it worked.

Verbally demanding to see helped the energy arrive. The piece I was looking for was inside Damon's head. This time I completely ignored the story.

"Remove the demon hardware anchor from Damon's head," I said, "and fill with light."

In my mind, the demon needed two anchors, like in Damon's real body, so I was surprised when the whole shadow exited Damon's clone without a second round of clearing. The possession of Damon's body stopped.

"Disconnect the demon from Damon. Fill with light."

I was the only one who could see the demon, and the hardware it was holding onto, floating away. The others saw Damon regain control of his body, panting for air.

"What happened?" Calder asked.

"Is it gone?" Damon coughed, rising to his knees. "I fought it."

"Fought what?" Tombo asked.

"What the hell?" Joseph asked.

"She got the demon out of his real body," Calder said to the others.

"It jumped into this one?" Tombo asked.

Damon was getting on his feet, still breathing heavily.

"Where is it?" Damon asked.

I shook my head. I didn't know, and all I could think about was how it still had those pieces of hardware and must be looking for another body to jump into.

Oh my God!

"How many more clones do you have?" I pleaded with Damon to know.

"Just the one in Scotland," Calder answered. "The rest are in pods and offline."

I sighed in relief. "Oh, thank God."

"Why?" Tombo asked.

"Can it jump into a body that far away?" Calder asked.

I started walking toward the train, barefoot, still half-naked and covered in a white leather cape.

"We need to get in touch with someone in Scotland and check," I said as they followed me into the train.

Damon pressed a button, "Malik, I can't call out from down here. We need you to check on everyone in Scotland, find out if my clone body woke up over there."

"Malik's not here right now," Caitir said, her voice strange over the intercom in the train.

Suddenly the train doors closed on us and started moving.

"Damon?"

He was busy typing furiously on the control screen as the train sped up quickly, pushing our bodies back.

"Are we all clones?" I called out, worried about the others.

When I saw all of them nod in agreement, my fear calmed.

It didn't take long for the train to reach a sharp incline and then we stopped. Hovering over the ground with the use of powerful magnets, the train itself started to make loud vibrational sounds while stuck in one place.

Damon came toward me, pulling me into him and whispered in my ear, "When you wake up, remove the demon from Caitir, or she'll kill us all."

"How do you know?" I stared at him.

"It wanted me to kill you. Caitir's mind is in Scotland, but the demon is anchored into her real body here. Her sleeping body. Her clone here already took the piece of demon back from inside you. It's awakened now. You're the only one who can stop her, so be careful!"

The intercom sounded again, "I wonder how long before the magnets give out at this angle," Caitir said. "It would only take the push of a button."

"Caitir," Calder said into the microphone. "Where's Malik?"

"Dead," Caitir said. "Now it's your turn."

As she disconnected the train's magnets, and the train plunged down, deep into the earth, I closed my eyes and held my breath. Waiting for the impact of the train slamming into the ground at too fast a speed to survive and hoping it would kill us instantly. A quick death wasn't as scary when you knew you'd wake up somewhere safe, or safer.

I wasn't sure where I'd land or how secure I'd be. I feared I would soon be hunted by someone who knew every inch of the bunker and how to use it against us.

It felt like no time at all had passed and I was back in bed in the bunker, waking up alone, my terror still existing within me. My mind was racing with the facts and what I needed to do. I was the only one with two active clones at home base. If I were the demon, I would have shipped everyone's consciousness off to Scotland and severed their connection to their real bodies, to deal with me alone.

Was she about to kill all of them too?

Hide and start the work? Or go get a weapon?

Could Caitir disconnect my access to all the rooms? The train situation says so. She could corner me anywhere she wanted. I sat up, closed my eyes, and imagined myself going after Caitir's darkness, starting with the first Ströngman box. I'd never felt so motivated or so filled with adrenaline, as I tried to stay quiet, whispering the words.

"Remove the Ströngman from the bone and from the body and fill with light," I whispered.

"Disconnect the Ströngman from the bone and from the body and fill with light," I spoke softly what I saw.

The list was there before me, a list like the one I'd used for myself, and for Damon, to heal sexual damage. Admittedly their trauma was different. Beyond removing the trauma, karma, darkness, torture, I remembered all the other terms too. Even though the images wanted to arrive, I was getting better at removing the distractions and focusing on the work alone.

Yawning and deep breaths were the best release too, and I tried to use them quietly while I was removing the energies of *Ritual Sacrifice*, *Possession*, and *Being Forced to Agree to Rape*.

Once I removed the Ströngman and reassociated Caitir's mind, I heard the intercom activate.

"I'm going to kill you, you do-gooder. Come out, come out wherever you are," Caitir's voice sounded.

Oh shit! She found me!

"You can't protect her from me," Caitir said over the intercom. "I'm going to kill everyone you love, and your bodies are going to help me," she said, obviously speaking to Damon.

"Gellion, concentrate!" I heard Damon say too.

He was right, it was distracting me, hearing her threats.

"I've activated four of them. They're headed your way," she said.

I ignored her threats and closed my eyes, focusing on her second Ströngman trauma.

"Remove the Ströngman from the bone and from the body and fill with light," I whispered. "Disconnect the Ströngman from the bone and from the body and fill with light."

"I'm coming for your Gellion," Caitir said.

I started removing the dark energy from her trauma box as if I were emptying buckets from a sinking boat.

Remove trauma, karma, darkness, torture, fear, abuse, damage, being bound, having no choice, pain, agony, ritual sacrifice, possession, and being forced to agree to rape, being forced to swear allegiance to the darkness.

It was clear the second trauma box carried a perpetrator who wanted more from Caitir, from the ritual of hurting a child. When the imploded box was handed back and devoured the perpetrator, the vision of it reminded me of the demon. Both tried desperately to hang on to the soul they wanted to torment and devour.

Before I could reassociate Caitir's mind, there was a loud banging on the door. I heard the intercom activate again.

"Damon, Damon, Damon. You've been keeping secrets from me. How are you able to access the computer from so far away?" She whined at him.

It comforted me that even while apart Damon was working to protect me still.

"If you won't let me in, I'll have to blast my way through."

I moved instinctually away from the direction of the door but didn't get very far before I heard a loud beeping and a flash hit my eyes, followed by the shockwave of a blast that sent debris in my direction. My body slammed hard into the floor, the wind knocked out of me.

I woke up to my leg being pulled by the ankle, my body being dragged across the slick hallway floors. My body hurt, and I must have made a noise because Caitir dropped my leg, turned around and stabbed me with a big syringe filled with fluid.

"Ah!"

I started screaming as the liquid that entered my leg burned through me. I tried to get up but immediately fell backwards and the burning turned to a total loss of control over my body and a stinging pain, as if a poison had taken over.

"What did you do to me?" I slurred, losing control of my mouth.

"Just a little mutated spider poison. It's a paralytic. My plan won't work if you wake up free and clear in another body," she said, taunting me.

Her eyes looked dark, almost black to me, like she wasn't really Caitir anymore, which was somehow comforting. The horror of losing all control of my body yet feeling the pain of her dropping me while trying to get me onto a gurney was also something quite distracting.

"Ow!" I moaned.

"Oops," she giggled, not caring how much it actually hurt to hit concrete.

I groaned. Once I was strapped in, she was wheeling me forward.

"Did you know spiders don't come from here?" she asked me, but all I could do was moan and blink. "Neither do demons," she said, giggling again. "They're not native."

She spoke with a high-pitched voice, like she was someone else, and terribly giddy. I closed my eyes and tried to continue the work in my head, without being able to speak or use my hands to simulate removal and light-filling work. Reassociating the pieces of Caitir from her second trauma box was like trying to reconstruct a movie in the dark, starring myself as the hero. I'd never felt more self-doubt in my life.

As if someone, somewhere were trying to send me a message, I saw something playing before me. All over the world I saw women and men and children, all abused, all desperate for healing, all of them doing this kind of work in the dark, in their dreams, and in their waking moments too. Many of them sleeping in the same house as their abusers, or the same bed. So much darkness created between them and inside them, long before they even knew each other.

The ones in my vision who were able to see it, able to understand that the darkness was passed down to them, created and perpetuated, they were suddenly able to remove it, and they were doing the work in silence, in prayer, with a desperate heart. If all those people could do such work, to remove the hand of the demon within their loved ones, in the dark, in the silence, in that quiet and protected place of prayer that usually goes unanswered, then I could too.

The safest place inside myself was the memory of that first

successful removal outside the Buddhist temple, in the crystal on the mound. I saw myself there again, staring into the crystal, watching myself do the clearing. Astral layer after astral layer away, doing the work far from me. I jumped there, like hopping from one rock to the next to cross a stream, until I felt like my mind had found that reality where I could be strong and swift until I was sitting there, the sun beating down on my face in the cool Autum breeze.

I saw myself remove the darkness of the separation between Caitir and her disassociated piece from childhood. Several rounds and there was nothing left of the girl who'd been stuck in a box. Unlike the removal work, when the demon noticed that good was replacing bad, the reassociation portion didn't seem to affect Caitir, or seemingly went unnoticed.

Moving onto the third Strŏngman was like going on autopilot because all the ideas and words were there and ready. Yet when I began and watched myself *remove the Strŏngman from the bone and fill with light*, Caitir stopped rolling the gurney, turned and hissed at me then pulled out a taser and zapped me.

"Ugh!" I groaned.

As I shook and convulsed and felt all the pain, searing up and down me, it activated a new level of burning along the same nerve lines being pinched by the spider poison. When she finally released me, all I could do was work hard to calm myself enough to figure out how to breathe again.

Caitir was wheeling me into the lab where the cloning pods were waiting. When I'd gotten a few solid breaths in, I *disconnected the Strŏngman box from her bone and filled with light*. This time she screamed and grabbed her head, as if she were in pain, then hit me on the head with the butt of the taser before zapping me again.

As I worked to breathe, Caitir had moved to the computer to use the robotic controls within the cloning lab. Pods from the deeper storage area were being retrieved by robotic arms along the facility. All of them were copies of Caitir. She walked back to me just to shock me again.

"I've already woken up four Damons, and sent them after your real body," she said before she let go of the taser button.

My real body?

I didn't wait for my breath to return, I just started using my mind to remove Caitir's childhood devastation from the last box, in the quickest terms I could think of applying to the work, for my desperation to get through it.

Trauma, out, light, in.

"Stop that!" she screamed at me.

Karma, out, light, in.

The taser hit me again.

Darkness, out, light, in.

"You bitch," she hit me in the face. I knew I was bleeding but ignored the pain and braced myself for the onslaught of more.

Torture, out, light, in.

Fear, out, light, in.

"Stop it! I'm gonna kill you! Ah!" She started screaming.

Abuse, out, light, in.

Damage, out, light, in.

Being bound, out, light, in.

The taser was sending my consciousness out, the searing burn shooting through me, as she kept the pulses coming at me until I was frothing at the mouth, and sick to my stomach.

I held out for one last affirmation.

Having no choice, out, light, in.

And then I was gone, and relished the idea of being unconscious, sweet oblivion until I woke up free from her torture.

My breath caught and I was panting, as my eyes flew open. Except, I wasn't anywhere new, only pulled back into the clone on the gurney, then punched in the gut. Being paralyzed was beginning to piss me off.

That hurt! Big sigh. *Focus Gellion!*

Pain, out, light, in.

She stuck another syringe in me, except this time it was in a vein. When she pushed the liquid in, instead of a burn that set me on fire, this burn took the pain away, and sent me into sweet nothingness, or rather just on the edge of it. I searched my mind for the feeling that had never been mine before. The closest I could consider was when I'd been given morphine to relieve the incredible pain, only to realize it wasn't strong enough, so they gave me something even stronger. The warmth of that relief, mixed with the release of all worry or desire to engage in thought, was the closest to this.

"I'm about to kill your girl," Caitir said into a tablet she'd picked up, and her voice echoed out across the intercom. "She just won't cooperate."

"You can't kill her," I heard Damon's voice say back. "She's safe."

"You think she's safe inside your little escape pod? Aw, that's adorable."

"You don't know which one she's in."

"I have four Damon's on their way, about to find out."

"But aren't you glad to be free of me?" Damon asked.

"My job was to help you!" Caitir screamed. "Guide you to stay in the dark and continue the evil here. You betrayed your oath!" The scream of indignation was low and guttural, verging on animalistic.

"See, so you're glad to be free of me, to have your own body to control, to experience the freedom to do what you want."

"I'm made for destruction and harm, to keep you on the path. I can kill other people you love. Maybe old Gell will stop pissing me off if I slit someone's throat."

I fought the stupefaction, holding onto the irony of where I'd just been in reactive torture, to where I was now, relieved and verging on apathetic.

Focus Gellion! Agony...um...um...

"You want me out of Caitir so bad, let's get me out!" She screeched as she pulled my gurney and dragged me out of the lab and down the hall to their avatar slumber observation rooms, while on missions.

Agony, out, light, in.

When she reached the door it was locked. She pressed a button on the tablet. "Nice try. Say goodbye to your precious cousin," she said.

494

Unwanted arousal, out, light, in.

Smack! She hit me in the face.

"That's it, I'm done playing nice!" And she grabbed my hand and stuck my ring finger in her mouth and bit it off!

I felt all of it but couldn't scream, just a deep sound of torment muffled from within, especially at the tugging. Then it was the image of my missing finger that was so shocking! I'd never quite felt that kind of terror, not even in the river. I screamed inside yet more muffled sounds escaped from me.

I took a deep breath in, only to feel the urge to yell more. This time my body gave way to the horror coming from inside me, and the cry out echoed throughout the hall. The pain from my finger existed despite the paralysis.

"You hear that? That should distract her for a minute," Caitir said to Damon over the intercom.

My real body is safe.

"Your real body is safe, Gellion," Damon said over the intercom, as if he were reading my mind, to save my sanity.

Fuck this demon!

Demonic Caitir picked the electronic lock to get into the resting chamber of her original body, and the source of her DNA code. When the door opened she shoved my gurney inside and let go, walking past me toward the bed as my gurney hit the wall. The real Caitir lie motionless in a sports bra and shorts. She had a beautiful tattoo across her torso, wrapping around to her midback. I realized their tattoos were about identity and connection. Coming back to yourself and knowing yourself had to be easier when the embedded art confirmed it.

Demonic Caitir was holding a surgical scalpel and held it over the face and body of her mirror image on the bed.

"If you kill her while you're still connected to her body," Damon's voice sounded out, "you die too, having failed."

"I have not failed," it disagreed.

"Will your Lord reward you for your time here?" Damon

questioned, taunting. "Knowing that we save children and punish the Satanists? Would your Lord consider that a success or failure?"

"I enjoyed myself in your absence."

"You alone, in a clone. You never made me act like you."

"Oh yes I did, for many, many years. And you were mine. You and her," she said, sitting on the bed, leaning on unconscious Caitir, tapping the scalpel's edge on Caitir's cheek. "The torment was great!"

"Not if you lose your power. You can still redeem yourself," Damon interrupted. "Right now, you're connected, tied to a body you can't take over. It wasn't until she separated the hardware that you finally got your freedom. Are you free inside my clones?"

I could see her face struggle, considering Damon's words.

"Why not just leave. Take your new bodies and do your evil elsewhere?"

"I don't see how I survive if I leave any of you alive. Killing you all is still a solid plan."

"You know the rule, demon. Blood is blood anywhere and everywhere, except for a copy frozen in time, made before the healing, made from the darkest version of self. You can keep the hardware, and you can keep the copies, but only if you don't kill the originals."

"Just let good old Gell finish the extraction?"

Demonic Caitir started jumping up and down like she was struggling with the idea of it, of leaving without taking a human life with her. I continued the work in silence after pushing the pain of my missing finger off to the side.

Ritual sacrifice, out, light, in.

Possession, out, light, in.

She screamed out, upset, then laughed, like she was trying to push past her own discomfort. I continued as quickly as I could.

Forced to agree to rape, out, light, in.

Forced to swear allegiance to the darkness, out, light, in.

In my mind, when young Caitir gave back the box to her abuser and it imploded and devoured the perpetrator, the vision of it reminded me of the demon inside her. It tried desperately to hang on to the soul it had tormented.

Reassociation was quick but next came the portal removal, a portal placed inside by the power of the abuse from a trinity of evil, cursing her whole system.

"Remove the blood curse from the body," I said out loud, having regained my voice, "fill with light."

"Remove the portal. Fill with light."

Caitir was growling at me, at my voice coming back to me, and trying to tolerate me doing work against her. Though the work was being done on the real Caitir's body, not the clone being used by the demon, I could tell she was fearful of it. In my mind's eye I saw the demon's shadow shimmer off the blood of Caitir's sleeping and tattooed form, and concentrated itself into her demon hardware, which was throbbing and pulsating with purple sparks of color.

Like Damon, Caitir was infected with many pieces of the Demŏnware, but this time my vision could find the anchors quickly, the ones with the most shadow protection.

"Remove the anchor Demŏnware from Caitir's pelvis. Fill with light."

She couldn't help herself, and I saw her coming at me but could do nothing to stop her wrath. Despite finding my body more receptive to my commands, my chest was strapped down. The scalpel was sticking out of my stomach, where she'd left it. Gaining her senses back, she backed away with her hands up and shrugged her shoulders.

"Oops. I forgot the new plan."

"Remove the other anchor Demŏnware from Caitir's heart. Fill with light," I said, while pulling the scalpel out of my abdomen with my tingling but no-longer-paralyzed hand.

"Disconnect the demon from Caitir. Fill with light."

Though I was trying to figure out how to cut that first strap across my chest, inside Caitir's tattooed-self and unconscious body I could see the Demŏnware leaving, retrieved by the demonic hand. Once the anchors were gone from the body, the dark hardware began rolling away from her. The demonic shadow was retreating, all of it, all the pieces of demonic hardware leaving Caitir and entering her clone with black eyes before me. A demon who'd left a sliver of itself in me, and a larger portion in them, was now removed from all of us and acting on its own.

Its face was still covered in the blood of my bitten-off finger, and she looked utterly deranged. I was sure I'd never seen a living demon, as the imagery of it before me was only familiar from stories of horror, and never real life. It was more dangerous than I could imagine, I was sure, and it was free from its shackles.

By the time the hardware had merged with her, I'd managed to cut myself loose from the chest strap and was sitting to get the strap off my legs. Everything tingled and burned as I forced my extremities back to life.

"I can kill you both now," she said.

As I slid off the gurney, standing between her and the unconscious body of the real Caitir, I held the metal gurney using it as a barrier between us. I still had the scalpel and when I looked at my hand, still bleeding from its missing finger, causing me pain, I grew a bit belligerent.

"Go ahead and try it," I said, kicking the gurney in her direction, so she'd have to take a defensive stance, "and I'll cut you open and watch you die."

She didn't run, but she didn't come at me either, her eyes looking around, analyzing the situation.

"MARI?" I called out.

"I disabled her," demonic Caitir said.

"MARI, re-enable your operating system," I said, hoping for a miracle.

"Hehe," she chuckled. "You have no idea how brilliant this mind is, and everything she knows. Oh, the destruction we will do."

"I'm not jealous of my friend. I'm amazed by her, amazed she survived and fought you, and I will protect her right to be free of you."

"You gave me exactly what I needed to multiply myself," she replied, her eyeballs moving erratically from side to side as her body shook, like a lizard stepping out of its old skin and shedding away to become something newer. "They're coming."

I knew I was doomed. She had reinforcements and I had none, so I did the only thing I could think of doing, which was force her out before the reinforcements arrived. So, I kicked the gurney at her again, and followed it, jumping onto it to get close enough to lunge with the scalpel.

I sliced her chest open when she moved her neck back to avoid my reaching her throat, as she shoved the gurney away, and I jumped back to keep the barrier between us. The door was still open and not far from her, and though she was crushed by the gurney I'd heaved at her, she rammed me and slid away through the open door. It was the exit I hoped for, so I pulled the gurney away and closed the door shut, locking it and looking for furniture to reinforce its closing.

"Damon?" I called out but got no answer. "I don't know what to do," and my hand was killing me. I slid down to the ground, against the blockade, adding weight to it.

"Gellion!" I heard Damon yell. "I need your help! I can't keep them out for much longer!"

I was in too much pain to think and because I hadn't tourniqueted the wound, I'd lost a lot of blood and was growing dizzy. As I cradled my hand the thoughts of what to do next were terrifying, but I was running out of time. I shoved the scalpel into my throat to end my connection to my mutilated body. It was terrifying and really hurt and I got cold and then it was over.

Waking up in Scotland wasn't a shock, except for the state of my body, which had all its fingers attached. When I pulled the bandages off I noticed the miraculous healing of my skin, which was simply shedding where I'd been infected with Shingles and Chickenpox boils. I grabbed whatever clothes were closest and was running for the stairs on the way down to the observation room.

No one was inside, and while I wanted to call for help, I had no idea how. The only thing that indicated a need for help was a red button. I pressed it and it did exactly what I hoped, and sounded an alarm, and all the monitor screens came to life.

When Caitir arrived, breathless, I felt terrified until she made eye contact, and I remembered not to fear her.

"Remove the blood curse of the demon. Fill with light," I said, sighing to see the Scotland copy of Caitir hadn't been overtaken, and also had no Demŏnware inside.

She ran to the monitors and started typing. Within moments all the cameras from the bunker were streaming into the multiple screens all over the walls.

"Show me Damon," I demanded.

"Oh my God!" Rosie called out as she entered the control room.

"You need to go back. All of you. Damon needs help."

"Look there he is," Rosie said, pointing to a screen in the corner of the room, as Eamon arrived.

"What the hell's going on?"

Caitir zoomed into the camera that showed Damon in a section of the bunker I'd never seen, defending his position with real weapons aimed at copies of himself.

"Where's Malik?" Caitir asked.

"She killed his clone."

"How did this happen?"

"I removed the demon, but it was still connected to the blood curse inside the clones. It possessed them. Now, it's trying to kill my real body before I finish," I said, sitting down at the desk chair, staring up at the four copies of Damon, using lethal force to try to get to my real body.

I tuned everything else out and started addressing the first copy of Damon.

"Remove the blood curse of the demon," I said, speaking of the copy I'd been focusing on. "Fill with light."

"Remove the Demŏnware in the head," I said, knowing it had to be there. "Fill with light.

"Remove the Demŏnware from the heart, fill with light," I sighed.

Nothing happened, the clone was still firing his gun. There had to be more pieces anchored into him, so I kept going.

"Remove the Demŏnware from the gut, fill with light," I yawned.

"Remove the Demŏnware from the pelvis, fill with light," I panted.

Damon had nineteen pieces of Demŏnware left, and if I divided by four clones, it meant the current guy must have one left. It was hiding. I looked hard until I could see it in the gut.

"Remove the Demŏnware from the gut, fill with light.

"Disconnect the demon from Damon, fill with light."

It worked!

The clone fell to the ground, as if hit by a bullet in battle.

"Go, Gellion!" I heard Caitir say, as a second clone dropped to the ground.

"I haven't done that one yet," I said. "Must have been Damon."

I focused on the third clone there, removing the blood curse, removing the pieces of Demŏnware, and disconnecting the demon. When the clone dropped to the ground, I felt relief.

Then a loud burst of gunfire sounded behind me!

Rosie dropped to the ground, dead. When I turned around and saw Eamon charging at Damon's Scotland clone, who was pointing a pistol right at me, I froze. Caitir leaped toward me as Damon's clone squeezed the trigger one last time before Eamon disarmed him, and they began fighting.

Caitir fell to the ground and on the monitor, the last demonic Damon had breached through the entryway and was fighting the real Damon too. Eamon and Damon were both in battle against Damon's powerful clones, but only one of them was fighting with their original body, Damon in the bunker. So, I focused on helping my real body first. Over and over, hand motions of scooping and filling.

"Blood curse, out, light, in."

"Demŏnware out of head, light, in."

"Demŏnware out of heart, light, in."

"Demŏnware out of gut, light, in."

"Demŏnware out of pelvis, light, in."

"Demŏnware out of...uh...um...the heart, light, in."

Damon had lost the upper hand and was being strangled.

"Disconnect demon, light, in."

Then the clone went lifeless on top of him, releasing his neck. I sighed deeply at the feeling of relief. Damon and my real body were safe again. I turned around to Eamon fighting for his life, to protect me. Moving away as Damon worked to get to me, removing the demon from the Damon Eamon was fighting.

"Blood curse, out, light, in."

"Demŏnware out of head, light, in."

"Demŏnware out of heart, light, in."

"Demŏnware out of gut, light, in."

"Demŏnware out of pelvis, light, in."

"Demŏnware out of…um…pelvis, light, in."

"Disconnect demon, light, in."

Though the clone stopped moving on top of Eamon, a knife had been shoved deep into Eamon's chest, and he was quickly leaving.

I pushed the Damon clone off him.

"When you get to the bunker, there are five copies of Caitir. Don't trust them. Protect the real Caitir," I said then Eamon too died.

Covered in blood, I searched the monitors for signs of the Caitir clones, who would surely be attacking Damon next, to stop me from removing the demonic control. When I glimpsed the first one, I locked-in and started the process.

Blood curse removal, head hardware removal, heart hardware, gut hardware, and pelvis hardware. Light in!

I pressed a button thinking it was a way to communicate.

"She's coming for you, Damon," I said into the console. "Be careful!"

I searched the monitors for another demonic Caitir clone. One appeared carrying a large machine gun and was moving quickly toward Damon's position. I ran through the removal quickly.

Blood curse, Demŏnware, Demŏnware, Demŏnware, Demŏnware, fill with light.

She stumbled a lot but didn't fall. A final piece of Demŏnware appeared and its removal finally took the demonic copy down.

But the third demonic Caitir wasn't far behind and had already started an assault on Damon's position using heavy duty gunfire. Before I could even begin the work on her, Damon returned fire and her body was destroyed.

The fourth was hiding, and the fifth had turned her wrath on the real Caitir and was trying to break through the barrier I'd set up inside. I ran through the removal quickly. Blood curse, Demŏnware, Demŏnware, Demŏnware, Demŏnware, disconnect, fill with light.

I was shaking realizing there was only one clone left, but that she was clearly hiding. I knew I should calm myself and see if I could find the last clone's energy signal, to end the battle once and for all, but I couldn't locate her when I closed my eyes.

"Bring the last Caitir clone before me," I said pretending she was there, hoping it would work.

"Blood curse, out, light, in."

"Demŏnware out of head, light, in."

"Demŏnware out of heart, light, in."

"Demŏnware out of gut, light, in."

And then she appeared on the monitor, walking toward Damon's defended position.

"She's got a rocket!" I yelled into the console as I pressed the button to speak, and then I saw Damon jump into what looked like a reinforced clone pod, the lid closed, and the pod entered an opening in the wall.

"Demŏnware out of pelvis, light, in."

"Demŏnware out of...uh...um...the pelvis, light, in."

The cameras were gone, except for the one behind the last Caitir clone, who had dropped the small launcher from her shoulder.

"Demŏnware out of..." I looked, and waving my hands to remove whatever was keeping it hidden, "uh...the...heart, light, in."

The clone stumbled, as if it were a robot, running out of battery.

"Demŏnware out of..." and it was still trying to allude me, "the head, light, in."

She stumbled again, falling robotically to her knees, falling forward onto her hands, shaking from the center of herself.

"Disconnect demon," I waved my hands, "light, in."

She stopped, as the animation of movement receded, and then her body toppled to the ground as if someone had finally pulled the plug. I sighed great relief to see them all go limp and then my eyes searched for confirmation Damon was alive.

"Gellion," Caitir called out from inside the command center of the bunker with her parents behind her.

"It's done," I said. "I'm so sorry it took so long," I panted out to her. "Please tell me Damon made it out safely."

She smiled and said, "We think so, but we're about to go dig you guys out."

"Is everyone okay? Did everyone make it?"

"We're all okay, Gellion," Eamon said. "They kept their attention on you, and Damon."

"And Calder and Malik?" I asked.

"They're safe," Rosie confirmed.

"Tombo and Joseph?"

"They're good. They're just stuck in South America."

I started to smile then burst into tears and severed the video connection.

27

KARMA

All alone in the Scotland command center I sat, staring at the livestream of the aftermath, smoke still billowing from the escape room where Damon had taken my real body. I kept scanning each video feed to make sure it was really over, and though I saw no more threats, the worst carnage was in the area Damon had used to secure and defend us. The rest of the facility looked mostly unscathed, and I'd been assured no one had been lost to the demonic entity who tried to kill us.

Yet when I looked down and around me at the carnage it was clear that the four dead bodies of people I'd grown to love were too real in death for me to brush away. I had no idea what to do with them or how to stay there alone with all that blood. The shock of the experience, of watching bodies taken over by demonic energy looking to multiply pain, was something I couldn't make sense of. These forces had only existed in movies for me, until now.

Stumbling, trying to stay upright in the slippery blood, some of it on me, I found the gun Damon's clone had used to kill Rosie and

Caitir, and put several bullets into him, just to be sure. I didn't want the demon coming back somehow, through some loophole and having access to all those vulnerable children. It also meant Damon couldn't easily come back here either and I would be alone for a while.

With the panic subsided, of being hunted by a monster, the sight of blood was pushing me to move, and I left the command center. There wasn't anyone in the halls, so I kept going. My bloodied handprint worked on the elevator, and I went up to the highest level I could go to the hospital ward where all the children had been.

When I opened the doors to the hospital's wing everyone looked my way. It was profound, a large audience, not because I was on display, but because I could see something on display within all of them. An entire hospital wing full of people staring at me and all of them vibrated demonic hardware, Demŏnware, underneath and within their human layers.

I could see it all from far away, a purple glow coming from within them, except when I saw Father Jerzy. It was not within him. I only saw him, and the relief of that, of seeing that even amongst all those good and humble people, Father Jerzy was actually the purest, restored something in me. Damon had been so right to keep him around.

I stared at Father Jerzy, my energy and expression desperate for his attention. He looked up, saw me, and put down what he was doing and came my way. I waited for him in the hallway.

"Gellion?" he asked, walking toward me. "Is everything alright? I thought you were with Damon."

"I was," I said, shivering and shaking. "I need to see the sky," I said, grabbing his hands and holding them. "I need to see grass and trees."

"What happened to you?" Father Jerzy asked, looking down at me, splashed in blood.

"It's not my blood. Please, I'm begging you."

"Of course," he said, and then he walked me to a faraway area I'd never seen, and we entered another elevator.

My hands were still shaking, and I was laboring to breathe, and I began to feel like my throat was tightening. I couldn't stop flashing back to Damon's and Caitir's cold and heartless eyes, so devoid of color or life. I rubbed my throat and my once-missing finger with my hands to help the feelings subside.

The elevator ride lasted a long time but eventually we arrived someplace unfamiliar. After a short walk it was clear we'd entered a massive distillery, passing the facilities to reach its large indoor loading garage. From the smell of it, I guessed the distilling was for Scotch.

Coats hung on wall hooks near the doors leading out to the loading warehouse. Father Jerzy grabbed two for us before we stepped outside. Then he walked me through the covered warehouse and out to the property beyond.

It was the Scottish countryside, and I could see all that I needed to see to remind of what time of year I was in and how the Earth itself still existed, still turning as it should. The colors, even muted ones, helped me breathe and refocus, the living colors of Earth. The leaves on the trees were orange, yellow and some red between the evergreens, it was so beautiful.

There were remnants of frost everywhere, as the sun had only been up for a little while. The time difference was confusing, but I was so grateful to feel the morning sun hit my face through the shifting clouds. I let go of Father Jerzy's hand and started walking. There was a path from the distillery out into a wooded area. I didn't know where it went or what it was for, but I needed to go there, somewhere, and breathe. I couldn't stop touching or holding my neck, or rubbing my finger, the fear and terror of my life was too much for my consciousness to handle and the fresh air, the moisture of the chill, the noise of life all around me, were exactly what I needed to process my trauma.

The path was much wider than I assumed and the wooded area it went into was larger and older than I thought possible. It was so majestic and even a bit scary to recognize my insignificance next to the enduring environment. I was too easy to destroy.

The slope was manageable, and the path became more and more friendly the farther I went, with chiseled logs made into steps in some places, rock slabs and even rope rails placed all along the worn path. I didn't notice Father Jerzy still behind me until I'd gone a long way and exhausted myself. He smiled and panted a bit, also unable to speak for the effort. He had a cell phone in his hand, and he pointed at it, as if it were the reason for him not being right beside me.

I nodded and then surprisingly kept going, curious why the path had gotten better and better, needing something else to think about. I didn't know how long the path would be, going deeper into the forest and up the mountain, but eventually we reached an area that looked like a camping ground, as it was more open and had a giant firepit, and places to cook on the fire.

The area was prepared for guests, with fresh piles of cut firewood and supplies, tables, and benches too.

What is this place? I wondered.

Beyond the clearing and through the trees there was something else. It wasn't distinct at first as it was so well camouflaged, but eventually my eyes found the forms. The trees were overtaken by houses suspended in the air that looked like they were blending into the scenery.

Treehouses?

They were amazing and practically concealed by their very design. I turned around and looked for Father Jerzy, who was just entering the clearing, and raised my arms to ask about this place.

"It's a glamping spot. It's owned by the distillery," he said, winded as he reached me.

"And the distillery is owned by?"

"The family," he replied, with a look that said I should know that.

"Where are the guests?"

"Oh," he chuckled. "It's a very exclusive spot and requires extra staff, so it's mostly reserved for when it's really needed."

"When's that?"

"When the owners want to use it to relax, entertain friends, or for the staff, like people who've been stuck inside for far too long and need to get away and be someplace peaceful," he said, winking at me.

"Oh," I said realizing it was for the hospital staff, someplace to rejuvenate after taking care of traumatized children.

"Preparations started a couple of days ago. We learned some of our friends are on their way back from completing a long mission. They could use a place to heal and reflect. You look like you need a break too."

Not wanting to go anywhere else, I asked, "Okay, sure. Which treehouse is mine?"

"Whichever one you want," he chuckled. "They've all been cleaned and equipped. Take your pick."

It was then that I could stop, I could breathe, I could rest. I found a chair and took a seat and just stared at the trees, their horizon beautiful in the clearing. Father Jerzy put himself to work building a fire. My eyes found the flame and stayed mesmerized.

After a long time of just being, I felt thirsty, and the chill started to set in. When my mind could finally return to my body, to be present within my living state, I looked around at a second growing fire and wondered how much time had passed.

"Gellion, is everything alright?" Father Jerzy asked, looking at my blood-splattered clothes.

"No one's hurt," I reassured him, "but no, it's not alright. Nothing is."

"You really don't remember," he said, as if he were just finally believing it.

"I'm not even sure I'm Gellion," I said, feeling strange.

I was blonde-haired and blue-eyed with everyone outside of DC, which I'd never experienced in my memory.

"I recognize you," he countered.

"Damon showed me everything I needed to do, and used to do, with lots of visual aids. I rose to the occasion and learned but it's only because I have a brain that likes to fix problems and solve equations."

Father Jerzy smirked.

"Yes, it's true, he gave you a roadmap, and cheat codes for what to envision, but he couldn't make you be her. He also wasn't going to give up on you, not after sacrificing so much just to survive to this point. I must give Damon credit for his insatiable hunger for justice and salvation."

"If I am her, I've lost her. I'm not me anymore either. I can't even get back to me." I said it, even though I knew he didn't quite understand what I meant.

This wasn't just about my memory; this was about a comatose body that belonged to me that needed to wake up. I'd been forced to watch someone else hunt me, while I was left completely helpless to get myself to safety.

Father Jerzy sighed and offered me his hand.

"I spoke to Rosie. She asked me to show you something when you were ready and said that they would join you as soon as they could."

I took his hand and let him help me up, even though I didn't want to stand. He led me to the other side of the clearing, where I noticed the path I'd taken seemed to start up again beyond the campground. We went that way, up the long incline.

The path ahead was much more winding, to lessen the slope. At the end of the path there was an open but narrow cave, large enough for several people to enter and sit. Within, imported crystals were arranged around the edge, while large cushions, pillows and mats invited visitors to sit in the center of the crystal circle within the cave.

I stared at the easy and protected beauty of it, but didn't go in. Just beyond the ledge to the small meditation cavern, around the other side was a water feature that looked like a natural pool, with a small waterfall that poured into it. The water was perfectly clear, and I stood and stared at it in curiosity. There were several beautiful stone benches near the waterfall behind the view of the mountainside

"Is it a hot spring?" I asked.

"No," he said. "It's created, heated, treated, and sometimes drained, but we do use the water in the mountain below us as it's rich in mineral compounds good for the human body, and we keep it clean using Celtic salt instead of chlorine, which is also healing, so it is like a hot spring in that way."

I nodded.

"You should get in. It's freshly cleaned and heated for everyone coming to camp soon."

"I don't have a bathing suit."

Father Jerzy smiled with reassurance. "It's very private here and it would be good for you. You used to say being in water was the best place to quiet everything, everything but what you needed to hear."

"It's still true," I agreed.

"I'll bring you some towels and a robe. You can wear your underwear or go nude. No one is expected for a while, but I'll keep watch at the campsite. The group isn't scheduled to arrive until sometime early tomorrow anyway, so you have plenty of time."

He left and I took off my clothes but left my underwear on, and dipped my toes in. When I got in, the water briefly turned red around me as I moved, and I finally understood why Father Jerzy looked so concerned. Blood was coming off me from multiple places on my face and hair, much more than just a splatter across my clothes.

The hot pool was so relaxing and inviting, and it looked real but felt better, as the walls near the waterfall had built-in seating with water jets. It was warm enough to lull me into the deep realization that my level of fatigue was beyond normal. My body started to breathe deeply again as I worked through the mental anguish.

Father Jerzy returned with towels, a robe and slippers, and a glass of water, which he handed to me.

"Take as long as you want. Someone will bring up food in about an hour or so."

"Thank you," I said, and he smiled slightly, bowed with praying hands and left.

I closed my eyes and pulled before my mind the biggest concern that wouldn't stop playing. The horror of what had just happened made me scared of anything and anyone around me, as everyone was so new, despite the growing love I was beginning to feel for them all.

Yes, we'd survived Damon's fragile technology being weaponized against us. Yes, energetic healing proved to be real and powerful. Yet my mind was traumatized by the experience that demonic forces exist powerfully enough to overtake us, to overwhelm humanity when a human consciousness is vacant. The encounter drove home the defenselessness of the human-soul system and opened my eyes to the truth of the world as a much larger and more embattled structure of energetic truth; a truth no one wanted to see or acknowledge, including me.

My reality though was far bleaker if I couldn't reconnect my consciousness back to my real body. Eventually I wouldn't survive without going back and it was scaring me. I'd been pushed so hard to finish so much work... but had I finished any of it on me? I missed some steps, I was sure.

What's left for me to heal? What's keeping me out?

Pain. It had to be the pain stopping me. I hadn't had a reprieve from the pain, not really ever, since waking up twelve years ago.

Yet the miracle of Damon's way of life. Living through clones as an extended vacation from never-ending pain. Sure, it's been terrifying, but once I realized I'd survive the craziness of their world living in a clone, it was not nearly as terrifying as being in misery, inside my real body, especially going through surgery and recovery.

Under the water, I watched the movie of my life play before me, the biggest highlights being the surgeries and the recovery and the pills to get through it. Every time I'd gone under anesthesia, I woke up not knowing myself or knowing for certain who I was, only that I felt different from who I'd been, and it was never for the better. More jaded, more angry and bitter, and more horrified at the new ways in which I could hurt or look disfigured.

In watching the playback of my life, I'd consented to the cutting, consented to the medical model that wanted to slice, poison and burn me, with no guarantee of a cure; and a sure guarantee that there would be pain, compounding.

I hadn't been ready to look before, to acknowledge that the pieces of metal on Calder's examination table had abolished my consent. When the procedure parameters changed to include tracking devices, equipped with electroshock mechanisms, so did the energetic consequences.

The more time I spent dunked under water, able to shut out the world, the more other realizations were coming front and center. I remembered the moment clearly when my hand shook, unwilling to sign the form to go under the knife again that last time. I had to be convinced by men I didn't trust to sign away my body.

In the vision, the paperwork I didn't want to sign lit up, shining a bright light onto the surgery, and the true version of the events unfolded. In the water, my mind could see that the surgeon changed after sedation, the surgeon-monster working to cut and move and spread and insert and activate within my traumatized body something alien. The moment the Frankenstein surgeon implanted foreign metal, implanted immoral technology and active electricity, that was the moment the contract was shattered, and it became a crime what was lodged within me. A false consent, a ruse, a hidden perpetrator against me.

These mad scientists were Strŏngmen of a different kind; purposeful in their evil, but secretive and subversive as to be allowed their malevolence and celebrated for it, thanked. How could I form the proper trauma box for the excessive damage, when I'd never considered myself a victim of surgery?

I lay back to float, my face touching the cool air as I found my peace in the silence and a rhythm to the buoyancy of the warm and flowing water. Behind my closed eyes not only did I see these Frankenstein surgeons, but I also saw the massive amount of Demŏnware within them, propelling them, and just like these monsters their hardware existed covertly.

Demŏnware; the riddle within almost everyone.

Is the Demŏnware in me too?

The subversion, the evil, the pain, the torment. Calder had been right, what I suffered, without knowing I'd even been a target, was insurmountable. Of course I didn't want to go back to that reality, but I had to go back. The longer I stayed away, the harder it would be to face it and return to myself.

I hadn't considered trauma boxes beyond rape, and yet trauma that changes us can come from all kinds of places, all kinds of events and people. Surgical trauma, especially within the confines of consent, changes the way its damage is connected, but doesn't change the need to heal it and release the horror of being cut open off one's body.

If rape disassociates, leaving a construct attached to the body and tattooed on the bone, what had the surgeries and recoveries done to me, left in me, or tattooed onto me?

It must be connected somewhere.

I'd had six major surgeries after surviving the car accident, and when I thought about their trauma as a concept, I could see them absolutely nowhere on my body. The leftover damage existed in my very skin, muscle, tissue, and organs with scars for receipts. How could the construct of the surgeries not exist there also?

I was back to asking myself questions because the visions I'd had were stalled. I moved out of my floating position and went back under, wondering if clear water would offer a better backdrop than my imagination.

When I swam under and opened my eyes I saw a translucent Damon sitting across from me. We were young, playing the game "Operation" but the rules were different. Damon wasn't trying to remove pieces from the game without getting jolted, he was placing tiny metal pieces exactly where they'd need to go to create a permanent jolt, until there were enough pieces on the board to short-circuit the whole thing. When he was done he looked up at me and winked.

What the hell does that mean?

I came up for air and thought about it. Essentially all the pieces of metal that had been removed from me could have been working together, or against each other. That meant that each piece added to me changed my electrical system entirely. Did that mean I needed to look for how to heal myself by examining the insertion surgery? Or maybe the suffering it generated backward in time was where the trauma existed.

I'd never even taken an anatomy class, let alone considered the electrical pulses of a human's body, and how that energy could help create a system of torment against itself.

Jesus, this is so complicated! I cursed.

"Jesus," I murmured, letting my body sink down to the bottom of the pool to then push myself back up again. "Jesus," I said again, thinking about the actual Jesus, the healer.

"I need help God," I whined out to the universe as I treaded water back to the shallow end, annoyed. "Please help me see this. Please send your angels to help me see the answers."

It couldn't hurt to ask.

Then I took a deep breath and sat my butt down to the bottom of the shallow end of the pool, just deep enough for my head to sit under the surface, and hoped I'd get another vision.

This time I saw myself on a surgical table, and a surgeon was placing something small inside me. We were in a bubble, and the bubble was my force field, and just outside the force field were several other surgeons, all holding their own version of small and metal technology. They stood above the bubble, as if in a surgical observatory, just outside my energy structure, existing in a structure all their own.

I went up for a breath and when I sank down it looked different.

Now there were more people standing above the bubble, around the edge of the surgeon's observatory. Directly across from the Frankenstein surgeons were Eamon and Calder and Dr. Gladnick. Dr. Gladnick carried only a surgeon's needle and thread, but Eamon and Calder were carrying the same hardware held by the Frankenstein surgeons, except the hardware looked discolored.

Gross! I squealed inside my head.

When I looked back down at my body on the surgeon's table, all I could see was myself post-op, at present time. Like the game "Operation," the red-light nose flashed representing the parts of my body where I'd carried pieces of metal that didn't fit. With each area of my body, and each piece of technology, there were a total of three surgeons attached. The most gnarled was the Frankenstein surgeon who'd inserted the device, and the other two surgeons attached were

Eamon and Calder, who'd removed it.

The whole grouping was attached to my red speckled trauma, and there were six groupings for the six pieces of technology, with twelve surgeries for insertion and removal. The energetic connections I could see above myself, still inside the bubble, were overwhelming. I understood why my confused body didn't want to wake up, and why my consciousness had no desire to return to so much constraint.

The reality of both inserted and removed equipment within me had been met with a completely broken system, with barely functioning neuropathways. The electrical signal within my real body was barely operational. Past the surgeons' connections, the Gellion on the table was devoid of life force.

In the water, I sent her light and realized that I needed it too. Of course I was shut down! How could I not be? The light I asked for inside my head, because I couldn't speak under the water, arrived. I could see it, my tiny aura lit up, growing in size, as my battery core filled with energy too, and my chakras started to fill with force, starting the self-feeding tornadoes.

When my own body was done filling up with energy from source, from all things magnetized to meet our needs, the comatose Gellion started to fill up too.

Another breath of air, and this time it was clear that the surgeons in the observatory did not exist as a normal Strŏngman would. Their existence as observers made it clear the difference between force and consent. Their facades were simply a part of the story, unattached to my trauma, only attached to the surgery itself.

Eamon and Calder's connection left a different kind of vibration, their efforts in alignment with trying to remove trauma and correct the harm, unlike the Frankensteins. Brighter in color, purer in their lines and strands of connection, Eamon and Calder sat in direct opposition to the other surgical intentions.

Though my consent had kept the medical trauma from turning into a construct, it hadn't changed the intent of immorality and purposeful harm. The Frankenstein doctors had avoided becoming Strŏng-men, but something else was there. It was the Karma between us that blinked red.

I'd used the word *Karma* as a concept of something to remove between a victim and their abuser, knowing it meant "connection," but I'd never seen Karma as anything more than a word. It was large and boundless in its energy, and alive in ways that seemed strange. Karma looked so obvious when comparing surgeons who healed to those who purposefully harmed. The doctors could hide behind consent, as they hid behind the entire medical model, but couldn't remove or destroy their negative Karma.

It was easy enough to wrap a bubble around the dark red specks of negativity tied to each doctor and concentrated in my body, to pull it from me and hand it back to them and fill myself with light. One by one, it became so, no more would my body hold what they had committed. The relief too of feeling so much ugliness, intentionally given, now released from a comatose system, brought me to the surface of the pool to yawn and quiver it off me.

Once all the Frankenstein surgeons and their surgeries had been Karmically removed from my blacked-out body, the strands between my body and the good doctors disappeared too. Good Karma didn't need highlighting for removal, and I could see now that it had only been there to highlight all the bad that shouldn't be.

I watched for a time as the bad Karma swarmed around the surgeons instead of me, no longer mine, but given to them to carry and neutralize. As evil as they were, I doubted our Karma would impact them much. They played in darkness and lived their lives measured by it. That was when I realized I couldn't be the only one hurt by them. They may have even spent an entire career dishing out trauma.

So, I looked harder at them as surgeons and observed the strands of connection between these doctors and their patients. There was that same color of what harm they'd done that had never truly been consented. Karma created by the surgeons didn't have to be carried by their victim though. I might not have been able to touch ingrained trauma, but I could redirect Karma back to its creator.

"Remove bad Karma," I said, my hands outstretched seeking all the damage, "from all their patients, and give it back to them. Fill the patients with light."

The vision before me exploded like fireworks on the Fourth of July, as the doctors received back the red specks of perpetration from their patients all over the world. All the red specks of immorality and pain coming back to them. It was like watching an animation showcasing nuclear war and the fall out, except in reverse.

The amount of Karma that returned to these doctors was enough to suffocate anyone and annihilate them from within. I had no idea how their lives would be affected, if at all, but if returning the trauma from just me was enough to cause them any issue, returning all of it should do some justified harm.

The only thing left were the strands of connection between us and between them and their other victims. Breaking the strands of attachment was as easy as walking through a spiderweb which dissolved as I filled the spaces with light.

Fingers crossed.

I'd never thought of myself as vengeful, and though it felt good to hope for retribution, it was really more about stopping continued harm. It wasn't about the years I couldn't change, but about the years I still had left, to take away the power of all that damage. With a deep sigh of relief, I dipped myself back under the water and embraced the peace of the quiet. Behind my eyes I wanted to reconnect to myself, to swim inside my real body and merge with the sleeping girl on the surgical table. Yet there was a pulsating shadow over her, waiting to be resolved.

The last Strŏngman box I'd done on myself ended in Caitir and Damon absorbing a part of a demon we all shared. But I never finished the work. I had never reassociated myself, not with so much going on. When I refocused I could see her, the piece of teenage Gellion separated, waiting to join me, her living consciousness desiring to be whole. Reassociation was easy and quick beneath the water. As our consciousness merged, I felt her take over, pulling me down deep into the dark, the urge for air losing its power over me. I was consumed with the enigma of being immersed and returning home.

The blackness remained but my open mouth pulled air in deeply, as much oxygen as I could inhale.

"Gellion?" I heard a familiar voice say.

"Damon?" I croaked out.

"I'm here. How'd you get here. What happened?"

"Why's it so dark?" I whispered.

"We're stuck in the escape pod."

"From the bunker?"

"Yes."

"We didn't reach a destination?" I asked.

"The blast damaged the shaft. We got far enough to survive, if we're not still being hunted."

"Your clones are all down. I cleared and cleared until they all fell down. Your family's alive," I reassured him.

He sighed then fumbled around in the space until he turned a small light on.

"Why's it so tight in here?"

"These pods were made for one," he replied.

"Oh. Do they carry supplies? I'm so thirsty," I said as my unused mouth made it hard to talk.

"Hold on," he said, fumbling around with his long arms.

When the bottle of water reached my lips, it felt as if my throat had dried out in a desert. I coughed at the new feeling of moisture.

"Take it slow. You haven't had water in a long time. Just ice chips."

I coughed some more while sipping until my body calmed down.

"What happened?" He asked.

I told Damon everything I could remember after our clones died on the train. About the demon coming for me in Caitir's clone first, and how it backed down to be set free. How even his Scotland clone had tried to kill me, but his family sacrificed themselves to keep me safe. How their faith in me held me up and pushed me forward, and that my mind wouldn't stop until I got us all there. How I was almost too late before I finished the job.

"I've been stuck down here a while. How'd you get back?" He asked.

"I saw what I needed to see in that pool next to the crystal grotto," I said without extra detail. "There was stuff from the surgeries I had to clear. Couldn't come back until I dealt with it. Why am I so sore?"

"I had to manhandle you to get you to safety. You're probably bruised."

"Yeah, feels that way, but I'm only sore on the surface," I said confused. "Where's all the piercing and shocking pain I normally feel?"

"The metal instruments are gone. Your body has been in rehab since right after the surgeries. You've had laser treatments for scarring, more for nerve damage, and infrared for your muscles. We've had to rebuild some of your tissue, and we put you through multiple skin detoxes and chelation through the veins. In between that your body has been on a slow heal in the medbed."

"That's a lot. I wish you'd told me. I expected so much more pain when I returned."

"You didn't ask, and we didn't want to overwhelm you. It was a lot of work, and there wasn't any guarantee."

"I should have been here to help."

"No, no, it was better this way. Rosie said it would have hurt you to see yourself. It was pretty brutal, but we knew it would get better. We took the work in teams and used robotic arms and other technology to make it all easier. We owed you that much."

"How did you manage it?"

"You were vulnerable and helpless. Fear can really reframe behavior. I feared if I didn't commit to the care you wouldn't wake up. The longer I spent here, the more important it felt to get you to a better place before expecting you to come back."

I sighed for the care, both grateful and awkward to have been given a full reprieve from more surgical trauma.

"That's generous. I'm having trouble moving though."

"Well as much movement as we gave you, and laser sessions for your muscles, still not moving on your own for this long atrophied you a bit, that's all."

I was about to ask him how long he'd been stuck down there, but a loud grinding sounded, then some metal clanking and banging, and a few sharp scraping sounds and we could hear someone call down to Damon. Not long after that, someone tapped the top of the escape pod, latched a metal hook, and we started getting tugged.

The movement was jarring, a little precarious and slow. I caught my breath multiple times when it felt like we might be dropped, and Damon held me tightly. Breaths turned to yawns to help calm me through it.

"How are we not out of oxygen?" I asked, realizing how small the space was and that two people were breathing air meant for one.

"I grabbed extra tanks," he replied.

Clever.

When we finally reached the top and got lifted up and out then lowered down, it took a lot to pry the disfigured pod open. Damon jumped out first and turned around for me. I couldn't move my legs much and it was hard to lift my arms enough to rest them on Damon's shoulders as he lifted me, as others held him steady.

"She's back?" I heard Rosie ask.

Then other voices around us sounded joyful to see me.

I was swiftly in Damon's arms, and we were surrounded as they led us through the rubble, back to the hospital wing, and to a medbed.

"Really?" I complained.

"Please? I know you're still numb in places, and we need to make sure you're not injured," Damon pleaded.

I looked around at everyone there, Caitir and Malik, Calder, Rosie and Eamon, Tombo and Joseph, all of them surprised to see me back inside my real body, and curious if I was okay. So, I nodded and closed my eyes and waited for the medbed to finish.

"You look good, lass," Eamon called out from behind the computer.

"Bruised but otherwise fine," Calder reassured.

Damon picked me up again and walked me to a hospital bed that tilted upright and put me down. Caitir handed us both some water and Damon sat next to me.

"You might want to send someone to Scotland," I said to all the familiar faces.

"Don't worry," Rosie said.

"We've locked down the mess until we can get back there," Eamon agreed.

"Well, actually, I may have drowned," I admitted, "while I was reassociating myself? Father Jerzy was keeping watch and might be checking on me soon."

"Oh dear," Caitir said.

Damon laughed out loud.

"Not funny," I chided him with a guilty smile for how ridiculous it sounded.

"It's lowly to frighten a holy man," Tombo agreed.

"Our Scotland clones are still active," Joseph said, motioning to Tombo.

"Ours too," Calder said, with a backhand whack at Malik.

"Yes please," Rosie said. "Father Jerzy should be spared the upset."

Eamon added, "It might take all of you to transport Gellion's body without causing suspicion."

"Nah, we'll just fly in the helicopter," Calder nodded.

"Subtle, real subtle," Caitir derided.

"You got a better idea?"

"Duh." Caitir tapped her head and looked at Damon. "Your remote chip copies finished the passage behind the waterfall two months ago."

"Has it really been that long?" Damon asked.

"Another passageway?" Malik mocked.

"Another?" I asked.

"Oh, he's the king of secret passageways."

"Who knows how to open it?" Damon asked.

"Shouldn't be too hard to figure out, now that we know where it is," Joseph reassured.

"We're on it," Tombo nodded toward Damon.

"Please apologize to Father Jerzy," I called to them.

"Don't worry Gell," Calder called back, with a genuine smile. I wonder if he'd seen the surveillance video earlier. The more I suffered, the more respect I seemed to earn.

"Hey Gell," Caitir said, reaching out for me. "I, uh, don't really have the words."

"It's not exactly a normal conversation. What can you say?"

"Well, thank you."

"Didn't really have a choice. It was us or them. You okay?"

"I feel really weird."

"Better?"

"Yeah, maybe, I hope so."

"Yeah, me too."

"I'm glad you're back. Sorry you can't walk yet."

"But the pain is mostly gone," I said, trying to be hopeful. "I've had to learn to walk before, and without the extra pain it won't be so bad."

Caitir leaned in for a hug and held me tightly and then let go and ran off to help the others transition to Scotland. She and her parents couldn't join them yet, not until more copies of them could be brought online.

Rosie and Eamon were still standing close by, smiling at me, while Damon held my hand.

"We almost died today," Eamon said, coming closer, "by a demon and a blood curse within our child, and within our adopted son," he said, referring to Damon.

"Attacked by the same ancestral evil we've been trying to escape for a generation," Rosie added. "This is not the first time you've saved our children."

I shook my head, "You kept me safe long enough to finish it. You protected me so I could help. You believed in me even when I wasn't convinced, when it still seemed like bullshit."

"You proved us right in the end," Eamon said.

"Thank you for saving them, for healing them," Rosie said.

"I saw more trauma inside them though," I sighed.

"In the last twelve years, to survive here, the darkness we've collected has been great, even after you purged us of so much."

"We watched the surveillance, lass, you cleared her, even while being tortured."

"We're all alive and better off," Rosie agreed. "Just ask Damon. He seems different too."

"Different how?" Damon asked his aunt.

"Well, I'm not seeing the deviancy behind your eyes. It's like a gloom has lifted."

"Damon?" Eamon asked him. "Do you feel different?"

"Of course. Gellion is awake. We made it out alive. That alone would..." but Damon couldn't find the words. He squeezed my hand and said, "...but really, I started changing when she got here."

"Hmmm," Rosie said.

"What?"

"Not nearly as much as you should have. There's light in your eyes again. I hope we see more of these lifted spirits."

Rosie leaned in and kissed my cheek, then kissed Damon's.

Eamon shook Damon's hand and took mine in his and kissed my hand, "Glad to have you home."

"There's a bonfire tonight at the campsite," Rosie said, as they backed away smiling. "Hope you can make it."

"Can we make it?" I turned to Damon and asked. "Can your old clones come online safely?"

"You'll have to clear them all to be safe."

I nodded then looked around, feeling apprehensive being so close to the cloning pods.

"You're not afraid of me?" Damon asked.

"I thought I'd be, and I was, right after it happened. I picked up the gun you'd used to shoot Rosie and Caitir and put some bullets into your dead clone, to make sure the demon couldn't come back," I said, feeling sick about it.

"Yeah, it was uncanny to have to kill myself multiple times. Those black eyes."

"You saw that too? It made it easier to separate them from you," I admitted, "And when I woke up in the dark and your voice was right there, so calm, I wasn't afraid anymore. I knew I was with the real you, the one who'd almost died to save me."

"I prayed. I never pray, Gellion. I prayed for survival, for your protection, for us to endure and come back from this."

"I prayed too, to come back to myself. The stakes are higher when you know you could really die. I'd forgotten that. It was like a dream until it became a nightmare."

"I've never seen myself become a monster before," he mused.

"Well, Caitir was way more brutal. The demon bitch gnawed off my finger. It was awful," I said, chuckling uncomfortably at the memory.

"Inhuman," he whispered, and in the low light he reached for my hands and gently massaged all my fingers, demonstrating they were intact.

"What about you, you've mentioned dark thoughts around me. Do you have them now?"

Damon took a deep breath as if he needed extra oxygen to process the information and force more sensations into the places he shut off to function.

"The thoughts aren't there, but there also aren't any triggers forcing me to react."

"What are your triggers?" I asked.

Damon leaned in and kissed me, and despite my physical weakness I kissed him back, matching his energy.

"Hmm," he grunted, looking confused.

"What?"

"No trigger," he said, curiously.

"That's a trigger?" I asked, incredulously. "Just kissing me?"

He nodded. "It was."

"What else is a trigger?" I asked.

He shook his head and said, "Let's take it slow."

"Well, I'm not saying you're like Jekyll and Hyde, but inside your clone you were gentler, for sure. I guess those bodies didn't have to carry all that Demŏnware, like the real you."

"Let's wait for the adrenaline to subside before I answer."

"Before you try another trigger?"

He chuckled and held my hand to his cheek.

"We were really close to losing everything," he reminded me.

He touched my face as my expression changed.

"I hope I'm different," he said, trying to reassure me.

"Do you love me now?" I asked, because I couldn't help myself.

"You first," he retorted.

"When you were just a dream, even when you weren't a real person, I loved you," I admitted.

"I am real. The nightmare I brought with me was real too, unfortunately," he said, his face sad as he reached out for me. "In every moment that it could be possible for my deeply troubled heart to feel, I've never not loved you," he spoke as if saddened I'd doubt it after all this time. "I'll never not want you, Gellion."

"Just as I am, Damon?" I asked.

He pulled the palm of my hand to his lips and kissed me, keeping his eyes on mine.

"Just as you are," he said, "always."

I believed him, not because I felt it within my soul or my bones, but because my heart ached for it to be true. Like the longing of all people who've wandered the world alone and hurt for too long, I heard my internal cynic cry out to deny this new way ahead.

To carry on inside a life beside Damon Jairus was to choose a different reality, to be called to the service of redemption, and to believe it was meant to be, beyond loyalty or love, by something greater. Our lives were intertwined, he and I, long before I knew him again or that a different version of myself existed. My dreams warned me I'd risk everything to save him yet staying by his side and facing the demons together meant a chance to survive.

AUTHOR STATEMENT

This work of fiction was created entirely with my wits, skill, knowledge, research, life experiences, visions, dreams, creativity, talent, conversations, inspirations, blood, sweat and tears. This novel was written over the last thirteen years and meticulously word smithed over countless hours, by a real-life carbon-based human being.

Artificial Intelligence (AI) has played no part in the creation of this work of fiction. Furthermore, this author rejects consent for Artificial Intelligence (AI) to use this work of fiction, a copyrighted material, for AI learning/training. Unless explicit permission is given by me, AI is not to use *Demŏnware: The Spiritual War Within* on any platform for any reason.

AI is neat and growing exponentially. However, owners of and purveyors of AI platforms using copyrighted materials without the permission from the copyright holders, is not okay. An artist's original, authentic work comes from their very own human spark, and it is criminal to have their life's effort misappropriated by a machine for other's profit.

Very sincerely,
Sōl Una
Author and Carbon-based Human

ACKNOWLEDGMENTS

I'd be lying if I didn't acknowledge that this tale was inspired by other people's lives and ideas, both fiction and non. Real humans and their real abilities began this journey in my head, as their magnificent stories touched my heart. One day I will acknowledge them by name, when they too are ready to share their knowledge.

In my search to tell a story that incorporated my own supernatural experiences, I followed the growing number of conspiracies popping up online. The rabbit hole did not disappoint, for how deep and dark it could go. The conspiracy trend changed everything and set the backdrop for this story's world.

What Demŏnware became was beyond my own ability to write alone. The muses that arrived to take the inspiration and expand it into this narrative were at another level. The idea changed over time, as recent years have exposed world conspiracies that align with a different kind of "energy vampire" concept. Real people don't regenerate right away, so the plotline of damage and healing would have to migrate to include what human frailty really entails.

Yet the most important aspects are there. The transformative power of love, the importance of the fight of good against evil, and an exploration of what can happen when innocence is thrown into a corrupt domain. Though I could never seem to finish this book, the world around started changing and so did the pieces of the puzzle.

Encouraged by music, YouTubers, bloggers, researchers, anonymous and public survivors, and changing spiritual themes and ideas, I wrote and plotted my beginning. Inspired, I set to work to build the characters, explore their backstory and write their path ahead. Eventually I ended up here, compelled to keep telling Damon and Gellion's tales, even if they're sometimes painful.

Demŏnware: The Spiritual War Within is only just the beginning. I can't wait to share with you what comes next.

ABOUT THE AUTHOR

Sōl Una Amé is a parent to three children, a spouse, a daughter, a little sister, and an empathetic ear at a local health center. In Sōl Una's spare time, (ha ha ha!), the stories that arrive and beg to be told always include a fundamental idea that healing and spiritual abilities are the real superpowers, since they help give people their happy ending in real life.

Sōl Una's experiences growing up included time spent with people who could see energy, who could channel information, and who could take away pain with their touch. Through that lens, the coming-of-age story she wanted to write was too pure, AKA "bland" and needed to be injected with a lot more horror, to create a magnified deliverance.

Yet the realistic hardships these characters face demonstrates the power of an energy that keeps our lives healthy, and what happens to people when it's shattered.

This book takes an extreme view of both the light and darkness on Earth. However, in the midst of the drama there is a greater understanding of how trauma roots itself and what measures can be taken to heal; processes Sōl Una has seen others use.

www.ingramcontent.com/pod-product-compliance
Lightning Source LLC
Chambersburg PA
CBHW020244030726
47499CB00001B/53